THE BA[illegible] ORDER

Peter David

First published in Great Britain in 2010 by Gollancz
An imprint of the Orion Publishing Group
Orion House, 5 Upper St Martin's Lane, London WC2H 9EA
An Hachette UK Company

A CIP catalogue record for this book is available
from the British Library

ISBN 978 0 575 10022 0

1 3 5 7 9 10 8 6 4 2

Printed in Great Britain by Clays Ltd, St Ives plc

The Orion Publishing Group's policy is to use papers that are natural, renewable and recyclable products and made from wood grown in sustainable forests. The logging and manufacturing processes are expected to conform to the environmental regulations of the country of origin.

www.orionbooks.co.uk

The author wishes to thank the ingenious creators of 'Fable' for allowing him to play in their universe

Prologue

"PEOPLE GET THE HEROES THAT THEY *deserve.*"

It is a very ancient saying, spoken by someone who was, I have no doubt, far wiser and greater than I could ever hope to be. For I am not, and never have been, a Hero. I have been a king, a warrior, a politician . . . but not a Hero.

I have always envied those who were.

I hear that the king of far-off Albion is a Hero. I have never had the honor of meeting him although I would much like to. In my younger days, that seemed a possibility, but matters of state kept me here. I always figured there would be time enough in the future.

Now the end of my future looms before me, and I am filled with naught but regrets.

I find myself, day upon day, trapped in endless and oftentimes mindless meetings as various landed and titled individuals come before me and explain why they should have even more land and more titles. Or an endless stream of people with barely two coins to scratch together parade before me, presenting me with problems or disputes and expecting me to come up with some manner of solving them. On occasion I am able to. More often than not, they are trapped by the particulars of their circumstances, and I cannot change them because I cannot, with a wave of my scepter, reorder the entirety of society. Such engagements become a humbling exercise in the realization of how limited a king's power truly is.

They are waiting for me even now in the throne room, more people seeking my help or advice or who knows what else. Very likely, the Duke of Overland will step in and start adjudicating the less-pressing cases in my stead. Ah, the duke . . . when he first came to court, he seemed very much the Hero to me. Brave, noble, selfless. His emulation of the heroic ideal is why I made him one of my closest advisors. But since then, he has proven just as much the political animal as any other striving for power, if not more so. Pondering the vast gulf between what I thought the duke was, and what he is, is what has prompted me to dwell upon the nature of Heroes in the first place.

Then I remember that the duke is not at court although he is reportedly on his way back from an excursion. Running late, so I'm told. So they will be waiting on me, then. Let them wait. That is one of the few advantages of being a king. People wait on you and dare not say a word if you decide not to tailor your schedule to their liking.

Rather than sitting in the confines of my throne room—

a room so vast that it would seem insane that anyone could possibly find it limiting—I have taken refuge in the royal garden. It is a crisp day as I sit here, surrounded by thick green hedges and lush beds of flowers planted by previous occupiers of the throne, or more precisely, their queens. The air is getting colder these days, and I see it in the morning frost on the flowers. It will mark their annual march toward extinction, only to be reborn in the spring.

Would that humans had the same capacity for endless rebirth.

I hear a soft footfall behind me and quickly I am on my feet. The bones may be brittle, the muscles may have lost their suppleness, but the reflexes continue to serve me well, and though my body may moan in protest, at least it continues to obey my commands. I have a short sword in my belt that I carry routinely, and it hisses smoothly out of the scabbard. I whip it around to face the unknown intruder.

It is a man with a bemused expression and empty hands. His face is narrow and hawklike, and his gaze darts around as if he is trying to determine what might be the source of my concern, only to be profoundly surprised upon realizing that it is he. He is dressed in traveling clothes and obviously has been employing them for that purpose, for they are caked with dirt. "Greetings, sire," he says.

"Greetings," I say cautiously. "I thought you might be an assassin."

"If I were, I would be a rather poor one, given that I am unarmed and that you are supposed to be elsewhere. So if my plan of attack were to involve assaulting you

bare-handed someplace where you are not supposed to be, then I'd be advised to find another vocation."

His words seem reasonable to me, and slowly I sheathe my blade. "Who are you, then, and what business have you here?"

"I am no one of importance. A mere lover of horticulture. Whenever I am hereabouts, I make sure to take in the royal garden."

"Which is intended to be for the exclusive enjoyment of the king."

"And will you have me beheaded for enjoying the flowers?"

"Kings have beheaded men for less." I shrug. "Enjoy them as you wish. In the grand scheme, it is of no consequence." I lower myself back onto the bench.

"I did not mean to intrude on the royal contemplation," he assures me.

"I contemplate nothing of consequence. I contemplate Heroes."

"How can you say that Heroes are inconsequential," he says, sounding surprised at the notion.

"Because there are no more, save for the king of distant Albion—at least, so I hear—and he is roughly my age. Once he has departed this sphere, Heroes will be of no more consequence than any other extinct species."

"Extinct? Never."

"You know the world in which we live as well as I," I say. "Once Heroes bestrode the land, and they were beloved and revered."

"And now?"

"Now?" I shrug. "Now they are treated with contempt.

With suspicion. Any who would pursue the noble calling are made to feel ignoble and so become mere sell swords or hedge wizards or similarly waste whatever talents they might have. The vast majority never even explore their potential, and thus their talents lie fallow while they lead mundane, unexceptional lives."

"A very sour view of the world, Your Majesty."

"Sour but no less accurate. What is it . . . ?" My voice trails off a moment before I recover it once more. "What is it about humanity that there is such a need to tear down Heroes? I cannot comprehend it."

"The pendulum swings and continues to swing and never stops. Heroes were once far more revered than they are now, yes, I concede that. And over time, people have grown suspicious because . . . well, because they are fools, I suppose.

"The truth is that people always want what they do not have while being dissatisfied with that which they do have. They had Heroes, and they became suspicious and distrustful and drove the profession nigh to oblivion. But nearly is not the same as completely."

"The time for Heroes has passed, and whatever you may believe about pendulums, oh nameless one, there is nothing to say that such a time will return."

He looks at me with something akin to pity. "You say that there are no more Heroes, and I am telling you that you are wrong. That may be a shocking notion for a king to have to face, since kings traditionally are surrounded by people who seem obsessed with trying to convince them of their infallibility."

"And you believe otherwise?"

"Belief indicates a lack of facts. I despise beliefs. I embrace only knowledge."

"So you have knowledge of Heroes, then." I keep my tone even and skeptical, not wanting to hint that there is the slightest bit of hope left within me.

"Yes indeed."

"Firsthand?"

"Seen"—and he taps the side of his head—"with these very eyes, as surely as I am seeing you."

"Tell me of them."

"It is a lengthy tale," he warns me. "A tale of such enormity and scope that some would dismiss it as a mere fable."

"I would hear it and dismiss it as nothing." I stretch and wince as I feel pain seizing my spine. "If it is all the same to you, I shall lie down upon this bench."

"You are the king. You may listen however you wish."

I lie down upon the bench, interlacing my fingers and resting them upon my chest. The position eases the spasms in my back, and I sigh gratefully. "Speak, then, and I shall attend."

"The tale begins in Bowerstone. You know of it?"

"It is in Albion, I believe. Beyond that, I know nothing of it."

"Bowerstone"—and the man is already warming to his tale—"in many ways is at the forefront of what Albion has become . . . and, by extension, what it has left behind. Once Albion had been a land where magic held sway. Eventually, technology supplanted much of it, like weeds overrunning a lush and green forest. At the time my story starts,

the advent of technology and the growth of the population had already caused Bowerstone to expand beyond an acceptable size for any city, much less a pit such as Bowerstone. If you expand a dung heap, you just end up with a far greater stench.

"Not that the entirety of Bowerstone was execrable. The immediate area surrounding Bowerstone Castle was quite nice. And one could actually spend a pleasant day wandering Bowerstone Market, with many respectable shops and the Cow & Corset Inn, where the meat was fresh and the wenches fresher. But then there was Bowerstone Industrial, a haven of so-called progress, belching smoke and fouling the very air. And then there was Old Quarter, a depressed slum filled with thieves and lowlifes. It is also the home of one of our protagonists, but we shall get to him anon.

"Instead, our story begins in the mind of a young man."

"How would you know what was in his mind?"

He had been about to move to the next sentence in his narrative, but his mouth remains open momentarily before snapping shut with an audible click. He pauses a few seconds, and then, his mouth in a firm line, says, "With all due deference to Your Majesty, this story will progress far more smoothly if you do not question me perpetually as I tell the tale. Please, I pray you, accept that I am the omniscient narrator of this 'fable,' and thus am somewhat . . . what is the word . . . ?"

"Omniscient?"

"Exactly."

I wave my hand magnanimously. "Proceed."

"Thank you, Your Majesty," he says with a slight bow

that is, surprisingly, devoid of any sense of irony. "So . . . the young man. His name was Thomas. Thomas Kirkman. He was a resident of a region called Millfields, near the lake. His father was a wealthy merchant dealing in textiles and simply assumed that Thomas would devote his full efforts into going into the family business since he was about to come of age. His mother, on the other hand, was of ill health and seemingly had been for as long as Thomas could remember. As for Thomas himself, he was a large, bold, and bluff boy with a disturbing tendency to say precisely what was on his mind regardless of the consequences. But he was also haunted by his original sin." He pauses. "You are doubtless wondering what that sin might be."

"Dare I ask?" I say drily.

"You are a king. The king dares all."

"What," I say, "is Thomas Kirkman's original sin?"

"He had the unadulterated nerve to not die."

Chapter 1

THE CREATURE WAS RIGHT IN FRONT of Thomas, right there, its mouth wide and its jaws slavering and its muzzle thick with blood. Its pointed ears were upright and quivering. Its fur was a dirty black, covered with debris and brambles from whatever bushes it had been hiding in, and when the creature roared, its breath washed over Thomas and caused his stomach to clench and his gorge to rise.

You can't smell things in dreams! You can't! This is . . . is no dream! Thomas's fear-stricken voice sounded in his head, and he tried to scream, but he was unable to find the breath to do so. The most he was able to muster was a paralyzed "urkh" noise that was hardly helpful when it came to summoning aid.

Thomas, lying on his bed, tried to twist away from the creature, but his body refused to obey the commands of his distraught mind. His attention remained fixed upon the blood that was all over the beast's mouth because he knew whose blood it was, and the notion that his blood was about to join it was overwhelmingly terrifying to him.

I don't want the same thing to happen to me . . . I don't want to end up like Stephen . . . please, no, please, no . . .

The creature grabbed one of his shoulders and began to shake him violently. This prompted Thomas to discover his voice, and it erupted from within him like uncorked champagne exploding from a bottle. Thomas screamed at the top of his newly liberated lungs. There were no words; it was pure, inarticulate horror spewing into the air.

Surprisingly, the creature actually seemed taken aback. It shook him even more, and then it spoke.

"Thomas!"

The fact that the monster was suddenly speaking in an understandable tongue was enough to shock Thomas to a halt. He stared uncomprehendingly at the beast with its fearsome yellow eyes, except instead of savagery, they were filled with confusion. *"Thomas, wake up!"*

With those words, it was as if a veil had been lifted from Thomas's mind. Slowly, the monster that had been looming over Thomas, threatening his life, dissolved like morning dew dissipated by the sun's rays. In its stead was the face of his father. He was jowly, with a gleaming, bald head that always seemed beaded with sweat regardless of whether it was hot as hell or cold as hell. His room likewise came into focus. It was a simple affair in terms of furniture, with only a single dresser and a bed with a lumpy mattress and a threadbare sheet.

The reason for this was that Thomas's father was a big believer in teaching his son how to properly apportion money. Rather than furnish the room himself, his father told Thomas that he had a certain amount of money available to him every year specifically designated to be used for room furnishing and that he was free to use it as he saw fit.

But Thomas set little store in such things as mattresses or dressers or even clothing. Instead, his entire focus was on books.

Lots of books.

Copious numbers of books. Books that were stacked everywhere, in no particular order, and yet somehow Thomas was always able to locate whatever particular volume he might be seeking at any given time.

"Thomas—!"

"I'm awake, Father," Thomas said with a croak, sitting up in bed. His nightshirt was soaked with perspiration, and his long, thick brown hair was likewise hanging damp around his face. "I'm awake—"

"What was hammering through your skull, boy?" said his father, stepping back. He glanced around suspiciously at the books as if they were the source of all his problems. "More foolishness gleaned from your endless collection of nonsensical tales?"

"They're not nonsense, and no," said Thomas.

"What was it, then?"

"I don't remember."

"You don't." His father did not sound particularly convinced, which was largely due to the fact that Thomas was an abysmal liar.

And Thomas knew perfectly well that his father was aware of his obfuscation. He tried to look his father in the eyes but wound up lowering his gaze, staring fixedly at the sheet as he insisted, "No. I don't."

His father considered pushing the matter but then shrugged it off, as if he had issues of far greater import on his mind. "You need to see her," he said.

"Her?" It was at that point that Thomas abruptly realized the earliness of the hour. The sun was not yet above the horizon. His father had always been an early riser, but this was excessive even for him. "Her who? Mother, you mean?"

"She began coughing, and she will not stop."

"Did you send for a doctor?" Even as he spoke, he tossed aside his blanket and settled his bare feet on the floor, which seemed unconscionably cold.

"Yes. And he suggested I send for you. He said that now would be a good time for you to see her."

Then did his father's meaning become clear to him as the last dregs of slumber fell from his mind. Forgotten, or at least shunted aside for the time being, was the snarling creature from his dreams. Instead, his focus was entirely on his father's concern for his mother. Not that his father was ever the most demonstrative of men, but even so, his worry was palpable.

Thomas followed his father out into the hallway and up the stairs to their bedroom. The doctor was standing just outside, holding his satchel loosely, a look of carefully contrived sorrow upon his face. "I have made her as comfortable as possible," he said, "but beyond that, there is nothing I can do."

"I'm sure you tried your best," said Thomas.

He stopped in the doorway, however, and even though he had known what he was going to see, it still wasn't easy for him.

His mother was lying in bed, looking wasted and wan. For a moment, he wasn't even sure if she was still alive, and then he saw her chest rise and fall ever so slightly, and a faint rasp sounded from her chest. "She's breathing easier," said his father, and Thomas found that distressing because she still sounded awful to him.

Then her mouth moved as if it was a tremendous effort of will, and her voice barely above a whisper, she said, "My son . . ."

"I'm here," said Thomas, and he crossed the room and sat upon the edge of the bed. He took her hand, and it felt cold as death already. He knew that sensation all too well, for he had felt it once before, and it was something that he would never, ever forget. "I'm here, Mother."

"I'm so glad. I . . . I need to tell you . . ." She squeezed his hand with all the strength that her frailty enabled her to display.

"Tell me what?"

"I . . ." A cough seized her, but she suppressed it. "I . . . forgive you."

He heard a sharp intake of breath from his father. "You . . . you do . . . ?"

She nodded, and even that seemed to require tremendous effort. "I blamed you . . . for your brother's death. It is a terrible thing to admit . . . but I did. And I should not have . . . it . . . it was not fair to you . . ."

Thomas was a swirl of emotions. "That's all right. Mother, I know that you love me. I've always known that."

"Yes. And the truth is . . ." Her body shook, trembling, and she forced herself to continue. "The truth is . . . if only one of my sons had to survive . . . I'm so relieved it was you."

"Mother, don't say things like that—"

"I'll say what I wish . . . what I need to say . . . the truth is that . . . that you have potential . . ." The three-syllable word had taken great effort for her to say, and she had to regain her strength before she could continue. "Far more . . . than your brother ever did . . ."

He wanted to tell her that that was ridiculous. That Stephen had had as much potential, if not more, than Thomas ever did. That Stephen had been smart and business savvy and also brave, so brave, and the fact that his life had been cut short by the—

Thomas stopped short. Even in his own head, the events of his past as he had remembered them had been subjected to such criticism and contempt that he censored his very thoughts.

"It's true," she said, as if he had spoken. "Your brother . . . he had very little worth. All he cared about were his books and his legends and tales of heroic adventure. He was never going to be of any use to your father.

Heavens know he was of no use to me. Not like you." And she squeezed his hand. "Not like you, Stephen."

Thomas felt as if his heart had just been crushed.

"The world would be so much poorer without you in it, Stephen. And you . . . you made up that . . . that insane story . . . about a balverine killing your brother . . . you didn't want to admit that you weren't able to save him . . . so you said it was something unnatural . . . that no mortal could have stopped . . . I forgive you that. I forgive you everything, Stephen. At least you're still here . . . instead of Thomas . . ."

His jaw twitched, and he saw his father looking at him with both despair and warning. "Yes, good thing for that," said Thomas, trying to keep the misery out of his voice and not entirely succeeding.

She didn't notice his tone. "Good thing," she echoed, and then she closed her eyes and let her head slump back. She shuddered once more, and there was a rattle in her throat that Thomas recognized immediately, for he had heard it on that long-ago day in that last, final moment of his life.

Then she was gone. And with her, she took the last dregs of Thomas's childhood. And he had no idea what she had left behind.

Chapter 2

JAMES SKELTON WAS A TOWHEADED lad, with a ruddy complexion and arms and legs that seemed determined to outstrip him when it came to physical development. Just when he thought he had the damned things under control, there would come another growth spurt, and suddenly he was tripping over his own feet or knocking things over with his elbows because he had turned around too quickly.

Not that it was difficult to knock things over or find other things to trip over in James's incredibly crowded home. Situated in one of the grimier, more run-down regions of Bowerstone Old Quarter, the house was only a notch or two above the category of "hovel," wherein resided James, his mother, his two surviving grandparents, a lazy bastard of an uncle, and six siblings. James was the second oldest of the brood, all of whom had been born one after the other over a period of six years. There was a permanent sense of frustration and claustrophobia in the home, and the children slept in shifts since there was insufficient bed space. All of the kids were actively employed in jobs ranging from apprentice ironsmith to apprentice beggar.

James had, as far as he was concerned, the best job of the lot of them because he was the only one who didn't complain about it incessantly. Not only that, but it was the only job that got him out of his section of town and into someplace that didn't perpetually carry the stench of offal mixed with blackened air. It brought him to Millfields and the home of Thomas Kirkman. According to Thomas, their house was relatively modest compared to some of the others, but as far as James was concerned, it was nothing short of palatial.

It was a crisp morning, the sun's warmth not having yet done much to warm it up. These days with the seemingly permanent haze of smoke that hung over the city, the sun was oftentimes fighting to penetrate it and not always succeeding. James ran as quickly as he could, striving as always to maintain his balance since his unfortunate gawkiness presented a constant challenge to remaining upright.

Other servants lived with their masters, but James did not reside at the Kirkman house. There were several reasons for this: They did not have a separate servant's quarters; and Thomas's father, when asked by his peers about the absence of live-in help, would sneer and say, "Why should I spend good money putting food into other people's mouths? What service are they going to provide me while I sleep? Let them feed themselves breakfast and dinner and not breathe my air in their slumber."

So James would hurry every morning from his home, such as it was, to the Kirkman residence, to serve in Thomas's employ and do whatever it was that Thomas required. He had operated in that capacity since both of them were quite young, and in more recent years, he had functioned less and less as a servant and more and more as Thomas's friend. A paid friend, by all means, but a friend nevertheless.

He was surprised to discover, on this particular morning, that the front door to the manor was standing wide open rather than closed as it normally was. The discovery was enough to cause him to slow his run to a trot, and then to a halt. It seemed odd, to be standing in front of the house that he had entered so many times and to find himself hesitating at the threshold. Then he heard the sounds of heavy footfalls coming slowly, methodically down the stairs, thump, thump, one at a time. The pattern was enough for him to figure out that it was two men who were carrying some sort of burden.

Then he saw two men dressed in black emerging into the daylight, carrying a stretcher between them, and there was a body on it covered with a shroud that reached up and over the head. But James didn't have to see the body beneath it to know whose it was.

"Poor Thomas," he muttered. It wasn't as if he was unsympathetic to the woman whose corpse was beneath the shroud, but at least her lengthy suffering was over.

Thomas, though, had been left behind, with a father who was hardly the most nurturing of men. On the other hand, at least Thomas had come of age and was in command of his own future even though that future seemed to be already set as part of his father's business.

As the men walked past with their burden, he said, "No hearse?"

One of the men shrugged, and said, "Busy elsewhere, and he wanted her gone as soon as possible."

"When's the funeral?"

"Ain't gonna be one," said the other man with a look of obvious disgust. "Said he didn't see the point in it. That they'd all had plenty of time to mourn her while she was dying, and no point in everyone sitting around and being . . . what'd he say?"

"Lachrymose," the first man said.

"Right. Lachrymose. We take her back to the charnel house, we burn her, and we'll be bringing back the ashes directly. No fuss. No muss."

"And no big cost."

Slowly, they both shook their heads, making no effort to hide their disdain for such a mind-set, and then continued on their way. James Skelton watched them go, scarcely knowing what to think of such a thing. Then he turned and headed into the house. Normally, he would have gone straight up to Thomas's room, but under the circumstances, he wasn't sure what his destination should be. But then the question was quickly settled when he heard an abrupt, frustrated, and very loud, *"Damnation, Thomas, not this again!"* It was coming from upstairs, and James didn't hesitate to sprint up the stairs to what was, as it turned out, the study of Thomas's father.

The man was in a fine lather, and he didn't even notice when James appeared at the door looking concerned. He was circling Thomas, who was seated in a chair in the middle of the room. It seemed like some manner of grand inquisition. "Could you possibly have picked," he was raging, "a worse possible time to—"

"*I* didn't pick it!" Thomas said plaintively. "*Mother* brought it up! When she was talking about how Stephen died! Well, actually how *I* died, but . . ."

"You died?" James spoke up, confused.

Thomas turned and saw that James was standing there, his face aghast. He wasn't the least bit embarrassed at having a witness to this confrontation. The Kirkman family had no secrets from James by this point in any of their lives. Still, he obviously felt the need to clarify the statement he'd just made. "Mother, while she lay dying, got everything jumbled in her head. She thought Stephen was the one who survived the balverine attack years ago instead of me . . ."

"There you go again! There are no such bloody things as balverines!" his father shouted. "Certainly not now, if there ever were! They're from another time, another age—"

"A better one," Thomas shot back. "An age of magic and wonder and heroism."

"Oh, balls, boy!" said his father with growing impatience. "When the hell are you going to live in the world we have rather than your world of books?"

"I need those books to keep me sane around here!" And now he was on his feet, bellowing in fury. "I mean . . . come on, Dad! How else? The way you talk to me every day, you make it pretty clear how disappointed you are in me. Even though I'm there, every day, down at the market, working as hard as any employee."

"You're supposed to be working harder! You're supposed to be working like someone who's going to own it all one day! You're—"

And James could take it no longer. Tossing aside decorum, uncaring of his relative status in the world, losing sight of who he was and what he was supposed to be, James's voice rose above both of theirs, silencing them with his outrage: *"For crying out loud, a woman has died here today! Will the two of you please knock it off? Show a little damned respect!"*

Thomas and his father were both stunned into a brief silence. It was Thomas who found his voice first as he said, very softly, "You're right."

"He's *right*?" Thomas's father was now speaking once more, but he was reacting very differently from his son. "*He's* right? He's a servant!"

"Even servants get to be right now and then, Father. I'm sorry I spoke so harshly to you. I know that you're doing the best you—"

His father wasn't paying him any attention. Instead, his gaze was fixed upon James, and James felt his knees going slightly weak. "Your services will no longer be required here. Get out."

"James, stay put," Thomas said immediately. He turned

to his father. "James is my servant. More than that, he's my friend. He's two years younger than I am, but he's a yard smarter. He's not going anywhere."

It looked as if half a dozen replies danced across his father's lips. Ultimately, he said nothing at all. Instead, he turned and strode out without a word. Thomas, who had been standing, sank back into the chair with a low sigh. He slumped back, putting his hand to his forehead. "I'm sorry you had to see that, James."

"I've seen worse," said James. "You want to tell me what happened?"

"Why not? Who else am I going to talk to?" he said mirthlessly. "You're pretty much all I have in the world right now."

James chuckled at that. "I've been telling you for a while, you need to find a girl."

"There are plenty of girls interested in me," said Thomas, and he sounded more annoyed by it than anything. "They see me as the son of a wealthy merchant and figure I'll be able to provide them a lifestyle they'll find pleasing. I want a girl who loves me for me, not for my father's purse."

"That's fair enough, and I'll wager you'll find her."

"Really." It was not a question but rather a flat assertion of skepticism. "James . . . even my mother wasn't in my corner. So I think you'll understand if I don't hold out a lot of hope in that regard."

"She wasn't in her right mind, and you know that."

"She may not have been in her right mind, but that doesn't mean she wasn't speaking from her heart . . ."

"Your mother loves you . . . loved you," said James. "You must know that. So does your father, although I imagine it's hard to—"

"Do you believe me?"

The question caught James off guard. "Believe you?"

"Yes."

"About what?"

"You know about what."

"I swear to you, Thomas, I really don't."

"The balverine."

"Oh. Well, I—"

A dagger was hanging at Thomas's hip. James had grown so accustomed to it that he had paid it no mind, but now Thomas pulled it out of the scabbard and held it up in front of him. "Stephen's dagger," said Thomas, his eyes fixed upon it as if it were a hypnotic flame. "He dropped it that day, fighting the balverine. Fighting to save my life because I'd been stupid enough to go into the woods at night on a dare. He dropped it, and it fell near me, and the balverine gutted him, James. It gutted him. I saw the insides of my brother spilled out upon the ground like a spilled plate of noodles, and then the creature came at me. It grabbed me and roared at me, and I faced death at the hands of something that seemed like it stepped right out of one of my books. And it didn't realize that I had grabbed up the fallen knife just before it took me, and I drove this knife"—and he jabbed it forward—"right into its eye. Right into the damned thing's eye, James, and it dropped me and grabbed at its face, blood pouring down, and I ran. I ran and I felt like every step I took, at any point, the thing would leap upon me from the darkness and drive me to the ground and finish the job. If I hadn't been such a damned coward—"

"Coward!" James could scarcely believe it. "Thomas, you were a child! Nothing but a child! You're beating yourself up because you didn't press a momentary advantage that, if you had, would have ended with there being two corpses in the woods instead of one that night? That's as ridiculous as . . . as—"

"As balverines being real?"

James shifted uncomfortably from one foot to the other. "It could have been a normal wolf."

"But it wasn't."

"But it could have been . . ."

"But it *wasn't*! Come on, James, you sound like my father!"

"You don't have to be insulting," James said defensively.

"Do you seriously think that I couldn't tell the difference between a normal, mangy wolf and a creature from hell?"

"I think it was dark, and you were young and terrified, and your mind might have built it up to become something torn from the pages of your books."

"That it *might* have."

"Yes," said James. "Because it *might* also have been exactly what you say. I mean, I heard rumors . . ."

"Rumors from the huntsmen who found my brother's body," Thomas said, nodding. "That there were footprints far bigger than any wolf's. I heard them, too. But they were shouted down"—and his voice was rife with sarcasm—"by those who knew so much better about such things. You ask me, they were warned against the prospect of hurting our city's precious economy by possibly starting a panic."

"That's entirely possible."

Thomas looked down as if his feet had suddenly become of tremendous interest to him. "At least once a week, sometimes more, the thing stalks my dreams, James. I've tried to read up on them, gone through all my books, learn everything I can. But I haven't found much beyond references to other volumes that I haven't been able to acquire. Sometimes I think the books that the legends are referencing are also legendary. The more knowledge I have, the more I'm prepared . . ."

"Prepared for what, Thomas? What in the world are you preparing for?"

At that, Thomas chuckled softly. "I don't know, James. But when I see it, I'm sure I'll . . ." Then his voice trailed off, and his nostrils flared, confusion crossing his face. "Do you smell something?"

"Smell something? No, why? What do you—?" Then he stopped, detecting it as well. "Wait, yes. Something . . . burning, I think. The house!" And his voice rose in alarm. "The house is on fire—!"

"No, it's coming from outside. Why would . . . ?"

Then his jaw dropped, his eyes widening, and he bolted from the room before James could determine what in the world was happening. James sprinted after him, but Thomas had already covered the stairs and was out the door and yelling at the top of his lungs before James could reach him. When he did emerge from the house seconds later, he could scarcely believe what he was seeing.

Thomas's father had gathered all of his son's books, created a small pile in front of the house, and ignited them. Thomas was waving his arms, and howling, *"You gormless teat! What the hell have you done?"*

"I've done you a favor, is what I've done." In contrast to his son, Thomas's father didn't sound at all angry. It was as if all the anger had been burned away from him in the fire. Instead, he was resigned and yet confident, convinced of the rightness of his actions. "You're not a child anymore, Thomas. You're of age. You have responsibilities. It's time to put aside the playthings of your youth—"

"Knowledge isn't a plaything!"

"Knowledge of what? Balverines?"

"And hollow men, and banshees, and . . . and the Triumvirate! The three greatest Heroes in the—"

"Knowledge of nonsense is of no use in the real world."

The flame was crackling furiously, smoke billowing from it and caking Thomas's face. He looked like a primitive creature bounding around a fire as part of some arcane ritual. Gesticulating wildly, he cried out, "*What do you know of the real world?* You've never wandered beyond the confines of this . . . this cesspool of a city! There's a whole wild world out there that you could experience, but you don't have the wit or imagination to realize it!"

"My wits kept you and your mother in a fine house for the entirety of your life, so I'd show a little respect if I were you."

With that pronouncement, he turned from his son and walked away. "I'll be down at the market. Join me there when you feel like honoring the memory of your mother and embracing your responsibilities as a man."

Then he was gone, and the only sound in the air was the crackling of the flames and Thomas's ragged breathing.

Thomas said nothing for a time, instead simply staring at the fire as it consumed the last of the books and burned itself out. James had never felt more helpless. Uncertain of what to say, he chose to remain silent.

"James," Thomas finally said, his voice so soft that James had to strain to hear it, "could you get me some water from the well? I'll need to wash up."

"Sure," said James, and he hastened to the well. He drew up two buckets as quickly as he could and hurried back to the house, the water sloshing violently around the tops of the twin buckets. James staggered under their weight and almost lost his footing as he made his way to the cistern.

He stopped, however, upon seeing that Thomas had emerged from the house once again. Thomas was dressed for the road, with a cloak and hood draped around his shoulders. He had also paid a visit to his father's well-stocked armory, for his father was both an avid hunter and also relentlessly paranoid that outsiders might show up and try to steal his money. He had a crossbow dangling from a holster in his left hip and a sword strapped to his right. There was a pack slung upon his back that was bulging with what James could only assume were supplies: easily transportable foodstuffs, changes of clothes, money, and whatever else one would need for a journey. Seeing the pails brimming with water, he said, "Good. Put them down." James did as he was instructed and Thomas went over to them, dipped one of the trailing ends of his cloak into one of them and used it to wipe soot and ash from his face.

"Are you, uhm . . . going somewhere?" asked James.

Thomas looked up at him with a raised eyebrow, and there was gentle amusement in his voice. "Isn't it obvious?"

"It . . . somewhat is."

"Then why did you ask?"

"Just trying to be polite. Where are you going?"

"East."

"Anywhere east in particular?"

"It is said," Thomas informed him, "that the true spirit of Albion resides in the lands to the east. Supposedly you can still see Heroes there if you look very closely. I'm going to go see for myself." He hesitated, and then his jaw tightened. "There's nothing here for me anymore, James. I don't belong here. I need to see things that are greater than anything I've ever experienced outside of my books."

"Balls," said James, and was inwardly pleased when he saw Thomas blink in surprise at the response. "This isn't about books, or narrow-mindedness, or even the true spirit of Albion. This is about balverines. Even more, it's about the balverine that killed your brother."

"No."

"Yes, it is. You want to find the one-eyed thing, assuming it still exists, and you want to kill it and cut its head off and shove it in your father's face, and say, 'See? See here? I wasn't lying all those years ago.'"

"If I did that," said Thomas with resignation, "my father would claim it was some sort of trick. Or the head of some sort of singular freak of nature. He would never, ever accept what I presented him as fact. There's no proving anything to him."

"Then why—?"

He thumped his fist into his own chest. "I need to prove it to myself. I have to see at least one of the damned things with my own eyes. For the past ten years, I've had nothing but my father and my mother openly disbelieving me, disputing me, dismissing me . . ."

"You must be running out of words beginning with 'dis.'"

"This isn't a joke, James."

"I'm sorry. But isn't maybe part of it that you're starting to wonder if perhaps they weren't right? That you were a scared child with an overactive imagination and a guilty conscience who built a simple wolf into something that it wasn't."

Slowly, Thomas nodded. "Yeah. And I just . . . I need to know, James. I need to know, and this is the only way I'm going to find out."

"Are you planning to come back?"

"I really don't know."

"Then you're not leaving me much of a choice."

The comment appeared to take Thomas off guard. He looked askance at James, his eyes narrowing in suspicion. "What exactly do you mean by that?"

James walked over to Thomas and clapped a hand on his shoulder. "The truth is, Thomas, the only part of my life that's remotely worthwhile is being associated with you. So the idea of not seeing you for the rest of my life just isn't acceptable to me."

Thomas visibly tensed. "So you're going to try and stop me?"

"Hell no. I'm going with you. What?" And he laughed. "Do you really believe I'm going to remain behind in this piss hole of a city while you're off adventuring in the lands of the east? Don't be ridiculous."

"James . . . it could be dangerous. I'm of age; you're not. It's not fair to ask you to . . ."

"You're not asking me to do anything," James pointed out. "I'm telling you what I'm doing. Besides, you need me."

"I really don't. I won't lie, James; you've been a good friend. But there are some things"—and his voice deepened, taking on a manly tone—"that I just have to do alone. Good-bye, James." He shook James's hand firmly, turned away, and started walking.

"Thomas," James called after him.

With a faint sigh of exasperation, Thomas turned, and said, "What?"

"That way is north."

Thomas tried to laugh dismissively, but then he looked uncertain. "You're sure?"

James chuckled. "Thomas . . . you get lost in the marketplace. Hell, you've gotten lost in your own house."

"Only that one time," Thomas said defensively.

Ignoring him, James continued, "I, on the other hand, have a superb sense of direction. I always have. And if you're going on any sort of trip, and you have the slightest hope of not getting lost, you're going to need someone at your side who—at the very least—can keep 'east' consistently in his head and his feet on the right path. Besides, you think I don't want to see a balverine? Or a hobbe, or a hollow man, or a kraken or whatever other creatures are out there that anyone in his right mind would be running from rather than seeking out? You think I don't want to see a genuine Hero? You think I want to spend my whole life in this place? Besides, if by some chance you manage to find your way, survive, and make it back here, I'm going to have to listen to your endless tales of adventure. To hell with that. So unless you've got a better reason for my not coming, like maybe that you're tired of my company . . ."

"We have known each other forever, James, and I have never tired of your company," said Thomas. "But . . . what of your family? You're simply going to take off?"

"If you can take leave of your senses, I can take leave of my family. Frankly, it'll be amazing if anyone in my family notices that I'm gone." He shrugged. "One less mouth to feed."

The two young men stood there for a time, regarding each other, sizing each other up. The one who had come of age, and the other who—if matters did not turn out as they hoped—might not live to reach that milestone. Then Thomas stretched out his hand, palm up, and James reached out and gripped Thomas's forearm firmly. Thomas likewise returned the grasp, and they shook once on it.

"Do you need to return home? To get your things?"

"I come from a poor household. I've nothing worth taking."

"Then wait a moment." Thomas went back into the house and emerged a few minutes later with a traveling cloak and a short sword. "Here. My father's. I doubt he'll miss them, and even if he does . . ."

"It is better to ask forgiveness after the fact than to ask permission and be denied?"

"Pretty much. So . . . east?"

"East," James said firmly.

"AND DO THEY INDEED EMBARK ON AN *easterly course?"*

The odd man who is telling me this tale gives me a quizzical look. "If they did not, Your Majesty, then it would not be much of a tale, now, would it."

"No. No, I fancy that it would not. I am curious, though, about how you know of it. Of how you know the conversations that the lads had, the very thoughts that run through their minds."

"You have asked me that already, but because you are king and are due all deference, I shall reiterate: For the purposes of this tale, I am omniscient. There is nothing connected to this adventure that is not known to me."

"And how came you by all this knowledge? Who are you? Or are you more 'what' than 'who'?"

"I am nothing more and nothing less than what you see. Now . . . may I continue?"

I feel a faint coldness in my arm and shake it briskly. It dissipates as if embarrassed that I have taken notice of it. Then I stare at my hand for a time. This prompts the storyteller to regard me with curiosity, and prompt, "Majesty—?"

"There were some who claimed," I tell him, "that when a Hero walks down the street, they could tell he was a Hero because he was surrounded with a glow."

"A glow?"

"Yes. A soft radiance that might have been shone down from above or radiated from within; it was hard to determine which it was. And you could tell just by looking that this was someone who had made nothing but positive choices in his life, always striving for the common good. Always taking the proper path when two ways were open."

"Just by looking, you say?"

"Indeed."

"Their imagination, surely."

"I would have thought as much. Still . . . it is comforting, is it not, to imagine that the choices we make enable others to see us in such a literally positive light?"

"I can see how comfort would be derived from that, yes. So . . . shall I—?"

"Continue?" I wave toward him with my now-fully-functioning hand, the momentary weakness having passed so completely that I am left wondering if I had imagined it. "Yes, by all means, do. Our young bravos headed toward points east, did they?"

"Indeed they did."

"A long way to walk."

"True enough, but Thomas had sufficient funds that several days later, they arrived at a central hub, where they were able to buy passage onto a coach. It helped that they were not particularly fussy about which direction they were heading, as long as it was toward the place where the sun rose each morning. After all, what better place to find enlightenment than where the sun first kisses the sky?"

Chapter 3

THOMAS WAS NOT ACCUSTOMED TO having people laughing in his face. Giving him dubious looks, or chastising him, or perhaps just shaking their heads and turning away while muttering disdainful comments, yes, all of that and more had he experienced.

This man, though, was laughing outright. He was round and heavyset, sitting opposite Thomas and James and swaying side to side as the rocking coach barreled down the highway. The horses' hooves stamped out a steady tattoo on the dirt path, and if they slowed, the coachman would shout "Yah!" every so often, which meant nothing to the horses, but then crack his whip, which did indeed mean something to them. The fellow passenger had already introduced himself as a merchant on business to Rookridge, the town for which the coach was bound, and just to pass the time, he had tried to prompt the lads to tell him what their own business was. Thomas had been evasive in that regard for much of the trip, but the merchant, whose name was Sutter, had managed to wear him down so that as their destination was merely a few hours on, he judiciously told him as much detail about the matter as he felt comfortable. No need to dredge up the entire tragic story of his brother, certainly, but he let down his guard sufficiently to describe precisely what it was that they were hoping to encounter.

This prompted the laughter, which so overwhelmed Sutter that he had to start coughing mightily, as if his lungs might be expelled from his chest, before he could compose himself.

"Balverines! Seriously?" he finally managed to ask.

James gave Thomas a cautioning glance, and Thomas was able to discern the unspoken message: *No. Not seriously. Tell him you were not serious. Tell him you were joking. We do not need this grief.*

He considered the silent advice and rejected it. Instead, he tilted his chin defiantly, almost as if challenging Sutter to take a swing at it, and said, "Yes. Seriously."

"But they're the stuff of myth and legend, boy!"

"So are Heroes, but we have one sitting on the throne of Albion."

"The last of a dying breed, I'll grant you that . . ."

"And," Thomas pressed, "the tales speak of the creatures that they fought against. If Heroes exist . . . even one Hero . . . then why not the monsters that challenged them?"

"Because," said Sutter, his face still red from laughing so hard, "people need to spin tall tales in order to make the accomplishments of the Heroes seem the stuff of legend. That's how people are, boy. There's just a need to make things bigger than they are. To build them up so—"

"So they can tear them down?" James piped up.

That prompted a moment of silence from Sutter, and then the merchant shrugged. "That's a valid enough point, I suppose. Heroes have fallen into disfavor, that's certainly true. But they've only themselves to blame, strutting around and acting as if they're so much better than everyone else."

"Maybe," Thomas shot back, "they really were better than everyone else. And maybe people didn't realize it because the Heroes were so good at disposing of the creatures and races that lurk in the shadows that people stopped being afraid and eventually forgot what it was they were afraid of in the first place."

"It's a worthwhile theory, boy," said Sutter. "But an even simpler theory is that all the balverines and their ilk were simply exaggerations that got out of control and took on lives of their own. Myth and legend were fine back in the days before we became more civilized, more technological. But the science of technology tends to drive out the backwards thinking of superstition and nonsense. Balverines are just overgrown wolves, and hollow men are simply poor bastards who were incorrectly pronounced dead, as happens from time to time if an incompetent physician cannot detect a heartbeat. And the terrified devils come out of their comas to discover they've been prematurely buried and claw their way back to the surface. Nothing supernatural about it. About any of it. Certainly not enough to go gallivanting around Albion looking for evidence of it."

Thomas was steaming at Sutter's words, but James rested a calming hand on Thomas's forearm even as he said, "You make a reasonable case."

"I am a reasonable man. I'm sure you'll find quite a few of us in your travels. Then again, you may also find one or two fools who will lend credence to nonsensical tales of balverines and the like. Pay them no heed, young masters." And he settled back into his seat, closing his eyes. "Pay them no heed."

Astoundingly, he was actually able to fall asleep despite the bumpiness of the ride. Under his breath, Thomas muttered in a nasal imitation of the merchant, "Pay them no heed," and James laughed softly. "What is it with some people of the older generation, that they talk like they're giving a formal dissertation?"

"It's called being pedantic," said Thomas, and then added, "Pay it no heed." Both of them laughed at that.

Several hours later, as the sun crawled toward its apex in the noon sky, the coach came rolling into Rookridge. The merchant woke up minutes before they arrived and, as the coachman opened the door for them from the outside, bade Thomas and James a good afternoon and much luck on their adventures. Then he walked away, shaking his head, and an annoyed Thomas was sure he heard the man chuckling and muttering, "Balverines," under his breath.

"The man's an idiot."

It was the coachman who had spoken. He was a much older man, possibly—Thomas felt—the oldest man he had ever seen, with thick white hair that hung in front of his face and beard stubble that protruded at random points from his cheeks in an odd patchwork fashion. His eyes were deep and looked hollowed . . . or perhaps haunted, and only one seemed to fix on them properly, the other crusted over. He was quite skinny except for his arms, which were disproportionately larger and rather well muscled, which explained how one of such slight appearance would be able to control a team of horses. He nodded in the direction that Sutter had walked, and continued, "A bleeding idiot, y'ask me," in a deep, cantankerous growl. "Doesn't know what the hell he's talkin' about."

"You could hear our discussion?" Thomas was astounded. "How? You were on top of the coach, and the horses' hooves were thunderous . . ."

"Long years of practice." He tilted his head slightly, his gaze shifting from Thomas to James, and back. "Balverines, eh?"

"Yes."

The old man coughed deeply and brought up a wad of spit that he expelled on the ground nearby. Thomas noted that it was tinted red. "The parents of the Hero of Southcliff were attacked and killed by a white balverine, or at least so it's said. They're among the most dangerous of the breed although some say the frost balverines are worse."

"Have you ever seen one?" Thomas said eagerly.

"No, and I'll be perfectly happy to reach the end of my days—which are probably coming far sooner than either of us would like—without ever having done so. But'cha don't have to see something to know something. Where there's smoke, there's fire, ya ken what I'm sayin'?"

"You're saying that with all the talk of balverines, they have to have existed in order to spawn it. And other creatures, too?"

"Most like." He spat again. This wad looked even darker red than the first, and he coughed a few times in order to clear his lungs. "Say what'cha will about the creatures of the night—and I could say plenty—but at least they're natural."

James exchanged a confused look with Thomas. "I thought they were unnatural, actually," said James.

"Pfaw!" The coachman snorted contemptuously at James and turned away from him, apparently having decided that he wasn't worth his time. Instead, he said to Thomas, "Machines are unnatural. Technology is unnatural. Great belching clouds of black smoke are unnatural. Balverines and dragons, scorpions and screamers . . . some of those things were old when the world was young. They have every right to be crouching in the shadows, waiting for unwary travelers such as you"—and he poked Thomas in the chest with a gnarled finger—"to let down your guard. They are beings of purest nature, and if they're recoiling from the damnable technology and the rotting of magic that passes

for the world today, then who can rightly blame them. I certainly can't. Can you?"

Thomas shook his head. "No, sir. I sure can't."

The coachman seemed to be trying to determine whether Thomas was being sarcastic. When he evidently decided that Thomas was not, he crooked that same finger that he'd been poking Thomas with a moment earlier, motioning the young man to draw closer. Thomas did so.

"Windside," growled the old man.

"I beg your pardon?"

"You want to be going to Windside."

"I do?" He looked to James, who shrugged. "Never heard of it."

"And Windside likes it that way." He pointed toward a distant mountain range that looked to Thomas to be about a day's walk. "Those mountains yonder are called Mistpeak. Just stay on this path and follow it up into them. Ain't navigable for horses; if you're on four legs, you'd have to be a mountain goat. But on two legs, you should be okay, especially if you pick yourselves up walking sticks in town to help steady you. Can't miss Windside; the buildings cling to the sides of the mountain more like bats than human structures.

"And what's in Windside that's worth all that effort?"

"The Library."

"Which one?"

"Just the Library," he said to Thomas with a sour look, apparently annoyed that Thomas had felt the need to ask. "It's got books on the exact sorts of things you want to find out about."

"Not sure that's a worthwhile use of our time," James said.

The coachman gave him yet another disdainful glare. "Wasn't talking to you."

James bridled at that, but Thomas put out a hand, cautioning him to silence, as he said, "What James means is that, well . . . I've been reading about these creatures my entire life." Then he saw the old man shaking his head. "I . . . haven't been?"

"Whatever you've been reading is tales retold, diluted, watered down, and gotten wrong, and with major pieces of them left out. That I can promise ya. Written by poseurs who heard stories from people what heard other stories. Ya want the real facts? Go to the source."

"And the Library is the source?"

"One of 'em, aye."

"Well . . . uhm . . . thank you," said Thomas, and he stuck out his hand to shake that of the coachman. The coachman, rather than taking it, looked at it suspiciously and turned, shaking his head. He hitched the horses to a post at the depot, and then walked away.

"We're not doing it, are we?" said James the moment that the coachman was out of earshot.

"I don't see why not," said Thomas readily.

"Well, how about that there's snow up there, which probably means that it's damned cold. And that the person who suggested we do it is some guy who drives horses for a living."

"And he's also the first adult not to treat me like I'm an idiot."

"Yes, but he treated *me* like I'm an idiot."

"Maybe, but that doesn't bother me as much." Thomas grinned. "Come on."

"Where?"

"To get some walking staffs. Also some gloves and wraps for our boots. Wouldn't want to freeze our feet or hands off."

"You realize we could die up there."

"At least we'd wind up well preserved."

With that, he headed off toward the local market. James reluctantly followed, muttering to himself about cold weather and coachmen who obviously didn't know when to keep their big mouths shut.

Chapter 4

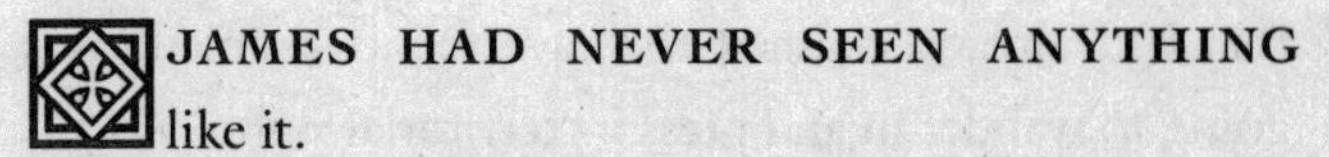

JAMES HAD NEVER SEEN ANYTHING like it.

That, in and of itself, wasn't all that surprising. Anything that he was witnessing that didn't look like either a run-down slum of a neighborhood or a moderately fancy manor—the two environs in which he had spent his fairly sheltered life—was by definition outside the realm of James's experience and thus was unlike anything he had ever seen. The more correct way to think of it was that it was unlike anything he had ever considered imaginable. In point of fact, the town of Windside seemed insane in its conception, to say nothing of its very existence. It was a town that by all rights should not have been there at all because James couldn't fathom *why* it was there.

"Who the hell would want to live here?" he gasped as he watched his own breath drift from his mouth.

He drew his cape more tightly around himself and was grateful for the gloves and boots that were keeping their extremities warm, or at least moderately so.

It had indeed taken them a full day and part of a night to reach Mistpeak, and they had found a convenient cave at the base of the mountain to camp in overnight. This was luxurious by contrast considering some of the places they had wound up camping during their sojourn thus far, because although Thomas did indeed have money with him, they had had to be judicious in its spending and thus had spent many a night sleeping under the stars. Still, even though the cave was relatively luxurious in comparison to their unsheltered stays, James kept waking up every so often, convinced that some large creature that had already claimed the cave for its domicile was going to wander in and press its territorial rights. Fortunately enough, that did not occur, and the only menace James had to face that night was Thomas's occasional, but nonetheless fearsome, snoring.

When the night had rolled over into the morning, they had emerged from the cave, stretched, eaten the remains of some heavily salted beef they had picked up at the market the day before, and then set out upon the path that supposedly would wend its way up to Windside. What had amazed James was the steady drop in temperature as their relative altitude climbed. It became progressively colder. At first it was barely noticeable, but the farther up they went, the more steadily and dramatically the temperature fell around them. The rocky trail became steeper, and soon every step that James was taking required effort and force of will. He was vaguely annoyed to see that, on the other hand, Thomas wasn't allowing himself to be the least bit deterred by his surroundings. They could have been strolling along a pleasant path in the forest for all that Thomas was willing to acknowledge the difficulty of their surroundings.

"You could at least *try* to make it look like you're straining," James had chided him. Thomas had simply grinned back, his smile the only thing visible within the darkness of the hood pulled up over his head.

Hours crawled one into the next, and the trail was getting narrower. It was becoming readily evident why horses would have been useless in this endeavor. There were points where the boys had to walk sideways in order to squeeze through, and James got himself hung up on his cloak several times, uttering profanities all along the way. "How much farther?" he had said at one point.

"How should I know?"

"Because coming up here was your idea!"

"Technically, it was the coachman's idea."

"Great!" James had shouted, his voice rising. "So we followed some nameless . . ." Suddenly something overhead caught his eye, something falling directly toward Thomas. *"Watch it!"* he cried out, and, grabbing the confused Thomas, he yanked him back toward himself. A column of ice, as long as a man and sharp as a javelin, crashed to the ground right where Thomas had been and shattered into fragments.

Gasping, Thomas and James stared at it, and then slowly and softly, Thomas said, "You might want to keep your voice down. Unless you feel like bringing down a ton of snow or ice on our heads. That's what loud noises do around here."

"So . . ." He looked around nervously. "You're saying that if I lose my temper, it could kill us."

"Pretty much."

"Wonderful."

That had been all the inspiration James had required to keep his mouth shut as they continued on their way. The path widened out a bit so that they were able to walk more normally after a time, but James was becoming increasingly concerned as the sun made its way across the sky, and no village presented itself. He was not enamored of the prospect of trying to find somewhere to make camp should night fall. For all he knew, Thomas's snoring would be sufficient to bring a drift down upon them. and they would freeze to death, buried alive beneath tons of snow. But he elected not to say anything of his concerns to Thomas because he had no desire to come across as someone who was constantly complaining. This was a quest, after all, and one did not whine about a quest even though the exact parameters of it were still a bit unclear to him.

They approached a blind corner of the type that always made James a bit apprehensive since he had no idea what to expect from around the other side. When they turned it, however, Thomas stopped in his tracks, and, as a result, James bumped into him with such force that the two of them almost went to the ground in a tumble of arms and legs.

"I'll be damned," said Thomas, and James was beginning to suspect they both would be when, as he dusted snow off his leggings, he saw what it was that Thomas was reacting to.

"Windside?" he said, and Thomas nodded, and replied, "Has to be."

There it was, just as the coachman had described. Spread out before them was a small valley that miraculously had taken shape right in the heart of the mountains. Neither of them would have thought the town could possibly be there if they hadn't been practically right on top of it.

The coachman had further been correct about it seeming as if the town had grown directly out of the sides of the mountain. There were small buildings in the valley, but there were also homes that appeared to be built right into the mountain itself. There weren't many, scarcely a handful. "Why would anyone live here?" said James wonderingly. "For that matter, *how* would they? Where do they get food? It's too cold for anything to be grown up here."

"I don't know," said Thomas, "but what I do know is that we're not going to find out anything standing right here." With that pronouncement, he headed toward the nearest building, which could reasonably be taken as an inn considering it had the word "Inn" scrawled on a sign that was dangling outside, flapping in the breeze and banging up against the building.

They entered and were promptly greeted with a chorus of, *"Close the door!"* because the wind was blowing so stiffly that it nearly ripped the door right out of Thomas's hands. James stepped in behind him, and Thomas forced the door shut. There were several people, scruffy-looking men, scattered about the run-down interior, which consisted of a few tables and chairs, most of which looked a bit crooked. With the door safely closed, the men took the measure of Thomas and James, snorted collectively in disdain, and returned their attention to their drinks. A tavern wench, with a large bust and larger attitude, approached them with a swaying motion as if she were on the deck of a ship. "What can I do fer ya?"

"We, uhm"—and Thomas glanced around—"were hoping to get a room for the night."

She looked them up and down. James thought she was trying to decide whether they were going to cause problems or not. "One room left upstairs," she finally said, apparently concluding that they were harmless. "Second door on the right. Tight squeeze, but it'll do ya . . ."

Suddenly, without any warning, she slammed her foot down on the floor. "Stupid wee beast!" she snarled downward. Then she looked back to the boys. "Got some vermin running around under the floorboards and in the wall. Ain't gonna be too bothersome for ye, is it?"

Thomas shook his head, and James did likewise. "No, not at all," said Thomas, and he reached into his purse and extracted the requisite two silver coins. He flipped them to the wench, who scrutinized them and then bit down on one of them. "You're supposed to do that for gold, actually," said Thomas.

She glared at him. "Telling me how t'do my job?"

"Nuh-uh," he said quickly. She didn't appear completely satisfied with his hurried response but chose not to press the matter. "Also, I was wondering if you might point us in the direction of someplace called the Library?"

"It's at the top of the stairs."

"Stairs?"

"Go out the door," she said, "look straight across the valley, and ya can't miss it."

"Okay, well . . . thank you," said Thomas. "We'll just put our things in the room and—"

"Actually, we're in kind of a hurry, so we'll drop them off when we come back," James said quickly, and then he pulled Thomas toward the door. "Just keep the room ready for us; we'll be back before you know it."

"I doubt that," she said, and that sounded rather ominous to James as they exited the inn.

"What was that about?" Thomas said in irritation the moment they pushed the door shut behind them.

"You really want to leave everything we own in the world in that room so that anyone could just walk out with it?"

Thomas was about to toss off an annoyed response, but then he paused and saw the wisdom in James's words. "All right, good point. So where are these stairs that she was talking ab . . . ?" Then his voice trailed off, and James saw where he was looking.

Directly across the valley, just as the wench had said, was a flight of steps. It seemed to go on forever, up the side of the mountain, and there was a fog bank that obscured whatever was at the top. They were just barely able to make out a vague shape that looked like a large building, which James took to be the Library they were seeking.

"Oh, perfect," muttered James. He turned to Thomas. "Seriously?"

"Seriously," Thomas affirmed, and James had to acquiesce. After all, they had gotten this far, so what was one flight of stairs? One incredibly long flight of stairs?

"Fine. No problem," said James.

BY HALFWAY UP THE STAIRS, JAMES WAS ready to throw himself back down. By the time they had made it three-quarters of the way up, James was ready to throw Thomas back down and then sit and point and laugh derisively as Thomas's sure-to-be-broken body thudded and thumped all the way back to the ground. He knew that it was an illusion, but it still seemed to James that no matter how much closer they drew, the end was never in sight. His breath became increasingly ragged, and his temper frayed.

Thomas, by contrast, remained in disgustingly good spirits. "Almost there," he said for what seemed the tenth time. Each of the stairs creaked under their footing, and James continued to be concerned that one of them would snap under their tread. Fortunately—or unfortunately, depending upon one's point of view—the stairs held up, and the Library remained attainable.

"Well—" Thomas started to say at one point, and James turned to him, and snapped, "If you're going to say, 'Almost there,' Thomas, I swear to—"

"Actually, I was going to say, 'We're there.' "

"What? Oh." James had been looking down for a time, focusing on his footing and keeping his face shielded from the increasing wind. They had reached a landing, a widened platform that was just a few steps shy of the top. "Okay, well . . . good. That actually went way more smoothly than I—"

"Don't move." Thomas was speaking very softly, and James had to strain to hear him. "Not a muscle."

"What?" He looked around. "What are you—?"

"I said don't move!" His voice dropped even lower, to barely above a whisper. "We're being hunted."

This time James did not respond orally. Instead, slowly, he turned his head in order to look in the direction in which Thomas's gaze was fixed. There was a snowbank positioned about ten feet away from them, and it didn't seem especially threatening as near as he could tell.

But then the snowbank moved ever so slightly, and then it rippled, and then it stretched and flexed its muscles, and that was when James realized that the snowbank had two small, yellow, vicious eyes that were staring right at Thomas and him. They narrowed as James made eye contact with them, and then he was able to discern the large head at the front of a sinewy body that was clearly ready to pounce. It was some sort of large cat, and its lips drew back in a snarl to reveal a fearsome row of teeth.

James's legs trembled, and suddenly that hideous home from which he had fled was starting to look a lot better to him. He remembered being told that animals could smell fear. If that was the case, this one was smelling pure, stinking terror.

"When it leaps," Thomas said, never looking away from the beast, "you go to the left, I'll go to the right."

"And we're doing that . . . why?" James was surprised by the evenness of his own voice.

"It'll be distracted, indecisive, for just a moment, and—"

While Thomas was busy explaining, the great cat leaped with an earsplitting screech designed to freeze its prey in its tracks.

It was partly successful, because although Thomas immediately leaped to the right as planned, James was riveted to the spot. The roaring beast came straight at him, and the only thing that prevented it from crashing into him and digging its claws into his flesh was Thomas's lashing out with his foot as he flung himself away, catching James in the hip and knocking him aside.

The white-furred cat landed between the two of them, its oversized head snapping this way and that. James saw that the creature wasn't solid white; there were small black spots all over it, faint but possible to see since it was close enough.

After a second's uncertainty, the creature apparently decided that James was the easier target. It whirled, its tail snapping straight out, and James saw its haunches go tight in preparation to leap upon him. He fumbled at the short sword dangling from his belt, and then the cat lunged for him.

James braced himself for the charge, and then he heard a scream of pain and was surprised to realize it wasn't his own voice. The cat was staggering and a still-trembling crossbow bolt was sticking out from its rib cage. James might have been the easier prey, but Thomas was now the more immediate problem, and the beast clearly was deciding to attend to him. Thomas was trying to nock another bolt as quickly as he could, but he was rushing. In his haste, he dropped the bolt and it clattered away from him, rebounded off the edge of the stairs, and fell away. There was no time for him to pull another from the quiver, and yet it didn't stop him from trying.

And just as the beast was about to attack Thomas, James's sword came clear of its scabbard. He swung it around, part desperately, part blindly, and he got lucky. The blade sliced across the cat's back right leg, severing the large tendons and hamstringing it. The beast screeched, this time not out of any desire to terrorize its victims but instead in pure agony. It tried to twist in midair, landed hard, and its hindquarters collapsed.

"Hah!" shouted Thomas. Disdaining the crossbow, he instead withdrew his sword and moved forward, preparing to put it out of its misery.

But James remembered that there was nothing more dangerous than a wounded animal. Before he could shout a warning, the cat pushed off with its still-functioning left hind leg and cleared the distance between it and

Thomas with a single thrust. It knocked Thomas off his feet and down he went, the sword tumbling from his hands. The creature was all of six inches away, and it brought its claws upward, ready to strike, and given one second, it would have torn away Thomas's face.

James tried to stab forward with the sword, knowing that he was going to come up short. Which was why he was as surprised as anyone could have been when the beast fell forward and lay there, unmoving. Its body shuddered once and then exhaled its last. For a moment James thought it was some sort of trick and then realized the absurdity of that. What possible reason would the cat have for trying to fool them, presuming it was even capable of such sinister thinking? Thomas had been totally helpless.

Nevertheless, James picked up a hard, cold stone and threw it with all his strength at the unmoving cat.

It continued to unmove.

He looked up to Thomas. "How did you do that? How did you kill it?"

"Me? I thought you did it."

James returned his short sword to its scabbard and crouched next to the animal. He saw something protruding from the base of the creature's skull. "What the hell—?" he said, and touched it gingerly. "It's a hilt."

"Of a dagger?"

"Other than our hovel being mortgaged to one, that's the only kind of hilt I know." He looked around nervously. "But where'd it come from? An invisible creature, maybe—?"

"I think it more likely that it was thrown."

"By who?"

"Whom."

"By whom?"

"Couldn't say." He looked around, squinting, trying to see some evidence of anyone else around. There were enough shadows to hide a dozen knife-throwers, and if they were not of a mind to be spotted, then they were going to remain unseen. He called out, "Whoever you are, we're very grateful! If you want to come out so we can thank you properly . . . ?" His call received no reply. "Ooookay," he said with a shrug after several moments of no response. Then he started to reach for the knife, but James grabbed him by the wrist, and said urgently, "No! Don't!"

Thomas gave him a quizzical look. "Why not?"

"What if pulling it out brings the creature back to life? What if it's supernatural in origin?"

"That's ridiculous."

"More ridiculous than balverines?"

Thomas was about to toss off a dismissive reply, but then the wisdom of James's words sank in, and he withdrew his hand, nodding. "Okay, fair enough. I mean, it's not likely, but we can't be too careful. Come on." And he clapped James on the shoulder. "Let's get up to Library before . . ."

"Before what?"

"Before we find out that this one here"—and he touched the cat with his toe—"wasn't hunting alone."

"Now you're the one with a fair point," said James,

and they quickly covered the remainder of the distance to the Library, both of them scrupulously watching the immediate vicinity lest another beast leap upon them.

THERE WAS BUT ONE LIBRARIAN PRESENT when they arrived. Thomas expected that there was going to be some involved wrangling necessary to gain access to the Library, but he could not have been more wrong. "Knowledge," said the Librarian, an elderly man with a thick white beard and disheveled hair, "should be free to all. You can take all your swords and war hammers and guns constructed by the hand of man, and none of them equals the power from information that a single book can provide you."

Privately, Thomas was of the opinion that a book wouldn't have done them a great deal of good against the animal that had tried to devour them out on the stairs, but he was a guest there and felt that it would have been impolite to say anything. But he exchanged a glance with James and could see that his friend was thinking the exact same thing. They shared a brief smile, and then Thomas settled down to business.

He found a sizable tome labeled *Creatures and Grotesqueries.* The book was thick with dust, apparently not having been read in some time. When he opened it, the spine creaked with the weight of years of accumulated knowledge. And the smell of it! What was it about mustiness that caused it to smell like wisdom?

The pages were of far thicker paper than any of the

books he had at home. Indeed, his old books seemed downright flimsy in comparison. He turned each page carefully, determined to make sure that he didn't tear any of them. When he reached the section labeled "balverines," he lay the pages down as flat as he could and began reading.

James wandered aimlessly around the Library, looking in wonderment at the shelves upon shelves of books. The Librarian walked alongside him, watching him with a raised eyebrow. "Have you read all of these books?" said James after a time.

"What would be the fun in that?"

"I don't understand."

The Librarian smiled through his dry and cracked lips. "The true joy of residing in this environment, day after day, is wondering what new bits of wisdom I might acquire in the process of perusing another volume in this vast and glorious collection of tomes."

"All right," James said cautiously, not sure that he really got it but deciding that if the Librarian knew what he was talking about, well, at least one of them did.

About an hour later he found Thomas hunched on the edge of his seat at a long table. There were now half a dozen books open to different sections, and Thomas's lips were moving softly as he read. "Well?" said James.

Thomas did not answer immediately, and when he did respond, it was in a voice hushed with awe. "It's amazing," he said, "how limited my books were in their scope."

"You're finding a lot about balverines here?"

"I'll say." He dragged over one of the books he had set aside and flipped through some pages. "Did you ever hear of the balvorn?"

"Uh . . . no."

"A monstrous beast of unknown origins. Fearsome beyond anything that anyone would have thought possible. Supposedly, in ancient times, it killed hundreds—maybe thousands—of people."

"Until it was finally destroyed?" he said hopefully.

"Actually, there's no record of the balvorn ever being slain although one would hope that it would be long gone to dust by now."

"One would hope that, yes."

"However, its handiwork remains to this day. Apparently only one person ever survived the attack of the balvorn. It doesn't say how he managed to pull that off, but he might have been better off if he hadn't lived. Because his reward was to be transformed into a creature that was smaller, but no less vicious, than its progenitor. I'd read that they spawned others of their kind through their bite, but I'd never seen anything about this very first of the balverines. Apparently"—and he shook his head in disbelief—"there have been actual instances of people rounding up balverines and pitting them against each other in pits of battle. Which is kind of a problem since the balverines were just as likely to find a way to leap out of the pit and attack the audiences as they were each other."

"What else?" In spite of himself, James was finding this information fascinating.

"Well"—and Thomas ran his finger along one of the

lines of meticulously rendered print—"the most aggressive and dominant of the balverines are white balverines. Supposedly, the white balverines are people who were slain by balverines during a full moon, at midnight. Something about that combination seems particularly potent." He started turning the pages of other books. "The book I'd really like to find here is something called the *Omnicron*. It appears to have a lot of detailed information about . . . well, about everything. I've checked the Library's files, and supposedly there's a copy here somewhere, but I went to where it should have been, and there's nothing there. I wonder if—"

"Wait . . ." James leaned forward, looking at the book over Thomas's shoulder. "Go back to what you were saying before."

"About what?"

"That balverines were once humans?"

"Well . . . yes. Why, what did you think?"

"I thought they were . . . I don't know. A separate race. So being a balverine is like having a disease?"

"I guess."

James sat down, perplexity on his face. Thomas turned in his chair and looked at his friend. "James—?"

"That's just . . . it changes things."

"Changes what things?"

"Well . . . if I were attacked by a balverine, I'd feel badly about killing it."

"Why in the world—?"

"Because they didn't ask for it, Thomas. They didn't ask to be made over into those . . . those things. You said it's spread by the bite? So if I get bitten by one of them, and I'm changed into a balverine, people will hate and fear me. For all we know, the people that they were . . . they're still in there somewhere, trapped in their brains. Inside every balverine there could be a person trying to get out."

"Perhaps several people if they feasted."

"Thomas!"

Thomas slammed the book shut, causing dust to fly from it, and he was on his feet, facing James. "I don't give a damn, James. So they didn't ask to be that way. So what? Neither did nymphs or scorpions or hollow men or whatever else is out there that crawls or swims or flies. They are what they are, and any of them would just as soon kill me, so I sure as hell better not hesitate because otherwise they'll manage to do it. If you've got a problem with that, tell me now, because if you do, then maybe you should think about going back home."

The air seemed to chill between the two of them. Thomas looked away first, dropping back down into his chair and turning his back pointedly to James.

James's jaw tightened. "Fine," he said between clenched teeth, turned on his heel, and strode away.

And Thomas started to call after him, but then caught himself and went back to his reading.

JAMES STRODE THROUGH THE LIBRARY, more agitated than he had ever been. Thomas had been the one constant in his life that was remotely worthwhile, but when his friend had lashed out at him that way, it was as if he didn't even recognize him. "Maybe he was possessed," he said to himself sarcastically. It certainly would have explained a good deal, but he knew that wasn't the case. He felt as if he had seen a side of Thomas that he hadn't known about before. What else, he wondered, was Thomas hiding?

He turned the corner and discovered the Librarian seated at a table, studying a book. The Librarian looked up at him and took immediate note of his agitation. "Problem, young sir?"

"No problem. No problem at all."

It was clear from the Librarian's look that he didn't believe that for a moment. "Tell me, young sir: Why are you here?"

"To learn about things. You know that."

"Yes, but why? Young people nowadays"—and he made an expression of disgust—"have no interest simply in knowledge for its own sake. The deterioration of the human spirit is a truly tragic thing to witness for any who have a sense of history. That is all that Heroes are these days, I fear. History. Here"—and he tapped the book in front of him—"look at this."

James hesitated. Something warned him against doing as the Librarian bade, but then he mentally scolded himself for such unseemly cravenness. It was an old man who just wanted to show him something in a book. *Are you determined to go through life jumping at shadows?*

He leaned in and looked where the Librarian was indicating.

"Your friend reads of balverines, who live to the east, when they lived at all," said the Librarian. "Of far more interest than monsters of the east are the Heroes of the east. Three formidable ones of true legend. Rather than obsessing about the worst that humanity has to offer, why not dwell upon the best?"

"How formidable were they?" said James, interested in spite of himself.

"I said the best, and I did not overstate. Balverines trembled in their presence, and hollow men bent to their will. Or so the legends claim," he added with a shrug. "It is hard to say of a certainty because, well, people talk, and they can exaggerate. That is the nature of legends, after all."

James was studying the texts. The Librarian was certainly right; page after page of text discussed their amazing accomplishments. In times of great crisis, people turned to these three Heroes to have their problems solved and their needs attended to, and apparently these Heroes never once let them down. Evidently, with their combined skills, they were capable of just about anything.

"It says here that nothing had ever defeated them," said James. "Apparently they died peacefully, in their sleep. Hunh. Doesn't seem like much of a death for Heroes. Heroes should die in battle with their teeth sunk into the throats of their opponents."

"And you would know this from personal experience?"

"Hardly," James admitted. "I suppose it's easy for someone who isn't a Hero to decide how others should lead their lives, or end them." He read further. "It says here they were each buried with some sort of weapon. Supposedly those weapons have great power—"

"And is that what your conspiracy is interested in?"

"What?" James, who had been bent over the texts, started to stand upright. "What are you talking ab—?"

Suddenly, the Librarian's hand was on the back of his head and slammed his skull down into the book, causing it to strike with such force that James thought the world was spinning around him. "Tell me!" snarled the Librarian in his ear, his voice no longer elderly. Instead, each word was crisp, the voice deep and resonant. "Do not think for a moment that you can fool me!"

"I . . . I don't understand! Fool you—?"

"Heading east, searching for balverines? What is your true mission?"

"That's it! That's all! I swear!" James tried to struggle against the old man's grip but didn't begin to make even the slightest progress against it.

"You're not searching for the power of the Heroes to use for your own selfish ends?"

"Are you *insane*? I never even heard of them before you brought it up!"

"And your friend?"

"I think maybe he heard of them. But even if he did, it wouldn't matter. He's looking for—"

"Balverines, yes. So you say. And why, pray tell?"

"Because his brother was killed by one and he wants . . . I don't know! Peace, I guess."

No reply came. It seemed as if the man was considering

his words. Then the hand withdrew. James gasped, sucking air in deeply, because the man had been pushing hard against James's throat, and he'd been having trouble breathing. He took a moment to gather himself and then stood and turned to face the man who had been abusing him so.

There was no sign of him.

He stood there, gasping, looking around, and was about to go in pursuit of his assailant before he realized that that probably wasn't the best idea. But why in the world would some librarian be attacking him? Asking him about conspiracies and such? It made no sense.

"Excuse me," said an elderly voice from near him, and even though it was soft-spoken, it caused him to jump. He grabbed for his sword and saw an elderly woman looking at him in confusion, her head cocked. She didn't seem to notice that he had his hand on his hilt, or perhaps she was just so old that she didn't give a damn if he cut her head off. "What are you doing here? Only scholars are supposed to be using this facility. You look like a vagabond."

"The . . . the Librarian said we could . . . that . . ." His hand involuntarily went to the back of his head. "I . . ."

"What Librarian? There's no one overseeing this facility save me. And you shouldn't be here."

"But . . . the old man—"

"You're blathering. There are no old men here. Just a young man who's making no sense. And I will thank you to leave now."

"I . . ." James stopped himself. There was no point in arguing with this withered crone. How was he to convince her that some strange man was wandering the halls of the Library posing as someone who was supposed to be there? And even if he did accomplish that feat, what was to be gained from doing so? What was the crone going to do? Sound an alarm?

Far better to just get out of there as quickly as possible.

He moved through the towering shelves, his thoughts racing far more quickly than he was able to keep up with them, and suddenly a figure stepped from the shadows into his path. Once again, he started to go for his sword until a familiar voice said, "I'm sorry, James, did I startle you?"

"*No!* No, not at all, Thomas," said James, trying not to let any sound of trembling be evident in his voice. "I was just . . . I—"

Thomas put out a hand. "I'm sorry. I shouldn't have snapped at you like that."

"Oh. Well . . . all right," said James, and he shook Thomas's hand firmly.

"No, it's not all right. You're my only true friend in the world, James, and you deserve better treatment than that."

"Don't worry about it."

"You won't be leaving?"

"Of course not. If I did, who would you have that you could abuse?"

"That's very true." Thomas said it with a straight face, but he wasn't able to maintain it, and they bo broke into laughter. He draped an arm around James's shoulders. "Come. I'll buy you as decent a meal as this rathole of a city can provide, and tomorrow we'll get out of here." He glanced around. "Have you seen that nice Librarian guy? We should really thank him for his help."

"We don't need to thank him for anything, actually," said James. "Come, I'll tell you over a drink because drink always makes the incredible far more credible."

Chapter 5

THE INN WAS REASONABLY BUSY THAT evening. Hardened travelers sat at the tables, chewing on what passed for meat in the place. There was one traveler who seemed to stand out among the others, though, as least as far as Thomas was concerned. He was seated toward the corner, his back firmly against the wall. He didn't appear focused on any individual; instead, he seemed to be watching everyone there all at the same time. He resembled to Thomas nothing so much as a snake that was basking on a rock, prepared to strike at any time but otherwise perfectly content to be left alone. He appeared middle-aged, and he had a narrow, hawklike face with a high forehead and thin hair graying at the temples. His eyes were half-lidded, as if he were partly asleep, yet for some reason Thomas had no doubt that he was entirely awake. His hands were resting lightly on a tapered black walking stick. His clothes were of a higher caliber than others around him. For one thing, they were freshly laundered, and the black material was fine rather than coarse. Cotton or perhaps even silk although Thomas didn't exactly have an expert's eye for such things. A gray greatcoat was draped over the chair next to him. He looked as out of place there as the boys themselves, but Thomas wasn't going to worry about him if he didn't appear to be presenting any manner of threat.

Thomas looked down at the plate piled with thin, barely cooked strips of meat, which was identical to the serving placed in front of James. As the serving wench turned away, wiping her hands on her apron, Thomas said, "Excuse me." She turned back to face him with ill-concealed annoyance. "Just out of morbid curiosity, what sort of meat is this exactly?"

"Snow cat," she said. "Fresh killed. Eat it and like it." Shaking her head in a way that made it clear that she didn't gladly suffer fools—or anyone, really—she walked away from them, leaving them staring at the unappetizing repast.

"Think it's the same one that tried to kill us?" said James. "That would explain why the beast wasn't where we left it on the stairs. Someone found it and—"

"And brought it here. Makes as much sense as anything."

"We're eating something that tried to eat us. Guess we had the last laugh." There were no utensils on the table, so he simply picked up a slice and bit off a piece.

More accurately, he pried it off with his teeth. Then he chewed slowly and with a great deal of effort before forcing himself to swallow.

"Well?" Thomas prompted.

"I stand corrected. The beast got the last laugh after all."

Suddenly, there was an explosion of noise from upstairs. It was a door slamming open and a big, burly northerner, all bristling beard and cold fury, stomped to the top of the landing and bellowed, *"Which one of you bastards did it?"*

Such a challenging declaration was impossible to ignore. Immediately, the men in the main dining hall of the inn were on their feet, and if the northerner was outnumbered by five angry men to one, he didn't seem especially concerned about it. "I'll take all of you together! For all I know, you were all in on it!"

"This isn't our problem," James said nervously.

"I'll go through every one of you and break you apart piece by piece until it's returned, starting with you!" And he pointed at Thomas and James.

"Now it's our problem," said Thomas. He stood and looked at the northerner in what he hoped was a placating manner. "Look, fella, uhm . . . I don't know what's going on, but I swear you—"

"He lost a ring." It was the hawklike man in the corner who had spoken up. His eyes were now fully opened, and they were glittering with amusement. "About yea large around," he indicated with his thumb and forefinger, "and a glittering sapphire in the middle."

"Yes! Exactly!" raged the northerner. "And if you stole it, then I'll—"

"Save your threats. I have taken nothing of yours."

"Then how do you—?"

"Because you were wearing it earlier this afternoon. Then you went upstairs to sleep off all the alcohol you consumed during the day, and when you chose to grace us with your presence just now, the ring was no longer on your finger. I assume that you removed it along with other trinkets—"

"I did not!"

"Then it must have slipped off your finger while you slumbered."

The northerner was coming down the stairs one shaking step at a time. Each thud sounded like a thunderclap. "If it had slipped off muh finger," he rumbled, "then I'd have found it on the floor! Or under the bed! But it wasn't there! I looked! I crawled around on the floor like a damned fool before realizing that one of you lot must have taken it!" He stepped from the bottom stair onto the floor with such force that pans hanging on the wall nearby shook violently. "All I found was this!" and he held up a small, half-eaten biscuit. "Somebody's idea of a joke, obviously! I'll show yuh who's laughing last!"

"Did you lock your door?" James spoke up.

"Of course I did!"

James continued, "So you're saying that someone picked the lock on your door hoping that you would be sleeping in there—and would also sleep through them coming in there in the first place—on the off chance that they might be able to find something worth stealing, either right off your hand or maybe being lucky enough to find a valuable trinket lying around on the floor? Come on. Does that make *any* sense to you?"

"Yes!" said the northerner, but he said it with a healthy measure of uncertainty. He hadn't even managed to convince himself, much less them.

"Okay . . . I'm glad it works for you," James said, trying the best he could to keep any hint of sarcasm from his voice. The fact was that the northerner could still pick him up and break him in half if he were so inclined. "But you'll understand if we find it a bit, uhm . . . dubious."

"The only thing I care about being found is muh ring," said the northerner, who was obviously starting to get himself worked right up again. James took an involuntary step back, certain that this entire business was going to start spiraling out of control very quickly.

He glanced toward Thomas, but Thomas seemed fixated with staring at the floor.

"Well?" thundered the northerner, clearly ready to keep true to his promise of assaulting everyone there—beginning with Thomas—until his ring was returned. The other customers were now glancing nervously at each other. None of them was especially enthused about the notion of taking on such a behemoth of a man. Even though they outnumbered him, somehow the odds still seemed tilted in his favor.

That was when Thomas looked back to the behemoth, and said with a calm voice, "Let me take a look up in the room."

"So you can put it back and hope yer not caught?"

"I don't have it, but I have a thought as to who might. Come along with me if you feel like it. In fact, it's better if you did, so you can see for yourself." With that, and without bothering to see if the northerner was in fact going to follow him, Thomas started up the steps.

The northerner looked puzzled. James had a feeling that the northerner was unaccustomed to people speaking to him in a reasonable manner, particularly when he was being belligerent. The bruiser shifted his gaze to James and looked comically quizzical, although James suspected that laughing at the man would be about the worst thing he could possibly do. Instead, James opted for the chivalrous course, bowed slightly, and indicated with a gesture that the northerner should precede him. The northerner did so, albeit with a skeptical grunt.

James also noticed that the hawk-faced man was watching the proceedings with what seemed a keen interest. James wasn't altogether sure that that man wasn't the one responsible for the ring's vanishing and was getting some twisted amusement over watching them run around in frustration.

Thomas was waiting at the top of the stairs and, when the northerner was in sight, pointed, and said, "That's your room?"

"How would you know that," said the northerner, his suspicions aroused, "if ye weren't already in it? Eh?"

"You knocked the door off its hinge when you barreled out of there yelling."

"Oh." Slightly abashed, which James wouldn't have

thought possible, the northerner said, "Aye, I, uh . . . I did do that."

"That's going on your bill!" the tavern wench shouted up from below. He answered back with an inarticulate growl, and she backed off and settled for glowering up the stairs at him.

Thomas stopped at the doorway of the room, the northerner right behind him. The rest of the northerner's supplies were stacked up to the right of the small bed, the mattress upon which looked as if it had been permanently bent courtesy of the man's weight. James noted with worry that most of them appeared to be weapons shoved in a large duffel bag.

The northerner looked in confusion at Thomas. "Aren't yuh going t'go in?"

"No," said Thomas. "I don't have to. I see what I'm looking for."

"The ring?"

"Not the ring." He was rummaging around in his purse and came up with a handful of coins. He sifted through them, and James couldn't imagine what he was looking for.

"Then how are yuh going t'find it?"

Thomas selected one silver piece and held it up. It glittered nicely in the light, much more so than any of the others had. Thomas nodded approvingly and then flipped the coin across the floor. It bounced a few times before landing at the far side of the room, which wasn't all that large and therefore not all that far. "Now," said Thomas, "we wait."

"Wait for what?" The northerner was looking increasingly impatient and was clearly getting angrier. "How long are we supposed t'wait?"

"As long as it takes although it shouldn't be too long . . . if you stop talking, that is. The more you talk, the longer it's probably going to require." Thomas looked at him blandly. "Do you have some other pressing engagement?"

It didn't seem possible that the northerner could scowl even more fiercely than he already had, but as it turned out, that was the case. Nevertheless, his beard bristling as if in response to his indignation, the northerner lapsed into silence.

Nothing happened for long minutes. The coin simply sat there. Others in the inn, curious due to the lack of fighting or, at the very least, the severe mauling that had failed to ensue, crept up the steps to get a better look. The stairs creaked under their treads, and James would do his best to shush them, although it wasn't as if he had much clearer an idea of what was transpiring than anyone else.

And then, just when it seemed as if the northerner's admittedly limited patience was at its end, Thomas's eyes narrowed, and he pointed. "There," he said, so softly that it could scarcely be heard.

There was a loose plank in the floorboard at the far corner. Thomas had been eagle-eyed enough to spot it even when no one else had. Now the board moved ever so slightly, and a small pinkish nose emerged from beneath. Because the light was dim, and the men at the door remained unmoving at Thomas's behest, the owner of the nose grew confident, thinking itself unobserved. Seconds later, it had emerged from the plank. It was a small, gray-furred rodent, larger than a mouse but smaller than a rat, with its eyes set up higher on its head than a typical rat's would be. It skittered across the floor straight toward the coin and picked it up in its tiny claws. It gnawed on the coin for a moment and then, even though it clearly wasn't any manner of food, turned and scuttled off with it back toward the plank.

"What the hell—?" breathed the northerner.

"Shhh!" Thomas said sharply. The instant the creature had disappeared beneath the plank, Thomas was inside the room and on his knees. He preemptively put a finger to his lips, indicating that everyone else should remain quiet. Now they could all hear the skittering of the tiny creature under the floorboards. Thomas followed it, putting his head against the floor so that he could hear it more clearly. He followed it as it made its way around the room. Seconds later Thomas was crawling under the bed, and then he stopped. He waited a few moments, and said, "Someone slide me a dagger." Unsurprisingly, the northerner was able to produce one instantly. He knelt and slid it carefully under the bed. They heard a faint scratching, then Thomas emerged from the bed. He extended the dagger to the northerner, hilt first, and then indicated the bed. "Push it aside," he said.

"But what was that thing?"

"It's called a pack rat. I heard something scuttling

around under the floor downstairs earlier on. When you told me what had happened, I remembered it. They're pretty common in more deserted areas in the land. If they see something sparkly and are carrying something when they do, they tend to drop whatever it is they have in their paws so that they can grab up the shiny item. And I think its nest is right under there."

The northerner, needing no further urging, yanked aside the bed and revealed an "X" on the floor that Thomas had carved into it with the dagger. "Now," said Thomas, "you can use the dagger to pry up the—"

The northerner dropped to one knee, drew back his huge right fist, and slammed it into the floor right on the mark that Thomas had etched upon it. The boards offered no more resistance than would have a thick piece of paper.

"Or you can just punch through the floor," said Thomas with a faint sigh.

He yanked up the floorboards, and there was an outraged squeal from beneath. There was the pack rat, looking up at them in great indignation, chittering at them and obviously scolding them for the intrusion. The northerner let out a roar like a wounded lion, and the pack rat, apparently realizing its precarious position, opted to bolt from there as quickly as it could. "I don't believe it," growled the northerner, staring down into the hole. He reached in, and his large hand emerged with a fistful of brightly glimmering trinkets. Most of them were more or less junk, but there were a few valuable-looking items in there. One of them was his ring, which he quickly slipped onto his oversized finger. And there was Thomas's coin, which the northerner flipped over to Thomas, who caught it deftly.

"What about the other things in there?" said James.

The northerner glowered at him in that way that only a northerner could. "Adequate payment for my inconvenience," he said.

James was about to offer protest, but Thomas put a hand on his arm and shook his head, indicating that seeking further hostilities with the beefy man would probably not be in either of their best interests.

Minutes later, they were back at their table in the main room. No one was saying anything to them. Some of them were even looking resentful, which Thomas couldn't quite understand and said as much to James in a low voice.

"Maybe they're just ingrates," said James with a shrug.

"Or maybe," said a low, clipped voice, "they would have welcomed a brawl, and you spoiled their fun." The hawk-faced man who had been off in the corner had pulled his chair over to them and was now leaning forward, resting his hands on the handle of his cane. "Of course, they also know on some level that you did them a favor since that behemoth would undoubtedly have massacred the lot of them single-handedly. But they'd never admit to that. So they have no choice but to glower at you in vague dissatisfaction." He paused and allowed a small smile to pull at the edges of his mouth. "A pack rat. You're astute."

"What's a 'stute'?" said James uncertainly.

The man stared at James for a moment as if trying to determine whether he was serious or not. Then, apparently, he decided it wasn't worth the effort and turned back to Thomas. "Of course, if you had not become involved, I have little doubt that I would have been able to figure out the fate of the ring myself. But your intercession was welcome."

"Was it?"

"Yes. It saved me the minor effort of having to climb the stairs." He inclined his head slightly in lieu of extending a hand to be shaken. "Quentin Locke. Pleasure to meet you officially."

"Thomas Kirkman," said Thomas, and he nodded toward James. "James Skelton."

"Young Master Skelton," said Locke, "seems to have taken a dislike to me."

Thomas looked questioningly to James. James simply shrugged, and said, "I don't like boastful people."

"Really. Then you must have little patience with Heroes since they are renowned for standing upon street corners and declaiming their greatness for all and sundry. How will you be Heroes if you do not embrace the proper mind-set?"

"What makes you think we want to be Heroes?" said Thomas.

"Why Thomas, don't you know?" James said sarcastically. "Mr. Quentin Locke here knows everything. After all, he would have been able to figure out about the pack rat if he could only be bothered to climb a flight of stairs. He said so himself. Easy to figure things out after the fact."

"Indeed." Locke gave James no more than a cursory glance. "You come from a poor family in Bowerstone. Multiple siblings of which you are the second oldest. You have a fondness for sweets that you do not indulge as much as you would like, and you are only barely literate. You attend this young man"—and he nodded toward Thomas—"as a servant although you are as much friend as he has ever had. And you, Mr. Kirkman," he continued, "are a well-off son of a textile merchant, your mother died recently, and you have boundless antipathy toward your father and an excessive interest in balverines."

The boys sat stunned at this litany. It wasn't as if he was telling them anything they did not know, but the fact that he knew it as well completely blindsided them. "He's a wizard," whispered James. "You're a wizard."

"He's right. You're a wizard."

"Hardly."

"How did you know all that?" said Thomas.

"I know what I know, and that is all *you* need to know, save this." And he leaned forward, and said in a hushed voice, "There is more danger on your path than you could possibly anticipate. There are things going on, forces at work, that could swallow you whole unless you're careful."

"Are you sure?"

"I am as sure of this as I am that the northerner will come to you in a manner that you will perceive as threatening but which actually is not. Be ready for all things." He pulled slightly on the handle of his cane, and the boys were surprised to see it come loose from the walking stick to reveal the gleaming edge of a blade attached to it. There was a sword secreted within the cane. Quentin Locke nodded once to acknowledge that they had seen what he was showing them before sliding it back into place. He touched his brow, as if tapping the brim of a nonexistent hat, and said, "We will see each other again, I have no doubt." And with that he rose from the table and was out the door.

The boys regarded each other with an equal mix of amazement, skepticism, and amusement. "What the hell are we supposed to make of that?" said James at last.

"He said he wasn't a wizard."

"Would someone who was a wizard admit to it, in this day and age?"

"A good point," admitted Thomas. "Still . . . I suppose maybe he was some sort of eccentric making lucky guesses." But he wasn't entirely convincing even himself, much less James.

Suddenly, James was half rising to his feet defensively. Thomas turned to see what James was looking at, and there came the northerner, gripping a musket in his hand.

"Oh no," muttered James.

Thomas was likewise worried, his hand moving toward his sword.

If the northerner saw the defensive gesture, he gave no indication. Instead, he laid the gun down on the table and stepped back. "I don't understand," said Thomas.

"This is for you. Oh, and this." And he tossed a small leather bag onto the table next to the rifle. "Some ammunition. Wouldn't be of much use without it."

"I . . . still don't understand."

"I can't abide being in any man's debt. Against the northern creed. We give weapons as thanks."

"That's . . . interesting," James said slowly. "Just out of curiosity, how often do northerners get attacked while they're trying to express their gratitude?"

"More often than ye'd think. People are just ungrateful, I guess."

James nodded. "That's probably it."

"Anyway"—and the northerner patted the musket—"use it wisely. Have yuh ever fired one before?"

"No. I imagine that it's like a bow?"

"Yes, except the recoil can knock out yer teeth if you're not careful." He smiled broadly for the first time, pulling back his lips. There was a gaping hole in the middle.

"I'll be careful."

"Good man." He patted Thomas on the shoulder, nearly dislocating it in the process, and then turned and walked away.

"Well," said James in amazement, staring at the newly acquired rifle on the table. "What do you think of that?"

"I think," said Thomas, "it's rather interesting that that's the first time in my life anyone has ever referred to me as a man instead of a boy. I have to say"—and he grinned broadly—"I rather like it. It all worked out well."

James raised his glass. "To the pack rat."

"To the pack rat," agreed Thomas, and they clinked glasses.

As they did so, the tavern wench came over and

slapped down a piece of paper between them. Thomas looked down at it and arched an eyebrow. "What's this?"

"The bill for the hole in the upstairs floor that's there thanks to you."

"But we didn't punch a hole in the floor!" James protested. "The northerner did!"

"Then *you* tell him to pay," she said.

James was about to continue to complain, but Thomas, with a heavy sigh, reached into his money purse and pulled out the requisite amount. The wench pocketed it with a disdainful look and walked away.

"Stupid pack rat," muttered James.

I FROWN, PUZZLED, SOME BIT OF INFOR-*mation niggling at me. That's how it often seems to me these days. That there is always something I am trying to recall and it is just beyond me, just out of reach.*

"Locke," I finally say, as the narrator of this little fable stops and looks at me in guarded surprise. "Quentin Locke."

"Yes," says the speaker, and then adds almost as after-thought, "What of him?"

"The names of Thomas Kirkman and James Skelton are unknown to me, although I mean no insult to what I am sure are two sterling young men . . ."

"You are the king. You can insult whomever you wish if that is your desire."

"That is as may be, but the point is that the name Quentin Locke is known to me. Or . . . perhaps someone else with that name, or a similar name . . . ?"

"He has relatives. They tend to get around."

"Thomas and James."

"Pardon, Your Majesty?"

"The boys. You left them in the tavern, so to speak."

"Ah. You were prompting me to continue. A thousand pardons, Majesty, I should have understood immediately." He settles back into his narrative. "The two hardy lads—or more precisely, one who was a man and the other who had aspirations to be so—departed upon the next morning and made their way east.

"Hunting was not always plentiful, however, and the travelers were not always sanguine about spending their nights sleeping out under the stars, particularly as—the farther east they went—the more inclement and even unpredictable the weather would become. But taking up residence indoors naturally cost money, and although Thomas was not without financial resources, it was easy for them to become depleted. And so—"

"They took up jobs? Resorted to thievery?"

"Neither extreme, as it turns out," he tells me with a smile. "James, as it so happens, was quite proficient in games of skill and chance for monetary benefits—"

"You mean gambling."

"I do. He was quite the cardplayer, was James Skelton. Thomas, as honest as the day is long, did not have the requisite control over his demeanor. He was an abysmal liar and therefore not particularly adept at bluffing or discerning when it was better to withdraw from a game or push hard for further gain. James, by contrast, was a skilled reader of others' moods and temperaments. Plus he was wise enough

to win just so much and no more. Not enough to garner ill will or engender anger or confrontation, but more than enough for their purposes, particularly as they moved from town to town.

"And all along the way, Thomas would inquire of balverines. For every fifty people he would ask, from forty-nine of them he would receive laughs or disdainful looks or pitying stares followed by the invariable shaking of heads and mutters of, 'Some people' or 'A grown man, believing in such things. Imagine!'

"But there was always the one in fifty . . . the one in fifty whose voice would drop to a hush and who would look around fearfully as if concerned that creatures might leap from the shadows cast upon the walls by firelight from a nearby hearth . . . who would nod and speak of the creatures that Thomas sought. They might tell a tale of having come upon one themselves and reveal a vicious scar that was a souvenir of the encounter. Or they might claim to know someone, or know someone who knew someone else, although the more distant the source, the more elaborate the description.

" 'Where to find them, then?' Thomas would ask.

"And they would look at him as if upon a lunatic, and they would ask why in the world someone would seek out such creatures instead of determining where they were and then taking pains to head in the exact opposite direction. And Thomas's face would be set and determined, and he would simply say, 'I have my reasons.' 'So do madmen have their reasons for what they do, but that does not make them any the less mad,' would be the reply, or some variation

thereof. Finally, though, the advice would always come down to the same thing. 'East,' he would be told. 'East is the way of the balverine. Last I've heard, last I knew, last anyone knew, they all withdrew east.'"

"Why?" I interject. I am aware that this man, this spinner of stories, dislikes interruptions, but then again, I am king, and royalty does have its privileges. I know that and so does he, and so although there is a brief flash of impatience upon his face, he does not give voice to that impatience. "Why east?"

"Why do you think, Majesty?" he says.

I give it some brief thought. "They would have been either running away from something . . . or toward something. If the former, then—were I to hazard a guess—it would be away from the things of man. Balverines are creatures of myth and magic, and mankind has developed into a race that deplores such things. Mankind . . ." And I despise saying the words aloud, but it is all too true. "Mankind is becoming tame in its view of the natural world, and balverines are by definition unnatural and untamed. Thus would they flee such deplorable concepts as science or industrialization and seek more . . . primal climes. If it is the latter, on the other hand—if they are running toward something . . ."

"Then what would that be?"

"A good question. Is it one to which you have the answer?"

"Mayhap."

"Well then"—and I gesture languidly—"proceed."

"As you wish, Majesty." And he bows slightly and, I

have to think, a bit mockingly, but I indulge him as a king would a jester.

"Farther east, then, did our young would-be Heroes travel. The more time that passed upon their expedition, the most resolute they became that they would eventually reach their goal, although what would happen then, neither of them could begin to guess. All they knew is that nothing, absolutely nothing, would stop them."

Chapter 6

"CAN WE GO HOME NOW?"

Thomas gave James the sort of annoyed stare with which James had become extremely familiar in the many weeks that they had been heading steadily in the direction of the rising sun. "A little setback, and you want to go home?"

"A little setback?" By the look of him, James seemed as if he wanted to burst out laughing but was too incredulous to do so.

The two of them were standing on the edge of a ridge, having just hiked their way through a challenging but not insurmountable series of hillocks. James was even coming to appreciate the new sights, sounds, and even smells that they were encountering. The trees, plants, wildlife, and even the air itself underwent subtle changes, and it gave James a true insight into the wealth and variety of environments that Albion had to offer.

But when they came around the side of what turned out to be the final hillock in that particular day's journey and stood upon the ridge, staring forward at the new obstacle in their path, James wasn't sure how to feel. After all, they were on a quest with no discernible destination or termination in mind, or at least in James's mind. If there was something clear in Thomas's mind, he had been doing a superb job of keeping it to himself. The uncertainty of their situation had brought James to a place where, if they were unable to proceed any farther and be forced to turn around—and thus never find themselves face-to-face with balverines—then he, James, wasn't going to be particularly upset about it.

On the other hand, he was a devoted friend to Thomas and knew how much it meant to him that he accomplish his aim, however ill defined that aim might be.

But when he found himself standing next to Thomas, staring at an endless vista of rolling blue waters, he blurted out, "Can we go home now?" without even really thinking about it. It just seemed self-evident that that was going to be the next order of business. So when Thomas described it as "a little setback," James was properly astounded.

"A little setback?" He made a sweeping gesture toward the horizon. "You call that *little*?"

Indeed, it was hard to argue with James's point. What was stretching out before them down below was nothing less than an endless vista of blue water, rolling steadily toward the shore.

"It's a sea, Thomas! It's a bloody *sea*!" James continued.

"I know it's a sea, James. I can . . . uh . . . see."

James shook his head and stared with an air of hopelessness at the newly discovered obstacle. "Maybe they all meant some other 'east.' "

"That's the only definition of east of which I'm aware," said Thomas.

The sun was leaving no uncertainty in the matter. It was still midmorning, and the glowing orb was positioned serenely in the sky. Unless the entirety of the cosmos had reoriented itself at some point during their travels, east definitely lay ahead of them, and there was a massive body of water making sure that they weren't going to be heading that way anytime soon.

"There's probably land on the other side," said Thomas.

"Probably?"

"Definitely." His hand covered his brow as he endeavored to see farther. "I'm definitely sure I see a hint of land on the horizon."

"And how do you suggest we get there? Flap our arms and fly?"

"We'll get there the same way that anybody gets where they want to go when water's in the way. We'll go by boat."

He continued down the path that wound steadily through the hillocks. James hustled to follow him, and said, "Thomas, I hate to bring this up, but I don't know how to sail. And unless you've been hiding some talents from me, you don't either."

"I'm not suggesting we captain and crew a vessel ourselves, obviously."

"Obviously," said James, to whom it had not actually been obvious at all.

"We'll hire someone to take us across. We have the money for it."

"You mean *I* have the money for it."

This comment prompted Thomas to stop, turn, and face his friend. He did not appear angry; instead, he just looked disappointed. He stopped so abruptly that James almost collided with him from the back and prevented that only at the last second with strategic deployment of the walking stick.

"Is that what it's come to, then?" said Thomas. "We've been sharing everything the whole trip, no questions asked. Food, money, resources. What's mine is yours and the other way around. And suddenly we're going to start keeping watch on whose is what?"

Absolutely. That's absolutely right. I've been more than keeping up my end of this entire insane affair, and now when geography itself is trying to tell us something, that's where I'm drawing the line.

And he saw the defiant look in Thomas's eyes, but also one of hurt, even betrayal.

He lowered his gaze, and said, "Of course not. We're a team. Whatever I can do to provide for this"—and he allowed a small smile—"this mad adventure, I'm there for it. But"—and he now looked back into Thomas's eyes—"who do we hire? For that matter, where do we hire them?"

"It's a sea," said Thomas, visibly relaxing at the reaffirmation from his longtime friend. "Where there's a sea, there are going to be port cities. We head down to the shoreline and start walking until we find what we're looking for."

"Which way?"

"Pardon?"

"Which way," said James, "do we walk? The land stretches off in either direction."

Without hesitation, Thomas said, "South."

"Why south?"

Thomas shrugged. "Because south is usually warmer."

James smiled broadly at that. "I like the way you think," he said, the mist emerging from his mouth not unnoticed.

They made their way down from the hillocks, treading carefully and nearly stumbling over some treacherous roots that seemed to exist solely to trip them up. Once they reached the shore, they turned and headed south.

THE FIRST VILLAGE THEY CAME UPON WAS little more than a few ramshackle homes strung together supposedly—according to the residents—for mutual protection. It was a ludicrous notion since, as far as Thomas and James could discern, even an army composed of twenty addled cripples armed with unstrung crossbows could have laid waste to the place. But they didn't dwell on it beyond wishing the residents good day and continuing on their path along the shore. This eventually brought them to a city called Seaside, which appeared to have a small but busy port. There was a permanent aroma of brine in the air, and James had to step carefully over the seemingly endless stream of rats that were skittering around the docks. One particularly fat one approached him with far more audacity than James was comfortable with, and he swung his walking stick at it, using it like a cudgel. The rat dodged away and ran, stopping only to give him a glare with its beady eyes.

"James! Over here!" It was Thomas calling to him, and he turned and saw that his friend was standing on the deck of a brigantine. Next to him was a well-dressed man in a long coat and a tricorn hat perched jauntily on his head. He was thick browed with a salt-and-pepper beard, and had a pleasant enough expression. His very presence seemed to inspire confidence, and James trotted up the gangplank. "Captain Rackam, this is James Skelton," Thomas said by way of introduction. "James, the captain here is giving us passage."

"I hear you're heading toward Blackridge," said Rackam.

"We are?" said James, looking questioningly at Thomas, and then quickly amended, "I mean, we are."

"Shorewall is where we're bound," said Rackam. "We have some cargo to transport over there, so it's not as if we're going out of our way. Blackridge is not too far, a couple day's journey. Provided"—and he lowered his voice, glancing around with sudden fearfulness—"we don't run into any opposition."

"Opposition?" echoed James, and now Thomas was looking uncertain as well. "You mean like . . . pirates?"

"Pirates? Pirates are the least of our problems. We need to beware"—and his voice went even lower, barely above a whisper—"*the kraken.*"

James gulped deeply, and Thomas looked pale. Rackam glared fiercely at them from beneath his furrowed brow, and suddenly his entire expression lightened, and a booming laugh issued forth. It shook his whole body, and Rackam clutched at his ample belly, which was likewise jiggling with mirth. Crewmen who were prepping the ship for departure stopped momentarily to enjoy their captain's amusement before they returned to their duties. "I'm sorry, lads," Rackam finally said when he managed to compose himself and catch his breath. "Just me having some fun. The look on your faces, though . . . it was worth it."

"So there are . . . no krakens," Thomas said. "I mean, I've read about them, and they're supposed to be . . . well . . . rather formidable."

"'Formidable'? That's an understatement, my lad," said Rackam. "According to legend, nothing can stand up against one of those monsters. Like a force of nature, they are. But that's just legend, like I said. Ain't no such thing, if ever there was one. Least not that I've ever seen, and

I've been sailing these waters since I was about your age. So I wouldn't be worrying about it none if I were you."

"Oh, we're not worried, are we, James?"

"Not at all," James said hastily.

"So"—and Rackam clapped his hands together briskly—"you have payment? In advance, as agreed?" He looked from one to the other expectantly, and Thomas in turn looked to James.

"Right, right, of course. How much are we talking about?" said James, removing his money purse from within the folds of his cloak. Thomas told him the agreed-upon price, and James carefully counted it out before handing it over to Rackam.

"Excellent," said Rackam cheerfully. "A pleasure doing business with you." He raised his voice, and called, "Mr. Sawkins!" A deeply tanned man with intricate tattoos running the length of both arms approached. "Mr. Sawkins, see our passengers to their quarters, would you, please?"

"This way, gents," said Sawkins with a gravelly voice.

He led them belowdecks, where there was a small, unfurnished room with a couple of bedrolls in the corner. James looked to Thomas uncertainly, and said, "This is where we're staying?"

"Finest accommodations we've got," said Sawkins, and he laughed coarsely before turning and walking away.

"Nice," James said.

"I know it doesn't look like much . . ."

"It doesn't look like anything." He dropped down

onto the floor and looked up at Thomas. "Are you sure about all this, Thomas? Have you verified anything about this Rackam fellow?"

"He comes highly recommended."

"By who?"

"By others along the docks."

"Which means," said James slowly, "that they could all be in on it together."

"It? What it?"

James was ready to answer quickly, but then he realized he didn't actually have an answer. Just a general, free-floating, unnamed concern. "Nothing," he finally said. "I'm just not thrilled about depending upon anyone except ourselves."

"We'll be fine, James," Thomas said with confidence.

It was a confidence that James did not feel, but he chalked it up to his natural tendency to see the worst of any situation, which he had always believed provided a natural balance to Thomas's occasionally infuriating optimism.

THE GENTLE ROCKING OF THE SHIP ONCE IT had set out from the harbor had lulled James to sleep as he lay on the floor of the cabin. That in and of itself was surprising to him since he wouldn't have thought it possible to obtain any slumber under the circumstances: being in a strange environment, in the company of men—some two dozen crewmen—none of whom he knew. But they had been traveling steadily enough that he was far more exhausted than he would have thought, and thus into a deep and dreamless sleep.

It was the growling and the high-pitched, abbreviated shriek that awoke him.

He sat up, momentarily bewildered, uncertain of where he was in that way that oftentimes happens when one awakens in someplace strange. In the dimness of the cabin, illuminated by a single porthole, he wasn't sure what he was looking at. Then, when he did see it, he jumped back, crying out in confusion.

There was a rat mere inches from his face, but it was dead. Stone-cold dead and being held in the jaws of what was possibly the most unruly dog he had ever seen.

It was a mutt, that much was sure. Some sort of terrier but with several other breeds mixed in, with disheveled brown-and-black fur and a left ear that had been partly chewed off in some fight long ago. Likewise truncated was its tail, which was wagging fiercely and was little more than a stub with a bald patch where once fur had been.

There was a deceased rat hanging from its teeth. Its body was still twitching slightly, but that was clearly final spasms from a rodent already well beyond its death throes. James fancied it was the same one that had been snarling at him on the wharf but tended to think that was more his imagination than anything else. Even James Skelton, with his highly developed sense of perpetual persecution, didn't think that one dumb animal had pursued him onto a boat just to try and settle a score. But then again, who could say for sure?

"What the hell—?" came Thomas's incredulous reaction. He was on the far side of the room and had already gained his feet. Despite the fact that the boat was rocking, Thomas moved with it, having adjusted so quickly to the movement of the ship that one might have thought he'd been on the ocean before. This prompted a flash of jealousy from James, who never failed to marvel at how quickly Thomas was seemingly able to adapt to any situation. "Where did that dog come from? And what's—? Is that a rat?"

"It was," said James, "but it's certainly not anymore." He locked eyes with the dog, who was regarding him with an open stare and mild curiosity signaled by a tilt of its head. The dog then lay the dead animal at his feet, barked loudly several times as if announcing its triumph, and then simply stood there with its tail wagging even faster to indicate that it was obviously in a rather cheery mood.

"Scratch its head," said Thomas.

"*You* scratch its head.

"Oh, fine," said James, "but I've never been much for animals." He obediently scratched the dog's head, and the dog flattened its ears and pressed its skull up into James's hand. For good measure it rubbed the rest of its body against James's leg.

"I think he likes you," said Thomas.

"Everyone likes me." He scratched the dog's head harder and even smiled. "I guess I'm in no position to be a snob. Near as I can tell, that rat was going to take a piece out of me, and the dog stopped him cold."

"Good for him, then. You should—"

"What the bloody hell is going on down here?"

It was the irritated voice of Sawkins, who had been passing by the cabin and stuck his head in, probably upon hearing the barking. "Where did that mongrel come from?"

The question surprised both Thomas and James, and they exchanged confused looks. They had both just assumed that he belonged on the ship. Judging by the sailor's annoyed tone, they had jumped to a false conclusion.

"Come on, you!" shouted Sawkins, and he strode forward purposefully. The dog slunk back and growled, but Sawkins didn't hesitate. He yanked his belt out from his trousers, batted the dog's snarling attack aside as if he were dealing with a recalcitrant two-year-old, and then lashed the belt around the dog's throat so deftly that only a matter of seconds had passed from the discovery of the dog to its being effectively overwhelmed. The dog tried to snap at Sawkins, but he effortlessly yanked the teeth clear of him, and in moments the dog was whimpering pathetically. Sawkins then dragged the animal up and out of the cabin, and just before it was hauled out the door, it cast a quick, pathetic look in James's direction.

James hesitated just long enough to grab up the fallen rat, and then he took off after them, Thomas following. They sprinted up the short ladder to the main deck just in time to see Sawkins yanking the dog toward Rackam, who was stepping down from the bridge and regarding the animal with a suspicious stare. "And what have we here?" he asked.

"Mangy mutt from the docks, cap'n," said Sawkins. "Must've crawled down into the hold and fell asleep there in some nook."

"Well, over the side with it," Rackam said impatiently. "We have no time for stowaways, especially the four-legged kind."

This was obviously the answer that Sawkins wanted, and he started to haul the dog toward the side of the ship.

"Let him go!" James had just emerged from belowdecks, and now he was crossing quickly, going right up to Sawkins and not backing down despite the intense glare from the seaman. "I said let him go!"

"You said?" Rackam was addressing him, and it seemed he didn't know whether to be amused or annoyed, and settled for something in between. "You're a passenger on my ship, Mr. Skeleton—"

"Skelton."

"—and I don't see where what you have to say means a damned thing." He nodded to Sawkins, who started to pull the dog toward the edge.

Thomas put a hand on James's arm, trying to restrain him, but James shook it off and stepped forward. The amusement that had been visible in Rackam's face moments earlier evaporated, leaving only the annoyance behind, annoyance and something more that would have been a warning to James had he been paying attention. "It means a damned thing because being a passenger on your ship makes me a paying customer, and besides"—

his mind raced, and he blurted out the thought before it was fully formed—"that's my dog."

"*Your* dog?" Rackam wasn't buying it for a second. "I didn't see you bring it on board."

"He ran on ahead. I'm actually glad you found him because I was worried he'd been left behind."

"Look, boy," said Rackam, "I don't know what your game is, but I know that dog. It hangs around the wharves, scrounging what it can and hoping someone feeds it."

"Look, I wouldn't, for a second, think to challenge you when it comes to, you know, seamanship or maritime skills," said James, digging deep into himself and finding resolve he hadn't even known was there. "But by the same token, I'll bet that you're no expert on dogs. So there's no way you can be absolutely certain as to whether you're looking at the same dog as was back on the wharves or one who just happens to look a hell of a lot like him but has in fact been my close companion for years now."

"*He* has."

"Yes," said James firmly. "*He* has."

"It's a female."

James blanched. "A female?"

"Yes. Even I, a humble nonexpert on dog breeding, can discern that little fact."

James looked to Thomas for help. Thomas cleared his throat, and said weakly, "Right. Well . . . that *would* explain the litter of puppies last year . . ."

"Wait!" James cried out, as Sawkins prepared to heave her over the side. "Please!"

"'Please' is a good start," said Rackam, "and not a word you've used yet in this discussion. That bit of courtesy will garner you an extra minute or so." He gestured for Sawkins to wait, and Sawkins did as ordered although it was clear from his expression that he wasn't happy about it.

"Look, Captain," said James, "she saved me from a rat that certainly didn't have my best interests at heart. You could use a good rat catcher on this boat—"

"Ship," Rackam corrected him sharply.

"Right, sorry. Ship. A good rat catcher on the ship. And besides, I'll"—he harrumphed deeply in an *of course I forgot to mention this but it should have been obvious* manner—"I will naturally pay for her passage."

"Pay for it."

"Of course." He reached into his coin purse and pulled out a fare equivalent to what he had paid for himself. "And you don't even have to find her separate quarters. She can bunk with us."

Rackam stared at James, obviously scarcely able to believe it. "You'd pay full rate of passage for a mutt?"

"No. I'd pay full rate of passage so that I don't have to watch a creature who just saved me from a rat bite get drowned."

The captain stroked his beard for a moment, then put out his hand. James, seeing it, let out a sigh of relief, put out his own hand, and shook the captain's firmly.

Rackam looked at him askance, and then said, "The money, you idiot, not your bloody handshake."

"Right. Yes, of course." And James hurriedly proffered the agreed-upon sum. Rackam took it from him, counted it quickly to double-check, and then said quietly to Sawkins, "Release the bitch."

It appeared as if Sawkins was about to offer protest, but he then thought better of it and let go his hold on the dog. She trotted across the deck as if she had not just narrowly avoided a watery grave and rubbed up against James's leg.

"Enjoy your honeymoon cruise with your girlfriend, Mr. Skeleton," said Rackam, and then he laughed loudly, and the rest of the crew joined in.

"Skelton," James corrected him, but so softly that no one heard him, nor would it have made any difference if anyone had.

Thomas stepped in close to his longtime friend and slowly shook his head in disbelief. "That was a hell of a thing," he said in a low voice. "What were you thinking?"

"I was thinking exactly what I said: That I wasn't going to stand by and just see a helpless creature thrown into the sea."

"You realize," Thomas pointed out, "that you could have been tossed into the sea right along with it, and there wouldn't have been a thing I could do to stop them."

"Oh, I don't believe that for a moment."

"You think they wouldn't have done it? If you'd continued to give backtalk to the captain? They take these things seriously, James."

"Oh, I believe all that," said James. He was crouching next to the dog, scratching the underside of her chin. She was clearly enjoying it and looking up at him with huge brown eyes that seemed to say that he was the center of her world. "But what I don't believe is that you wouldn't have found a way to stop them. That's what you do, Thomas. You find ways, when no one else can. You," he continued with confidence, "would have found a way to save my sorry ass, and the dog besides."

"It's kind of you to say so, but—"

"No buts," said James firmly. "I'm no brownnoser, Thomas. I'm not trying to blow sunshine up your skirts. I'm just telling you what I think is true."

"Well, let's hope that your life doesn't come down to counting on my supposedly bottomless wellspring of cleverness."

"There are worse ways to die," said James, "than counting on your friend only to have him let you down."

Thomas stared at him blankly. He didn't have to say anything; his bewilderment spoke volumes.

"Uhm . . . yeah," James said uncomfortably, scratching the back of his head, "that sounded better in my head."

BOTH THOMAS AND JAMES ENDURED A period of adjustment with shipboard life, particularly when it came to the steady swaying of the vessel. They adapted to different aspects at different speeds. Thomas, for instance, was far steadier on his feet than James, who staggered for hours and had an unfortunate tendency to fall over if there was any chop at all. On the other hand, James had the far stronger stomach and wasn't the least bit put off by the vessel's nauseating rocking, while early in the voyage, Thomas hung over the edge and vomited up the rum and salted pork that had served as their main source of nutrition since boarding the ship. Their mishaps served as endless fodder for the sailors, who found their problems a diversion from the occasional tedium of shipboard life.

At one point, while Thomas was slumped on the deck, his head whirling from the nausea of seasickness and feeling the right fool, one of the sailors sauntered by. He was the oldest of the crewmen that Thomas had seen, with a few stray wisps of hair clinging stubbornly to his head and skin so dried out by the sun that it looked like old leather. He said cheerfully, "Feeding the kraken, were ye?"

Thomas looked up at him in confusion. "Feeding the—?"

"That's what we call it when ye empty the contents of yer stomach into the old briny. Some people believe a kraken gulps it up and follows, looking for more."

"Do they." He adjusted how he was seated on the deck so that he wasn't slumped over anymore. The motion made his head swim all the more, but he worked as best he could to shake it off. "The kraken wouldn't exactly be known for its discerning palate, then, I take it."

The sailor stared at him blankly. "What?"

"Never mind," said Thomas, shaking it off. But now

his interest was caught, and he said, "Captain Rackam said there were no such things as krakens. That they were just yet another creature of myth that maybe never was and certainly isn't anymore."

"Oh, I've no doubt he said that," said the old sailor, and then he lowered his voice and suddenly seemed deathly serious. "But I've been around a bit longer than the captain, aye, I have. And there's more at the bottom of the sea than most men would want to admit because it gives 'em comfort to believe otherwise. Yet ships still get lost at sea every so often, young master, and it's easy to blame the elements or pirates or what have ye." Then, with a low growl, he said, "It's man's own fault, it is."

"What is?" Thomas didn't quite understand what he meant by that.

"All this"—and the old sailor made a face of unrestrained disgust—"this invention. Technology. Industry and such. Things were fine as they were, but there ya go, with men who think they know so much making all their so-called improvements in the world. Pushing creatures of myth and magic into the shadows and the recesses of men's imaginations. Did they think there'd be no price for that? Did they truly believe that those selfsame creatures wouldn't, at some point or 'nother, take a stand and start pushing back? Ye know what a volcano is, boy?"

Thomas nodded.

"Myth and magic, it's like a volcano. And men and their inventions and technology and industry, it's like they been trying to shove corks in the top o' one of them volcanoes. Try to bottle up the forces inside. And ye can't do it. Ye can't, because ye know what happens, sooner or later?"

"It blows."

"Sky-high." The old sailor nodded. "And anyone what happens to be around when it comes, well, they get good and cooked. You get what I'm sayin'?"

"I think so," said Thomas slowly.

The old sailor regarded the sea with what appeared to be the greatest depths of suspicion. "There's something building in the world, boy. Something big and something bad, and I ain't sure that any of us are gonna survive it. The pushback's comin', count on it. Just hope that you're nowhere around when it happens."

The old man turned away, and Thomas suddenly blurted out, "What about balverines? Do you know anything about balverines?"

"Why?" He arched one of his bushy white eyebrows.

"Because"—and he squared his shoulders, and said with as much bravado as he could summon—"I'm looking for them."

For a long moment, the old man said nothing, and then he said brusquely, "If that's the case, ye best hope the kraken takes ye." Then he stalked away, shaking his head and muttering in disgust about young idiots and their fool, antiquated notions of quests.

It did little to lift Thomas's spirits.

Chapter 7

LYING IN THE CRAMPED QUARTERS that he was sharing with James, Thomas was all too aware of the fact that the ship was starting to rock increasingly. He was hardly a seafaring individual, but he was certainly able to tell when there was a change in the conditions that the ship had been experiencing, and that was most definitely happening now.

"A storm," he muttered. "It *would* come rolling in now, when we're supposed to get into port tomorrow morning." He glared upward toward the skies, even though obviously he couldn't see them since he was belowdecks. "You couldn't have held off," he asked the unseen clouds, "for one more day?" His stomach had only recently settled into something manageable, no longer determined to eject food from him forcibly at the slightest provocation. And now a new challenge was being presented it? It just didn't seem fair somehow.

Then he heard roaring laughter, a demented giggling, and a minute later, James made his way down into their quarters, the dog right behind him. He hadn't given her a name yet, despite Thomas's urging to do so, since he wasn't convinced that the animal wasn't going to take off the moment they reached their destination. "If I don't give her a name," he had reasoned, "I won't feel betrayed and abandoned."

"You worry about things that don't bother any normal person," Thomas had said, but didn't push the matter.

So now came James and his nameless pet, and he seemed entirely too pleased with himself. That self-satisfaction immediately prompted a trill of alarm in the back of Thomas's head, but he tried to tell himself that he was being paranoid for no good reason. "What's with you?" said Thomas. "You seem in an awfully good mood."

"I am indeed." James grinned like a fool. He pulled out his money purse and held it up for inspection. "Notice something different?"

It was hard not to. It was bulging, so packed with coins that their outlines could be seen pressed against the sides.

"You didn't."

"I most certainly did."

"You *gambled* with these men? These sailors?"

"They invited me," James said in mild protest. "They were playing at cards, they challenged me—"

"Which was it? Invited or challenged?"

"A bit of both, actually. They obviously thought I'd be easy pickings, Thomas." And it was clear that the notion irked him. "Now they know differently."

"James . . ." Thomas was shaking his head. "What were you thinking? Were you thinking at all?"

"It's not as if I cheated! I won fairly!"

"I know! You always win fairly! But have you forgotten that that hasn't stopped you from having major problems with sore losers? And the only way you've avoided getting the crap kicked out of you was that we've gotten out of there, sometimes as quickly as humanly possible?"

"So? I still don't . . ." Then his voice trailed off. "Oh."

"Yes. Exactly. 'Oh.'" Thomas had gotten to his feet, and he was standing several feet from his friend, his arms folded, regarding James with exasperation. "There's nowhere to go on this vessel. Putting some distance between yourself and a pack of sore losers isn't an option. Unless you're about to suggest we jump overboard and throw ourselves on the sea's mercy."

James, who had been waving the sack of coins around with such pride and relish, was now staring at it with as much enthusiasm as if he'd been holding a bag of pus. "What should I do? I mean . . . I could just return it . . . but won't that seem like I'm admitting that I cheated? Like I have a guilty conscience, trying to make things right even though I didn't do anything wrong?"

"I'm not sure. Maybe the smartest thing to do is ask the captain. He knows his men best, after all." He paused, and then, eyes narrowing, he said, "Was the captain one of the players?"

"No."

"Then we should be thankful for small favors, I suppose. Toss it here. Let's see how much there is."

Obediently and reflexively, James lobbed it toward Thomas.

It never got to Thomas's outstretched hand.

Instead, the dog, which was between them and apparently under the impression that a game was being played, leaped up with unexpected enthusiasm and snagged the bag of money between her teeth.

"Poxy cur!" James shouted. "Give it here!" He lunged for it, but the dog—still thinking it all a game—deftly dodged him and bolted from their quarters.

"Oh, *fantastic*!" said Thomas with a moan. James was already out the door after the fleeing animal, and Thomas hesitated, wondering if he should bother to go in pursuit as well. This was, after all, James's problem. But Thomas had noticed that James's problems tended to become his problems as well. Even as he headed out after James and the dog—the latter being easy to track because there was no great trick in following James's string of outraged profanity—he was already coming to the conclusion that they would have been far better advised to have let Sawkins toss the damned beast overboard when he had originally wanted to.

Down, down into the bowels of the ship did James and Thomas pursue the dog. Obviously, she was heading for the place where she felt the greatest safety: the hold of the ship, where she had first stowed away. Why the hell couldn't she have stayed there, hunting rats, slinking around, and keeping out of their way and not needlessly complicating their lives?

The smell of brine became stronger in Thomas's nostrils, and the rocking of the ship was becoming even more severe. Several times, as Thomas clambered down short ladders chasing after the continued cursing of his friend, he staggered and nearly fell, catching himself at the last moment. He jumped down from another short ladder and landed on what he realized was the bottom of the vessel. His boots hit water: not much, not enough to make him think that the ship was sinking. But it was enough to make him believe that there was a slow leak somewhere, and the sides of the ship could stand with some maintenance.

That was when he realized that he wasn't hearing anything from on ahead. Not the dog barking and not the stream of profanities from his companion. "James," he called tentatively. "James—?"

"Thomas," James's voice floated from the darkness ahead. "I think you need to see this."

There was naught but darkness ahead of him for a moment, and suddenly light was glowing. It illuminated James's face, and Thomas realized that James was holding up a lantern that must have been hanging from a peg nearby. "I should see a lamp?" said Thomas, not quite understanding what it was that James was trying to show him.

"No. This." James raised the lamp higher and turned

a key in the bottom, causing the light within the lantern to burn a bit more brightly. When he did that, it gave Thomas a better view of their surroundings.

There was an amazing assortment of things, from rugs to perfumes, foodstuffs to clothing, and weapons, all kinds of weapons. They were on slightly raised platforms to avoid any chance of seepage getting into them and damaging them.

"So what? We knew they had cargo; they told us that."

"But of such variety? There's no rhyme or reason to it. And this." And he held up tags that were attached to one of the tapestries. "It says 'Property of W. Maheras.' "

"Maheras." The name was familiar to Thomas. His brow furrowed as he tried to recall why that should be, and then it came to him. "He was a merchant. My father had some dealings with him. And then he ran into major financial difficulties because he had a shipment that was stolen by . . ."

He stopped, his throat closing up, paralyzed by the dawning realization.

"Pirates," said James, who had already had sufficient time to process that which Thomas was only now just grasping—including the immensity of their situation. He was rummaging through other materials in the cargo. "This store of wine, from another merchant vessel that was raided. There's no telling how long some of this has been down there."

"They sell or trade as need, and live off that which can be of use to them," said Thomas.

"What do we do? What the hell do we do?" said James, and then he froze, his eyes widening.

Thomas realized immediately that James was looking behind him. He turned and saw, standing on the ladder that led down into the hold, Rackam. Despite the rocking of the ship, which was becoming increasingly violent as the storm built in intensity, Rackam was standing perfectly still. Still as death. He was holding a pistol in his hand, and it was leveled at Thomas. Despite the extreme jeopardy of their situation, Thomas could not help but be impressed by the fact that he kept staggering this way and that, fighting not to be thrown off his feet, while Rackam remained unperturbed.

"If it makes you feel any better," Rackam said in what was almost a purr—like a lion studying helpless prey and enjoying the anticipation of a kill—"we were likely as not going to dump you over the side tonight anyway. You are, after all, rather well-funded young men, and there's no earthly reason to deliver you to your destination with your wealth intact, let alone with your lives still within your bodies. But Master Skeleton here made the decision that much easier for us. Not just easier: pleasing."

"All right, now you're just getting my name wrong deliberately simply to annoy me, aren't you?" said James.

"I'll be having your money now," said Rackam. "All of it."

James stared at him levelly, and then said with what seemed to Thomas absolutely supernatural calm: "What money?"

Rackam was clearly in no mood for trading words with James. "I was hoping you would cooperate and then head up to the deck on your own, so that my men wouldn't have to haul your dead bodies topside. But"—and he shrugged—"we will do what must be done." And he shifted the gun so that it was now aimed squarely at James. The cocking of a hammer on a gun produces a sound like none other in the world, and that singular noise was like an explosion in the cargo hold.

The sound of it catapulted the dog from the shadows nearby. The dog, which had been relatively meek in fighting to defend her own life, was unstintingly, unhesitatingly vicious in responding to a direct threat to James. With a snarl, she leaped through the air, bounding once off a crate, and clamped her jaws on Rackam's extended arm a split second before he fired. The shot went wide, exploding harmlessly against the bulkhead. The gun tumbled from Rackam's hand, and the pirate captain roared and cursed and tried mightily to shake the dog off his arm. But the distraction was enough to cause even the seasoned pirate to lose his footing, and the dog managed to drag him off balance, the animal given additional sure-footedness by dint of her being on all fours. Rackam went down, pounding furiously on the animal, who resolutely refused to let go of Rackam's arm.

"Go! Go now!" shouted James, gesturing frantically for Thomas to head up the ladder while Rackam was distracted. Then he turned toward the weapons and grabbed up a cutlass, a large, fearsome-looking blade.

With a roar, he charged straight at Rackam, who was on the ground, wrestling with the dog.

The instant he drew within range, Rackam lashed out with one booted foot, catching James directly in the pit of the stomach. James doubled over, staggering, falling against the ladder that Thomas was already halfway up. Briefly distracted, the dog's hold on Rackam's arm loosened, and it was just enough for Rackam to yank his arm free and then shove the dog away. He grabbed for his fallen pistol, reached it, swung it, and fired it into the shadows into which he had thrown the dog. There was a pained yelp from the darkness, and then Rackam turned his attention back to the boys.

They were gone.

Thomas and James sprinted back to their quarters, quickly gathering up their gear. "What about the dog?" said James, but the look Thomas gave him immediately quieted him. Thomas knew he should be angry with his friend for bringing up something as relatively trite as an animal when their own lives were at stake, but he really couldn't blame him. The dog had saved their lives just then against Rackam's weapon. Certainly that should have entitled the animal to some loyalty on their part. Perhaps James was the one with the right idea, but in any event, Thomas was hardly in a position to discuss it just then.

He checked his rifle to make sure it was loaded, then slung it over his shoulder and grabbed his other weapons and supplies as well. James whipped his newly acquired cutlass through the air once or twice, nodded approvingly, and then shoved it through his belt. From outside, they could hear the howling of the wind and deafening roar of thunder. "Now what?" James called, trying to get above the noise that was surrounding them.

"We grab a lifeboat!"

Going topside seemed unthinkable, but waiting around in their cabin for Rackam or his crew to come after them wasn't exactly an option either. James nodded and then followed Thomas.

They emerged into chaos.

Sawkins was at the wheel, lashed to it so that the huge gouts of water wouldn't knock him over the side. The night sky was black as pitch, the moon afraid to show its face, and lightning ripping across the roiling clouds providing the only illumination. The sails were furled since they would have done no good under the circumstances. When Sawkins saw Thomas and James emerge onto the deck, he shouted at them, gesturing wildly for them to get back below since he was unaware of what had transpired belowdecks. They ignored him, instead trying to stagger across the deck to get over to the lifeboat. Sawkins screamed at them, demanding to know what they thought they were doing, but the wind carried his words away . . . not that it would have made any difference even had they heard him.

Thomas made it to the lifeboat first, grabbing on to the ropes that were holding it in place, but before he could loosen them, a blast of water slammed over the side and hammered into him, lifting him off his feet, crashing into his body with the force of a thousand blows.

Thomas had no chance and was thrown backwards, and the only thing that prevented him from being knocked clear to the other side and off the boat was James, clutching onto the main mast for dear life while making a desperate, all-or-nothing grab for Thomas as he hurtled past. James snagged Thomas's wrist, and Thomas felt a sharp pain lance through his shoulder as the force of the sudden stop nearly yanked the arm from its socket. He shoved the pain away into the furthest recesses of his mind, figuring he would deal with it later should there actually happen to *be* a later.

They both clutched onto the mainmast for a few seconds, hoping that the furious seas would subside long enough for them to take refuge in the lifeboat and get clear of the ship. Thomas knew that the odds of their survival in a small vessel in these waters were minimal, but if they stayed on the ship, their chances were nonexistent.

Then their hearts sank because suddenly the deck was awash with far more than vicious waves.

Rackam had emerged from below, murder in his eyes, and the rest of his crew was following him. Even that old sailor, the one that Thomas had been talking to, was among them, waving a sword in a threatening manner and looking as ready to deal death as any of the others were.

Thomas and James were still closer to the lifeboat than anyone else, but with all the pitching and rocking that the ship was undergoing, it was impossible for them to release their grip on the mainmast without risking being hurled bodily off the side. Rackam's men, far more practiced at dealing with vicious pounding from the environment, were making their way toward the boys. Rackam had obviously reloaded his pistol because he was gripping it tightly in one hand while wielding a sword in the other, maintaining his balance like an expert tightrope walker as he advanced on the boys, with his men following him.

Thomas would not have thought it possible for the ship to lurch more violently than it already had, but he would have been wrong. The ship abruptly shuddered with such force that even the sure-footed Rackam and his men were thrown down, and the vessel rose partly out of the water, as if another wave were lifting it up. It did not, however, slam back down again. It seemed, at first, as if the ship had run aground on some manner of atoll or reef. Perhaps it had even struck another vessel that had been long ago sunk and now existed only to be an obstruction.

But then the ship slammed back down into the water, apparently rolling off whatever it was that it had run into. Rackam and his men looked around, confused. Then they dismissed it from their concerns, focusing instead on their reason for having ventured onto the deck during the worst storm in memory.

Abruptly, the ship shuddered again, as if the subsurface reef had somehow pursued them. Perhaps there was indeed a derelict ship beneath the waves that was being pushed around and used as nature's battering ram to continue pounding the pirate vessel.

And then there was a scream. Despite the pounding

of the surf, despite the roaring of the lightning and shrieking of the wind, still was that scream heard. Even though it had been produced by a human throat, it sounded inhuman, likely because the situation that was prompting it was beyond human ken.

It was one of the crewmen, and something had grabbed him around the middle. Because of the darkness, it was impossible to discern what it was at first.

As near as James could determine, it was some sort of snake. It was pale, incredibly pale, wrapped around the sailor's middle, and the sailor was continuing to scream and pound at it in a vain effort to make the huge reptile let go. *Some sort of serpent that the wave washed up onto the deck,* Thomas thought, and that seemed to make sense.

It stopped making sense, however, when the sailor was lifted off his feet and yanked skyward. Ten feet high, then twenty, and that was impossible, just impossible. How in the world could a snake, even a serpent, hoist the man in the air like that? How long and powerful was this creature, anyway?

"Hellllllp!" shrieked the pirate, his terror-filled voice once again carrying over the cacophony of the storm, and then he was gone, just gone. Yanked downward abruptly by the serpent and under the surface.

There was no sign of either the man or the snake.

Rackam froze where he was, unable to comprehend what he had just seen, the boys seemingly forgotten.

Then came an explosion of water. Not a wave leaping over the side of the wildly rocking vessel but an actual detonation of something violently displacing it, and suddenly there were serpents crawling all over the deck, slithering across it, seeking out contact. Their coils were everywhere, and most insane of all, Thomas couldn't see their heads. Their bodies just seemed to end in points.

That was when he realized. That was when they all realized. If they hadn't been distracted by everything that was going on—the boys' attempted escape, the tempest tossing the ship, the hammering waves—it would likely have come to them sooner. As it was, even experienced sailors could find themselves in situations where there was too much happening to readily grasp.

Now the serpents were grasping them. Except they weren't serpents at all.

It was the old man, the elderly sailor, who was the first to give voice to what they had all come to understand. *"Kraken!"* he shouted, and, oddly, there was no fear in his voice. Instead, there was almost a sort of twisted satisfaction, as if he was faced with death but felt it was utterly worth it in order to be proven correct. Thomas couldn't be sure under the circumstances since rain was pounding in his face, but it even seemed as if the old man was smiling.

The ship shuddered violently yet again, and it shook Thomas and James from their temporary paralysis. Thomas screamed in James's ear, *"Go! Go for the lifeboat!"*

"That thing is in the water! You want us to get closer to it?"

Once more the ship trembled, and then there was a sound, a terrifying sound. When one is chopping down a tree, there is always that moment when the point of no return is reached, an earsplitting cracking and snapping that indicates the tree is about to give way to the demands of gravity and begin its death-fall to the ground. That was the sound they heard at that moment, towering above the fury of the storm because it was so much closer.

Thomas grabbed James by the shirtfront, and shouted, *"It's breaking apart the ship! We're going to be closer whether we like it or not! We might as well be floating!"*

There were sudden screams. The tentacles—not serpents, obviously—were seeking new victims.

"Good point!" yelled James.

Sawkins had been snagged around the leg, and, his arms pinwheeling, he was hoisted high into the air, howling for help that wasn't forthcoming. Those pirates who were armed with pistols were firing everywhere, and their shots were rebounding harmlessly from the kraken's hide. Rackam, shrieking curses at the beast, had pulled out a sword and was hacking away at one of the monster's limbs. He was screaming incoherently, telling the creature to get the hell away from his ship. Even though the sword wasn't penetrating, the force of it and—perhaps—the pure fury of the ship's captain, caused the tentacles to recoil for a moment, as if trying to determine the true nature of this harassing creature.

Then the tentacles lashed forward, as quick as the huge snakes they resembled. One of them wrapped around Rackam's ankles and the other around his upper torso before he had time to react, and then Rackam was lifted up, up, struggling, writhing in the creature's grasp.

He had barely enough time to cry out one final time in defiance, and then the tentacles twisted in opposite directions and Rackam was torn in half, blood geysering in all directions, splattering across Sawkins, who had been close enough in the creature's clutches to witness his captain's fate. Sawkins shrieked at what he'd seen, and then he was gone, dragged off the ship and down into the depths.

And the old sailor who had warned against the advent of the beast stood perfectly still. He made no move, took no action against the tentacles. Instead, he remained utterly immobilized, and the boys watched with astonishment as the tentacles went around all sides of him but never came into contact with him. It was as if he were standing in the middle of a snake pit but was invisible to the inhabitants therein.

Then a splintering line that ran the width of the ship began to appear. Somewhere below, somewhere unseen, the beast was applying pressure to the ship's underside and was systematically cracking it like a large seagoing egg. The boards beneath their feet were splitting apart, and Thomas and James were out of time. They dashed toward the lifeboat even as the boat angled against them. The tentacles were everywhere, and they dodged between them, bounding like dancers, the tentacles snapping at them and trying to ensnare them.

The few remaining crewmen tried to follow their lead, but the boat was breaking in half, and they were too far down. The angle against them, the pirates slid backwards, some of them off the boat entirely, others into the grip of the tentacles. The only one still standing was that same old man, and Thomas had a brief moment where the two of them locked eyes. The old sailor brought his arm up and saluted gravely, and then a huge wave slammed up and over the teetering aft section of the ship, and the old man was gone.

Thomas and James lunged forward and grabbed the rail of the ship just as more water pounded over them. They barely held on, and then Thomas yanked at the ropes that secured the lifeboat to the side of the ship. The knots were holding them tight, water-soaked and impossible to deal with.

"*No time!*" shouted James, the cutlass in his hand. He swung it around with incredible force, and it was at that moment that Thomas came to the realization that James was considerably stronger than he was. Either that, or sheer terror and a desire to survive were enough to increase anyone's upper-body strength.

The blade sliced right through the rope, parting it effortlessly. The lifeboat tilted wildly, hanging at a sharp angle, and then James leaped straight up to avoid one of the tentacles that was slithering across the deck. Thomas followed suit, clutching on to one of the support ropes from the rigging, and used his own knife to hack through the remaining support ropes. There was a squeal from the overhead pulley as the boat's weight caused it to give way, and the lifeboat fell away and down into the darkness.

"*Now!*" shouted Thomas, and James required no further urging. He couldn't clearly see where the boat was, but he could see where the ship was going. The tentacles were now everywhere, pulling in opposite directions as they had with the late Captain Rackam. He had been ripped apart in a matter of seconds; the ship, while far larger, wasn't going to take all that much longer.

Thomas leaped clear of the ship, as did James. He hit the water and went under, and for a split second he had a glimpse of something beneath. It was vast beyond comprehension, and he thought he briefly saw a huge eye, and then a second. Thomas couldn't swim, but desperation propelled him where knowledge could not. He emerged upon the water's surface, gasping for air, and then his salvation emerged from the darkness. It was the boat, with James already in it, fumbling with the oars in an effort to draw closer to him. He needn't have bothered; the waves were doing the job of bringing him straight toward Thomas with such force that, had Thomas been a hair slower, the prow would have crushed his skull. As it was, he was able to twist to one side just in time to avoid getting his head bashed in, and a second later he grabbed on to one of the oars as a cresting wave drove the lifeboat past him.

"Come on! Come on!" James snarled between gritted teeth, leaning on the oar and seesawing it so that Thomas was practically catapulted into the boat. The tiny vessel rocked so violently from the impact of Thomas's forceful entry that it very nearly capsized, but James threw himself in the other direction and righted it. Water lapped over the sides, and Thomas grabbed a small pail that was tied to the inside of the boat for just this situation and

proceeded to bail out the water as quickly as he could. James, meanwhile, manned the oars, necessity serving as a particularly apt teacher, using them to steady the boat and navigating the waters with impressive deftness for a beginner.

Then something lunged out of the water at them and James, with a startled cry, nearly tried to strike it with one of the oars. He held up at the last second and gaped in astonishment.

It was the dog, paddling furiously, desperation in her eyes.

"I don't believe it," Thomas said. "That damned animal has more lives than a cat." Even as he spoke, he put down the bucket he was using to bail and stretched out a hand. He grabbed the frantically swimming animal by the scruff of the neck and hauled her toward the boat. Then he let out a cry as the dog, desperate to get on the source of very meager safety, clawed at his chest and even scratched his face before tumbling onto the bottom, water splashing up around her. "Poxy cur!" he cried out, and cuffed her, but she snapped her head away and deflected most of the impact. She didn't snarl in response, though; instead, she looked at him with apologetic eyes and then started eagerly lapping at the water gathering on the bottom.

"It's salt water! It's no good for you, Poxy!" James shouted over the thundering all around them and pushed the dog away from it with a shove of his foot. The dog looked surprised, but she didn't continue with her endeavors to drink it.

"Poxy?" Despite the severity of their situation, Thomas found the strength to half smile. "That's her name now?"

"Well, I called her that, and you called her that. So it seems fitting someh—"

Poxy suddenly started barking, and if it was possible to discern fear in the voice of a dog, then the terror that this animal was feeling could have been perceived by a man who was deaf and blind.

James paused only long enough to rack the oars, and then he threw himself backwards, landing atop the dog, clamping his hands around her muzzle, and hissing, *"Shhhhh!"* The clearly frightened dog started to fight out of reflex, but then immediately appeared to understand the need for silence. James angled himself so that he was lying under the narrow bench that stretched across the boat and provided a seat for whoever was manning the oars.

Thomas instantly followed James's lead, dropping to the bottom of the small boat, rolling himself into as small a target as he could possibly make himself. The three of them lay there, paralyzed, too scared even to breathe. If they had been able to cease the beating of their hearts, they would have done so. In fact, it seemed a distinct possibility that that might just happen.

A tentacle had emerged from the water and was moving slowly across the boat.

It's going to crush us, thought Thomas. *It's going to crush this boat just like it did the ship. I've led us into a fool's quest, and this is the end for both of us.*

Except the lifeboat was so small that it was, in and of itself, indistinguishable from dozens of other pieces of flotsam and jetsam that were bobbing in the water, a mute reminder of the sailing vessel that had been endeavoring to traverse the seas only minutes earlier. The tentacle slid into the boat, but rather than touching the bottom, the tentacle rested on the rower's bench. It then moved across it tentatively, looking for . . . well, Thomas didn't like to think about what it was looking for. It was mere inches above the boys, neither of whom were moving, and even the newly christened Poxy was able to restrain her natural desire to start barking at it or challenging it in some manner. Thomas could see that she was trembling against James, her fur still matted down from the water. High above, the lightning continued to shatter the darkened sky, the waves bouncing them around. And Thomas was utterly convinced that he could still hear the screams of the pirates being ripped apart or dragged down to their deaths in the murky, surging sea.

The tentacle had now made its way across the bench, probing delicately, and Thomas braced himself, waiting for it to haul the entire ship beneath the water.

And then it withdrew.

Just like that, the tentacle withdrew, hurriedly, seemingly losing interest. Seconds later, it was gone, and although the ship was still bobbing violently in the water, the kraken appeared to have moved on to something else.

Thomas could not for the life of him imagine how it was that they were still alive. He wanted to stay where he was, flattened on the bottom of the boat and doing everything he could to avoid possibly being noticed by the tentacles making their triumphant return. But that didn't seem to be a viable option, not if they wanted to have a prayer of keeping the boat from tipping over.

James realized this at the same time, and, sitting up, he grabbed the oars and started rowing. It seemed an eternity ago that he had boasted to Thomas that his presence on the excursion was a necessity because he has an infallible sense of direction. Never had that been put more to the test, or been more necessary to any possibility they might have for survival, than at that point in time.

Poxy remained at the bottom of the boat, taking up a position under the bench and keeping her head covered with her paws. She might well have been a valiant rat catcher and even assailant of pirates within the relative safety of a boat, but it was clear that she was not exactly at her ease in the middle of a roiling sea. But neither were they, so it didn't seem fair to hold the dog to a higher standard. Her flank was near Thomas, and he saw a gash in her hindquarters that he had no doubt was a gift from the barrel of Rackam's gun. *Well,* thought Thomas grimly, *the dog is still alive, while Rackam died.* So it was obvious who was the final victor in *that* little confrontation.

"Do you need help?" he called to James, who was continuing to row with all the considerable strength in his arms.

"Not right now! I'm pretty much in control! Trying to do it together might be more trouble than it's worth!"

"True," said Thomas, who hated to admit that since he despised the notion of simply lying there and not serving any purpose. He pulled himself upward and steadied the prow as best he could, trying to offer a counterbalance every time the waves threatened to upend the boat.

Then, in the near distance, he heard what could only be described as an unearthly scream. It was like nothing he had ever heard before, like nothing he thought anything living would have been able to produce. It was deep and sonorous. Shielding his eyes as best he could, he tried to see through the chop and the spray, through the darkness that continued to be broken almost entirely by lightning and nothing else.

And then, for just a moment, a cloud moved aside, and moonlight flooded from on high, and Thomas was able to see something that seemed as if it had been ripped from a primeval time before humanity strode the earth. At that moment, the notion that there were dividing lines between myth and magic, between reality and legend, dissipated, and Thomas saw the world through a prism that provided an image of a world that could not possibly exist.

A vast, perfectly shaped undersea creature that Thomas could only conclude was a whale—a creature so astoundingly big and so beautifully and meticulously crafted by nature that Thomas had to choke down a sob lest he be unmanned by the sight—lunged in slow motion out of the water at least a mile away. It was not alone. The kraken was wrapped around it, its tentacles encircling it like a twisted perversion of a lover's embrace. For the first and only time, Thomas had a brief glimpse of the kraken's vast body beyond its tentacles, shaped like a spear, clinging onto the whale's skin. The eerie noise that Thomas had heard seemed to be coming from the whale, and he could only imagine what it signified. Was it a bellow of defiance? Was it a desperate cry for help that would never come? He did not know, nor would he ever. It was obvious that the presence of the whale had been what had drawn the kraken away from him, and with any luck would keep the creature away long after he and James had vacated the area. That was assuming, of course, that they managed to accomplish that seemingly impossible feat.

But James was undaunted by the challenge that the high seas were presenting. He rowed unrelentingly, indomitable, his jaw set, unwilling to give even an inch to the seas that were battling him.

The waves pushed them higher, higher, and then the boat tumbled down the far side, and James deftly kept the valiant little vessel on an even keel. They completely lost track of how long they continued to fight to survive: It might have been minutes, or hours, although it most certainly wasn't days. James continued to row, and Thomas saw that his friend was becoming exhausted. His arms were moving as if they were leaden, and he was grunting with every stroke whereas earlier he had rowed with facility. Finally, he could stand it no longer. "I'm taking over!" he shouted.

James tried to shake his head, but he scarcely had the

energy even for that. Thomas pulled himself across the bottom of the boat, avoiding standing up lest he cause the entire thing to topple. Realizing that their mutual safety was far too important to be jeopardized by his pride, James waited until Thomas was in place and firmly gripping the oars and then slid off the bench with a moan. *"Which way?"* Thomas shouted. In response, James pointed off to the right, and Thomas obediently sent the boat careening in that direction.

And as they continued to try to put as much distance as possible between themselves and the site of the pirates' violent demise, the cries of the whale eventually subsided and then disappeared entirely.

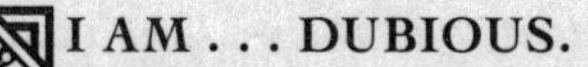

I AM . . . DUBIOUS.

The storyteller ceases his narrative and regards me with what I could best describe as mild surprise. "A problem, Majesty?"

"They survived an encounter with a kraken?"

Slowly, he nods. "Yes, Majesty, as you have heard . . ."

"I find that difficult to believe," I tell him after a long pause. I stand because I have been seated for a time, and I am feeling a distant tingling in my legs. I both hear and feel the creaking in my knees. When I take a few steps forward, it requires everything I possess not to display a limp.

"Arthritis in the right knee causing you to limp, Majesty?" the storyteller says without hesitation.

I am irked by this. It is foolish, I know, but despite my advanced age, despite the very obvious betrayal in every way imaginable that my body has foisted upon me, I nevertheless do not want to appear at all fragile. Yet this man, this spinner of fables, is able to discern immediately the pain that has taken up residence in my leg joint.

I am about to deny it out of hand, but I see in his eyes that he would not be fooled. It seems foolish to me that I should allow pride to dictate my response. I am, after all, a man of accomplishment. A king. Why should I be the least bit concerned about displaying frailty in front of this . . . this no one.

It is foolish pride, nothing more.

"Yes," I say, and add, "and in my hip as well, if that is of any interest to you."

"I was aware of that as well, but I did not wish you to think I had developed a curious fixation on your hip."

I stare at him for a moment, and then I laugh loudly. The noise startles even me; it has been quite some time since I actually laughed about something. It is not . . . kingly, perhaps. Not appropriate to one of my station.

He smiles slightly in response. He does so awkwardly; it does not appear to be a normal expression for him. Then the smile fades, and he says, not ungently, "Human frailty is nothing to be ashamed of, Majesty."

"It is nothing to be proud of, either."

"It is the price one pays for not dying."

"Not dying," I tell him, "may be an overrated experience."

"Living is not a pastime for the faint of heart," he says. "And the commonality of the human experience is that no one gets out alive."

"How fortunate that you have come here to me so that you can share your pointless homilies and inane observations,"

I say, driven more by my own unwanted pain than anything he has said or done. "To say nothing of your increasingly unlikely narrative."

"Unlikely?"

I say again: "A kraken? They survived a kraken?"

"It is as I have said."

"No one survives such an encounter."

"Indeed." He appears thoughtful. "If that were the case, then how would any know of the existence of such a creature, much less be able to lend name to it? Sailors would simply be lost at sea, unable to pass on legends of a monstrous tentacled being. The expression, after all, is 'living to tell the tale.'"

"Still . . . two callow youths on their own in a rickety lifeboat in the midst of a storm?"

"And a dog. They had a dog," he reminds me.

A silence stretches between the two of us, and then the storyteller says, "Majesty, you simply have to ask yourself: Do you desire for this story to be true?"

I surprise myself with my lack of hesitation. "Very much."

"Then your wish"—and he bows slightly, albeit not mockingly—"is my command."

I sit back down, trying to ignore and refusing to acknowledge the audible creak of my knees. "So our young Heroes are adrift in the water, the storm raging . . ."

"The storm, as it so happens, subsided before much longer."

"The fate of the kraken?"

"Unknown. Perhaps it died in combat with the other great behemoth of the seas. Perhaps it triumphed and was so sated in its devouring of its vast prey that it settled to

the sea bottom to digest it. Whichever the case, it did not return to harass the lads further. So in that regard, they were fortunate."

"And then—?"

"Then it turned out that James's instincts had proven true yet again, as the rising of the eastern sun verified. For the dawn of a new day revealed that land was beckoning to them."

"Safety."

"Well," says the storyteller, "safety may have been another matter entirely. It is all relative, you might say. The boys had encountered piracy and a mythic creature upon the seas, but it was not as if there was a lack of evil or menace on the land, as well you know, Majesty."

"Indeed I do."

"So they achieved landfall—Thomas, James, and Poxy Cur, as she was to be known—and made their way to the town of Blackridge. It did not take them long to get a sense of the place in which they had landed. They were immediately struck by the fact that it seemed far less industrialized than all that which they had left behind. Even the most backwards, least impressive sections of Bowerstone seemed tremendously advanced in comparison.

"The sky seemed to be permanently overcast, and the forests . . . which had been beaten back to a large degree in Albion . . . seemed to be everywhere, lurking just on the edges of the town at all times, as if waiting for the residents to lower their guards just for a moment so that the trees could overrun it and reclaim the territory for their own. It would turn out that much of Blackridge was like that;

indeed, most of the country was, as they would continue to explore it. There was a feeling of the arcane in the air that was unique in their experience.

"As for the residents of Blackridge, their view of the world, and the things about which they worried, well . . . that was somewhat different as well . . ."

Chapter 8

THE MASTER OF THE HOUSE BLANCHED when he saw Poxy, and snarled, "Is that your . . . your creature?"

Thomas and James, bone weary, wet, exhausted, and wanting nothing but a place to dry out, looked in confusion from the innkeeper to the dog and back again. "Yeah," said James, who was hardly in the mood for any manner of grief from anyone, much less a bowlegged tavern-owner with a foul attitude that was only matched by his equally foul breath.

"How long have ye had it?"

Something warned James to lie immediately, and he said without hesitation, "Raised her from a pup. If you're in the market for one, you can't have her."

The master of the house squinted at James as if he had just been speaking in a foreign tongue. "Why would

I—?" Then he stopped, waved off the notion, and instead said, "Never mind. Just keep the damned thing to yourself, understand?"

"Yes," said James, who didn't understand in the least but was too fatigued to care. Thomas was in the same state of mind, and he simply nodded.

Minutes later, they were in a small room, which was furnished with a pair of bedrolls and nothing else. Poxy growled at them, and James said, "Go ahead, girl." The dog promptly leaped upon the bedrolls, and an assortment of round insects, some almost as large as the palms of their hands, scuttled out in all directions. Poxy immediately took great delight in bounding about and stomping on as many of the bugs as she could catch before the last of them had scurried to safety in the cracks and crevices of the room.

Without having to say a word, James picked up the bedrolls, dragging each of them between two fingers of either hand, and shoved them out into the hallway. If the window in the room had not been little more than a crack in the wall, he would have tossed them out of it.

They didn't say anything for long moments; instead, they just sat on the floor in a daze. Then Thomas said, "Something to drink?"

"Absolutely," James said so quickly that Thomas didn't even get the last word out in its entirety.

Minutes later they had cracked open a couple of newly acquired bottles of God-only-knew what it was. The uncertain brand or type of alcohol they were about to pour down their throats was of no consequence to them. All that mattered was drinking as much as possible, as quickly as possible, as if doing so could wipe away what they had seen and experienced. Thomas had also acquired some manner of dried-out meat, which he doled out between himself, James, and Poxy, the latter of whom sniffed it suspiciously and didn't seem particularly thrilled at the offering. Then she made a noise that sounded like a grunt and ate it grudgingly.

James's head was swimming when he finally got around to speaking. "I'm sorry," was what he said.

Thomas stared at him, squinting, trying to determine why it was exactly that there seemed to be more than one James in the room. He chalked it up to simply being the most recent of the exceedingly odd things that he had experienced since he had left home. "You're sorry? For what?"

"I got too full of myself, playing games with those pirates, beating them." He was speaking with excessive slowness. He sounded as if he were trying to remember how to pronounce every single word before it left his lips. "If I hadn't done that . . . if I hadn't gotten them angry . . ."

"You're being ridisculous," Thomas chided him. Then he frowned, and said again, "Ri-dis-cu-lous," continuing to mangle the word but at least enunciating it meticulously. "They were *pirates*, John."

"James."

"Whoever the hell you are. The point is . . ." He stopped, frowned, his eyes bleary. "*What* was the point . . . ?"

"Pirates."

"Right. Exactly. They were pirates. You heard the captain, right before he was ripped to pieces . . ."

James raised his half-empty bottle of whatever. "To Captain Rackam. He died a man of parts."

Thomas burst out laughing, as did James. So overwhelmed with mirth was Thomas that he actually fell over, dropping the bottle, but there was no harm done since he had just emptied it. The bottle rolled away as Thomas held his stomach and continued to howl with laughter. James was laughing as well, but in a fashion that sounded more like a long, sustained hiccup.

"That's . . . that's not funny," Thomas said as he gasped for breath. "That . . . that's really not funny, James. You should be ashamed of yourself."

"I am. I truly am." But he didn't particularly sound it.

"It was a horrible thing . . . what happened to him . . ."

"Not much worse than what he had planned for us."

At that observation, Thomas finally did manage to get himself under control, his face darkening. He remained lying on the floor, but he pointed at James, and said, "Yes. Exactly. What he had planned. You said it yourself. The fact is, you forced the issue. They were humoring us, probably because it amused them to do so. But we were never going to make it to port alive. If not for you . . . and if not for your stupid dog . . . they'd probably have murdered us in our sleep. Apologize?" He blew air disdainfully. "*I'm* the one who should be begging *your* pardon."

"How do you figure that?"

"How do I—?" He was astounded that James even had to ask. He propped himself up on one elbow. He tried to look James in the eyes, but James had appeared to develop the inconsiderate attribute of wavering from one side to the other, not to mention unaccountably dividing every so often for no discernible reason. Thomas closed his eyes so he wouldn't have to look at him. "How far back do you want me to go? To my own stupidity and overconfidence in choosing pirates to be our means of crossing the sea? I went with the first boat—"

"Ship."

"—whatever. The first ship that was willing to take us, without even giving thought to checking with anyone else."

"You said you checked around."

"Barely. Casual inquiry, at best. Hell, probably they were all pirates at that wharf. I should have figured that could be a possibility. Stupid!" he snapped at himself and, for good measure, struck himself in the side of the head with the base of his palm. This proved to be an astoundingly bad idea as Thomas's eyes crossed, and he fell off his own elbow, to be left lying prostrate once more. Deciding that he would be well-advised to simply stay where he was, he continued while reclining. "Then how about the fact that this whole crazy trip was my idea in the first place? If I hadn't talked you into this—"

"Talked *me* into this?" James continued to lean against the wall; since it graciously provided support, tumbling over wasn't an issue. "I talked you into bringing me along, remember?"

"Yes, I remember, but if I hadn't suggested it—"

"If, if, if," James said, and then added a snort for good measure, "How much do you want to play that game? Endless second-guessing of everything in your life. That's the problem with smart, well-read people like you, Thomas. You're always thinking, thinking, thinking about the road you already walked and trying to wonder whether it would have been better if you'd taken the right fork instead of the left fork or the left fork instead of the right fork. Well . . . fork that. You can 'if' this all the way back to when we first met as children, and it'll still all come down to the same thing."

"Yeah? What thing is that?"

James leaned forward and started to topple. Poxy quickly stepped in, and James leaned on her so that he didn't fall completely. Thomas couldn't help but notice that the dog hadn't bothered to provide support for him. "The thing is: I would not have missed this for the world."

"Really." Thomas wasn't convinced. "We've almost been eaten several times, we almost drowned, we almost—"

" 'Almost' means nothing."

"It means we could have died and were damned lucky not to have. I mean, be honest with me, James. You can't be having a good time."

"It's an adventure. Of course we're not having a good time," said James matter-of-factly. "When you're on an adventure, the good times are had from a distance. You remember everything you went through and laugh about it and marvel at the fact that you're still alive."

"That's assuming we're still alive to marvel at it."

"Of course we're still going to be alive," James said firmly. "You said it yourself. The number of 'almosts' that have lain between us and death have been piling up, and yet here we are. By any reasonable measure, we *should* be dead. But we're not. Do you know why?"

Thomas shook his head.

"Me neither," James said with a twisted grin. "But I'll tell you this: We two, we're not meant to wind up in the belly of some beast or at the bottom of the sea or lying out to be carrion bait. Because if that was our destiny, then we'd have met it already. The fact that we're here proves that we're going to succeed in our goal."

"What's scary is that that actually makes some measure of sense," Thomas admitted. "Because I'm pretty sure that it actually makes no sense at all, which just goes to show how much I've had to drink."

"The fact that you're lying on the floor pretty much makes that clear."

"So . . . what are you saying? That we don't have to worry about fatal mishaps because there's no way we can fail?"

"Oh, there are plenty of ways that we can fail. We still have to be careful, watch our backs, and everything else that men who are not destined for success have to do. Triumph isn't a given; you have to work for it. But I'm just sure that we're going to reach our goal and find the balverines."

"At which point . . . ?"

"They'll likely rip us apart."

Thomas laughed loudly once more, a reaction that

some part of him couldn't begin to fathom considering there was nothing remotely funny about the comment. It drove home to him the truth of the lunacy upon which he had embarked: that even if somehow he did manage to accomplish his goal, he might well be bringing them directly to their deaths. He had no real idea what success in this mission would ultimately look like. The head of the balverine who had slain his brother mounted on a pike? It was beyond unlikely. It was preposterous.

There was only one true, realistic outcome.

"We're both going to die," Thomas said. "We're barreling at full speed toward a confrontation that we cannot possibly survive. That is what success is going to look like: our corpses."

"Then they'll be well-preserved, thoroughly pickled corpses!" James declared loudly. "To success!" And he raised the mostly empty bottle and finished draining it.

"To success!" Thomas said, just as loudly and raising his hand, which was bereft of bottle.

Neither remembered much of anything after that.

THEY AWOKE AT ROUGHLY THE SAME TIME, but neither of them was particularly inclined to stand up. Instead, they simply lay there on the floor, staring glassy-eyed at each other, as if they had just awoken to discover, much to their mutual surprise, that they were about to be dropped into their graves.

"Am I dead?" James said after a time.

"No."

"You're sure?"

"Yes."

He started to sit up, and the world spun around him so violently that he had no choice but to thud back to the floor. The noise startled Poxy awake. She raised her head, looked around, then glowered at James to make sure he was aware of her lack of approval for rousting her. Then she settled her head back on her paws and closed her eyes once more.

"Why," said James with a low moan, "am I *not* dead?"

"Well . . . because no one killed you."

"Why didn't they? Why couldn't they do me that favor? Some random assassin, maybe, coming to me in my sleep and slitting my throat. Then I wouldn't have to wake up feeling like this."

Thomas was now sitting up, squinting against the few shafts of daylight that were filtering into the room. "James," he asked tentatively, "are my legs longer this morning?"

"What?"

"My legs. Are they longer this morning than they were last night?"

James studied them for a bit. "No," he finally decided. "They look pretty much the same. Why?"

"I could swear that my feet are farther away than when I last looked at them."

"No. Same distance. Still attached to your ankles. But I think my tongue is about to fall out of my mouth."

"You'd be lucky," said Thomas. "I wish I didn't have a tongue. Then I couldn't taste anything, and I wouldn't feel like I have a mouth full of sewage."

"There's only one thing to do."

"Yeah? What?"

"Drink some more. I liked how that felt."

Thomas coughed roughly, which brought up some phlegm that he spat into the far corner of the room. It struck a roach that had been trying to make its way across the floor and knocked it over onto its back, where it lay with its legs frantically waving. Thomas watched it until he lost interest. "We can't keep drinking, as tempting as that might be. We've made it to the eastern lands. Now we keep heading east."

"Sounds like a plan," said James

"And one that I absolutely intend to put into action right after I go outside and vomit."

"An even better plan. Let me know how it goes." And then he flopped back onto the floor and fell back asleep.

Between Thomas's extended bout with nausea and James's thundering headache that pounded in his skull as if someone were striking him repeatedly with a club, they were not fully themselves until the sun had crawled nearly to the noon hour. They ate a simple meal of bread and cheese since the innkeeper didn't exactly have much variety, nor were they feeling especially hungry, although Poxy certainly fed eagerly enough on table scraps.

Finally, packing up their effects, they took ready leave of the inn, with the master of the house continuing to glare suspiciously at the dog. The boys remained as clueless that day as they were in the evening as to why Poxy was garnering those sorts of suspicious and angry looks from the innkeeper but were willing to chalk it up to the idea that he simply despised canines.

But as they walked about the undersized, underdeveloped city, James slowly began to realize that the master of the house had not been alone in his objections to Poxy. There were not many people out in the streets, but those who were quickly crossed to the other side of the street when James and Thomas passed by, and the dog was the subject of much discussion and many sidelong and suspicious glances. Poxy was blissfully unaware, of course, but it was impossible for the attention the dog was drawing to escape the notice of the boys.

"What the hell is going on around here?" James finally said in exasperation to Thomas, only to discover that Thomas was paying him no mind. Instead, he saw, to his surprise, that Thomas's hands were trembling as he held a sheet of paper in his hand. He had plucked it off the outside wall of a tavern. It was hardly unique; from where they were standing, James could see copies of the hand-scrawled notice running up and down the length of the main cobbled street, as if the poster were concerned that they would be remiss if someone should be able to walk ten feet without encountering it.

"Look at this. James, look. Can you believe it?"

"It is truly astounding," James said drily. "It looks to be some sort of flexible material—possibly made from trees—with writing upon it. Here I thought writing could only be chiseled upon stone tablets."

"You're a riot, James."

"My head is still throbbing. You're lucky I'm walking. Asking for jokes that are funny is just way too much. What is all this about—?"

"A woman . . ."

"That's when the trouble usually starts," James said ruefully.

"A woman," Thomas pressed on, with a warning look to James that he should not make light of the situation, "is looking for help over the disappearance of her daughter. A daughter that she swears was taken by a balverine."

"Taken by—?" He took the paper from Thomas and read it. It was exactly as Thomas described it. A local woman was seeking out a Hero to investigate the disappearance of her daughter, and she was convinced that a balverine, or possibly balverines, were responsible.

"She wants a Hero and believes in balverines," said James in wonderment. "It's like we've stepped back in time or something."

Thomas said, "The eastern lands seem to be more backwards than where we came from."

"No kidding. Maybe it's because they're way less industrialized. Hell, maybe that's the problem with machines in general," said James.

"You lost me."

"Well, it takes work to believe in what can't be seen. The whole purpose of machines is to make life and tasks easier. Industrialization takes the wondrous and makes it mundane. How can people be amazed in a world of mundanity?"

"I don't know what you're talking about," said Thomas. "Believing in the unseen requires no effort at all. Faith is a convenient substitute for thought."

"I'm not sure I agree."

"And I'm not sure I care," Thomas said firmly, waving the sheet of paper in James's face. "All I care is that, back home, the whole idea of Heroes is considered quaint, out-of-date, even arrogant. To say nothing of how people look at us like we're idiots every time we bring up balverines." James couldn't refute that; he knew it to be true. "And here," continued Thomas, "is a woman who is reaching out for help. Screw the reasons for it. All I care about is that if we can find her daughter, maybe we can find the balverines we're looking for."

"And once we find them?"

"We save the girl, hopefully without getting killed."

James thought about it a moment and then nodded approvingly. "Okay, then. Let us see a mother about a daughter."

IT TOOK ONLY A BIT OF ASKING AROUND TO locate the home of the woman who had put up the flyers. Everyone in the town knew her, and although they continued to cast suspicious glances at the dog, they didn't hesitate to point Thomas and James in the right direction so that, within the hour, they were standing outside a house that was only a step or two up from a hovel, situated on a decent-sized piece of land that served as a not-particularly-prosperous farm. Thomas rapped on the door with as much authority as he could muster. They heard some shuffling about from within, and then it creaked open to reveal a man so massive, with a sullen glare so inherently threatening, that Thomas stepped back and almost reached for his sword out of reflex. The man had a thick chin to which some grayish whiskers were clinging, a low-hanging unibrow from beneath which piglike eyes glowered, a wide nose that appeared to have been broken at least twice, a mass of salt-and-pepper curls . . .

. . . and a shapeless dress that hung almost down to his thick ankles.

"Who are ye?" said the man in a voice that was surprisingly light and even female in nature . . .

It's a woman. Holy hell, it's a woman.

Thomas could see that James was coming to the same conclusion and looked equally stunned in the realization. Rebounding as quickly as he could, Thomas held up the flyer that was fluttering in a stiff breeze. "We—" And his voice cracked slightly, so Thomas cleared his throat and began again. "We are here because of your notice. Because of your daughter."

"Aye, but who are ya?" she said again. "Yer not from around here. I can tell from yer accent, yer clothes, yer—" Then her eyes widened as she looked past Thomas. Quickly, she reached into her home, grabbed something that he couldn't see, then shoved him out of the way as if he weighed nothing and came out wielding a muck-encrusted spade. She came right at Poxy, bellowing a string of profanities. Poxy bounded back, her ears down, barely escaping the sweep of the digging implement.

James had been momentarily paralyzed by the unexpected assault, but with a moment to adjust to the situation, he leaped onto the woman's back and clung to it like an infant monkey to its mother. *"Hold it!"* he shouted, and the female behemoth backpedaled quickly, a move that confused James right up until she crushed him up against her home. Fortunately, the wood of which the sides were composed was not particularly sturdy, and instead of breaking every bone in his body, the impact caused him to crash right through the house and wind up lying on the floor of the room that served as the living room, dining room, kitchen, and, for all he knew, privy, at least judging by the smell of it.

In the street, she continued to swing the shovel at Poxy, who dodged this way and that, desperately avoiding her but clearly reluctant to vacate the area since she had no desire to abandon her masters. The woman continued to bellow imprecations at the dog, and the entire business might well have gone on all day if she hadn't heard the distinctive cocking of a crossbow. She turned, still holding the shovel defensively, and Thomas was standing a safe distance away with his crossbow aimed at her.

"I could be using my rifle right now," he said with a calmness that he didn't quite feel, and thus had to force his voice to remain flat and even. "But I'm not sure I could shoot you without killing you. I'm a bit more confident with this that you'll survive it. So that should tell you that we're not here to hurt you . . ."

James staggered out the front door, bracing himself against the frame since the world was still spinning around him a bit. "And it should further tell you to stay the hell away from my dog," he added defiantly.

"It's evil," she said with a snarl, clutching the shaft of the spade so tightly that her beefy knuckles were turning white.

"Why do you say that?"

"Because all dogs are evil. They're cousins of balverines."

"That's utterly ridiculous."

"Ayuh?" she grunted. "That beast . . . it's waiting. Waiting for ye to lower yer guard so it can tear yer throats out in your sleep."

"She's been with us any number of times that we've been asleep," James said, "and our throats are just fine. Why didn't she kill us then since she had the opportunity?"

She fixed her angry gaze upon Poxy, who backed up with her tail between her legs and a faint whimper. "She's verrrry crafty," said the woman.

"Look, I don't mean to be rude here," said Thomas, "but we really don't have to put up with this kind of abuse and suspicion. We came here because we thought you needed help. Not to be assaulted or to have our dog—"

"She's my dog," said James.

"—or to have his dog maligned."

"Then why do you travel with the creature in the first place?"

"Because . . ."

"Because," James said abruptly, "we are balverine hunters from a far western land. And this dog, whom you would so readily try to dispatch, is one of our greatest weapons in that endeavor. She's a tracker. She helps us track balverines. And we have tracked them here, to this land. Fate and our four-legged ally have led us here, but if you have no interest in our services"—he shrugged in what seemed a significant manner—"then we will be on our way. Isn't that right, Thomas?"

"That is indeed right, James," Thomas said, nodding. He backed up, keeping the crossbow aimed at the woman. James followed suit.

Abruptly, the woman dropped the spade. "Wait," she said sharply, and the boys both held their places. "I might have been . . . hasty."

"At the very least," said James.

"I am a woman alone, of limited means. But if ye can help me, I'll pay whatever I can."

"This is not about payment," said Thomas. James looked at him in a surprised way that said, *It's not?* Thomas quickly shook his head, and continued, "This is about trying to aid your daughter . . . although if I understand your flyer correctly, I'm not sure how much aid we could provide. Not if she's really been kidnapped by balverines. I hate to sound cold, but she's probably dead by now—"

"That isn't what concerns me."

"It's not?" Thomas and James exchanged confused looks. "Then what . . . ?"

"If yer truly hunters," said the woman, "then ye'd understand."

It took a moment for comprehension to dawn upon Thomas, but then it did. "You're afraid," said Thomas, "that they've transformed her into one of their own. That they've made her into a balverine."

Slowly, she nodded, and then, to their astonishment, thick tears began to roll down her blubbery face. "I can't have that for my little girl. I can't have her live like that. Ye understand what I'm saying."

"You're saying that if we find she's been changed . . ."

"Ye put her down as ye would any rabid animal. As we would a dog." And she looked distastefully yet again at Poxy, wiping the tears from her face with the back of her arm. "As we have all dogs hereabouts, lest they turn out to be agents of the balverines."

Thomas could scarcely believe what they were dealing with. It was almost literally a case of night and day. They had departed a land where balverines were considered nothing more than fables that were used to scare recalcitrant children, and arrived on foreign shores where balverines were taken so seriously that innocent animals were slaughtered lest they prove to have some sort of tenuous connection.

"If this is not an indelicate question," James said, "what is your husband's opinion about this?"

"He's dead," she said flatly. "Robert is dead, the useless fool. Come inside. I'll tell ye about it." She turned her back to them and headed back into the house with the manliest stride that Thomas had ever seen in a woman, not to mention a few men. She left the spade lying on the ground, which might have been her way of conveying that she no longer intended to pose a threat to them. On the other hand, Thomas had a feeling that—were she so inclined—she could likely beat them to death with her bare hands. His gut instinct, though, was that they would be safe enough. It was only at that point he realized he still had the crossbow armed and leveled. He unnocked the bolt and hung the crossbow back on his belt.

"You sure that's wise?" James muttered.

"We handled a boatload of pirates. We can handle her."

"We barely escaped them," James corrected him, "and only with the 'help' of a kraken, and something tells me the kraken would take one look at her and swim in the other direction."

Thomas chuckled softly, unable to disagree.

THE WOMAN GAVE HER NAME AS "MRS. MULlins" without providing a first name. She offered to brew some tea and prepare them a meal, but Thomas very quickly said that it was not necessary since neither of them was hungry. The haste with which he spoke surprised James, but then he realized the reason for it. Thomas still did not trust the woman: For all he knew, she might try to poison them or at the very least knock them out so that she could take another pass at the dog without having to contend with them. This seemed a reasonable cause for concern, and so James simply nodded his agreement with Thomas.

"My husband and daughter were in Underwood, the forest not far from here, gathering herbs for my medicines. I brew up home remedies, y'know," she said. Thomas, of course, had no way of knowing that, but he simply nodded as if it were a matter of general information. "They thought they were safe because it was during the day, and the balverines only come out at night. But this particular day, the full moon was high in the sky as sometimes happens. And I guess that's all the balverines need to do their . . . their hideous deeds."

Thomas was sitting on a rickety chair, and he leaned forward carefully lest it shatter under him. "Have you ever actually seen a balverine with your own eyes?"

"Seen? No. But every so often we hear them howling deep in the woods. They wouldn't dare venture into town because they know that we're ready for them. Balverines don't have the stomach for direct confrontation with those who are prepared to battle them."

This didn't sound exactly right to Thomas. From all that he had read, balverines weren't exactly shy when it came to attacking, especially if there was a pack of them. But who knew for certain? Perhaps there was only a single balverine making his presence known in the town, or—if there was indeed a pack—they tended to range away from the town and content themselves with preying on forest creatures. Anything was possible when dealing with creatures of the supernatural.

"There is a path that leads deep into Underwoods, and a crossroads about a mile in. It was at that crossroads that Robert and Hannah—that's my daughter's name, Hannah—that they had their . . . their encounter." The woman's beefy hands were clamped together, the fingers interlaced, fidgeting with each other. "There were three of the creatures. Robert tried to put himself between them and Hannah, but he had no chance. They just . . . they tore into him, ripped him to pieces, tore him apart, and devoured him right then and there, right in front of Hannah. Flesh, muscle, bones, made no difference to them. They just ate it all. The only thing left of him was some blood-smeared tatters of clothing. And Hannah they dragged away, screaming the entire time. I . . ." She paused, and then pressed on. "I figure either they wanted to save her to . . . to eat her later . . . or else they wanted to make her into one of them. It's been two weeks, and I want to know either way. I want them killed either way."

"I don't get it," said Thomas. "How do you know what happened? Your husband, dead, your daughter, dragged away. That doesn't leave any witnesses."

She thumped the side of her head. "Aye, of course. I forgot t'mention: that boy."

"What boy?"

"Young Samuel." Her face twisted in disdain. "He's been sniffing around my Hannah ever since she started growing breasts. He was following after her that day, hanging back a distance. He comes from fair hunting stock, so he has some measure of woodcraft, I'll give him that. He saw it all happen, hiding behind some brush. Hiding! Little gibbering gnat. Ye'd think that he'd have tried to intervene instead of just cowering and letting her be dragged off . . ."

"If he'd have done that, he'd most likely be as dead as your husband," James said. "And you'd have no first-hand account of what transpired."

"That's no excuse for cowardice," said Mrs. Mullins, "and don't think I didn't tell him so. He comes here, tells me what happened, and brings me to the crossroads to show me. There's blood everywhere, on the ground, on the trees. But none on him, that was for sure, because he kept himself good and hidden. I reamed him right and well, don't think I didn't. I reamed him and told him he had no business standing by and letting them do that to my husband and little girl. He cried," she said in disgust. "Cried like a wee baby, he did. He ran off, and no one's seen him since. I may well have shamed him into heading off after them."

"You mean," Thomas said slowly, "that you 'shamed him' into setting off after balverines and very likely going to his death?"

She shrugged. "It's of no never mind to me what happened to him."

Thomas bristled at that. "Perhaps it's of a never mind to his own parents. Did you stop to consider that?"

"All I considered is my own kin. I don't give a damn about him and his."

"Yes, that's pretty obvious." It was at that point that Thomas was starting to feel disinclined to do a damned thing to help this woman. *Let her stew in her own juices for the rest of her life. Her husband and daughter are better off dead than having to live with this creature.* But he then dismissed such thoughts as uncharitable. He was hardly seeing Mrs. Mullins at her best. Furthermore, he remembered all the anger, all the hostility that had permeated him for so long after the death of his brother. It was anger that he carried to this day and had been partly responsible for fueling his departure from home in the first place. If that cold fury still burned so brightly within him even after all these years, how much more furiously did it sizzle within the breast of this woman, who had lost them so relatively recently? It was difficult for him to do, but he needed to dig down and find compassion for this woman.

Besides, she wanted them to seek out balverines, and that was their mission objective anyway.

And then James asked a question that seemed a complete non sequitur. "Has it rained?"

"Rained?"

"Since she was taken. Has it rained since that day?"

She frowned, obviously having to bring all her limited mental capacities to bear on the question. Then, slowly, she shook her head. "No, as a matter of fact."

"Do you still have them?" James said suddenly.

"Them?" Now she was completely lost. "What them?"

"The tattered remains of your husband's clothing."

"James," said Thomas, regarding him skeptically, "why in the world would she still have—?"

"Ayuh. In a box out back."

Thomas shifted his astonished gaze from James to Mrs. Mullins. "You *kept* it? Why would you keep something like that?"

"I waste nothing. It's the way I was brought up."

"Okay, then," said James, who didn't appear to think that was at all unusual. "I'd like that, and also anything that your daughter wore. Anything that might still have her scent."

"How are you going to follow her scent?"

"I'm not"—and James pointed proudly to Poxy—"she is."

"She?" Her voice dripped with distaste for the very notion. "You expect her to lead you to her own kind?"

"She's a dog, not a balverine. They're not her own kind. It hasn't rained, so with any luck, the spoor—although hardly fresh—won't have been washed away. And," James went on, becoming increasingly heated, "if you people hadn't been so stupid as to make sure to dispose of every dog in the area, you could easily have used one of them to track down your daughter. Your superstitiousness only crippled your ability to help them. So you think about that while you're getting us what we need."

She glowered at him, but he failed to burst into flames or transform into an oversized icicle or simply drop dead as a result. Having failed to accomplish that, she turned on her oversized foot and waddled out to get the required items.

The moment she was out of earshot, Thomas turned to James and gave him a look that did not radiate confidence. "You're going to use Poxy as a tracker?"

"That's the plan."

"James, come on. I know you think highly of this animal, and she certainly has her talents as a rat catcher. But training a dog to follow scents takes a long time. Just waving something under her nose and then expecting her to follow the scent . . . especially when several weeks have passed . . . I just don't see it working."

"We know nothing about her pedigree, Thomas. Who she belonged to or anything like that. For all we know, she *is* trained to do what we need her to do. So I say we give it a try. Besides, do you have a better plan?"

"Not really," he admitted.

"All right, then."

Mrs. Mullins returned a short time later with the bloodied, shredded remains of a tunic that Thomas safely assumed had been her husband's. In her other hand she was holding a hairbrush. "This was my daughter's," she said, waving the hairbrush. "Got strands of her hair still in it, so I'm figuring this might be exactly what ye need."

"That could be of use, yes." James took the hairbrush and the cloth, making a face as he handled it, and carefully put the two of them into separate pouches of his pack. "A crossroads, you said?"

"Yes. The main road leads right up to Underwoods. Follow it in, and you'll get to the crossroads."

"Okay, then." Thomas bowed slightly since that was what the situation seemed to call for. James did not. Clearly, he was still steamed over the way in which the burly woman was regarding his dog. It seemed to

Thomas that James had a good deal invested in a dog that he had only acquired scant days earlier.

They emerged from the house into a day that had become overcast, but otherwise the weather appeared to be holding up even though there was a nip in the air. "So now we head to the crossroads?" said James.

"We head for the crossroads," Thomas nodded. "And we see what happens next."

Chapter 9

"MAIN ROAD" WAS SOMETHING OF AN overstatement. There was in fact only one road through Blackridge, and they were able to follow it readily enough toward the Underwoods. They were relieved to get out of town because the glares they were receiving from the townspeople they passed since they had a dog in their company were becoming tiresome. In several instances, some of the men stopped and turned and looked as if they were ready to try and assail Poxy, but Thomas would have his hand resting with significance on his rifle while James kept his on the pommel of his cutlass, and that was generally enough to send a mute warning to anyone who was even thinking about trying to start difficulties.

"This whole thing with the dog reminds me of something I read about in a history text," said Thomas, as they walked the main road. "An outbreak of disease about a century back, in a seaside city called Port Manteau. It swept through the city, killing one person in three. And Port Manteau had a fairly high cat population. So a group of superstitious idiots decided that the cats were avatars of demons and started killing all the cats. In no time at all, every single cat in the entire city had been executed in the belief that it would rid the city of the disease."

"Did it?"

"Actually, it aggravated it. Turned out that the disease was actually being spread by wharf rats, and the cats were the only thing keeping the rats in check. With the cats gone, the rat population exploded, and people started dying faster than ever."

James shook his head. "Amazing sometimes what people will and will not believe in. They think balverines and krakens are the stuff of legend, and in the meantime slaughter harmless animals out of fear. Did they ever finally manage to bring the disease under control?"

"In a manner of speaking."

"Meaning?"

Thomas stopped and looked glumly at his companion. "The local governor had his soldiers surround the city so that no one could leave, and then they fired flaming arrows at it by the hundreds."

"They torched the place?" James could barely speak above a whisper.

"They did. Houses, women, children, everyone. It was said that the stench from the burning flesh could be smelled from ten miles away, and the tower of black smoke was visible from twice that distance. The city was never rebuilt."

"No surprise there. Who would want to live or do business in something that had once been a huge charnel house?"

"No kidding," said Thomas. "And there are some who believe that to this day if you walk around the area where Port Manteau used to be, you can hear the terrified cries and agonized screams of the once-living residents, howling for help that would never come."

"By contrast with that, the occasional balverine assault would seem like no big deal. And yet"—and James scratched behind the dog's ears—"the people here still felt the need to try and get rid of the very animals who might have helped them fight the monsters they were so afraid of. Astounding how shortsighted people can be sometimes."

"Sure is."

They said little else as they continued on their way, and they were in Underwoods before they even quite realized it. There wasn't a clear line of demarcation between village and forest. Instead, the trees seemed to increase in number until they found themselves in the midst of the forest. There had been paving on the road when it was in the village, but as they moved out into the woods, it was replaced with the plain old dirt road that it no doubt originally was.

It didn't seem any different from any number of other forests through which they had traveled, and yet Thomas found himself far more alert than ever before.

The shadows seemed to stretch out toward him, and everywhere seemed to be potential hiding places for balverines. They had come a long way from the realm where such creatures were considered harmless beings of myth.

A snap of a branch caused Thomas to jump two feet, and his sword was out of his scabbard and in his hand as he whirled to face the new threat. All he saw was James standing there, lifting his foot off a branch and not knowing whether to feel chagrined or amused. "Are you all right, Thomas?"

"I'm fine."

"All evidence to the contrary." James watched as Thomas sheathed his sword, and then said, "I didn't mean to startle you . . ."

"I startled myself. I just—"

"You just what?"

Thomas hesitated, and then said, "I know what I saw the night that my brother was killed. I know in my heart that it was a balverine, and such things were real. That's why we're here; that's why we set out on this quest. Except I've spent so much of my life being told that I was wrong, that I was imagining things, that I was crazy—that my brother wasn't killed by a balverine because such creatures don't exist—that it's just weird to be faced with the reality of it. There was always some element of . . . I don't know . . . safety in thinking, in the back of my mind, that it was a delusion on my part. Now I'm in a place where there are people so worried about balverines that they slaughter dogs. It's just requiring a bit of adjustment on my part."

"Well . . . adjust fast, okay? You can't be jumping at every sound."

"I'll be fine. Don't worry about me."

"I'm not," James said cheerfully. "I'm worried about me. I don't need to accidentally startle you and wind up with my head on the ground before you've had a chance to realize that it's me."

Thomas laughed at that. But then he stopped laughing and likewise stopped in his tracks. When James looked at him quizzically, Thomas simply pointed.

There was a crossroads just ahead.

"Odd," Thomas said after a moment, "that balverines would take refuge in a forest that's so relatively 'civilized' that it would have not one but two roads through it."

"Why odd? If they're looking for human prey, why would they spend all their time in forests that are never traveled and unlikely to see anything except the occasional lost soul? They'd want to position themselves along a busy road."

"Yes. Yes, I suppose that makes sense."

Slowly, they approached the crossroads, Thomas keeping a wary eye on the shadows, which now seemed even more fraught with peril than before. Everything was quiet. *Still as the grave,* he thought. It wasn't nighttime, the primary domain of the balverines, but daylight hadn't prevented the creatures from assaulting Robert and his daughter, so that certainly didn't serve as a guarantee of safety.

Once they reached the crossroads, they stopped and stood there for a few moments. It was definitely the same one, because although time and weather had washed away some of the blood, the trees were still stained with it, and some of the ground was stained as well.

Poxy stared around curiously, showing intense interest in a squirrel that was perched on a branch overhead and looking down at them mockingly.

"All right," Thomas said to James. "Now's as good a time as any to test your theory."

James removed the bloodstained piece of tunic and held it up to the dog's nose. Poxy stared at it with curiosity.

"Get the scent, girl," said James, and when Poxy made no move toward it, he pushed the cloth forward up against her nose. "Get the scent," he said again.

Poxy drew her head back, trying to get away from it, and James stubbornly kept moving the cloth back and forth in order to keep it in front of her nostrils. Thomas watched this for a minute, and then said, "James, I think you're wasting your time. This is—"

"*Wait!* She's *got* it!" James said excitedly.

It appeared that James was right. Poxy had suddenly taken a renewed interest in the cloth that he was holding in front of her, and her nostrils were flaring. And Thomas could have sworn that there was something akin to understanding in her eyes, as if an old instinct, possibly long forgotten, was being reignited.

And then, with as much confidence as any trained bloodhound had ever exhibited, Poxy went to the center of the crossroads and began sniffing around.

"I don't believe it," said Thomas. "This is incredible."

"Ha," said James dismissively, as if the outcome had never been in doubt. "That's my dog, is all."

At which point Poxy suddenly bounded up and down, barked excitedly, and then started down the road to the right. She stopped briefly to turn and bark again, clearly wanting to make sure that the boys were going to be following her.

They set off after her immediately at a brisk trot, moving at a moderate pace since they had no idea how far they were going to be following the dog, and they did not wish to wear themselves out. Poxy could easily have left them in the dust, but every time she started to put any major amount of distance between them, she would stop, turn, and wait until they were close enough so that she could continue on her path without losing them.

As it turned out, they didn't have to go all that far. In fairly short order they found that the road was leading them directly to a farm. A pig farm, as it turned out, which was something they were able to determine easily enough with their own noses. They may not have had the olfactory prowess of Poxy, but it was hardly required because the smell of the swine was quite pungent, and the wind was carrying it directly to them. Poxy barked with greater excitement as they drew within view of the farm. There was a ramshackle house, a barn, and a large pen in which a number of oversized hogs were feeding and grunting and acting like pigs. Poxy bounced around, running up to the pigs, barking eagerly, and then running back to Thomas and James with her tail wagging. Clearly, she was expecting to be praised.

"Great," said Thomas, walking over to the pigpen and looking down at the inhabitants. His nose wrinkled in disgust. "This is a dead end."

"She seemed so sure," James said, visibly disappointed. "It was a nice try, but I think we—"

The air exploded around them.

Thomas was so startled that he tumbled headlong over the fence and into the pigsty. The pigs bounded backwards, snorting and grunting in indignation that an uninvited guest had entered their pen.

James darted behind a tree, Poxy right with him, as there was a second explosion that chipped a huge piece of bark off the tree. "What in the—?"

"I have you now!"

A burly man with fiery red hair was lumbering toward them, and he was wielding a rifle that looked significantly larger than Thomas's. He was the one who had shouted at them, and apparently the diatribe was only just commencing. *"Came back for more, did you? Well, you'll get more than you bargained for this time! This time I'm ready for you!"*

Making sure to keep himself shielded behind the tree, James called out, *"What the hell are you talking about! We've never been here before!"*

"You expect me to believe that?" demanded the man who was approaching them. "You think I don't know what's what? You!" And he swung his rifle around to get a bead on Thomas, who was lying on the ground behind one of the pigs. "Get out here and die like a man!"

James rapidly calculated the distance between himself and the crazy man with the rifle, and realized there was no way he could cover it without presenting an easy target. That wasn't about to deter him, though; not when it came to Thomas's life being on the line.

And suddenly Thomas was up from behind the pig, his right arm moving in a blur. Something hurtled through the air, and the man let out a shriek of pain as a throwing knife buried itself firmly in his upper chest. Even as the hilt was still quivering, Thomas was bolting out of the pen and vaulting the fence in one quick stride. The man tried to bring the rifle to bear, but Thomas had scooped up a fistful of mud and threw it squarely into the man's face. It blinded him, and he got off another shot, but it went wide. Thomas darted in quickly and grabbed the barrel of the rifle and shoved it straight up so that it presented no threat. Then he drove a knee squarely into the man's groin with an impact that James could feel from where he was standing. The man opened his mouth and tried to groan, but he couldn't gather his breath to do so as Thomas yanked the rifle completely clear of his grasp. The man sank to his knees, his eyes looking ready to leap out of his head. "You . . . bastard," he managed to gasp out, and then he slumped over, his hands over his crotch, as if he was concerned that Thomas was going to strike him there a second time.

Thomas picked up the fallen rifle and held it across

his body in a nonthreatening manner, but in such a way that he could aim it quickly at its owner if such an action was required. With one hand, he made a vague effort to brush some of the crusted mud off himself. Over in the pen, the hogs were still snorting in irritation and letting him know that they did not appreciate his intrusion.

"Now listen to me carefully," Thomas said with remarkable calm. "We don't have the slightest idea what you were going on about. Why don't you tell us, and perhaps we can help each other . . ."

"You buried your damned knife in my shoulder!"

"*You* were going to *shoot* me!"

"*You* were going to steal another one of my pigs!"

Thomas looked to James in confusion, apparently hoping that James had some idea as to what the man was talking about, but James was as clueless as Thomas. "What the hell are you *talking* about?" James said.

"You know what I'm talking about! Two weeks ago! One of my pigs disappeared! And now you strangers show up here, poking around my animals! Who else would it be? Criminals returning to the scene of the crime! *Damnation!*" That last was as a result of the man trying to pull the blade out of his shoulder and yowling in pain.

Thomas rolled his eyes, and said, "Lie down. Don't move. James, get over here and bring the pack."

James did as Thomas bade him, and Thomas knelt next to the man who had, moments earlier, been ready to shoot him. "What are you doing?" demanded the wounded man. "Are you going to try and kill me now—?"

"I have a sword, I have a rifle—two rifles, counting

yours—and a crossbow. If I wanted to kill you, it would prove no great difficulty. Now be quiet and try not to squirm. James, come help hold him down."

The man let out a yelp, but he was still too much in pain thanks to the combination of the knife and the brutal kick to the groin. James pushed him over with ease, and when the man tried to sit up, Poxy trotted over, placed one of her paws on his chest and growled in his face. The sight of her bared teeth was enough to cause the man to stop moving and stare up into her muzzle with undiluted terror.

Slowly, carefully, Thomas withdrew the knife from where it was embedded and quickly pressed a cloth against it to stanch the bleeding. "You've got damned good aim," the man said grudgingly. "Looks like you didn't hit an artery or anything vital."

"I was aiming at your heart," said Thomas.

The man grunted.

It took Thomas and James only minutes to dress the wound. Again displaying grudging respect, the man said, "Not badly done for amateurs."

"And you're a professional?"

"Former soldier of fortune."

"And now you're a pig farmer?"

He shrugged and then winced at the pain the thoughtless gesture had caused. "Family business. My father was old, needed help, and I came here. We do things for our fathers."

Thomas's lips thinned, and he simply said, "Yes, I suppose we do." James said nothing.

The former soldier of fortune looked from one of them to the other. "So you really had nothing to do with my stolen hog?"

"Not a thing," said Thomas, and he quickly laid out for the man the circumstances that had brought them there. "I suppose the dog just smelled the pigs, and that's what brought her here," he concluded, but then he frowned. "Except . . ."

"Except what?" said James.

"Well . . . that's just a hell of a coincidence, don't you think? That one of his hogs was stolen right about the same time that that Robert and Hannah vanished?"

"You're thinking that a balverine might have done it? That that's what Poxy was tracking?"

"That's a possibility . . ." said Thomas. "It explains some things, but—"

"Balverines?" The soldier-turned–pig farmer regarded them skeptically. "In this neck of the woods? Ain't no balverines around here."

"The townspeople believe—"

"The townspeople don't know their backs from their fronts. They jump at shadows and believe that danger lurks behind every corner. *Used* to be balverines in these parts, and their legend still keeps everyone on edge. But they ain't 'round these parts. Not anymore."

"Why not anymore?"

"Because"—and he had a smile of pride—"me and some others drove 'em off. One of the last things I did before I hung up my sword. Me and some of my mates, we rooted

’em out and sent ’em packing. Last I heard, they retreated farther east. So if you’re truly mad enough to go seeking them, then that’s where you’re going to want to be.”

“But I don’t understand,” said James. “If there are no balverines around here, then why did some of them show up to attack Hannah and her father? Why did they drag her off?”

“I suppose it’s possible,” said the pig farmer. “A stray couple of pack members wandering far afield.”

“Or . . . it might be something else,” said Thomas, but he made no attempt to elaborate.

“Well, if you find my pig, or find who took it, there’s a reward in it for you if you either return the animal or put the thief’s head in my hands.”

“We’ll definitely keep that in mind.”

They departed the farm then although Thomas had taken the precaution of removing the remainder of the ammunition from the man’s rifle without his knowledge. That way, if he suddenly decided to avail himself of the opportunity to fire upon their unprotected backs, he would not be able to do so. And by the time he reloaded, they would be long gone.

“So now what?” James said. He was still obviously chagrined over Poxy’s inability to bring them to their quarry although he supposed he couldn’t blame her. The aroma of the pigs must have been powerful, even from the distance they’d initially been standing.

“We go back to the crossroad.”

“And—?”

"We try again."

"We do?" James said in surprise. "But she's just going to bring us right back to the pig farm, won't she?"

"Not necessarily. We've got the other item, the hairbrush. We use that this time." Thomas looked down at Poxy, who had stopped briefly to chew on some shrubs. "I think you were right about her, James. I think she does have some tracking capability. How good it is, we're about to find out."

James scratched his chin thoughtfully. "What's going through your mind, Thomas? You're thinking something, but damned if I know what it is."

"I don't want to say just yet. Let's see how matters play out."

That seemed needlessly cryptic to James, but he decided not to press Thomas on the matter. This attitude was very much in character for him: Thomas didn't like to voice opinions unless he was completely certain of them.

Returning to the crossroads, James removed the hairbrush from his bag and, once again, held it under Poxy's nose. This time she got the idea even faster than before. She buried her nose in it and withdrew with an annoyed little yelp as the bristles from the brush scratched her tender nose. She shook her head, making an irritated snuffling sound, and then sniffed the brush more cautiously.

Then she started moving in a circle around the crossroads, sniffing the ground industriously. James considered this to be a good sign; at least she wasn't heading straight off right back down the road that they'd just come from. She seemed to understand that she was looking for a different scent this time. The only question that remained was whether she was going to find it.

After a few more moments that seemed to crawl past, Poxy's tail suddenly stiffened, and her ears flattened. She growled low in her throat, which made James think for a moment that some sort of threat was imminent, hiding behind a tree or some brush. Then James realized that Poxy was in fact reacting to something that was no longer there; she had instead picked up a scent that she obviously considered extremely threatening.

"She's got it," James said with growing excitement, and Thomas nodded in agreement. "Go find her, girl! Come on!" And he clapped his hands briskly. "Go find her!"

Poxy required no more urging. Instead, she bounded away, this time continuing straight down the path rather than moving to the intersecting crossroad. Thomas and James set out after her, moving at a full-out run yet falling behind nevertheless. As before, every so often Poxy would stop, turn, and wait for them to catch up before she continued on her way.

This, however, was not destined to be as short a trip as their first attempt to track down the missing young girl. Instead, they continued through the woods for hours. The sun moved irresistibly through the sky, and every so often they would have to stop to rest, eat from their meager supplies, and regain their strength. During those times, Poxy would return to them with what appeared to be great impatience, so eager was she to have them continue following her.

The early evening stretched into night, and they were still in the woods. Neither Thomas nor James was ecstatic about their situation, because if the pig farmer had been wrong—and there was every chance that he was—and the balverines in fact stalked these woods, then the boys would be tremendously vulnerable. But there was no choice for it, and so they made camp in the midst of a natural ring formation of boulders, thus providing them some minimal protection. James then went into the woods, borrowing Thomas's crossbow, and within the hour returned with a newly caught and deceased rabbit that he expertly skinned while Thomas started up a campfire. They cooked the animal over the fire and ate their fill while Poxy—who seemed to understand that there would be no more tracking this evening—managed to chase down a pheasant for herself. Unlike the boys, she preferred her meal raw.

"I don't like just sitting here," grumbled James, "when we could be following her—"

"She's been gone for a while, James. I wouldn't be concerned; one more day shouldn't make all that much difference in the grand scheme of things."

Thomas sounded entirely too relaxed about the whole thing; James was now more sure than ever that Thomas had thoughts he wasn't sharing and was burning to know what was going through his friend's mind. But he knew Thomas well enough to be sure that he would tell him when he was good and ready.

They took turns sitting guard while the other slept, passing the rifle between themselves. Truthfully, neither of them knew how firearms would fare against such creatures, but simply having it in their hands was enough to give them some measure of confidence.

When the morning sun barely crawled onto the horizon, they downed a mean breakfast of bread that was rapidly becoming stale and was one day away from being inedible. James, foraging in the immediate area, found a spring where he was able to refill their water containers. Once he and Thomas were ready to move out, he pulled out the hairbrush and held it up toward Poxy's nose as he had the previous day. Poxy sniffed it, this time taking care not to bump her nose against the bristles, and moments later was back on the scent. By this point, Poxy had managed to develop a steady pace that didn't threaten to leave the two of them behind, so she no longer had to keep stopping to wait—with growing impatience—for them to catch up.

The forest began to thin around them, a development that both pleased and disappointed Thomas. It appeared, at least from what they had encountered or, more precisely, failed to encounter, that the pig farmer had been correct. There were no balverines in this forest although very likely the mere threat of them was enough to make sure that the villagers never wandered particularly deeply into it. So that was something of a relief since they had been able to pass through unmolested. On the other hand, since finding such a creature was their top priority, it was disappointing and frustrating that they had not managed to encounter any.

Poxy kept them on the trail and then, about half a

day's journey farther down, they came upon another village that was so similar to the one they'd departed that for a short time Thomas feared that they had gone in a tremendous circle. This worry was quickly set aside, however, as whatever chance encounters with passersby they had resulted in nods or smiles or comments of "Good day to ye," without the slightest bit of hostility directed toward Poxy. Whatever feeling the locals might have had toward balverines, it certainly didn't extend to their views on dogs. In fact, James and Thomas even saw a few other dogs wandering around the area, and Poxy almost let herself get distracted until James managed to refocus her with a sharp word and a wave of the hairbrush.

The roads continued to be unpaved, which was of benefit since they weren't entirely sure how the scent would have stood up if it had transitioned from dirt to pavement. Then Poxy abruptly veered off onto a side road, and the two of them followed her as she eagerly led them along.

Ahead of them, they heard a steady clanging that signaled they were approaching the shop of a smithy, who was steadily hammering away on his anvil. It was there that Poxy was bringing them. Thomas and James shrugged to each other, unsure of what to expect, but they gamely trailed behind the dog and moments later walked into the smithy's shop.

Sure enough, there he was, an older man with the sort of massive forearms that one would expect of a man in his profession. He was wearing loose trousers and no shirt but instead a leather apron, as well as thick gloves. Wielding tongs in one hand and a large mallet in the other, he was hammering out a horseshoe and building up a good deal of sweat as he did so. He didn't notice them until James loudly cleared his throat, and then he looked upon them with kind eyes as he set his tools down. "How can I help you boys?" he said.

"Well, actually, we're . . ." And unsure of how to approach it, James said, "We're looking for Hannah."

"Oh," said the man, and automatically he turned as if he were about to call out a name. Then he hesitated, whatever he was about to say dying in his throat, and slowly he turned back to them. "Who might you be?"

"I think a better question," Thomas said, taking a step forward, deepening his voice to sound more authoritative, "is . . . who might *you* be?"

The man had put down neither hammer nor tongs. In fact, as the mood in the small building grew chillier, he seemed to be gripping both of the tools tighter. "Considering that you happen to be strangers here, and this is *my* shop, I don't see where you get to be asking *any* questions. In fact, as far as I'm concerned, what you get to do is get the hell out of here."

"We're here," Thomas said slowly, "because her mother is worried about her."

"I don't know any Hannah, and I don't know her mother."

"Really. Because it seemed to me that you were about to call out for her when we first arrived."

"You're wrong."

"I don't think I am."

And then something in his voice changed, and his gaze became very fixed upon them. "So you're looking for Hannah, are you? On behalf of her mother?"

"Yes, that's right," said James, wondering why the smithy's tone had suddenly become so stilted. "We just told you that—"

He had about two seconds worth of warning, enough time for the sound of steel hissing from a scabbard, and James spun, yanking out his cutlass and bringing it up in a purely defensive manner, blind, instinctive. A sword came crashing down upon it that he managed to deflect through the wildest of luck, the two blades running the length of each other and clashing together at the hilts. The other sword was in the hand of a young man with wild hair and wilder eyes.

Their gazes locked, and James was filled with anger, with an unnameable rage, that this person had tried to assault him from behind in such a cowardly manner. He focused all that fury, envisioned it as if it were a ball of black energy within him, and he drove that blackness directly into the eyes of the young man who was shoving against him. It froze his attacker in his tracks, and James brought his fist up and around in a short, quick jab that took his assailant on the side of the head, sending him down to one knee. He pointed his sword at the young man's throat, and if his assailant was giving any consideration to trying another attack, the growling Poxy's face a mere inch from his dissuaded him. The young man froze.

The smithy, meanwhile, came straight at Thomas,

wielding the long tongs as if they were a bludgeon. They were not designed as such, but then neither was a fireplace poker, and one could certainly stave in someone's head with such an instrument. Thomas dodged back, grabbing for his own blade, but the smithy struck him on the arm with the tongs before he could pull it. Thomas cried out, losing all feeling in the arm, and fell back against some chains hanging from nails on the wall. He grabbed the chain with his still-functioning left arm and whipped it around as fast and as hard as he could. He got lucky; the chain snaked around the smithy's throat, cutting off his air. The smithy dropped his makeshift weapons to try to remove it, and Thomas yanked as hard as he could. It hauled the smithy off his feet and slammed him into the wall, which shook violently from the impact. Before the smithy could recover, Thomas yanked again, hauling the smithy the other way. The smithy stumbled and tripped over his own feet, crashing noisily to the ground. The impact yanked the chain out of Thomas's grasp, and instead of trying to grab it again, he yanked out his sword. The smithy pulled the chain clear of his throat, and whispered hoarsely, "You bastards . . . I'll kill you . . ."

"Not," James called out, "before I kill him. I assume his death would mean something to you."

It was at that moment that Thomas suddenly realized that he had no idea if James was bluffing or not. Up until this moment, neither of them had been in a position where they would be forced to take lethal action against an opponent. It was one thing to contemplate having to kill a monster in order to survive. But slay another human being, especially in order to fulfill a threat? Thomas wasn't sure if he himself was capable of such a thing. But when he looked at James, he saw a burning coldness there that made him think that not only was James capable of doing such a thing, but that he would think nothing of it.

Whether it would have come to that or not would not be known, at least not at that moment. Because the tableau was disrupted by an alarmed female voice that cried out, *"What's going on here!"*

It was said that if one wishes to get an idea of what a daughter will look like twenty years hence, one need only look at the mother. In the young woman standing in front of them, with pale blue eyes and an expression so frightened that all the blood had drained from her face, there were the general hints of Mrs. Mullins. But she was far smaller and delicate, which gave Thomas enough reason to hope that the girl—presuming she was who Thomas suspected her to be—might escape that undesirable fate.

"Hannah?" said Thomas tentatively.

The young man whom James was holding at sword point shouted, *"Don't answer him, Hannah!"* and then promptly winced in mortification.

"And you," Thomas continued, addressing the young man as if he hadn't spoken, "would most likely be Samuel. And you, sir"—and he turned to the fallen smithy—"are Robert?"

James, who had been grinning at the young man's

slipup in revealing the girl's identity, suddenly looked bewildered, as if he had wandered into the middle of a play and was desperately trying to get caught up on the plot. "Wait . . . *what*? I thought they were—"

"Dead. That's what they wanted people to believe, wasn't it," Thomas said, but it was not a question.

There was a deathly silence, broken only by the low growl of Poxy, who was not yet entirely convinced that there would be no further attacks.

Then Hannah came forward, her hands clenched to her bosom, and she said, "If you are bounty hunters, please . . . we'll pay you more than she did, I swear. I . . . I don't know how, because we're hardly rich, but if you'll be patient—"

"We're not bounty hunters," said James. "We're . . ." He looked to Thomas, and then squared his shoulders and, trying not to sound self-conscious, said, "We're Heroes."

Hannah looked surprised, as did the two men. "Heroes?" she echoed. "Seriously?"

"We're trying to bring it back into style," James said with a shrug.

"But . . . you've been trained? I wasn't even aware that any halls remained—"

"They're keeping a low profile," said James.

Thomas was feeling increasingly uncomfortable with every passing moment. "Who and what we are is far less important than your present situation," he said, endeavoring to shift the emphasis back to them. "You understand why we're here?"

"I'm not sure *I* understand why we're here," said James. "Your mother, your wife, and . . . well, she's nothing to you, really," he said to Samuel, "but this woman back in Blackridge, she's in mourning for you. She misses you terribly."

"Of course she does," Robert said heatedly. "Misses having us as her servants. Misses brutalizing us, dominating us, making our lives a living hell. That's what she misses, I can guarantee you that."

"And if we went back," Hannah spoke up, "there would be more of the same and worse besides." Abruptly, she started to yank up her skirt, and James immediately looked away, unsure of what she was intending. "I want you to see this," she insisted.

"I assure you, there's *nothing* there that we feel is *any* of our business," James said.

"James," Thomas said softly, "I think you need to see this. Do as she's telling you to."

Confused but attending to his friend's words, James turned back, and he gasped when the sight met his eyes.

There were bruises along her legs. Most of them had faded with time, but there was still enough evidence of them that he could determine they had, at some point in the recent past, been extremely severe. There was also a huge gash down her right thigh. There was no shame in the girl's eyes; instead, there was pure defiance.

"When . . . did those happen?" he managed to say.

"When did they not?" she shot back. "Pain and injuries have been part of my lot in life for as long as I can remember. It didn't matter the reason—a dropped dish, a less-than-respectful word, or not performing a chore with sufficient alacrity. This gash"—and she pointed to the scar—"is when she struck me a glancing blow with a whip."

"A *whip*?"

"One of a number of weapons she keeps around in case of balverine attack. She believes they fear the noise of the whip crack."

"I never heard that one, and I think that the whip crack would slow them for maybe a second before they ripped you apart," said Thomas, and then he gestured toward her exposed legs. "I think you've, uhm . . . made your point."

She dropped her skirt back into place. James, meanwhile, turned to Robert. "But . . . if she was like this, your wife . . . if she was so brutal . . . why didn't you fight back?"

"Would you like to see *my* array of scars and bruises?" He prepared to lift his shirt.

"No. No, that's quite all right," James said hurriedly. "But . . . look, if you don't mind my asking: Why did you marry her in the first place?"

Robert sighed heavily in that way people do when they are reflecting upon the follies of their existence. "I used to drink heavily. I suppose the two of you are too young to experience what it's like to wake up on a cruel morning and discover that the attractive, charming woman sharing your bed is far less so upon the return of your sobriety."

"Ouch," said James.

"Indeed. And when that unwise assignation results in

your child being carried within her belly, well . . ." And he shrugged. "If you're a man, you take responsibility for your actions and come to feel that whatever happens is happening because you deserve it."

"But it reached a point," said Hannah, "where we could no longer stand it." She moved over to her father then and took his hand firmly, looking at him with great sympathy. "You're in that sort of situation, and you feel trapped. It's hard to describe. The biggest challenge is overcoming that feeling and taking it upon yourself to break free of it."

"And you did it with the help of Hannah's friend, Samuel," said Thomas, nodding toward the young man whom James had had at sword point earlier. "Friend or . . . more than friend?"

"Far more," said Hannah, and then gently she rested her hand on her own belly.

It became blindingly clear to James at that point. "You're up the spout, with *his* child," he whispered.

"No drunken assignations required," said Samuel.

Hannah nodded, and then she reached out and took Samuel's hand, squeezing it tightly. "And if mother found out, I can't even think what . . . it's unimaginable . . ."

Thomas and James could imagine it all too easily. Any reaction, from her mother murdering Samuel to beating her daughter so comprehensively that she lost the child . . . anything was possible. If the woman bruised her daughter over a dropped dish, how would she react to something like this? Not well, that much was certain.

James at last understood. "So these two"—and he

indicated father and daughter—"went off into the woods, and Samuel, you came running back with the entire story about the balverines, knowing that the woman's superstitions would cause her to believe you . . . but wait, no. That wasn't all. The blood . . ."

"Courtesy of a stolen pig," Thomas said. "You stole one from a local pig farmer . . ."

"A runt," said Samuel defensively, as if that somehow made it more acceptable. "It wouldn't have been worth much to him anyway."

"Then you brought it to the crossroads, slaughtered it, spread the blood all over while father and daughter went on ahead, after Robert changed shirts and gave you a torn one that you could soak in the pig's blood. That's why," Thomas said to James, "the dog went straight to the pig farm. She was just following the scent of the type of animal whose blood it was."

"Ah. Well . . . good girl." James petted the top of her head approvingly. "I knew there must have been a reason for it."

"What happened to the actual carcass of the pig?"

"We took it with us," said Robert. "Served as a decent meal for our first few days here."

"And this business? You're a blacksmith—?"

"This was not," said Robert, "something that was simply embarked upon. I prepared for this carefully. Set up this business ahead of time so that I would be able to provide for my daughter and"—he nodded toward Samuel—"my future son-in-law. Keeping my plans hidden from my wife was tricky, but not impossible."

"And that brings us back around to you," said Hannah. She stepped toward James, and Poxy immediate growled in warning. James softly shushed his dog, stroking the back of her head to indicate that he was not facing any threat. "You can't tell her. You just can't. If you tell my mother, she'll show up here, and—"

"And what?" The skepticism in James's voice was evident. "Drag you back home, kicking and screaming?"

"Possibly," said Robert. "Or she may be so filled with fury that she'll just kill us all here."

"This is ridiculous!" James said in exasperation. "It's unmanly, that you should be so afraid of a single woman! You should stand up to her, face her, tell her that she has no business terrorizing you like that! And whatever she's done, she at least deserves to know that her family didn't die at the hands of balverines!"

"James," Thomas said firmly, "that's not our decision to make."

"What?" James turned to Thomas, astonished. "How is it not our decision? The woman asked us to provide her some sort of definitive word of her family! I know that you're all about hunting down balverines, but me, I was thinking that we were supposed to, you know, keep our word to the woman who sent us on this task in the first place!"

"You wish to locate balverines?" Robert said abruptly. "I can tell you where you can find them."

"And we should believe you?" said James. He folded his arms and regarded Robert with derision. "A man who came up with a whole plan to fake his death because he was too afraid to be honest with his own wife?"

"Believe me, do not believe me: It is entirely up to you," Robert said. "But if it is balverines you seek, I can tell you where to go and who you can speak to about it."

"To whom we can speak?" This last interested Thomas tremendously. "What do you mean?"

"There's a man. He came through Blackridge a year or so ago, seeking to do business."

James was about to express disbelief, but he was distracted by Hannah's reaction. There was fear in her face, and her voice trembled slightly as she said, "The tall man?"

"Yes," said Robert, nodding. "The tall man. His name was Kreel. Kreel the huntsman was how he introduced himself around town."

Unconsciously protective of her unborn child, Hannah automatically wrapped one arm around her stomach. "I did not like him. I did not like him at all. Death unseen walked arm in arm with him."

"And what did this Kreel the huntsman want?" said Thomas.

"He wanted to see people die."

"Hannah!" said Robert sharply.

But she did not back down from the tone in her father's voice. "That's what he wanted, Father. Let's be honest with them. None but a sadistic madman who wants to lead others to foolish, needless deaths would be endeavoring to offer excursions into balverine territory."

"I met him too, this Kreel," Samuel now spoke up.

"Hannah has it exactly right. He claimed that he had spent his life hunting balverines. You ask me, that's a career choice that's enough to make any man cold and brutal. He claimed he had killed many of them, and that he had decided to enlist others on balverine-hunting expeditions. He said that he knew our village had a keen interest in the creatures and thought there would be potential customers eager to take him up on his offer."

"And did anyone?" asked Thomas.

Robert shook his head. "Not to my knowledge, no. Kreel did not seem particularly concerned. He simply announced that it was the collective loss of the townspeople and returned whence he came."

"And where was that? Where can this Kreel be found?"

Robert hesitated, and then said, "Your word. Your word that you will leave us to ourselves and tell my wife nothing of this."

"You have my word."

"Thomas!" James had spoken with such vehemence, such astonishment, that the tone of it startled Poxy. "What about—?"

"You have my word," Thomas repeated firmly. "We'll get out of here, and you can live your lives as you see fit."

"They're Heroes, Father," Hannah said. "That alone makes their word good enough for me."

Robert gave it a moment's more consideration and nodded, satisfied that he and his makeshift family would remain unmolested. "Sutcliff," he said. "Kreel is based in Sutcliff. It is said that the forest there is a major hunting ground for balverines. If you seek them, and a guide to take you to them, then Sutcliff should be your destination."

"And that would be—?"

"Due east from here."

"Yes, that figures." Thomas bowed briefly and stiffly to them. "For what it's worth, I think what you have done is answer cruelty with cruelty. She really is in mourning for you, your wife . . . your mother."

"And me?" asked Samuel.

"Honestly, she didn't seem to give a damn about you," said Thomas. "But however nasty she is on the outside, she's as grief-stricken as any mother and wife would be. I just want you to know that, in case it makes you think about going back to her someday. Who knows? She might be so glad to see that you're alive that you won't have to be worried about your safety. Plus, I hear that grandchildren can work wonders on people. Just think about it is all I'm saying."

"We shall," Robert said, although there was little in the manner in which he had spoken that led either Thomas or James to believe that any of them were actually going to do it.

JAMES SAID VERY LITTLE AFTER HE AND Thomas took their leave of the small blacksmith shop. Any questions or attempts at casual conversation resulted in only short, barely articulate grunts. Even Poxy could discern that there had been a change in her master's demeanor, and she stayed close by his side and whimpered every so often to make her concern known.

With the sun lowering and no inns in sight, they made camp just off the road, at which point Thomas could stand the silence no longer. "You are upset," he said.

"That's ridiculous. I have no right to be upset," said James. He sat a short distance away, his legs curled up and his chin resting upon his knees. "Where does it say I'm entitled to have opinions? Only what you say matters."

"Stop it. You're being ridiculous."

"*I'm* ridiculous!" It had not taken much prodding on Thomas's part to spur James to vent his frustration. "You believed everything they said! Everything!"

"You saw the marks on the girl. Their story made sense."

"Their story was just that: A story! But you, you're so damned trusting, you just accepted everything they said at face value! What if the mother isn't the brute they say she is? That the father just decided he could do better elsewhere, and the daughter and her lover went along with it?"

"Come on, James. You saw that woman. She would have beaten *us* to death, given half a chance."

"She didn't know who we were! And what about the pig farmer! He promised us a reward if we could point him to the one who stole his pig. Which we can do now, except . . ."

"Except I gave my word—"

"Your word, not mine. Or are we back to insisting

that I've no say in it? Besides," he added before Thomas could respond, "you only promised not to rat them out to the mother. You didn't say anything about the pig farmer. Let Samuel deal with the consequences of his actions instead of us always struggling to keep our purses and bellies filled."

"There are more important things than money, James."

"Isn't it funny how people who have money always say that?"

"James—"

James put up a hand, and said brusquely, "Forget it, okay? Just forget it." He added in a formal tone, "You have made the decision and I, your humble servant, will abide by it."

Thomas was hurt by James's reaction. "James . . . come on. You know you've always been a good friend, not just a servant."

"All I know is that I'm tired of talking about these things, okay?"

That was most definitely not how Thomas wished to leave the matter, but it was clear that James was in no mood to continue the discussion. So Thomas lay out his bedroll and rested himself upon the ground, James following suit, pointedly lying with his back to Thomas. Thomas shrugged, hoping that James would be in a better mood upon the rising of the sun and that matters between them could return to normal.

He drifted to sleep and, for the first time in a while, the balverines came to him in his slumber. He was a child again, running through the woods with his brother next to him, urging him to flee, and then his brother went down, and this time there was not one balverine but a dozen. They were ripping him apart before Thomas's eyes, and he opened his mouth to scream as loudly as he could, but no sounds were coming out. He lay helpless on the ground, paralyzed with fear, and the balverines crawled over his brother's corpse and slowly approached him, their lips drawn back, their baleful glare fixed upon him, and then, with an ear-shattering roar, they leaped upon him.

He woke up a split second before they landed on him and sat up immediately, gasping, clutching at his chest, checking himself automatically to make certain that he had not received any fatal wounds. His pounding heart started to slow to something approaching its normal rhythm as Thomas moaned and remained upright, now fully awake and afraid to return to the realm of dreams, where the balverines were waiting to pounce upon him.

Thomas glanced over toward where James had been sleeping to make sure that he had not disturbed his friend.

James was gone. So was Poxy. And so was their gear.

Chapter 10

THE SUN WAS HIGH IN THE SKY WHEN James arrived at the crossroads and hesitated, trying to determine which direction would be best for him to go. It was an extremely bright day, and yet only a few slivers of sunlight were able to thread their way through the thicket of branches overhead.

"So what do you think, Poxy?" said James after a few moments of contemplation. "To the pig farmer first? Or to the mother? My inclination would be to the farmer," and he sat down, working it through. "And here's why. The farmer is probably going to want me to bring him to Samuel before he'll cough up the reward. But I doubt he'll have any interest in the father or the daughter; just the one who slaughtered his pig. So he'll be busy taking vengeance on the lad, and that'll give the father and daughter a sporting chance to get away from there before the mother shows up. On the other hand, Mrs. Mullins *should* have the opportunity to confront her runaway family. Maybe I can get her and convince her to stop along the way to pick up the pig farmer, and the two of them can travel with me. That way, everything is done all at the same time, and everyone can be satisfied all at the same time . . ."

His voice trailed off.

Poxy was studying him with her steady, unblinking gaze, and although he knew he had no reason to think of such things—that although his dog was bright, she was only bright for a dog and certainly didn't have anything approaching human intelligence—it nevertheless seemed to him that she was judging him somehow. That she was contemplating his motives and not liking what she was seeing.

"The woman has a right to know," he said to Poxy, "and the man has a right not to have his livestock stolen. You know that, right?"

If Poxy was to provide an answer, it was a mute one: She turned and trotted off into the forest, barking, perhaps in pursuit of a squirrel that she had noticed running past. He called after her in annoyance, but she didn't return. "Fine, Poxy Cur!" he shouted. "But don't expect me to be sitting here when you come back! I'm leaving! Now!"

But he did not leave. Instead, he remained there for what seemed an unbearably long time, staring off into the distance, his gaze turning from the direction of Mrs. Mullins to that of the pig farmer and then back again.

"Dammit," he said at last.

He turned around and had just enough time to let out an alarmed cry as Thomas plowed into him. They went down in a tangle, elbows slamming into their respective eyes and mouths and chests, and they thudded across the ground until they rolled to a stop. Then James threw himself off Thomas and kept going, skidding to a stop a short distance away and scrambling to his feet. *"Thomas! What the hell—!"*

"You were going back!" Thomas shouted, his face twisted in fury. James could not recall ever seeing him so filled with wrath. "You were going back to Mrs. Mullins or the farmer! After I told you—"

"After you *told me*?" James bellowed right back at him. "So much for the whole thing about how I'm not your servant! That I'm your friend!" He mockingly started bowing, his arms outstretched. "Yes, master! Whatever you say, master!"

"Don't be an ass!"

"Better an ass than a hypocrite with an elastic sense of values!"

"You don't know what you're talking about," Thomas said heatedly, advancing on him. His right hand was clenched, trembling, as if it were ready to strike James of its own accord. "It's not hypocritical to display some simple human compassion."

"Where's your compassion for the mother, eh?"

"Maybe she doesn't *deserve* compassion! Did you ever consider that? Maybe she's exactly what she was described as! You saw her! And there's no reason to doubt what they said about her and about how she made me feel!"

"*You*? How she made *you* feel?"

"I mean them. How she made them feel!"

"*Is* that what you mean?" James said challengingly. "You with your ideals of perfect heroism. Looking to have your own little glow of light following you around?"

"As compared to you? Do you know what happens to Heroes with dark alignments? The darkness starts showing up on the outside!" He approached James and started ticking off aspects on his fingers. "You grow horns! And your eyes glow red! And . . . and flies start following you around . . ."

"Oh, please."

"It's true!'

"You don't have an exclusive on what's true and what's false! There's plenty of information about the world that isn't in any of your books!"

"Yeah? Like what?"

"Like—"

"Well? Don't just stand there, James. Enlighten me. Tell me what—"

"Like that my father left us!"

Thomas stared at him blankly, taken aback by the statement, which he did not entirely understand. "What do you mean? I knew that. He died when you were—"

"Not 'left us' in that sense. I mean actually left us. Walked out on us. Said he was going out for a while and never returned. Your father may be far from perfect, Thomas, but at least you have one. And I swore, I *swore* I would never be anything like him because I saw what it did to my mother. But what did I do at the first opportunity? I ran out on my mother and on my family. I became exactly what I swore I never would become."

"You said they wouldn't miss you."

"They probably won't, but that doesn't make what I've done any better."

"Then"—Thomas was utterly perplexed—"why did you come? It's not as if I asked you; I certainly didn't beg you. Why are you here if you feel that way?"

"Because you were going, and I thought you needed me. And I figured I'd be letting you down if I didn't come with you." James shook his head, running his fingers through his hair. "How stupid does that sound? I mean, really. You're of age. I should have just left you to your fate instead of volunteering to come with you. I . . ." He sighed heavily. "I feel like I'm losing the will for this, the longer that we go on . . ."

"Ridiculous," Thomas said firmly. "You have more will, more determination, more resolve, than anyone I've ever met. And the fact is," he admitted after a brief hesitation, "the fact is that you were right. I would be lost without you, James. Truly lost. And . . . well, maybe I'm no different than you."

"Meaning?"

"Meaning I'm letting my feelings about my own family affect how I'm reacting to what we're facing now. I mean . . . no matter how many times I tell myself that the things my mother said on her deathbed were meaningless, it still hurt like hell. And so I wind up not being particularly sympathetic to Mrs. Mullins, you know? Although the fact that she tried to pummel us to death didn't do much to endear her to me either." He picked up a small stone and threw it in a random direction, watching it rebound off a tree. "Maybe you're right. Maybe we should tell Mrs. Mullins the truth and just let things sort themselves out."

"And allow their deaths to be on our conscience? Not sure I see the purpose of that. Let's face it, Thomas: If we take our mutual blinders from our eyes and give our best guess as to what really happened, it probably did play out exactly as father and daughter described. And if the mother finds them . . ."

"There will be more of the same, only worse," said Thomas. "Bruises that don't ever heal."

"Hard to heal when you're dead."

"You really think she's capable of killing them?"

"Oh yes," James said without hesitation. "You saw the woman. The *kraken* wouldn't have wanted any part of her in a battle. I mean, maybe its cruel to her to let her live a life of uncertainty, but it's only one person being made to suffer instead of three. Four, if you count the child that's growing in Hannah's belly."

"You say all this now," said Thomas, "and yet you ran off intending to inform on them. And you were going to tell the pig farmer for that matter, in order to get the reward."

"Yes," said James, "and I'm not proud of that. I guess I needed some time on my own so that I could come to my own conclusions. Conclusions that were, as it turns out, identical to yours, but at least I knew for sure that they were, in fact, *my* conclusions."

"Rather than just deferring to me, you mean."

"Pretty much. I was actually getting ready to retrace my steps when you decided to knock me to the ground."

"Sorry about that," Thomas said with obvious chagrin. "I just . . . needed to stop you."

"Well, next time, try shouting, 'Stop!' That'll work just as well." He flexed his shoulder tentatively, wincing as he did so. "You were lucky. If I had any warning at all, I'd have handed you your head."

"No doubt in my mind," Thomas said diplomatically.

James studied him, trying to determine whether Thomas was being sarcastic or not. Thomas kept his face carefully neutral. Finally, James lowered his arm, and said, "Horns? Seriously?"

"That's what I've heard."

"I'm sorry, but that really just wouldn't work for me. For one thing, I typically look good in hats, and horns would make head apparel problematic."

"To say the least."

"So"—and James rubbed his hands together briskly—"to Sutcliff, then?"

"Unless there is someplace that you would rather go."

"Any number of them. But Sutcliff would seem to be the place. Especially since we now have a name to ask for."

"You mean Kreel," said Thomas. "A man who claims to hunt balverines regularly."

"It would seem to make him the perfect guide."

"Yes. Which is enough to worry me," said Thomas, "since I've discovered that most things in life that seem perfect tend to be anything but. Still, he would give us—at the very least—a starting point." He glanced around. "Where is the Poxy Cur?"

"Oh, she'll probably show up in a few minutes." James, now standing, brushed off the dirt from himself. "You know how kids are. They don't like to hang around and see their parents fighting."

Thomas laughed at that and clapped James on the shoulder. Then, in all seriousness, he said, "I *would* be lost without you, you know."

"Yeah, I know," said James with an indifferent toss of his head. "I just wanted to make certain that you knew."

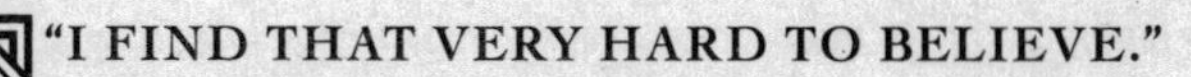

"I FIND THAT VERY HARD TO BELIEVE."

The storyteller stops and regards me with polite confusion. "What's that, Majesty?"

"That business with horns and flies and such. I mean, the thing with the glow is hard enough to swallow, but now I'm supposed to accept that negative decisions cause a demonic aspect to manifest? Honestly, how could that be possible?"

"Since you are asking, Your Majesty," the storyteller replies, "I should think that you would know that as well as anyone. How many times have you encountered individuals about whom you could make judgments based purely upon their appearances? A modest maiden, perhaps? Or a barbarian warrior? Does not a thief telegraph his intentions with his shifty nature? Or a swaggering brute his predisposition toward violence?"

"That is all true enough," I say, "but it is hardly the same thing as claiming that one's choices cause physical changes—"

"Can you not discern a glutton by his more-than-ample physique? The laborer by the quality of his hands? The dandy by the softness of his?"

"Again, there are exceptions, certainly . . ."

"No exceptions," the storyteller says with conviction. "Who we are, what we are, the type of person we are . . . all these things are discernible in a hundred different manners to one who is observant. It is all a matter of degrees. And Heroes are like other men and women, only more so. They are held to a far higher standard and thus operate on a grander scale than mere mortals. So if people look upon a Hero who is positively aligned, does it not make sense that they would perceive him as the essence of goodness? And by the same token, if his actions are negatively aligned, then such would be visible even to the naked eye of the most common of commoners. Certainly, horns and gleaming red eyes would be far in excess of the physical changes one would see in an ordinary, life-size individual, but Heroes . . . they are much larger than life. So naturally the manner in which their decisions impact on them would be larger-than-life as well, as least as far as observers are concerned."

I give that explanation some thought and find myself nodding slowly. "I admit that that makes a certain degree of sense. Very well, then, storyteller: I accept your explanation, at least for now. So"—and I gesture lazily—"you may proceed with your tale if you are of a mind to. As I recall, the lads had managed to salvage their relationship when it was teetering on the brink of total destruction, am I correct?"

"You are indeed, Majesty. Were you concerned that they would not be able to do so? That there would be an irreparable rift between them?"

"I was worried that might be the case and was hoping it would not be," I admit. "The lads are well matched in temperament and deserve to bring this quest to a successful conclusion united."

"Why do you believe that the quest will in fact be concluded successfully at all? You do not know that of a certainty."

"That is true," I say, "but it seemed a safe assumption."

"Assumptions are never, by definition, safe. Quests do fail, Majesty. Heroes do fall short of their goals. Many even die in the attempt."

"That is true, but who tells such stories? The fact that the story of Thomas and James is sufficient to warrant repetition by one such as you would seem to assure that it was fulfilled. What other reason would a storyteller have for describing their adventures?"

"A cautionary tale, perhaps. The mere telling of a story does not guarantee a happy ending. A tale of young love can end tragically in the deaths of the two lovers, their romance forever denied, at least in this world. That does not make the story any less potent."

"But these are not two young lovers of whom we speak. These are two friends upon an adventure. What purpose to tell their story if not to bask in their triumph?"

"To remind others," says the storyteller, "of the high price of failure."

I consider that, and then say, with a touch of worry, "Well, now, that is a consideration that is genuinely going to fester within me." I draw my great cloak around me even more tightly, for it seems to be getting colder still, and we have been outside far longer than I had anticipated when I first came out here. "Very well, then. Speak of these matters with no assurance of the outcome, and I shall hope for the best."

"As you wish, Majesty." And he leans back, his gaze drifting inward as if he is seeing the matters playing out before his inner eye. "James, as it turned out, was quite correct; Poxy rejoined them before they had traveled half a mile. She simply emerged from the woods as if she had not departed, her tail wagging eagerly in greeting. Together, the three of them retraced their steps and then kept on the road headed east. Every so often they would affirm from passersby that they were indeed heading toward Sutcliff, and the response would always be a ready confirmation. A few suggested that there were other destinations that might be more interesting and—to use their term—more modern. 'Modern' was, of course, a relative term, since much of the countryside was primitive by the standards of Albion to which James and Thomas were accustomed. But Sutcliff, by all accounts, was primitive even by the standards of Blackridge. There were no factories pumping out smoke, no great machine shops pounding out manufacturing. More than that, though, was the architecture of the place. The buildings were made of crumbling stone, with

gargoyles mounted atop in eternal crouches that made it seem for all the world as if they were ready to leap upon unsuspecting visitors. Some claimed that Sutcliff was a haven for all things uncanny, that hollow men haunted the cemeteries, and banshees drifted through the streets late at night. None of these were the boys able to verify personally; on the other hand, they weren't really trying all that hard since these were not creatures that they had any desire to encounter.

"Sutcliff itself was curiously divided, and in a manner appropriate to its name. The two sections were referred to as the Uppers and the Lowers. That was reflected along economic lines rightly enough—the working class, the farmers, the tradesmen, all resided in Lower Sutcliff, while the rich, the well-to-do, and the powerful were in far grander homes . . . 'grander' being a relative term . . . in Upper Sutcliff. But it was also a part of the geographic construction of the terrain. Lower Sutcliff was a vast valley that bumped up against the waters, while Upper Sutcliff was a hillside community that stretched around into—appropriately to the town's name—a towering cliff side. Residents on the highest peaks of Sutcliff could gaze down upon the residents of the valley, watching them in the way that eagles could look down upon ants and be amused at the way they scurried about their business.

"And in their travels, in addition to asking about the town, Thomas and James would every so often ask if anyone knew the name of Kreel. No one claimed to have firsthand knowledge of him, and some of them were doubtless speaking the truth. But others appeared to be lying,

for they would suddenly refuse to meet Thomas's gaze, or they would hurriedly remember an appointment and be on their way down the road. No fools were Thomas and James. They were easily able to discern the falsehoods uttered by those they encountered, and it was obvious that these people had no desire to dwell on the mysterious Kreel or even mention his name if it could be helped.

"They arrived in Sutcliff and continued in much the way they had until that point, hoping that fate would turn in their favor.

"As it happened, it both did and did not . . ."

Chapter 11

THE MARKETPLACE IN LOWER SUTcliff was bustling, a mass of humanity on a bright morning that was the first display of pleasant weather in a week, which was probably the reason for the copious number of people there. James and Thomas were drinking in the atmosphere, both figuratively and literally since there were shopkeepers there from local brew houses who were more than happy to sell samples of their wares.

It reminded James, in a wistful sort of way, of his home, except this was somewhat cleaner, a difference that he was inclined to chalk up to the relative lack of industrialization. For one thing, the air was far cleaner. He couldn't remember the last time that he had actually enjoyed breathing. He would take deep lungfuls of air into his chest and swore that he could taste the difference between what he was experiencing and what he had grown up with.

Moreover, city services were dedicated toward keeping the streets themselves as clean as possible, with a surprising number of people whose job apparently consisted of running around with brushes and scoops to make sure that all animal offal was cleaned up from the streets. For once James didn't have to watch where he was going lest he step into gifts left behind from horses. He wasn't noticing any dogs in the area, which made him wonder if the same superstitiousness from Blackridge was in force here in Sutcliff. However, people weren't glaring at him as he walked along with Poxy at his heel; in fact, they didn't seem to notice them at all, which was just fine with James.

The smell of cooking sausages caught his nostrils and drew him over to a stand, Poxy following eagerly. Her mouth was practically watering. The man behind the grill noticed the dog and, instead of trying to chase her away, pulled out an uncooked sausage from behind his counter and flipped it to her. She caught it on the fly and immediately gulped it down with such eagerness that the man, laughing, tossed her two more just to watch her excitement.

"How much for—?" said James, indicating the third sausage that Poxy was just in the process of gulping down.

"Buy something for yourself, and we'll call those bonuses," he said.

This naturally endeared the man immediately to

James and he pulled his purse loose from his belt and dug in generously. He had become so sick of the barely adequate food that they'd been eating at inns, combined with whatever they'd manage to catch themselves while traveling through forests, that this came as a pleasant change of pace. He wound up buying three, whereas, if not for the man's generosity with Poxy, he likely would have bought only one, maybe two. Relooping his purse around his belt, he tasted the first cooked sausage so fast that he wound up burning his tongue and proceeded more slowly with the second one.

Before he could eat the third, however, he felt someone bump into him.

Typically in such an encounter, the person doing the bumping would offer some sort of apology, occasionally earnest, sometimes perfunctory, and maybe even desultory. The one who had bumped into James, however, did none of those. Moreover it was done with enough force that James was convinced that it was deliberate.

Some sixth sense warned him, and immediately his hand went to where his purse was. Except, in this case, it was more accurate to say that it went to where his purse had been, for it was no longer there.

"Son of a bitch!" shouted James, and he whirled, just in time to catch a quick glimpse of the person who had bumped into him—a small form in a gray cloak—moving hastily through the crowd, trying to put distance between them. *"Stop him!"* he shouted, and instantly he was in pursuit.

It was everything he could do to keep the thief in

sight. The little cretin kept dodging this way and that, trying to insinuate himself between people who were going about their business and were utterly unaware that a sneak thief and cutpurse was trying to employ them as a means of escape.

James continued to shout *"Stop him!"* but no one made any move to impede the thief. Instead, they looked around in confusion, as if unsure what was being asked of them.

Then Poxy started barking furiously, and that was sufficient to get the crowd to part where James's cries had been insufficient. Suddenly, magically, James had a straight avenue right toward the sneak thief. Poxy sprinted ahead of him, covering the distance more efficiently courtesy of her four legs compared to his paltry two.

The thief darted to the right, trying to get away, but Poxy had his scent now, and people continued to scatter in order to get out of her way. Poxy caught up just in time to snag the trailing end of the thief's cape, and she seized it in her jaws. It yanked the thief to a halt, a strangled cry coming from him. He grabbed at the collar of his cape, trying to untie the bindings and free himself from it so that he could keep going. Apparently, they were tightly knotted, or else the thief was just nervous, because he fumbled with them for a few seconds that wound up costing him dearly. For it was sufficient time for James to catch up with him and slam into him, knocking him to the ground. The cape tore out of Poxy's mouth, leaving her with a mouthful of material.

James struggled furiously with the thief, who was trying to squirm free from his grasp. It was like trying to wrestle with an eel; three times did the thief nearly squirm free. Opting to go for a wrestling hold in order to immobilize him, James shoved his arms under the thief's armpits, brought them around, and clamped his hands across the thief's chest.

They grabbed on to two round, unaccountably soft projections from the front of the thief's chest.

He was so startled at realizing that he was grasping two handfuls of female breast that it was enough for him to relax his guard for half a second. That was all that was required for the thief to drive an elbow into his mouth, splitting his lip. It knocked James off her back and onto his own. She stumbled to her feet then and started to run forward, and might well have gotten away except Thomas stepped into view, sword in his hand and the blade aimed directly at the base of the thief's throat. The two of them had separated so that they could work the crowd more efficiently in their attempts to try to locate someone who knew the mysterious Kreel. But James's shouts for help had brought him running, and now he was blocking the thief's direct line of escape. "Don't move," Thomas advised.

Poxy was now at his side, offering similarly growling warning. The thief ignored the advice, turning to try and run back the way she had come, but James was back on his feet and blocking her path.

"Give it back," said James, his hand outstretched.

The young girl was glaring at him with the most

stunning green eyes he'd ever seen. Her hair, now visible because her hood had been pulled back, was fiery red, but her bearing and the upthrust tilt of her chin gave her something of a mannish look. "Give what back?"

"Don't try to bluff it through, missy," James warned her.

"Bluff what through, you sick bastard? You jumped on me, were groping me . . ."

"You stole my money!"

"I don't *think* so. You," she said preemptively to Thomas, "with the pigsticker. Sheathe it and get out of my way. If you do, then I'm just willing to forget all this."

By now the confrontation had drawn a sizable crowd. James was starting to get uncomfortable as he realized that what the onlookers were faced with was two strangers threatening a young woman who was claiming that she had been manhandled. If it came down to who the mob was going to side with, he wasn't thrilled with the odds coming down in his favor.

Suddenly, there was a bellowing shout of, "Make way! Make way for the magistrate's men! What's all this, then? What's all this?" James let out a sigh of relief because now the authorities had made their presence known. That relief lasted for exactly as long as it took him to realize that they, too, might well side with the young woman over the two out-of-town men.

The crowd separated, allowing four uniformed men to make their way through. They were armed with both swords and pistols, and their long blue coats with braid on the shoulders were very impressive-looking. Whoever this magistrate was, he certainly liked to keep his men well attired. The tallest of them, with furrowed brow and bristling beard, strode forward, and when he spoke, it was instantly obvious that he had been the one shouting up until that point. "So what's going on here?"

Before James could get a word out, the girl stepped forward, brazen as anything, and pointed accusingly at him. "He grabbed me and groped me and tried to steal my purse as well." And she had the unmitigated gall to hold up James's own money purse. The small brown leather sack, much smaller and less full than the one he'd lost at sea, dangled from her hand, tauntingly. "Fortunately, he never got near it."

"She's lying," James said heatedly. "She took it from me. I was the one chasing her. My friend will vouch for me." And he pointed at Thomas.

"Of course; he's his friend. His partner in crime," the girl said defiantly. "He and his animal blocked my path so that I'd be forced to stop, and then the one from behind came in to try and grab it. Grab my hard-earned money!"

James's heart was sinking as he saw how the people in the crowd were glaring at him, nor did the officers seem particularly sympathetic to him. He had to admire the young woman's technique: She had to be about his age, but she was as masterful an actress as a female twice her age. She had even managed to acquire a slight tremble in her voice, as if she were so shaken that she was striving not to burst into tears in the face of these horrible youths who had teamed up to rob her.

That was when Thomas said, very softly but with great authority, "If she worked so hard for it, then I'd think she'd know how much of it there was. In the purse, I mean." The edges of his mouth were turned in a smile.

Immediately, James's spirits, down in the cellar only moments earlier, buoyed considerably. She'd been too busy running to stop and count the contents. But James had been scrupulous about knowing exactly how much they had to spend at any given time.

"Makes sense to me, Sergeant," one of the men said to the leader.

The sergeant nodded, pulling at his bristling beard. "It does indeed. Give it here, miss, and tell me how much is in there. Do so accurately, and these young men will be punished to the full extent of the law."

The girl knew she was caught out at that moment; she had to have known. Yet still she tried to bluff it through. "Sergeant, I hardly think that's necessary. To punish them, I mean. Obviously, if they're such desperate scoundrels that they have to stoop to such foul means of survival, that sort of existence is punishment enough to—"

"Twenty three silver, five gold pieces," James said briskly. When the sergeant looked at him in surprise, he shrugged, and said, "I just figured, why drag it out? For that matter, if she were innocent, I think she'd be trying to prove it as fast as she could."

"Only someone who's guilty feels the need to prove anything; those with a clear conscience don't feel any urgency," she said with remarkable archness, but James could tell there was a false note to it, a slight crack in her demeanor.

The sergeant apparently could discern it as well. His hand motioned with growing impatience. "Have it over, lass. He's told us what his claim is about the contents; let's hear yours."

"Well, it's the same as his, obviously," she said, "since that's what's in there. But he had enough time to count it when—"

"When what?" Thomas said abruptly. "You said yourself he never got his hands on it. So when did he have the time to count it?"

The sergeant looked from Thomas back to the girl, and the truth of Thomas's words registered on him.

The girl smiled and suddenly she drew her arm back and threw the pouch as hard as she could directly at the sergeant's face. The towering official's reflexes were formidable; rather than ducking back or even being struck, his hand snapped up and caught the purse deftly. She didn't wait to see the result of her throw. Instead, she tried to bolt, but James was too quick for her and grabbed her firmly by the arm. Seconds later, the sergeant's men had moved in, and they had her immobilized between them, holding the struggling girl with her arms between them. She tried to kick at them, but the angle was wrong, and all she managed to do was scuff up dirt.

"I believe the truth of the situation has made itself evident," the sergeant said. He tossed the bag of coins to James, who caught it deftly. "My deepest apologies, young sir, for your inconvenience. I discern that you are a stranger to our city. I hope that this encounter will not give you a distorted view of it."

"Don't worry about it," said James, who could afford to be gracious under the circumstances. "So . . . do you need us to sign a complaint or something? Appear before a judge or even this magistrate of yours . . . ?"

"Unnecessary," the sergeant said briskly. "The rules about sneak thieves are quite clear. The magistrate has no time for such petty matters; he leaves it to me to implement the punishment, especially when the truth of the case is as evident as it is here."

And for the first time, the girl dropped all of her pretensions. Clearly terrified, she gasped out, "No! Please! It . . . it was my first time!"

"Your first time?" said the sergeant.

"Yes! I swear it was!"

"Very well, then. Since it was a first offense, I will give you the option of choosing which hand it will be."

The comment made no sense to James, but he saw Thomas blanch at the sergeant's icy tone, and then he understood. "Wait . . . you're . . . you're not going to—"

The girl was screaming now, nearly drowning out the sergeant as he raised his voice and said, "Which hand, missy? Left or right? Makes no never mind to me, but I'm a busy man, and I haven't got all day." As he spoke, he slid his sword out of its scabbard. There were tassels dangling from the golden hilt, and the blade glimmered in the sun like a thing alive. Even standing several feet away, James could see that the blade was razor-sharp.

And Thomas quickly stepped forward, coming between the sergeant and the girl. "Hold on, Sergeant. That seems a little severe."

"More like a little sever, actually," said the sergeant, which prompted a burst of carefully modulated laughter from his subordinates. But then he quickly turned serious. "Seeing as you're a visitor here, son, I'll excuse your getting between an officer and his lawful duty for the moment. But only for the moment. You'd be well-advised to step aside so that I can do what I'm bound to do."

"Yes, well, I'm unbinding you," said Thomas. "My friend and I are, I mean. We're not going to press charges, isn't that right, James?"

James hesitated.

"James."

"Well, she *did* steal my purse and then lie about it," said James slowly, "and if I hadn't been keeping such careful track of our money, then we'd be the ones who were in for it instead of her. And something tells me she wouldn't be doing a damned thing to help us. Instead, she'd probably be standing over where you are, laughing up her sleeve and deciding how she was going to spend our money."

There were agreeing murmurs from the crowd, and the sergeant said to Thomas, "Your friend is making a pile of sense, lad. You'd be well-advised to listen to him. Besides, this has already jumped over the 'pressing charges' stage and gone straight to the punishment stage. Which reminds me, girl, your time is up. If you can't make the choice, then I'll make the choice for you. Gentlemen, the right one."

"No!" she screamed, as the soldiers shoved her right arm forward. She tried to yank it away, but two men were holding her bodily; one man had her by the upper arm while the other was firmly gripping her forearm and extending it. Her hand was flopping about on its wrist like a frantic fish on a beach.

"Step aside, lad, now. *Now*," said the sergeant, no longer taking the affable tone of one trying to humor someone from out of town.

Thomas hesitated only a moment and then did as he was instructed.

The girl cried out, thrashed in their grip, tried to slam her foot down upon their booted insteps in hopes of dislodging them just enough, but it did no good. The sergeant stepped around so that he would have a clear angle at it even as he said, "I would suggest you all step back. There's going to be some blood, and you won't want to be close unless you're keen on being splattered." Immediately, the citizens did as they were bidden. "Right, then," he said briskly. "And keep in mind, young lady, that you only brought this upon yourself."

He drew back his sword, high over his head, like an executioner about to bring an axe down through the neck of a condemned man. And then in one swift motion, the blade sped through the air and down and sliced through the girl's outstretched hand, barely slowing, sending the hand tumbling to the ground and blood jetting from the stump. Her screech of pain was overwhelmed by the approving shout of the crowd that justice had been done.

At least that's what the sergeant probably *thought* would happen.

What *actually* happened, much to the surprise of the sergeant, was that another blade, seemingly extended from nowhere, intercepted his stroke and caused it to skid wide and harmlessly to the side.

James watched in shock as Thomas faced the soldier, his own sword outstretched, having been pulled from its scabbard with such speed that even James was astonished; he'd had no idea that Thomas was that quick. Thomas, for his part, stood with his feet firmly planted, the blade thrust outward and above the girl's hand, still quivering from the impact of the sergeant's sword crashing into it.

"I won't stand by and see such brutal justice done," said Thomas with astonishing softness of voice. One would have thought that he was making some casual comment to an old friend about some bit of historical trivia while having a picnic. "This is barbaric, and if you wish to punish her, then you'll be going through me in order to accomplish it."

"How dare you!" bellowed the sergeant. He turned to his men, snapped, "Hold her!" and then came right at Thomas.

Thomas stepped back, and his face was as calm as James had ever seen. The sergeant was a trained soldier, presumably one of the better blades in the city if not the best, but Thomas didn't seem the least bit perturbed. It was as if he was convinced not only of the rightness of his actions but that that rightness would carry him through and win the day.

The blades came together, this time with equal force. A quick encounter, a riposte, and then the swordsmen parted, assessing each other. "You have a supple wrist, boy, I'll give you that," said the sergeant with a growl. "And your footwork is competent enough. But you are still obviously a rank amateur. Surrender now, or I'll gut you where you stand."

Slowly, Thomas shook his head.

The sergeant came in quickly then, the blade moving faster than before. Thomas deflected it again, still acting only defensively, searching out some weakness in the sergeant's attack. There didn't seem to be any. The blades engaged and disengaged repeatedly, each time a little faster, and Thomas's confidence was visibly growing the longer he managed to hold his own. The sergeant's scowl deepened, and he tried another attack, and another, and Thomas beat them all back, searching the entire time for a weakness in the sergeant's attack.

Suddenly, he saw the sergeant leave himself open, and he thrust forward, his first deliberate attack.

The sergeant easily deflected it, and James realized belatedly that Thomas had been lured, for Thomas was momentarily off balance, and the sergeant took the opportunity to slam the hilt of his sword down on the back of Thomas's head. Thomas staggered, still holding on to his sword, but now he was vulnerable, and the sergeant lunged forward, driving his sword through Thomas's chest and out his back. The stunned young man fell to the ground, his life bleeding out onto the street, his quest never to be fulfilled.

At least that's what the sergeant probably *thought* would happen.

What *actually* happened, yet again to the surprise of the sergeant, was that Poxy leaped forward, snarling viciously and barking so deafeningly that one would have thought the hounds of Hell had been unleashed. Immediately, the sergeant jumped back, moving so quickly that his feet almost went out from under him. He recovered at the last second, and shouted to his men, *"Shoot that animal!"*

And that was when James stepped forward, and his gaze locked onto that of the sergeant, who turned automatically when he saw movement toward him.

And James pushed.

Not with his body. Not with his sword, which still remained in its scabbard. Instead, he pushed his mind, his personality, his pure focused willpower, right into that of the sergeant, overwriting the sergeant's intentions as a scrivener would undo a written mistake and write over that.

"You're not going to do that," he said firmly, as Poxy automatically darted behind him.

"*Excuse* me?" said the sergeant, incredulity in his voice.

"You are going to take us to the magistrate," James continued, and his voice was flat and unwavering. He kept on pushing, thrusting his willpower as if it were a spear, driving it as hard as he could, as deeply as he could, into the sergeant. He didn't actually know that he was doing it, and would have been unable to explain the technique if he'd been asked. All he knew was that something had to be done, and he was going to be the one to do it. Failing to do so literally never occurred to him.

"We will explain the situation to him, and we are going to tell him face-to-face that this law of his is"—and he glanced at Thomas—"brutal and uncivilized. And if he demands punishment at that point, then we will deal with it. But we are not going to allow this girl to be maimed on our behalf. That's just the way it's going to be."

If anyone in the entirety of Lower Sutcliff had been making a sound, they had fallen silent. Indeed, it seemed to James that the whole world had just become unnaturally quiet. In his mind's eye, somewhere back home, his mother and siblings were leaning forward to hear what would happen next without fully understanding why it was they were doing so or what it was they were listening for.

The sergeant stared at James for a long moment, and then said brusquely, "You have more balls than brains, I'll give you that."

Silence hung for a second, and then there was a loud burst of laughter from the onlookers. Then the sergeant pivoted on his heel and told his men, "Bind the girl's hands. These gentlemen and their mongrel will be accompanying us to the gaol, to await disposition by the magistrate."

"I hope he has a pleasant disposition," James said chipperly.

The crowd didn't laugh at that. Instead, they just scowled at him.

"Great," said James.

Chapter 12

THE CELL WAS DARK AND DANK, WITH the small window inset in the upper portion of the wall doing nothing to clear out the air and make it remotely breathable. There was straw scattered on the floor for no purpose that Thomas could imagine. It certainly did nothing to lessen the stink of the place. Nevertheless, Poxy seemed rather enamored of it, and she actually pushed a large clump of it together with her paws to fashion a nest for herself.

Poxy was situated directly between the two of them, with her chin resting on her paws and her eyes closed. James was seated on the far side of the cell from Thomas, although "far side" might have been a generous description. The cell couldn't have been more than eight feet from one side to the other. With Poxy stretched out at full length, James and Thomas had to keep their legs curled up in order to avoid kicking her.

They said nothing to each other for a long, long time.

Finally, it was Thomas who spoke first.

"You waited until the *dog* was threatened?" He seemed to be having trouble processing it. "*That's* where your priorities were?"

James shrugged.

"Seriously, James"—and Thomas cautiously stretched his right leg to one side in order to loosen it up—"they're going to chop the girl's hand off, and you say nothing . . ."

"I didn't say nothing. I said a lot of things, and all of them were true, and just because you disagreed with them doesn't make them nothing."

". . . and then you stand by when that sergeant was going to kill me . . ."

"I wanted to give you a chance to defend yourself, although frankly it was stupid that you went after him in the first place."

"But the moment the dog was threatened, *that* was when you jumped in?"

"They were going to shoot an unarmed dog," James said defensively. "That was just wrong."

Thomas didn't know whether to laugh or cry at that. "James, for crying out loud! Where are your priorities? They were going to butcher that girl—!"

"Actions have consequences," James shot back, "and I don't ask anyone to intervene when I make mistakes. I take what's coming to me and oh, by the way, so do you."

"And if the dog hadn't been there? If Poxy hadn't

been threatened, would you have left me to my fate as well?"

"Of course not." James sounded hurt. "If I hadn't been able to talk him out of it . . . if I'd had to draw on him . . . then that's what I would have done. I would have stepped in. You're my friend, for pity's sake. We're in this together."

"So you're not defending a principle, really. Just the person."

"I suppose so, yes. But I'm actually okay with that."

"Well, I'm defending the principle, James. Something is either dead right or dead wrong."

James made a scoffing noise. "You know why tales of adventure and heroism are printed in black ink on white paper, Thomas? It's because it's only there, in such fables, that the world is black-and-white. In the real world, it's all about shades of gray."

Silence then resumed between the two of them. With a deep and frustrated sigh, Thomas tilted his head back, closed his eyes, and tried to drift to sleep. He floated in and out of consciousness for a time, and at one point he turned and was startled to see that James was no longer sitting on the other side of the cell. He had come over to Thomas's side and was sitting about two feet away, leaning against the wall just as Thomas was. Thomas stared at him in confusion.

Gazing fixedly in front of him and not looking at Thomas at all, James said, "I'll say this, though. The way you took on that sergeant . . . that was bloody brilliant."

"Really." Thomas was confused by the praise.

"Because a little while ago, you said it was frankly stupid."

"It can be both. Probably some of the greatest acts of bravery in the history of mankind were the stupidest as well."

"I suppose."

"I mean"—and James turned to look at him—"were you scared? The man's a professional soldier. Did you really think you'd be a match for him?"

"I wasn't really thinking, actually," Thomas admitted. "My blood was pumping and there was a sort of pounding in my head and my knees were shaking . . ."

"They were not."

"You couldn't see it?"

James shook his head. "Not in the least little bit. You looked absolutely sure-footed, and cool as ice. I'd never have guessed."

"Was the sword steady? I was sure my hand was trembling as well."

"Rock steady. I'd never have guessed. And you had him going, I can tell you that."

"Nah. He was just toying with me. He could have done me at any time."

"That"—and he pointed at Thomas—"is a load of crap. I was watching him, watching his eyes. There were a few times when he was really worried. He would have this confident look, but then I'd see the confidence shake, just a little. I can read people, remember. I know what's going through their minds, and more than once, he was starting to wonder if he'd taken on more than he knew." Then James grunted softly. "All over a matter of principle to defend a sneak thief. Amazing."

"Well, what about what *you* did? That was amazing as well," said Thomas.

"What are you talking about? I didn't do anything."

"Oh, come on!" Thomas said firmly. "The way you looked at that man, the way you talked to him. It was like you were giving him no choice except to say what you wanted him to say. You talked to him like . . . I don't know, you were a king or something, commanding immediate respect and obedience."

James laughed. "You don't know what you're on about."

"I sure do. I know what I saw and what I heard. Here was a man with a sword and a gun, backed up by his troops, to say nothing of a crowd of people looking on who could have jumped in if they were so inclined . . . and you, with your hands empty, took control of the situation completely away from him. He had no idea what to say or do except whatever you told him to do."

"I startled him, nothing more. And amused him. It meant nothing."

"No, you imposed your will on him is what you did." Thomas contemplated him for a moment, as if truly seeing him for the first time in his life. "You know who did that?"

"Don't start."

"Spellcasters."

James rolled his eyes. "I told you not to start."

"I am totally serious, James."

"Yes, I know you are. That's what's so annoying. I'm

not a spellcaster just because I managed to convince a sergeant to throw us into gaol. If I was really some sort of spellbinder, I would have convinced him to let us go completely."

"And if I were a truly great swordsman, I would have been able to defeat him," Thomas said with growing eagerness. "For two guys who haven't had any training, we've been able to pull off quite a lot."

"Again: We're in gaol."

"But at least we're still alive. That's got to count for something. Who knows what we'd be able to do if we'd been able to spend a few years in a Guild Hall, honing our talents and reaching our full potential? You might be tossing around blasts of lightning with a wave of your hand, and I might be able to take on an army of men single-handedly."

With a heavy sigh, James said, "Those days are past, Thomas. You know it, I know it, and all the 'what-ifs' in the world aren't going to change that."

"James . . . the only thing that has *ever* changed *anything* in the world is 'what-ifs.' Without those, we'd all still be rooting around in swamps, primitive and afraid of terrifying creatures lurking just beyond the perimeter of the campfires."

"Yeah, well . . . all things considered, maybe we'd be better off back in the swamps."

Poxy, who had appeared to be dozing, suddenly lifted her head as if she was anticipating something. Moments later, they heard a noise at the door, the sound of a bolt being slid back, and the door opening with a loud creak.

Torchlight filtered in from the hallway, and a pair of guards dressed in the same manner as the sergeant had been were standing there waiting for them. They had their guns unholstered and, even though they were not aiming them at Thomas and James, the unspoken message was clear: *Make any sort of move against us, and we will blow your brains out.* The mute warning, once sent, was readily received. Thomas and James got to their feet, keeping their hands visible and at their sides. Poxy growled low in her throat, and James patted her on the head and quietly urged her to settle down.

"Come with us, if you please," one of the guards said.

"And if we don't please?" James said automatically. Thomas glanced heavenward.

The guards gave no answer. That alone was a response.

Turning to Thomas, James said with false joviality, "I don't think we're actually being given a choice here."

"I could kill you where you stand," offered one of the guards. He actually sounded rather keen to do it, no doubt because attending to corpses was someone else's problem, and he'd be relieved of the odious duty of dealing with the prisoners.

"That's okay," Thomas said quickly, before James could utter another of his dubious witticisms and get them both killed. "I think we'll come with you."

"As you wish." The guard sounded vaguely disappointed. His companion just looked bored.

Thomas toyed with the notion of trying to overwhelm the guards and flee the gaol. As quickly as he contemplated it, however, he set it aside. They'd been told that

Sutcliff was someplace that could lead them to balverines and was also the residence of the mysterious Mr. Kreel. That being the case, becoming fugitives would hardly serve their cause. They needed to face down the magistrate, present to them what Thomas considered the rightness of their actions, and then hope for the best. He was fully aware that matters might not exactly turn out the way that he was hoping, and having to fight their way out could wind up being the only option. Best, though, to let things play out before embarking upon that last-ditch scenario.

They were brought up a twisting flight of steps, with Poxy leading the way, James behind her, and Thomas behind him, with the two guards bringing up the rear. Ahead of them, at the top of the stairs, was a heavy door that was open wide, with another guard standing next to it, holding it open and glowering down at them. He looked especially suspicious of the dog. Thomas was starting to wonder if people suspected that Poxy was, in fact, the brains of the group. Considering the number of times that he and James seemed to fall headlong into danger, he was starting to wonder that himself.

They emerged from the door and were let out into a narrow courtyard with the open entrance to another building at the opposite side. More guards were lining the path on either side. Thomas recognized a couple of them from the squad that had originally arrested them. Not for the first time did he wonder to where the girl had been taken away. It would be coldly amusing if, once she had been separated from them, her right hand had been summarily chopped off, and she'd been sent on her way. That scenario tended to render all of their own actions as somewhat moot.

He discovered in short order that that was not the case. They were escorted into a room that was too large to be an office but too small to be a true court. There was an oversized desk at the far end, and a seating area off to the side that was crammed with onlookers. Thomas wondered if they were others who were waiting to be summoned before the magistrate, but then James and he were brought forward and made to stand several feet in front of the desk, at a respectful distance. More guards were standing to either side of the desk, clearly to act as a buffer should anyone have thoughts about attacking the magistrate. Certainly, that wasn't an option since their weapons had been taken from them upon their arrest. Still, Thomas found that he rather liked the notion that he and James were considered so dangerous that, even unarmed, they were treated as if they were capable of inflicting catastrophic harm.

The fact that they were the only ones brought forward told Thomas that the onlookers were just that: an audience who was there primarily to be afforded some entertainment. No doubt they were hoping for a good legally mandated thrashing or maiming or even—one could only dream!—a hanging. It was Thomas's sincerest hope to be able to disappoint the lot of them, the bloody vultures.

There were two doors to the front of the chamber: one to the right and another directly behind the desk.

The door to the right opened, and through it came his old friend, the sergeant, pushing ahead of him the young thief who had gotten them into all this trouble in the first place. She had a face so bereft of expression that Thomas had to think even James would have been daunted playing poker with her. Her hands were firmly bound behind her back, and she was wearing her hood up so that her face was almost invisible within. She deliberately dragged her heels, and the sergeant pushed her from behind, nearly causing her to stumble. He grabbed her by the back of her tunic and yanked her upright.

"We meet again," James said with surprising cheer to the sergeant. The sergeant said nothing in response but contented himself with scowling at him. That was fine with the boys; they were getting used to it. It seemed at some point or another, everyone they met scowled at them.

Not the crowd, though. Apparently amused at James's insouciance, a ripple of laughter rolled through the onlookers. This did not sit well with the sergeant, who gave them an evil look as if they had somehow betrayed him and, for that betrayal, would face a fate even more forbidding than what awaited the young men. The glare quickly restored order, but quite a few people were still smiling. For some reason, that cheered Thomas considerably.

Then the door behind the desk opened wide and immediately, as if on cue, everyone in the room promptly got to their feet. Thomas and James had no need to do so since they were already standing.

A cadaverous-looking man with a gleaming pate utterly

bereft of hair emerged from the unseen room behind the door and closed it firmly. Thomas took one look at him and felt a chill down his spine. He had an immediate instinct that things were not going to go well with this individual. The man, whom Thomas assumed was the magistrate, took his place behind the wide desk and sat with his shoulders hunched and his head thrust forward in a way that evoked a vulture. That, of course, suggested to Thomas that they were as good as dead. Immediately, he started reassessing the room in terms of how one might exit it in a hurry. Unlike the nimble-handed thief, the young men's hands were free. That could well prove to be a mistake if the situation called for them to attempt a sudden breakout should matters go against them.

He knew what he had said to James about taking a principled stand and dealing with the consequences of their actions. On the other hand, if it seemed that they were not going to get a fair hearing and that the magistrate's mind was already made up, with only the speaking of their sentence to be uttered, then Thomas didn't see any reason not to try to get the hell out of there.

"So," said the magistrate in a gravelly voice, once the spectators for that afternoon's entertainment had seated themselves. "You are the two young scoundrels who thought to undermine my law, eh?"

Oh yeah. This is going to go great, thought Thomas.

Still, there seemed no way that matters could possibly get worse, and so Thomas spoke his mind: "We felt that—"

That was as far as he got before a sharp impact on the back of his head staggered him. One of the guards had thumped him solidly with his fist, and Thomas felt as if his brain were bouncing back and forth inside his skull.

"You were not given leave to speak!" snapped the magistrate.

Poxy, seeing that Thomas had been struck, spun and growled ferociously at the guard who had hit him. The guard immediately went for his gun, and James instantly shouted, "Poxy! Down, girl! It's going to be okay!" He dropped to one knee and wrapped his arms around her to settle her. Poxy did not try to struggle from his grasp, but there was cold fury in her eyes, and she looked as if she was ready to lunge at the soldier if James let go of her for so much as an instant.

Thomas shook off the ringing in his head and didn't bother to point out that, since the magistrate had posed what sounded like a question, thinking that an answer had been expected was hardly out of line. Certainly it wasn't worth a blow to the skull. It was just a further indicator to him that they were not going to get a fair hearing. Because of that, he was already running through his head how the first thing he would do would be to move like lightning, yank the sword from the guard's scabbard, cut him down, grab his gun, shoot the sergeant, vault over the desk, take the magistrate hostage, and use him as a shield so that they could make their way out of the chamber. From that point on it was simply a matter of running as fast as they could.

It seemed a reasonable plan, with the only thing

deterring him being the fact that he had never in his life killed a person or come close to killing a person. Even when he had been fighting the sergeant, he hadn't been thinking much beyond defending himself and simply hoping to disable his opponent. In this case, disabling was not an option. He needed to kill or be killed, and he wasn't entirely sure that he could accomplish the former in order to stave off the latter. He supposed he wouldn't know until the moment came.

The magistrate stared at them for a long moment in a challenging manner, as if waiting for them to say or do something that would further earn his ire. The boys wisely said and did nothing, and he nodded once briskly as if satisfied that a lesson had been properly administered. Then he turned to the sergeant, and said, "And this is the young thief with whom they were in cahoots."

And that was the point where James stood, squaring his shoulders, keeping one hand resting steadily on Poxy's head. "You, sir," he announced in a voice as clear as a clarion bell, "are an idiot."

The magistrate paled in shock, and then, before anything else could be said, James suddenly pivoted and faced the soldier who was standing right behind him. The man's fist had been cocked, prepared to deliver a cuffing just as he had inflicted on Thomas, and James in full fury shouted, *"Try it! Try it when I'm looking at you instead of with my back turned! Try it, I dare you, because then you get to explain to your wife this evening how you got your fist shoved down your own throat!"*

The soldier stood there with his fist held exactly in the

same position, and his eyes were wide in shock as James's infuriated gaze drilled into him. Then, as if the man were nothing to him, James slapped the fist aside. "You," said James, "have no idea who you're dealing with." As if indifferent to any further threat that the guard might pose—or perhaps simply secure in the knowledge that Poxy now had his back—James turned to the others, and said, "*None* of you have any idea who you're dealing with. You, Magistrate, as I said, are stupid. Or, at the very least, woefully misinformed. If that's the case, then your problem is with whoever gave you bad information, not us." He began a slow pace, fixing his gaze upon each and every person there. Even the spectators were watching him raptly. "I'm going to be honest with you: I think what my friend did was a bonehead move. This girl is nothing to us except someone who tried to rob us. But he refused to stand by in the face of what he saw as an injustice, and he is going to explain to you, right now, why he did that, and you are going to listen to every word he has to say. Do you understand me? Do you *all* understand me?"

There was a deathly silence, and all eyes slowly turned to the magistrate. He had not moved so much as a centimeter since the beginning of James's outburst. He could just as easily have been a statue for all the outward signs of life he was displaying, and Thomas began to wonder if the man hadn't simply died from shock right there.

And then the corners of the magistrate's mouth began to twitch. His dry lips stretched a bit, causing cracks to appear. He trembled ever so slightly, as if he were having some sort of a mild fit, and then from his mouth issued a noise that sounded like a creaking hinge.

It continued and became rhythmic, and more sustained, and louder.

And Thomas realized, to his utter astonishment, that the magistrate was laughing.

The soldiers were too stunned to react; it was obvious that they had never seen anything quite like this. But the spectators, eager to remain in the magistrate's good graces, and seeing that there was implicit permission to be amused as well, promptly followed the magistrate's example. Within moments, the entire chamber was ringing with laughter.

James was looking in amazement at Thomas. He wasn't sure what the meaning of all this merriment was, but it stood to reason that it was going to be of benefit to them. And he leaned over and whispered, "Maybe you were right! Maybe my willpower *is* overwhelming!"

The magistrate was now on his feet, still laughing loudly. It sounded incredibly strange, as if it was an action that he had not embarked upon for a very long time. Then he leaned on his desk, putting one hand to his chest, recovering himself, although the spectators were still laughing loudly.

And then he reached into the pocket of his long black coat, withdrew a pistol, and aimed it straight at James. His face still displaying a rictus of a smile, he croaked, "I'm going to kill all three of you myself."

James and Thomas were frozen in shock. All the plans that Thomas had for how to escape death should it come down to it were blown right out of his head at the abrupt reversal of the magistrate's attitude.

The magistrate cocked the hammer on his pistol, and despite all the close scrapes that they had faced, the fact was that they had never been as close to death as they were at that moment.

Their salvation came from a most unexpected source.

"I wouldn't do that if I were you, Magistrate."

It was the young thief. Her voice was clear and firm, and there was not a trace of fear in it, as if the magistrate's intention to gun them all down by his own hand was of no relevance to her at all. Although her hands were bound, she managed to flip her head back so that the hood fell away.

"How dare you!" said the sergeant. "How much rudeness is the magistrate supposed to endure?"

But the magistrate was staring at the young girl and his eyes widened, revealing a latticework of veins. "Sergeant . . ." he said slowly, "is this the one whose hand you were going to cut off? This is the girl?"

"Yes, Magistrate," said the sergeant. "I apologize for her arrogance. I thought I had managed to beat it out of her, but apparently—"

The magistrate whipped his gun around, aimed, and fired.

The sergeant staggered, a look of astonishment on his face like nothing that Thomas or James had ever seen. More out of reflex than conscious thought, he reached up to his forehead, and his hand came away covered with blood. The sergeant's mouth moved in a vain attempt to form a question, but all that emerged was more blood, pouring down his chin, dripping onto the clean and pressed white shirt of his uniform. Then his knees gave way, and the sergeant collapsed to the floor, lying there in a spreading pool of his blood.

The girl had not been in the least bit startled. Rather, she stared down at the sergeant with a sort of indifference, as if the abrupt taking of a human life was of no consequence to her. Then she looked back to the magistrate, and said, "I would appreciate it, Magistrate, if someone unbound my hands. My wrists are starting to chafe."

"Do as she says!" the magistrate ordered. The soldiers had scarcely had time to process the fact that their sergeant was dead when one of them moved forward to release the girl's wrists. Then the magistrate turned back to Thomas and James and stared at them as if not quite certain what to make of them. This was someone whose entire world was carefully constructed in such a way that he knew all the components of it intimately and was able to control all of them. At least that was how Thomas saw it. But it was clear that he was utterly bewildered as far as the two of them were concerned. Settling for the simplest means of dealing with the situation, he pointed at them with one bony finger, and said, "Take them back to their cell. Do nothing to injure them. Nothing."

SO IT WAS THAT JAMES AND THOMAS FOUND themselves right back where they had been scarcely an hour earlier. As if they had never left, Poxy contentedly lay down, rested her head on her paws once more, and settled back to sleep.

"What the hell just happened?" said James.

Thomas shrugged. "Your guess is as good as mine."

James gently thumped his head back against the wall. "I can't believe that I actually thought I'd imposed my will on that . . . that gargoyle. What the hell was I thinking?"

"I'll tell you what I was thinking. I was thinking that here you were talking about *me* being brave? Suffering cats, James! At least I was holding a sword when I made my stand!" He laughed, incredulous. "Shouting at the guard, facing off against the magistrate. I've never seen anything like it."

"And it would have been the last thing you'd ever seen if it hadn't been for . . . I don't know *what* that was! That girl! The magistrate looked ready to piss himself! Who the hell *was* she?"

"Well," Thomas said thoughtfully, "she obviously knew the magistrate, and he knew her, and she knew he was going to know her."

"Meaning . . . ?"

"I don't know," Thomas admitted.

"Okay, well, that was useful."

"Whoever she was, though, I have a feeling we're going to find out. He told them not to harm us, remember. Obviously . . ."

"There's something about this that's obvious?"

Thomas nodded. "He's not sure of our relation to

the girl and doesn't want to do anything that's going to upset her."

"I'm not sure of our relation to her either, so at least we're on the same page in that respect."

They talked for a time longer, batting around theories, none of which were provable or even particularly convincing. Eventually, just as before, Poxy suddenly hopped to her feet and turned to face the door. Her body was tense, as if she were bracing for another possible battle.

Then they heard the voice of one of the guards saying, "This is the one, my laird. They're in here."

"Thank you. You're free to go." The voice was deep and confident and slightly lilting, and there was a slight burr to the words that sounded foreign to Thomas and James. Moments later, they heard a key turning in the lock, and the door swung open.

A man stepped into view. He was tall, close to six feet, with thick brown hair that had touches of gray in the wide sideburns. He was dressed entirely in gray, the only contrast being his voluminous cloak, which was of thick white fur. Even though there was no breeze whatsoever in the dank cell area, the fur seemed to be riffling, as if it had a life all its own. Poxy actually whimpered slightly and backed up, taking refuge behind James and peering out from between his legs.

"Greetings, my young fellows," he said in his booming voice. "You've created quite the stir in Sutcliff. My good friend, the magistrate, had a great deal to say about it."

James wanted to say defiantly that if the magistrate

was a good friend to this man, then clearly this man could not be any friend to them. But he decided to keep his mouth shut since the last thing they needed was his exacerbating the situation.

Thomas instead spoke up, and said neutrally, "I'm sure he did. Did he tell you that you could send the guard away and talk to us?"

The man laughed at that, his upper body shaking as if that were the funniest thing that he had ever heard. When he recovered himself, he said, "No, no, fellow. I am not one who has to ask leave of the magistrate. He has his uses, certainly, and he does a superb job of keeping order in Lower Sutcliff. But I don't have to ask his leave for anything."

"Who are you?" said Thomas.

He bowed slightly, and said, "Laird Ethan Kreel, at your service." And even as the last name sank in, he continued, "Or maybe I should say that you have been at my service?" He turned to his right, and said firmly, "I believe you have something to say, young lady?"

He pulled someone into view then from where she had been standing off to the side. It was the young thief. She looked severely chastened by his presence but nevertheless managed to summon a touch of her previous defiance. "Thank you for saving me from getting my hand chopped off," she said, while managing not to sound the least bit grateful at all. Indeed, she sounded more like she resented their intervention, as if unwilling to acknowledge, even after all that had happened, she was at all in their debt.

Her petulant tone was not lost on the laird. "You'll have to excuse my daughter. She has a mind of her own, which is a tragic inconvenience when it comes to women, don't you think?"

His daughter? The thought went through both their minds.

"Now, then." And Laird Kreel clapped his hands together and rubbed them briskly. "Let's get you out of his hellhole. You will come and be guests in my manse as a thanks for the service you provided us in saving my daughter from that foolish sergeant, who apparently was unable to recognize nobility when it was standing right in front of him."

"May I ask, my laird . . ." Thomas began.

"Oh, 'Kreel' will suffice. I do not tend to stand on ceremony."

"Okay, then . . . Kreel . . . I was wondering if you were the same Kreel who had been seeking participants for a balverine expedition?"

"The very same, yes. Why?" And he seemed to regard them with new interest. "Are you keen to join us? You're certainly brave enough, that much you have made clear."

"I would be keen, yes. We both would be," said Thomas, indicating himself and James. "But do you have any experience hunting them? Have you ever actually, you know . . . seen one?"

"Seen one?" Again Kreel laughed, and he indicated the white cape he wore over his broad shoulders. "Where do you think this came from, fellows? The pelt of a frost balverine, this is. Killed and skinned the bastard myself on expedition to the far northern wastelands. I'll be happy to tell you all about it."

"He'll be more than happy," said the girl ruefully. "In fact, if you want to shut him up, you can pretty much forget about it."

"Quiet, Sabrina," he ordered her. "You've indulged your disrespectful tongue enough for one outing, I should think. So, fellows"—and he turned back to them—"this meeting would seem to be serendipitous for all of us."

"I could not agree more," said Thomas.

At which point Sabrina actually smiled at Thomas.

For some reason, despite their imprisonment, their nonexistent trial, and the summary execution of the sergeant who had threatened them, James found that moment—Sabrina smiling—to be the single-most-disconcerting thing he'd encountered in the past day.

Chapter 13

"WELL," SAID JAMES, NODDING IN SATisfaction, "*this* is certainly a step up from our previous quarters."

That was something of an understatement. The guest room that they had been accorded in the mansion of Ethan Kreel was positively vast in comparison to the cell, with ornate furniture and two oversized beds. James flopped back on one of them and let out a contented sigh. "I swear, this is so incredible, I could sink into it, fall asleep, and never wake up."

"You realize that never waking up would be a *bad* thing, don't you?" Thomas pointed out.

"Oh. Right. I guess so."

There was a thick rug in the middle of the room, and Poxy took up residence on it. Even *she* looked contented.

"I don't suppose he'd let us move in here," James said

hopefully and only half-joking. "I mean . . . the size of this place! It's epic, Thomas! Epic!"

Thomas certainly couldn't disagree with that. The mansion was almost more castle than mansion. Three stories tall, designed in an "E" shape, constructed entirely of stone, with a combination of gothic gables and three towering spires, one at either end and one directly over the main entrance. They had passed other homes on the way, each of them similarly grand, but this was easily the most prominent in the area.

The guest rooms were on the third floor, which was the only one to have any corridors; on the bottom two floors, one room simply led into another and another, each more grand than the one before it. James felt as if being there had a dizzying effect on him, as if he were climbing a mountain, and the air was becoming increasingly rarefied.

James continued to lie stretched out on the bed, and then he looked at Thomas, who was leaning against one of the walls, looking thoughtful. "You know, there are actually some nice chairs here," James pointed out. "You could actually, you know, sit."

"Why was Kreel going around to different towns trying to enlist people for a balverine expedition? I'm just not sure I get it. I'd figured, from what I'd heard, that he was trying to get the money together to finance it. But you've seen this place. Obviously, he doesn't need the money . . ."

"Obviously, I do not."

They were both startled by the sound of Kreel's voice.

He was standing at the doorway, dressed casually, looking amused.

"You have a very soft footfall, sir. Not to mention an unnerving habit of hanging about doorways," said Thomas.

"When one is a tracker, one is accustomed to being able to move with a light tread," said Kreel. "As for doorways . . ." And with a shrug, he stepped into the room. "Now . . . as you noted, I obviously have no need of money. Whoever told you I was soliciting customers for a hunt apparently got their facts wrong. I was instead offering to *hire* people to act as servants on an expedition. They may have heard that money was involved and simply misunderstood."

"That does make a bit more sense," Thomas said guardedly.

"Of course it does. A journey such as this entails a great deal of equipment, ranging from tents to specialized weaponry such as silver bullets or silver daggers. If I'm on my own, of course, I'm perfectly capable of attending to my own needs. But several well-to-do individuals will be joining this excursion, and they are unaccustomed to having to carry so much as their own handbag." He shook his head and had a pitying expression, as if he could not fathom the sort of people who would require such aid. "In any event, I am pleased to say that my endeavors to that end were successful. I've acquired eight servants to join us. I assume, since you've come a long way on your own, that you will not need anyone to attend to you."

James was about to state that, in point of fact, he was Thomas's servant and that attending to Thomas was his job, but Thomas said quickly, "No, of course not. We can do fine on our own."

"I suspected as much," said Kreel. "And I, as I mentioned, am self-sufficient. So eight servants for the three individuals who will be accompanying us should be enough, don't you think?" Thomas and James nodded. "Excellent, then. Dinner, by the way, will be served within the next few minutes, so feel free to come down and meet the others in our sojourn tomorrow."

"How did they come to join the group?"

"Oh, word gets around," said Kreel. "I've taken others on such expeditions, and they tell their friends, who contact me and ask if they can likewise participate. That's the thing about the nobility, you see. One person hears about it, and the next thing you know, they all wish to be involved. You'll meet them."

"I'm not sure we'll fit in," said James. "We're not exactly titled individuals."

"Say that you are. They will not know. Tell them whatever you wish."

Thomas was surprised by the notion. "They won't believe us."

"Of course they will. You are in the home of a rich man. What else would you be but the sons of rich men, sent to spend time with me and learn the skills of hunting and tracking."

"Yeah, well"—and Thomas plucked at his clothing,

extremely worn from their time on the road and in harsh elements—"we don't exactly have the outfits to carry that off."

"Of course you do."

As if on cue, a servant came in, pushing a rack of clothing. The boys looked at it in surprise. As near as they could tell, it would all readily fit them.

"You were expecting to have guests of our general size and shape who would require clothing?" said James.

"Expect?" He chuckled. "You will find as you go through life, Thomas, that the wise man expects nothing but anticipates everything. By the way, you gentlemen are quite sure you do not wish separate quarters?"

"No, this will more than do," said Thomas.

"It is, of course, none of my business, but are the two of you . . . ?" And he looked from one to the other with a raised eyebrow.

Thomas didn't understand, but James did, and very quickly he said, "No! No, it's not like that at all."

At which point Thomas did comprehend, and he seconded James's assertion. "It's just that, we have been traveling together for so long now, and watching each other's back . . ."

"I totally understand," said Kreel. "Would that I had a traveling companion on whom I could count so thoroughly. Very well, then. I will see you later this evening."

He turned then and left the room, leaving the boys to sort through the clothing and be extremely impressed by what they saw.

* * *

THE ASSEMBLAGE IN THE VAST DINING ROOM was indeed a most regal one. Neither Thomas nor James had ever been to a king's court, and this was probably as close to one as they were going to get. There was an elaborate spread upon a vast table that included fresh-roasted mutton, potatoes that smelled remarkably sweet, cooked squab, sumptuous green beans, delectable cheeses, and much more. Wine flowed freely, and the combination of the food and the lofty company was more than enough to make the entire thing one of the headiest experiences the boys had ever had.

Thomas and James met the three highly placed individuals who were slated to be in the hunting party on the morrow. The first was Roland Shaw, Duke of Entwhistle, a cheery fellow with a ruddy complexion who was positively ebullient about the prospect of seeing "something mythic."

The second was introduced as Dean Simon Carter, the headmaster of a noted school of higher learning called the Hale Academy. Dean Carter was not yet nobility himself, but he was a widely respected academician at a school noted for catering to the youth of all the most highly placed families, and it was expected that he would receive his own title within the next year. Of all the people intending to hunt balverines, Carter seemed the least likely: an older man, slightly stooped, with bushy eyebrows and a strained manner as if he were uncomfortable outside a room filled with books. Perhaps,

Thomas reasoned, Carter was deliberately undertaking the adventures as a means of expanding his horizons.

The third participant was Lady Molly Newsome. She was the most unusual of the crew. She had apparently been married to one Laird Peter Newsome, himself quite an adventurer who had demanded in a wife a woman who could keep up with him. Not only had Molly met that expectation, she had in fact exceeded it. They had been inseparable for a number of escapades, and it was during a mountain-climbing expedition that an unexpected rock-slide had caught his lairdship off guard and swept him off a cliff, much to the screaming horror of his now-widowed wife. Molly Newsome had sworn that she would maintain the adventurous lifestyle that she and her husband had embraced and live every moment to the fullest. She certainly seemed every inch the adventurer: a tall, robust woman with red hair piled atop her head, twinkling eyes filled with merriment, and a voice like a trumpet.

They displayed some mild interest in Thomas and James, readily accepting Kreel's explanation for their presence. They were far more interested in conversing with each other, though.

Also present at the dinner were the eight servants Kreel had recruited for the hunt. It was unusual for servants to be allowed to eat at the same table as nobility, but Kreel was egalitarian in his attitudes. "We will all be sharing the same hazards of the hunt," he informed the assemblage, "and therefore it is only appropriate that we become accustomed to each other's company in more relaxed circumstances."

Because they didn't have to pretend to be more than they were, James found himself more comfortable interacting with the servants than with the nobility. Seated next to him at the table was a rather curious fellow whose name was apparently Bell . . . "apparently" since he was speaking with such a thick and unfamiliar accent that it took James a while to be confident in understanding what he was saying. He had a mane of hair that made him look more lion than man, and he was tall and muscular and seemed extremely impressed to be in the company that he was.

"Have yuh ev'r seen th'like of sich a gath'ring?" said Bell, looking extremely impressed at the company around him.

"Very impressive," said James.

"Demned near heroic, is what it is. Sutcliff is legen'dry fer it, y'know."

"Is it?"

"It is indeed," said Kreel, taking an interest in their conversation, seated several people away. "Sutcliff is renowned for its proud history of Heroes, and likewise its population of creatures of myth and magic."

"Why is that, do you think?" Thomas spoke up. "I mean, what's the big attraction of Sutcliff?"

"Well, now, I could explain it to you," Kreel began.

"And ordinarily he would," said Sabrina. She had been seated at the far end of the table, as far away from everyone else as possible, and that seemed as much her choice as anything else. It was the first time that she had spoken the entire evening. Thomas had never seen someone who seemed quite so determined to be disassociated from their father . . . unless, of course, he counted himself.

"However," Kreel continued as if Sabrina had not spoken, "we have one of the premier scholars in such matters present at our table. Dean Carter, would you care to enlighten the young fellows?"

"Well," said Carter, leaning forward and steepling his fingers, "I should emphasize that we *are* discussing legend rather than fact. I dislike the notion of elevating a fable to the status of absolute truth. Oftentimes, you'll find that myths are created in order to explain that which cannot be explained by rational means. The *fact* of the matter is that Sutcliff remains a location replete with beings that are considered, in many other parts of Albion, to be extinct, if they ever lived at all. It could be any number of factors: environmental, availability of prey, population, climate changes. Many more that I could not even begin to guess."

Sabrina made a loud snoring sound at her end of the table.

"Sabrina!" For the first time, Kreel did not sound amused at his daughter's deliberately provocative behavior. She retreated into herself and said nothing.

Carter, surprisingly, chuckled. "Do not reprove your daughter, my laird. My students would likely agree that I tend to perambulate around a subject before getting to the heart of the matter. Very well, then: The explanation that is rooted in legend has its basis in the tales of the Heroes Three."

Thomas perked up considerably at this. "Heroes Three? You mean the Triumvirate?"

"I," said Shaw, "have heard of a group called the Trinity. Is that they?"

"All one and the same. Different appellations for the same three," said Carter, warming to his topic. "Presuming they actually existed, their true names have been lost to antiquity. Supposedly they came together, the three of them, for each of them represented the absolute spire of learning for their respective disciplines. Individually they were formidable; as a team, they were absolutely invincible.

"The first was the Hero of Skill. Anything that came into his hand could be used as a weapon with unerring accuracy. Knives, spears. If he used a sword, he did not hack or slash, but instead always attacked with a thrust that inevitably found a vital organ. Some claimed that firearms were initially invented specifically for his use, for with a pistol or rifle, he was a marksman of exceptional mastery."

There had been other conversations going on up and down the lengthy table, but all of them had ceased. Instead, all eyes and ears were upon Carter. He was all too aware of it and clearly enjoying the attention.

"The second was the Hero of Strength. He was a premier swordsman, and unlike his more precise comrade of Skill, the Hero of Strength was like unto a berserker with a sword in his hand. It was said that the Hero of Strength was a massive bear of a man, as wide as a tree trunk and easily as durable. He wielded a sword that was said to be so heavy that none but he could lift it. And when he did . . . when he went into battle . . . nothing could withstand him. He could hack his way through an army of menaces, and all would fall before him.

"The third was perhaps the most formidable of all: the Hero of Will. He needed no weapon save his own mind and inner energies. He could conjure up lightning strikes, blasts of power that could annihilate enemies from a distance. None could withstand him.

"And when the three of them came together, there was nothing beyond their abilities, no quest that they could not fulfill, no goal they could not accomplish."

"Save one." It was Molly Newsome who had spoken, and when she continued, it was with an understandable air of melancholy. "Death. They could not stave off death. Immortality is one goal that eludes us all."

There was a moment of silence, for everyone at the table knew precisely why she had spoken thus. The shade of her late husband was obviously still hovering near her thoughts even though it had been several years since his disastrous fate. If there were any in the room who were uncharitable enough to think that perhaps the Lady Newsome had somehow sought to arrange her husband's demise and make it look like an accident, they would have dismissed the notion the moment they saw the haunted sadness in her eyes.

"Not to be insensitive," Dean Carter said gently, apparently aware of the pain that Newsome was feeling and the reason behind it, "but actually—according to legend—that is precisely what they did."

The Lady Newsome had seemed in danger of drifting into her own recollections, but this snapped her back to reality. "They defied death? Truly?"

"In a manner of speaking." He leaned his elbows on the table and interlaced his fingers. "According to the legends, death came to the Heroes Three through most pernicious means: a curse called down upon them through terrible magics. Had the Heroes been in their prime, they might yet have thwarted it. But their years were advanced, and their powers somewhat diminished. They fought back and fought back, but the curse was a truly irresistible force, and it drove the Heroes back and back, down and down, into a secret place deep beneath the earth. And there did the curse finally strike them down."

"But not before they were able to accomplish their final masterstroke!" Thomas jumped in, and then immediately looked abashed when all eyes turned to him. "I'm . . . I'm sorry. I didn't mean to—"

"No, that's quite all right," said Carter. "I'm merely a teacher; let us hear from one who is obviously a student of such things. Complete the tale, young sir."

"Uhm . . . well . . . according to what I've read," Thomas said, clearing his throat, "the Hero of Will joined the powers of the Heroes of Strength and Skill and, in one final burst of his magical prowess, imbued three power talismans with the essences of the Triumvirate. A pistol, a sword, and a gauntlet, for the Heroes of Skill, Strength, and Will respectively. Icons that, if worthy successors were to put them on, would make them—for a time, at least—Heroes on par with the originals."

"Very good," said Carter. "You read of them in your books, back in your home to the far west?"

"Oh yes."

"That shows how far the tales have spread, then."

"I read that they died peacefully, but I far prefer this version," said James.

"But," Thomas said eagerly, anxious to have holes in the stories filled in, "nothing that I've read details whatever happened to the icons."

"The icons remained where they were, with the bodies of the Heroes who had crafted them. Unfortunately, they were in the hands of the enemies who had brought the curse down upon them," Carter said immediately, as if he had been waiting for the question. "Posing an eternal threat to their enemies should anyone worthy manage to get their hands on them."

"Then why didn't the enemy destroy the icons and so remove the threat?" said Shaw. "Doesn't make much sense to me."

Carter turned to Shaw with a raised eyebrow. "You doubt me, my laird?"

"You? No. The story? Well, that is another matter."

"Laird Shaw is something of a skeptic," Kreel said indulgently. "He wishes to see things for himself before accepting their veracity. It is his nature to question."

"Understandable," said Carter. "Questioning is good; it is the only way to get at answers. According to the story, the power of the Hero of Will was able to keep their enemies at bay even after his passing; such was the force of his will. The enemies could not approach the icons, or come within range of the remains of the Heroes. They had to content themselves with guarding the entrance in eternal vigilance so that none would be able to get to them."

"And where exactly is this last resting place?" said Thomas, trying to keep the eagerness from his voice and only partly succeeding.

"Ah, there I cannot help you, young sir. There is purportedly one tome, called the *Omnicron*, that contains that information—that and much more ancient arcana—but I have never seen a copy of it. Fitting that a book about legends is nigh unto legendary itself."

"Fitting and convenient," said the ever-doubting Shaw.

This caused a ripple of laughter up and down the table, and Kreel said cheerfully, "Well, on the morrow, Laird Shaw's doubts about the reality of such mythic beasts as the balverines—the doubt that drove him to join us on this expedition—will be more than satisfied. Thank you, my good dean, for giving us some compelling background on the legends of Heroes."

"More than background, my laird," Carter reminded him. "Remember, it was an endeavor to explain why our land remains a source of such mythic power. The point was that wherever the Heroes are, their remains—and their puissance—are somewhere in Sutcliff or its vicinity. And that puissance draws mythic and legendary beings to this area, as honey draws bees . . ."

"Or flame draws moths?" suggested Thomas.

"That may well be the better analogy," said Carter.

"It is a weakness of such creatures that they are perversely drawn to that which can destroy them."

After the impromptu lesson about things legendary, the conversation broke back down into smaller groups. Thomas could not help but notice, however, that Sabrina continued to keep to herself. Except every so often he saw that she was stealing glances his way, and he wondered what—if anything—he should make of that. Ultimately, he decided that it was best to make nothing of it at all, for the young woman was clearly nothing but trouble.

Later, after dinner, the guests milled around, chatting with each other. Thomas saw that the Lady Newsome did not seem to be particularly interested in talking with anyone except Laird Shaw, who in turn was clearly finding the lady utterly engaging. Thomas wondered where that was going, if anywhere at all. From what he'd understood, her husband had passed quite some time ago, more than a respectable amount of time for her to contemplate other dalliances. And the way that Shaw was looking at her, like a hungry animal . . . well, if it wasn't lost to the casual examination of Thomas from a distance, then surely the lady was quite aware of it.

"Well, whatever," Thomas muttered with a shrug. "It is certainly none of my affair."

Dean Carter, being of humbler origin than his fellow travelers, seemed quite engrossed in chatting with the servants, particularly the one called Bell. It made sense that someone who was scholarly would be interested in speaking at length with the lower class from foreign lands. He would probably consider it a learning experience. Then Thomas reminded himself that he was from the lower class. Certainly his family—meaning his father and he—passed for wealthy back in Bowerstone, but most certainly not among this company. Mentally projecting it, he imagined that they could fit a dozen of his own house into this mansion.

Suddenly feeling a sense of disconnect from both his company and surroundings—and seeing that James was cheerfully occupied being on the periphery of the dean's discussion with Bell—Thomas wandered away from the gathering hall and strolled through the mansion, taking in the ornate sights. He wondered if living there every day of one's life caused a person to take for granted all of the splendor around: the artwork, the sculptures, the grand design of the place. Did it all become mundane thanks to constant exposure?

Maybe he could ask Sabrina about it.

That was a notion that he promptly dismissed from his mind, remembering that the one person in the entirety of the place that he needed to steer clear of was the young woman who had come close to getting both James and him killed.

Although . . . did he not bear some responsibility for that? If he had done as James had bidden, the girl would have posed no threat to their well-being at all. She would have been punished for her crime, forced to bear responsibility for her actions, and that would have been that. Thomas was really the one who had gotten them into their entanglement.

He ceased his musings about Sabrina, deciding that that way lay only madness. Instead, he focused on the new artistic marvel that was laid out before him.

He had entered a room that he could only think of as the mural room. That was because the entire room consisted of nothing but one vast mural: an incredibly accurate portrait of the very mansion in which they were. He wasn't quite certain that he understood the point of it. To his mind, aside from portraits, paintings should be of things that were far away or outside of the experience of the viewer. What sense was there in crafting a rendering of something that people could see for themselves by the simple expedient of stepping out the front door, walking five hundred paces, and turning around?

He supposed that the art was in the scope of the work, and in that regard he had to admit that it was stunningly impressive. The rendering was massive, taking up in their entirety three walls of the room. The attention to detail was meticulous: Every stone, right down to its individual shape, was represented in the mural. Some of them were irregularly shaped, and Thomas suspected that if he were somehow able to step outside and view the mural at the same time, that if he did a one-to-one comparison, the irregularities would match up. So that meant that some artist had either had a memory that bordered on the supernatural, or else that he had sat outside and first done a thorough portrait of the house that he could then transport into the mural room and proceed with his work there. The more Thomas thought about it, the more abashed he was that he had initially been dismissive of the work. One had to respect the dedication to the endeavor, if nothing else.

What was even more intriguing was that the proud spires that jutted from three points in the mansion had been done in bas-relief. Rather than being painted onto the wall, as was the case with the rest of the house, they were constructed from some other material—possibly the same stuff from which the actual spires had been made—and were affixed against the wall in exact proportion to the rest of the mural. It added a sort of three-dimensional effect to the entire thing.

"Why?"

Thomas jumped slightly, for the voice that had spoken had been unexpected and thoroughly startled him. He turned and saw Sabrina standing there, her arms folded, that same defiant tilt to her chin that she always seemed to have. "Wh-why what?" he managed to stammer out.

"Why did you interfere? When they were going to cut off my hand. You didn't need to, you know," she added. "I could have handled it myself."

"Considering you were about two seconds from having your hand lopped off, you certainly fooled me in that regard," he said tartly. "You know my reasons: I said at the time. I thought it an act of barbarism that no one deserved, much less a young woman."

"So that was it," she said smugly. "That I'm a young woman. Had I been a young man, I'd've been on my own."

"I didn't say that at all."

"You didn't have to. I know your type all too well.

The would-be Hero, jumping in to aid the damsel who he thinks needs his protection."

He ignored the sarcasm. "And is aspiring to be a Hero such a terrible thing?"

"It's way out-of-date, even in this country. You heard it yourself: Heroes live on in legend only."

"If that's how you feel, then what's the point of talking to me?"

She stared at him then, and her eyes seemed to devour him.

And then, completely out of the blue, she took his face in her hands and kissed him. It was hungry and filled with need, and at first he was startled, but then he almost melted into it.

He had kissed girls before, certainly. Flirtations, come-hither moments that ultimately went nowhere, or eager courtings from girls who he knew considered him good husband material and wished to make their interest known, almost as a matter of wise commerce.

This was not that.

There was no restraint anywhere in Sabrina. One moment she had been standing there, and the next she was kissing him with a consuming passion as hot as any flame. She thrust her tongue into his mouth, which startled him since no girl had ever done that before.

Then she withdrew, and it left Thomas staggering, as if a passing storm had just come in, pounding the area with its full and unbridled fury, then moved on just as quickly. He stared at her, uncomprehending.

And she said in a tone that sounded more accusatory

than loving or flattering, "It was a stupid thing to do, but it was also brave and rather sweet. Despite appearances, and the way I am . . . that wasn't lost on me. And I am . . ." She hesitated, and then concluded, ". . . thanking you for it. That was me, thanking you."

She turned away then but before she could take another step, he said, "Why?"

"I told you."

"No, I mean . . . not the kiss. Not that . . . I'm not left wondering about the way in which you thanked me. I mean . . . why did you disguise yourself? Engage in being a petty thief? You obviously had no need of whatever paltry sums you could have snatched in the marketplace. It just . . . it makes no sense to me why you would take such a terrible risk."

"It doesn't have to make sense to you," she said airily, "it only has to make sense to me."

"That's true, but it'd be nice if you could at least make an attempt to explain it to me."

"Does it truly matter?"

"Yeah. It does."

She continued to regard him as if she were dissecting him. Finally, she said, "I doubt you'd understand."

"Oh?"

"My father makes me crazy."

"Believe me, I understand," he said firmly. "In fact, one of the reasons I set out on this trip is that my mother had died, and—"

"My mother is also dead," she said. "Her life taken by balverines."

Thomas gasped, the entirety of Laird Kreel's attitudes suddenly made clear. "A balverine killed my brother as well, in my presence."

"I . . . am sorry to hear that," said Sabrina. Her voice softened, much of the abrasiveness that characterized her speech gone. "I was not there when my mother died. I have long been relieved for that fact. My father, however"—and the bitterness crept back into her voice—"was there. It was his fault that she died. Only his. I can't ever forgive him for that. But I can do things every now and then that I know are going to drive him crazy."

"Like indulging in criminal activities."

"Exactly like that. Unfortunately," she continued ruefully, "I can only go so far in defying him. It's like . . . I hear him in here"—and she thumped her head—"banging around, not leaving me alone. He has learned well from his exploits, and from his perpetual quarry, for he has his claws into me right enough. I cannot tell you how much I would like to break free of him utterly, renounce him, put him and this . . . this place . . . to my back forever. But I . . ." She paused, and when she spoke again, it was the heavy utterance of one who was forced, very much against her will, to acknowledge her limits. "I can't. Bottom line is, we all are what we are. I can pull against the ties that bind me to him, but they will never be broken."

Thomas stepped forward and took both her hands in his. "I used to think the exact same thing," he said. "You're maybe a year or two younger than I, and a couple of years may not seem like much . . . but you'd be amazed at how much they matter. What is unthinkable for you today, tomorrow you may be doing."

"I kind of doubt that," said Sabrina. "You don't know my father, and you sure don't know me."

"What is your favorite color?"

Her eyebrows arched. "What?"

"Your favorite color?"

"Red."

"You see," said Thomas, smiling. "Now I know you better than I did before. That's how things happen in life: a little bit at a time."

She laughed at that, and he was pleased to note that she had a rather musical laugh. *She should do it more often,* he thought.

Then she kissed him again, softer this time, but no less passionately. There was no hesitation in his returning it this time, and he felt a connection to her such as he had never known with any other living being.

They parted momentarily, and then her lips were firmly against his once more, and he felt as if he were falling into a deep, endless well, the world lurching around him.

She withdrew abruptly and it was as if he had suddenly crashed to the ground. She stepped back lightly, like a dancer, and laughed again, and then she turned and was gone from the room, leaving him wondering what in the world had just happened.

He returned to the gathering room where the social intercourse between the various guests was still going on. There was no sight of Sabrina. James noticed him returning and looked at him oddly. "Are you all right?" he said.

"Hmm?"

"You look quite out of breath. Like you've been running a marathon or something."

"I'm . . . fine. Couldn't be better." The words were spilling over each other and, to his own ear, Thomas sounded like a complete idiot. Apparently he sounded that way to James as well because James kept staring at him as if aware that there was something Thomas wasn't telling him. Ultimately, James turned away, apparently deciding that whatever it was Thomas wasn't sharing, it wasn't all that important to begin with.

The gathering broke up not long after, and Thomas and James went upstairs to their quarters. They talked about all that they had seen, and their impressions of the other guests. Thomas, however, kept his encounter with Sabrina a secret, close to his heart. It surprised him a little that he was doing so, for he had never felt as if there was anything that he could not tell James. James, supposedly his servant, and yet who was as much a brother to him as his actual brother, long dead.

Soon, with the lights out in their room, Thomas lay in his bed and had to admit that this was indeed quite possibly the most comfortable mattress upon which he had ever been. He expected that slumber would be quick in coming to him; it certainly had been to James, whose regular breathing and slight snoring—courtesy of his irregularly shaped nose, broken in a brawl at a rather young age—could attest.

But he was wrong. Instead, he lay there, staring into the darkness, unable to get Sabrina out of his mind. He would summon up the recollection of his lips against her, of the firmness of her body as his hands had caressed her. He was starting to think that he wasn't going to be getting any sleep at all; his body felt like it had too much blood in it.

There was a soft creak at the door.

He turned in the bed and looked, and gaped.

Sabrina apparently took after her father in one particular respect: She tended to look good standing in doorways.

She was, however, significantly less clothed than he. She was wearing a simple white shift, and somehow in the dimness of the hall light, it was practically translucent. He could see the entire outline of her slender body beneath it.

Sabrina said nothing. She simply stood there, allowing him to drink her in. He abruptly realized he had stopped breathing. He knew his heart was still beating because he could feel it thudding against his chest.

Then, ever so slightly, she gave the slightest nod before turning and walking away with that uncanny noiselessness she had inherited from her father.

You can't. You don't dare. You stay right here and just forget about—

His feet were on the floor before his brain had a chance to emphasize to him the importance of staying in bed. His chest was bare as well; he was clad only in breeches. Poxy lifted her head in lazy confusion at the sudden movement but, seeing no imminent danger, yawned and plumped her head back down. The floor was cold beneath his bare feet.

She just wants to talk. She has things to tell me that might be of use. Don't make more of this than it is. All these and more did he tell himself, and the entire time he hoped that he was wrong.

He emerged into the hallway, and he saw her disappearing around a corner, the slightest flutter of her nightgown indicating that she was indeed just down the way.

As he reached the end of the corridor, he glanced at the far end behind him. He thought, although he wasn't sure, that he saw one of the servants, Bell, coming around the corner. He ducked around after Sabrina, reasonably sure that Bell hadn't seen him although he wasn't sure why it would have mattered if he did. Thomas was of age; he needn't concern himself with what anyone thought . . .

Except her father. You're in his house. What you're thinking of . . . what you're fantasizing about . . . it's wrong, it's just wrong. You speak of principles; where are your principles now?

But the pounding at his temples was enough to drive any further thoughts right out of his head.

There was a door hanging open to his left. *It's a trap. That's it. It's some sort of trap,* he thought. *The absolutely last thing you want to do is go into that room. Turn around and run before it's too late.*

He entered the room.

It was pitch-black. He could see nothing at all.

He suddenly became aware of someone breathing behind him. He turned, and he had a brief glimpse of Sabrina standing there, her hand on the door. Slowly, she shut it. There was a single taper in a gold candle-holder, the flame flickering.

Thomas gulped deeply. He whispered, having no idea why he was doing so: "Did you want to see me?"

Her voice was low and amused. "Actually, I thought you'd want to see me." She reached up to the thin straps that were holding up the shift and slid them down her arms. With nothing to support it, the nightdress slid to the floor and gathered at her feet.

She stood there, nude in the candlelight. Thomas had seen countless sunrises and sunsets, and a vast blue sea, and mountains and forests and all the glories that the land and nature had to offer. Yet he knew, without question, that he had never in his life seen anything as beautiful as what he was beholding now.

Sabrina let him drink in the sight of her, and then she turned and blew out the candle.

He whispered her name in the darkness, and then her warm flesh was pressing against his. "Are you sure?" he said softly. "If . . . if you're doing this just to spite your father—"

"I'm doing this"—and she kissed him again—"because I want to take myself out of myself. Just for one night, I want to leave what I am behind. I want someone to make me feel like something different."

"And what do you want to feel like?"

"Like I'm yours."

Then she stopped talking and started doing things with her hands to him. And as she guided him backwards onto her bed, the last vestiges of both his clothing and his restraint were stripped away. There was only him and her and warmth and heat, and the rest of the world was gone.

MUCH LIKE THOMAS, I DISCOVER THAT I *have forgotten to breathe as well, and have to force myself to do so. I see the amused look on the part of the story-teller. "Wipe that smirk off your face, for I am not so old and infirm that I am incapable of wiping it from you myself."*

"Apologies, Majesty. I hope that I did not, in the graphic nature of my tale, embarrass you in any way . . ."

"Do not be absurd. An old man I may be, but still a man, and in spirit a young one. I had my share of fair young things in my life, and I . . ." I am suddenly wistful. "The young man who still resides within me looks at young women now, and lusts after them as much as he ever did. But he sees them as if from across a great divide, for age has distanced me from them."

"You are the king. Would that not enable you to indulge

in such dalliances as you wished? Who would dare refuse you?"

"Who indeed?" I say. "And therein lies the tragedy. For I would know that the only reason sweet young things with firm flesh and a well-turned ankle would be with me is for that very reason. A man in the depths of winter has no business with a lass in the bloom of spring, especially if she believes that she dare not refuse. That is simply the way of things."

"You are a man of true conscience, Majesty. And I hope that you do not think the less of young Thomas due to his lack of will with the daughter of his host."

"He hardly forced himself upon her. It sounds to me as if she was anxious to extend some hospitality of her own." I chuckle at my own witticism although it sounds more like a tired wheeze. Then I feel surprisingly ashamed of myself; it is hardly a dignified response for a king.

If the storyteller shares my negative opinion of myself, he is generous enough to keep that opinion to himself. Instead, he says neutrally, "Indeed she did, Majesty."

"Perhaps," I allow, "it was an unwise thing for Thomas to do. But youth is the time for men to make mistakes, and be driven by their passions. Knowledge may be gained from books, but wisdom can only be gained by experience, and mistakes are the greatest granters of wisdom. If one is afraid to make mistakes, then how will one stretch the bounds of one's world? One should not simply walk gently into walls; one should run into them at full speed." He looks at me oddly, and with an amused smile. "Did I say something entertaining to you, storyteller?"

"No, Majesty. Merely something with some foresight

that you are as yet unaware of. You will understand later in the tale. It is comforting to know that you do not hold Thomas in less esteem for his actions."

"Not at all. Were I in his position, I would likely have done the same. I never claimed to be pure of heart and chaste in mind and body. Why should I expect more of . . ."

"Of the Hero of a story? Is that not the point of a Hero, though? To have someone of whom we expect more?"

"Partially. But they also enable us to see flaws within ourselves. A flawed Hero can be as compelling, if not more so, than a noble one."

"I quite agree, Majesty. Shall I continue?"

"Best that you would." I look to the skies and see that the sun is crawling across the horizon toward its inevitable rest. "For I see that the day is determined to flee us despite our wishes that it do otherwise, and I've no mind to sit here in the darkness and listen to your words. The cold is already infesting these old bones, and the absence of sunlight will be of no benefit."

"I did not think it was quite that cold, Majesty, but if you say so, I shall continue."

"Please do."

"Very well." He pauses, gathering his thoughts, and then says delicately, "I shall not go into detail of the rest of that evening, save to say that Thomas's youth and stamina were well tested that evening, repeatedly."

I smile, warmly remembering that period in my life. The fires still burn within me, but they are tamped down somewhat by the passing of time. Yet I am still able to bask in the warmth of recollection.

"He did not remember falling into an exhausted sleep. All he knew was that suddenly her hand was upon his shoulder, shaking him gently, and she was whispering to him, 'The house stirs. 'T'would be best if you were not here when it—'

" 'Yes. Yes, of course,' he said. He clambered from the bed, the beginnings of dawn filtering through the window, and tried swiftly to yank on his breeches. He succeeded in upending himself and falling over. He felt like a complete fool, but he heard a gentle laugh and saw that Sabrina—lying on the bed, without covers, exquisitely naked—was amused by it rather than thinking him a fool.

" 'Fortunately, you were more graceful last night,' she said.

" 'I am . . . pleased to hear that.' He was continuing to whisper as he pulled up his breeches. 'I am . . . not terribly experienced in such matters.'

" 'Nor am I. But judging how I feel this morning, I would have to say we did it correctly.'

"He wondered what he was supposed to say next, but before he could speak further, she gestured for him to hasten from the place. He did so, terrified that the wrong person would be walking past and see him emerging from a room that he had no business being in. He placed an ear against the door, heard nothing, then insinuated himself into the corridor and hastened back to his own room.

"He opened the door with as much stealth as he was able, and it rewarded him by not so much as creaking. Even Poxy did not stir as he quietly closed it behind him, made his way to his own bed, and slid under the covers.

"And then James, who had seemingly been asleep, slowly raised his head and stared at Thomas through half-lidded eyes. For long moments there was silence, and Thomas wondered if James was even awake. Then James's first words of the day settled that:

" 'I hope she was worth it.'

"There was no judgment in his voice; it was too early in the morning for that. It was simply a flat statement. Thomas briefly contemplated posturing, or denial, or claiming that he had absolutely no idea what James could possibly be referring to. But they had known each other too long, these young brothers in all but blood, and Thomas smiled, and said, 'Completely.'

"James grunted, and then said, 'Just pray that her father doesn't find out, or he may decide to hunt you instead of balverines.'

"That was a concern that Thomas could not argue with."

Chapter 14

"ELDERWOODS, MY FRIENDS. ONE OF the great natural wonders of Sutcliff . . . and home to balverines."

Laird Ethan Kreel stood on the edges of a forest that seemed shrouded in darkness even though it was mid-day. A road ran along the perimeter, but there was nothing entering the woods themselves. As near as Thomas and James could discern, it was an area that had been untouched and untrammeled by human beings.

The entire expedition was gathered at the forest's edge. The servants were loaded down with the equipment that the brave explorers would require for survival. They were bearing up under the burden well enough although Bell seemed to be struggling a bit with his pack, even limping slightly, and James hoped that he wasn't overloaded. When he asked out of concern, Bell simply grimaced a bit, and said, "Nuthin I kenna handle," and spoke no more. Obviously, he was a prideful individual; James could respect that.

He wasn't entirely sure he still respected Thomas, though, considering that his old friend seemed rather distracted from the endeavor. It was hard to believe: Their entire voyage had come down to this moment, and Thomas's mind seemed elsewhere. James, of course, knew exactly where, and on exactly whom. *Why her? Why that spoiled brat? Maybe Thomas sees something in her. Yeah. He sees himself in her,* James thought mirthlessly.

Their trip to the woods' perimeters had been without incident. There had been much conversation and chatting between the members of the expedition; it was as if the previous night's get-acquainted gathering had simply been taken on the road. Conspicuous in her absence had been Sabrina, who had not departed with them that morning after breakfast and indeed had not even come downstairs.

Taking too great a chance with fate, as far as James was concerned, Thomas had nevertheless inquired of her father as to her whereabouts.

"Sabrina will not be joining us," said Kreel easily, as if it were a matter of no consequence. "She has very little taste for these hunts. She will be remaining back at the mansion, where hopefully my servants will do a better job keeping an eye on her this time so that she does not head off into the marketplace and cause more mischief."

This had been an answer that had saddened Thomas even as it had gladdened James. As the journey had proceeded, James had said in a low whisper into his friend's ear, "Be grateful she is not along."

"Why?"

"Because you do not lie well, remember? And if she were hanging on your arm, or otherwise displaying affection for you, and her father asked why there was such a turn in her feelings for you, I do not believe for a moment that you would do a good job of dissembling. That's why."

"You worry about too many things," Thomas had said carelessly, but it was clear that he knew that what James said was true.

Now the group had reached the forest called the Elderwoods, and they were studying it. It seemed that there was, for the first time, a hint of trepidation. And the very first one to display it was, of all members of the group, Poxy. For when they drew to the edge of the forest, the dog—who had been willing to take on everything from pirates to krakens to soldiers on behalf of her master—whimpered and backed up, her ears down, her tail planted firmly between her legs.

"Poxy?" said James in surprise, clapping his hands briskly. "Poxy. Come here, girl. Come here."

Poxy most definitely did not come there. Instead, she continued to retreat until she had taken up station a good twenty feet back, whereupon she dropped to the ground and simply refused to budge no matter how much James appealed to her to follow him.

"Well, *that* does not bode well," said Shaw. "The dumb animal is too smart to enter where the humans would dare to go. Should we be taking our lead from her, Kreel, rather than you?"

"Life is not worth living without risk, my laird," Kreel said calmly. "I have guaranteed none of you that we will not face any danger. Believe me, we will. All I can remind you is that I have survived any number of such expeditions, to territory far more hazardous than what is effectively my own backyard."

"Yes, about that," said Molly Newsome. "I admit to some curiosity about the fact that the balverine forest is within range of your home and yet you do not find yourself constantly assailed by them. Why is that?"

"A good question, my lady, and you need look no further than there for your answer." And he pointed at Poxy, who was still cowering some distance away. "The Elderwoods are a mystic haven, and there is a line of demarcation between the end of the forest and the beginning of civilization. Whether it is a natural one that has developed through time or one that was laid down by a wizard at some distant point in the past, I could not say. The result, however, is consistent: Beasts do not wish to cross it in either direction. The balverines cower within the Elderwoods, having no desire to step out into the exposed realm of man. By the same token, even the more modest beasts, such as Master James's dog, will have no truck with setting foot—or paw, if you will—within the confines of the woods."

"But we can enter?" she said.

"We are not beasts, my lady"—and Kreel smiled—

"although it may seem to you at times that men become beasts in your presence."

"They have at times," she said, and this caused a ripple of laughter among the assemblage.

"Very well, then," said Kreel. "Now . . . I would suggest that you keep your pistols at the ready. You have all assured me that you are familiar with firearms and have used them in the past. I will not lie to you: If any of you have boasted without foundation, then your personal jeopardy has been increased, for your pistols are your first, best means of offense. I have loaded them with silver bullets. Even a wound from silver is like unto acid upon the creature and will stop it in its tracks; a bullet to the heart or the head will dispose of one permanently. You all understand?" There were nods from all around. "Also, you have the silver-edged knives I have given you. Those likewise will prove fatal, although obviously the balverine would be at far greater proximity. Unless you are exceptionally skilled in the practice, I would not suggest using the knife as a throwing blade. The odds are that you will simply wind up weaponless. So . . . are we prepared, then?"

The members of the nobility looked at each other. It seemed to James that each of them was waiting for the other to say, "To hell with this; let's return to the mansion, drink and dine well in privilege, and speak no more of this ever again." But none of them did, and collectively they nodded.

"Into the woods, then," said Laird Kreel.

As they entered, the last thing James heard was Poxy whimpering after him, clearly asking him to remain with her and stay out of these darksome woods. For the first time since he had met her, James did not heed her. He wondered if it was a decision he was going to live to regret . . . or, for that matter, live through at all.

THE EXPEDITION HAD BEEN UNCONSCIOUSLY bracing itself for being attacked the second they entered the Elderwoods. Certainly, the environment seemed to invite it. The darkness of the woods was not simply some manner of illusion when standing out on the roadside. Having entered the woods, it seemed to envelop them as if they had wandered into the belly of the beast. The servants had torches with them that could be lit when the sun went down. For the time being, the very minimal daylight that managed to reach the forest floor, like an intrepid soldier fighting through overwhelming enemy forces, provided them with just enough light to be able to see ahead and around them. Even so, the shadows were long, and many leafless branches stretched above them, like skeletal arms ushering them to their doom.

However, despite the morbid character of their surroundings—or perhaps specifically because of its less-than-promising nature—they relaxed a bit when assault was not forthcoming within the first five minutes. When nothing happened within an hour, they relaxed a good deal. There was casual discussion back and forth, and

Kreel even took the time to point out things of interest, such as particularly old trees or curious rock formations.

The more they relaxed, though, the more tense Thomas became, so much so that James's accidentally bumping into him was enough to make him reach for the pistol tucked into his belt. His rifle was slung over his shoulder although that had likewise been filled with silver bullets. Then he saw that it was James, and he let out a relieved sigh.

"You've got to overcome that whole jumpiness thing of yours," James said chidingly. "You can't keep being ready to open fire every time someone steps on a branch."

"I'll be fine."

"I don't get you. This is what we've been working for, what we've been waiting for. You're finally getting your wish; you're knocking on the back door of the balverines, about to face them down. Who knows, maybe you'll even have your dream come true and wind up with the head of the balverine that killed your brother as a trophy."

"It won't bring him back," Thomas said as he stepped carefully over an upright rock that seemed to have been placed there specifically to trip him up. "Kreel's wife—Sabrina's mother—was slain by balverines. Kreel wears the pelt of one as a trophy, he's killed who knows how many, and Sabrina is still mourning the loss."

"I didn't know that about her," said James. "Then again, I don't know her as well as you." When he saw the look Thomas gave him, he added, "I don't mean anything more by that than what I said."

"Sure. Okay."

"Thomas . . ." And James lowered his voice even more, glancing to make sure that they were out of earshot from the others. "What are you going to do? About the girl, I mean."

"I don't know. Marry her?"

"After one night of passion? Are you insane? Passion fades, Thomas."

"Does it?"

"Well . . . so I've heard," he said, putting on an air of mild chagrin. But then he grew serious once more. "What, are you going to bring her home with you? Or maybe move in with her in her mansion? What kind of life would you have with her?"

"I don't know, James. I haven't worked any of it out."

James grunted in mild annoyance, but then said with false chipperness, "Look at the bright side. If you don't make it out of here alive, then hey: problem solved."

"You're cheering me right up there, James. If you—"

Suddenly there was the sound of something coming very quickly toward them. Branches were snapping, brush was shaking, and immediately Kreel gestured for everyone to draw into a circle, everyone with their backs to each other. "Weapons up!" he called out, and all of them obeyed, their weapons at the ready.

Thomas's pulse was racing, his eyes wide. He had unslung his rifle, hoping to cut short one of the creatures' charge before it got close enough to do damage to anyone. Dean Carter had his gun leveled and a distant look on his face, as if he were studying something from far enough away that he was not at risk. Laird

Shaw was grimly determined, holding his gun with two hands, keeping it steady. Molly Newsome appeared the most delighted of the three, swinging her gun in a wide arc, eager for something to unload upon. It occurred to Thomas that perhaps staring down death was her way of feeling close to her departed husband.

The eight servants were also armed, their guns out and aimed with varying degrees of confidence. Bell appeared the most prepared, and something about him seemed different to Thomas although it was not anything that he could quite put his finger on. As if he had been wearing his personality rather than inhabiting it and was now tossing it aside in favor of something new and more suitable to the occasion.

"Steady . . . steady . . ." said Kreel, and Thomas felt as if the shadows themselves were about to reach out and drag them off into the abyss.

And then the source of the noise burst out at them from two directions.

It was a pair of deer, a doe and a buck. Shaw, his nerves on edge, actually fired off a shot as the two animals nearly collided with each other ten paces away from the circle of hunters. They veered off at the last moment and then darted right past the band, the doe on one side and the buck on the other.

Then they were gone, and all was still once more.

The hunters looked around at each other, and then Molly Newsome chuckled. This laughter was quickly taken up by the others until it became a full-throated, unrestrained round of merriment at their own expense.

"That was—" began one of the servants as the laughter began to die down.

He didn't get to finish his sentence, as a balverine dropped down from overhead, landed directly in front of him, and clamped its jaws around his throat.

The servant's eyes widened, his mind unable to process what was happening, and then the balverine yanked its head back and tore the man's throat out. Blood fountained, splashing all over the balverine's face, and its tongue darted out and licked at it as the servant fell to the ground.

There was a collective shriek from the hunters, and they opened fire on the beast. It staggered under the hail of bullets but did not go down, and suddenly there were more of them, plummeting from the canopy of branches overhead and leaping out from the shadows as if they'd been wearing them as cloaks for concealment.

The servants started firing, and it was impossible to miss the targets because the balverines were not slowing at all. They tore into the servants, and if the curse of the balverine could be passed along through biting, it seemed there would be none who were going to have the opportunity to discover if it was true. There was no biting here, but instead rending of flesh and ripping out of organs, and veins and guts being yanked out and slurped down like gluttons at a feast. There was blood everywhere, and the warm splatting of organs hurled against the trees.

Thomas emptied his rifle into one of the balverines that was charging straight at him and, as with the other weapons, it did nothing to slow him. The balverine leaped straight at him and Thomas, reversing his rifle, swung it around like a club. The rifle slammed against the balverine's head and the stock shattered, the balverine being knocked momentarily to the ground. Thomas tossed aside the broken rifle and yanked out his sword. The downed balverine started to clamber to its feet, and Thomas whipped his sword around as hard and as fast as he could. It wasn't silver, but it was sharp nevertheless. His aim was to behead the creature; in that he fell short. Instead, the sword made it halfway through, lodging in the balverine's throat. It tried to howl but instead coughed up blood, and Thomas yanked hard on the sword, tearing it loose. The balverine, clutching its throat even as blood poured between its fingers, lunged for him, and Thomas sidestepped and brought his sword swinging around from the other direction. He connected with his target once more, and this time the force of the blow was sufficient to tear the beast's head from its shoulders.

Then there was another roar from directly behind him. Having no time to turn, Thomas desperately thrust the blade backwards under his arms. He heard an agonized yelp and tried to turn around, but in doing so he loosened his grip for half a second. That was all the time that was required for the balverine behind him to strike him in the back of the head. Thomas was sent flying several feet and crashed into a tree. He slid to the ground and tried to see what was happening around him, the world spinning from the blow he had taken to his head.

A balverine was crouched there with Thomas's sword buried in the upper part of its chest. With an annoyed growl, it yanked the blade out and tossed it aside. Then it advanced toward Thomas, and Thomas tried to grab for his crossbow, but he knew that there was no way he was going to have time to load the thing before the balverine was upon him. Even if he did, the odds were minimal that even a perfectly placed bolt would have the slightest effect.

Then Thomas saw Kreel, the laird himself, coming up right behind the balverine, and he had to think that he had never been so happy to see anyone in his life, ever. Kreel was going to save him and strike down the balverines with the force of his personality alone, and perhaps even wave his hand and bring the dead people back to life. Anything was possible when Laird Ethan Kreel was there.

Kreel cuffed the balverine on the side of its head as if it were a misbehaving puppy. "Not this one. You know better. You should all know which is which. Fool." He struck him once more, and the balverine growled in annoyance but then turned and loped away.

Then Kreel looked apologetically to Thomas. "Apologies for the inconvenience," he said, as if he had kept Thomas waiting too long for an appointment. "The bait I packed into the backpacks of the servants is supposed to draw them to who is food and who is not. As you can see, I am selective."

"W-what?" Thomas wondered just how hard he had

struck his head. Certainly the world already seemed on the verge of blacking out; perhaps this was some sort of delusion that was preceding unconsciousness. Maybe he was already out cold, and this was a dream.

Then Thomas was yanked to his feet, and there was a stink behind him of rotting meat that turned out to be the breath of a balverine that was holding him immobilized. From across the way he saw that James was being similarly held, and was screaming his name. Dean Carter, Laird Shaw, and Lady Newsome were likewise in the grasp of balverines and were already shrieking protest as they were being yanked away into the woods. The remaining balverines were feasting on the bodies of the downed servants, some of whom—horrifically—were still twitching. *They're eating them alive . . . blood and thunder . . . they're eating them alive . . .*

Kreel's smiling face swam back into view. "I know this is most confusing for you, fellow. But trust me when I say that this is actually a tremendous honor for you. You could have been the prey. Instead"—and suddenly his eyes were glimmering yellow—"you are going to be given the honor of being made a predator."

"What . . . what are you?" whispered Thomas, as a curtain of black seemed to descend over his eyes.

"I am Ethan Kreel, high laird of the Balverine Order," Kreel told him. "And you are about to become one of our number. But it must be done properly, lest you be reduced to the savagery of one of these poor creatures." And he gestured to indicate the other balverines, who were still picking through the remains of the servants. "Do not concern yourself; I assure you that all will be made clear."

And then all went black.

JAMES FELT AS IF HE WERE GOING MAD.

He was being dragged through the forest by balverines, hauling him along as if his attempts to pull clear of them meant nothing. They had taken his weapons from him, and he obviously posed no threat in a hand-to-hand situation. But where the hell were they taking him and the others? It made no sense at all.

A short distance away, Thomas was also being hauled along. Unconscious, he'd been slung over the shoulder of one of the balverines, who was carrying him along as if he were a bag of laundry. Carter, Shaw, and Newsome were farther ahead, their cries of terror having disappeared into the distance.

More in a display of defiance than with any expectation that it was going to do him any good, James abruptly brought his foot down and slammed it onto the paw of the nearest balverine. It let out a yelp and snarled at him, drawing back its claws as if ready to gut him like a trout. *That would be better than whatever they have planned for us,* he thought, and readied himself for death. He was surprised to discover it didn't require all that much preparation: to some degree, he'd been ready for death ever since embarking on this excursion in the first place.

"Ah-ah," a scolding voice said sharply, and the balverine backed off. James turned to see that Kreel had fallen into step alongside them. The balverines were making no threatening gestures toward him, nor were any holding him by the arms to prevent him from escaping. "He and his friend have been chosen. You know that." The balverine growled at him but clearly understood, although that didn't deter it from glaring fiercely at James in a way that indicated that—given the slightest opportunity—it would tear James to pieces.

James tried to speak, but his voice was so constricted with fear that at first it came out barely as a whisper. "Ch-chosen for what?" he finally managed to say.

"Why, to be added to the Balverine Order. We are a growing and influential group."

"You . . . you're an order of people that . . . that are friends with . . . with these monsters?"

"No, James."

He gestured for the balverines who were dragging James to stop, and they did so. Kreel turned to face him, and—just as Thomas had seen—his eyes transformed from brown into pale yellow. But there was more. His teeth began to lengthen and become sharper, and white fur began to appear on his face, his jaw distending into a muzzle. He held up his hands, and claws began to jut out from his fingertips.

He halted the transformation, seemingly through willpower alone, at a midway point between being a human and a full balverine. But James could see that that was where the metamorphosis was taking him.

"Do you begin to understand now?" Kreel said, his voice deep and guttural and sounding more like a snarling animal's than a human's.

"You're . . . you're a white balverine," he managed to gasp out, stating what was patently obvious. "But . . . you wear the fur of—"

"Of a former rival."

"You're a monster!"

Kreel's clawed hand lashed out and wrapped itself around the petrified James's throat. "We," he snarled, "are not the monsters. It is humanity that performs the monstrous acts. Hunting our kind into oblivion. Changing the world, remaking it into their image. Even though you have been gone from your home for a time, you still stink of industrialization and 'progress.' Albion was once a land of myth and magic. *Now* look at it! Forests being chopped down to make way for cities, which in turn pollute the air with their foul industry. Creatures of wonder being driven into hiding or away from the eyes of man altogether, while mundanity steadily increases its chokehold upon the collective imagination of the population. You've seen a world without greatness, without quests, without Heroes and fables of them. Do you truly think it an improvement over what once there was? Do you?"

And James's eyes locked into those of Kreel, and even though he could barely speak, still he managed to command with a hoarse whisper, *"Let go of my throat!"*

Kreel did so without even thinking about it, and then looked at his own hand in mild surprise, as if it belonged to someone else. Then he turned back to James, his eyes narrowed, cautious where he had not been before. "We are going to change things, James. The Balverine Order is making sure of that, slowly but surely."

"Change things to what?"

"To a world that is more suitable for our kind, James. One where we can run free without fear of assault and extinction. Where we can prey upon food with impunity. Where we can halt the building of cities and the annihilation of forests, take back the land, and live the sort of life to which we are entitled." He reached out with a single clawed finger and stroked the side of James's face. "And the way to do that . . . is to be in control. That's how we're going to do it, you see. By being—"

Suddenly Kreel's head snapped around as an infuriated barking came from just to his left. Bursting out of the brush, her teeth bared, snarling and snapping, came Poxy, barreling straight toward Kreel, defiance in her eyes.

She had come for James. She had overcome her fear of the forest, her trepidation, and—seeing James in the hands of the enemy—did not hesitate to charge her opponent.

"Poxy, no!" screamed James.

Kreel did not pause. He took two quick steps forward, meeting her charge as she leaped straight at him. He swung his hand as if swatting a fly and gutted Poxy while the dog was still in midleap. Poxy let out an agonized cry that mingled with James's own, and then the dog hit the ground and lay still. She scarcely had time to whimper, and then there was a rattle in her throat and a look of surprise in her eye that quickly faded and became blank.

James cried out and tried to get to her side, even though she was already gone, but the balverines holding him yanked him back alongside them. “You didn’t have to do that!” he howled at Kreel.

“I was attacked, and I struck back,” Kreel said calmly, taking the time to lick the blood from his claws. “That is the balverine way. You will understand that before very long, when you become one of our Order.”

Hot tears were running down James’s face, and he snarled in a manner that would have rivaled that of a balverine, “I’ll kill you. I’ll kill you, you bastard. You’re going to die.”

“I very much doubt that,” said Kreel, and then—as if James no longer mattered—he said, “Ah. We’re here.”

James was hauled into a clearing and, moments later, Thomas was dumped by his side. Thomas moaned softly, just starting to come around, and the balverines stepped back, releasing their hold on James. Neither of the boys were now being restrained, but balverines were ringing them, and escape was clearly impossible.

At that moment, though, James wasn’t thinking about escape. Instead, he was trying to comprehend just what exactly it was that he was seeing.

It was a temple of some sort. It seemed as if it had been carved out of solid rock, right into the side of a mountain, and it towered above them, at least fifty feet high. There was a large opening that served as a gateway to whatever was inside. There was what appeared to be a large, irregular circle with points chiseled into the stone, and it was only after looking at it for a few moments that James realized he was staring at a rendering of a wide-open jaw. The meaning was clear: Whoever entered there was effectively being swallowed up by those within.

There was a man standing directly in front of the temple entrance. Even in the dimness, he appeared familiar to James, and he couldn't quite place where he knew him from.

"It took you long enough," growled the man, and that was when he knew.

"You're . . . you're the coachman!" James said.

Thomas, who was clearly trying to shake off the unconsciousness that had settled upon him before, didn't seem to comprehend. "Coachman . . . ?"

"The one who suggested we go to Windside! To the Library to learn about balverines!"

"Kind of you to remember," said the coachman. He wasn't talking at all in the manner that he had been when they first encountered him. He sounded more polished and educated and even a bit contemptuous of them. "Tried to set you on the right path, hoping you'd get here sooner or later. I thought right from the start that you boys had potential. Good to know that I was right. Sent word on ahead to Kreel to be on the lookout for you."

"And here they are, sir," said Kreel with a touch of pride. "James, Thomas . . . this is Lugaru, the undisputed leader of our Order."

"We've met," said James tightly.

"Yes. Yes, we have," said Lugaru, but he was paying

no attention to James. Instead, he was focused entirely on Thomas. "And I want to say that it is going to be a personal pleasure turning you, Thomas. As one of our Order, you will travel the land, encouraging other young bravos such as yourself to join Laird Kreel in balverine hunts. As much as we have a dearth of Heroes upon the land, there is still always the possibility that more may rise. Yours and James's particular task will be to seek them out, bring them to us, and help convert them to our cause. Eventually, the Balverine Order will control all the nobility, all the richest and most powerful individuals, all the potential Heroes, and—with just a bit of luck—the monarchy itself. We will use that power and influence to remake Albion into what it was rather than into the pestilent rathole that it is currently being turned into. And you will be a part of that, Thomas."

"Go to hell," Thomas snarled.

Lugaru made a scolding, clucking noise with his tongue. "That is uncharitable of you, Thomas. Especially when you realize that I am being truly generous, all things considered."

"What 'things'?"

"Why . . . that I'm not seeking vengeance upon you."

And Lugaru began to transform. He did not reach a halfway point as Kreel had done and then pull back. Instead, he grew, larger and larger, black fur growing upon him, his face distending, bones audibly breaking and reknitting as they came together in a new form. The other balverines backed away, and several of them started to howl, and then all of them were.

Something popped out of his face, pushed out by the restructuring of the bones therein. It was a fake eye, crusted over so that it looked like it was a genuine one that had simply been overtaken by disease.

His clothes, hanging loose and shapelessly upon him, began to fill out as his size increased. Within moments, he had transformed into a full-sized balverine, his black fur rippling, his single glittering yellow eye locked upon Thomas. He spoke and the words were more animal growl than human, but still understandable.

"Vengeance," he snarled, "for taking my eye when I killed your mewling puke of a brother. But having you in my Order, under my rule . . . that is a far more elegant revenge, don't you think?"

THOMAS FELT AS IF HE WERE GOING MAD. He prayed that he was still unconscious and had yet to awaken. But he knew that, no, that was not the case. He was here, he was facing the monster that had killed Stephen, and now—apparently—was going to do even worse to him.

He screamed then, a howl of rage that itself was almost as far from human as Lugaru was. Lugaru laughed in response, a terrible thing to hear, and Thomas yanked at the balverine that was now holding him back. The balverine simply snarled, holding him tight, giving him no chance to escape.

And suddenly there was an explosion that echoed through the forest.

The balverine who had been holding onto Thomas pitched forward, and there was blood all over the fur on the back of its head. Just like that, Thomas was suddenly free, and then there was a second, similar explosion, and the balverine that had been holding James immobilized likewise pitched over.

Thomas's first instinct was to charge straight at Lugaru, even though he knew it would be suicidal. But that instinct was overridden by a loud voice shouting, with authority so commanding that it could not be ignored, *"Run! Run now!"*

They did as they were instructed, bolting toward the forest. With a roar, the balverines turned in pursuit, and then there was a rapid series of shots, and in quick succession four more of the balverines went down, grasping at their chests and keeling over.

Kreel and Lugaru were both far enough back that there were balverines in front of them who were taking the brunt of the shots. Kreel no longer held on to his human form; instead, he began to grow and change into a white balverine, howling fury that someone was daring to attack them in this manner. "Get them!" he bellowed, pointing at James and Thomas as they fled into the forest. *"Get them!"*

Thomas was certain this was about to be the shortest-lived escape in history, for there was no matching the balverines when it came to speed.

And suddenly one of the foremost balverines erupted in flame.

Thomas had never seen anything like it. The balverine

twisted around, screeching, batting at itself, trying to extinguish the fire, and then a second balverine went up. They staggered, pitched forward, and then, an instant later, the entire area in front of the temple burst in flame. It spread far more quickly than seemed humanly possible, and within seconds there was a virtual wall of flame between the balverines and the escaping boys.

Thomas tripped and fell over an extended branch, and then someone reached up from the darkness, yanking him to his feet. "Run," said a clipped voice, and he looked up, uncomprehending, into the face of Bell. "Run if you value your life. Both of you!"

The "both of you" comment referred to the fact that James had just stumbled into view next to him. "You're alive?" James said to Bell.

"Yes," said Bell, his thick accent gone, "and I intend to keep it that way. Come! Quickly!" With no further urging, he started sprinting into the forest, and Thomas and James ran after him.

James quickly took the lead, his typical ability to never get lost serving him well in the darkness of the Elderwoods. "Keep going!" Bell urged them. "The smoke and fire should cover our spoors. Plus they're pinned down, at least for a while. By the time the fire burns itself out, they won't be able to catch up with us. At least in theory."

"What the hell happened back there?" Thomas managed to say, trying to avoid tripping over more obstacles that seemed determined to throw themselves in his path. "Was that you shooting them—?"

"Yes, with silver bullets. Our host took it upon himself to make certain that the weapons you were all carrying were not genuine silver," Bell said grimly. "Naturally, I anticipated that and made sure to have my own ammunition with me. What I wouldn't give for some manner of moveable turret gun."

"But the flames—?"

"Flammable oil in bottles, stuffed with cloths that I ignited before hurling them. The brittle and dried-out nature of the forest made the immediate area particularly susceptible. With any luck, the whole damned place would burn down, but I seriously doubt we're going to be that fortunate."

That was when Thomas saw that Bell was carrying a walking stick tucked under his arm. It was familiar to him, and now so was Bell's voice. *"Wait!"*

"Waiting isn't an option."

"I mean, I know you! You're—"

At that instant, a balverine came leaping out of the forest straight at them.

There was a sharp hiss of metal, and Bell was now holding a long, slender blade that he had pulled from concealment within the cane. Without hesitation, he thrust forward with it, and the blade drove directly into the balverine's chest, piercing the creature's heart. The balverine fell back and was about to let out a dying howl that might well have alerted the others, but Bell reacted swiftly. Even as the balverine opened its mouth to cry out, Bell yanked out the blade and swung it with perfect precision. It didn't cut off the monster's head, but it didn't have to; it sliced expertly through the beast's vocal cords, aborting any outcry before it could be given voice.

Bell turned and held up the blade. "Silver-augmented," he said. "Particularly effective against the beasts."

"You're Locke! From back at Windside, at the tavern."

"I don't believe this," said James. "Did the whole damned town follow us here?"

"Hardly," said Quentin Locke. "I told you there was a conspiracy, and now you're neck deep in it. Now . . . I suggest we keep moving and get to the forest perimeter. There we should find what we need in order to go where we need to go before the balverines overtake us."

"And . . . and where's that?" said Thomas. But Locke was already moving, and Thomas had no choice but to run to keep up. "I said where's that? Where are we going?"

"To Kreel's mansion."

"Are you *joking*?"

"No. That is where we're going to find what will be required to put an end to this."

"That being?"

"Heroism."

"Heroism?" Thomas gasped, trying not to run out of breath as they sprinted through the woods. Behind them, the forest was alight with the flames. "But the only living Hero is the king of Albion! What are you saying, that we run and tell him what's happening and bring him back here?"

"A functional plan, but far too lengthy, particularly if we have any hope in hell of saving the others from the clutches of the Order. We are going to have to deal with Heroes far closer in proximity."

"Heroes? You . . . you can't mean us . . ."

"Yes and no, Mr. Kirkman," said Locke evenly. "We are going in *search* of Heroes. The Heroes Three. The Triumvirate. Whatever it is you wish to call them."

"But . . . but they're legends!"

"No, Thomas, they're quite real. And they are the only hope we have of putting an end to this Balverine Order and saving Albion from their unholy influence. I apologize for the melodrama, but there you have it."

"But even if they existed, aren't they long dead?" said James.

"Yes, Master Skelton. But last I looked, the three of us are alive. And that is going to make all the difference in the world."

Chapter 15

THEY'RE GOING TO CATCH UP WITH US. *There's no way they can't. Even if we're lucky enough to make it to the edge of the woods, once we're out into open land, there's simply no way that they're not going to overtake us.*

Those depressing thoughts kept tumbling through Thomas's frantic mind as they continued to sprint through the forest. Every shadow seemed to conceal a balverine ready to leap out at them. Every branch was a skeletal hand ready to snag them and drag them back into the woods. He was even sure at several points that he could feel the heat of a balverine's breath on the back of his neck, but he dared not look behind him because at any moment he could trip over something that could possibly cause him to twist or even break an ankle. At that point, James would have no choice but to leave him behind. Except he knew that James would never do that, just as he would never abandon James. They would either make it together or not at all.

When he wasn't giving thought to surviving the forest, he was trying to process what he had just witnessed. The monster who had slain his brother was the leader of some . . . some sort of balverine cult? Their quest had been monitored from the very beginning both by the balverines and by this mysterious man, this Quentin Locke. Had they ever been in control of their destiny at any point?

He asked the question of Locke as they neared the edge of the forest.

"Yes," Locke said in a no-nonsense tone. Amazingly, he didn't seem the least out of breath. "At any point, you could have turned back. Your determination to see matters through was entirely your own affair. Likewise, how this all ends is also in your control, at least for the moment."

"Meaning?"

"Meaning as long as they don't catch us. There. Through there," he said, pointing to a separation in the trees. It occurred to Thomas that Locke's sense of direction was as unerring as James's. He envied them; at one point he'd gotten lost inside the mansion while wandering from room to room.

The mansion.

Sabrina. What was he going to say to Sabrina?

Everything that she had said about her father, all of it now was understandable. She had somehow intuited what her father was, a secret that he must have been hiding from her. But he had only been partially successful in keeping his true nature from her. This was about more than just her blaming him for the death of her mother. Instinctively, she had sensed the evil within him.

How was he going to tell her?

It was starting to seem as if being killed by balverines had some advantages. If nothing else, it would spare him some difficult conversations.

They came staggering out of the forest, having quickly traversed at a dead run the distance the expedition had traveled at a slow walk. The mansion was very far in the distance, though, and Thomas knew that sooner or later the balverines would emerge from the forest and come after them. He now knew that Kreel's tale about balverines not desiring to leave the forest was nonsense. The beasts could come and go as—

He looked around. There was no sign of Poxy. He wondered where she had gotten off to.

What he did see, however, surprised him greatly. It was a groomsman, looking rather disheveled and not terribly happy to be there. He was there with four horses: One he was astride himself, the other three had their leads tied off around a tree, and they looked no more pleased to be there than their keeper. They were saddled and ready to go.

"Five more minutes, and I was gone. Heard screams like banshees in the distance, I did," said the groomsman, his voice quavering with fear. Thomas was about to clarify for him that it was, in fact, balverines and not banshees, but then decided that that probably wasn't the best way to handle the situation. Meantime, the groomsman continued, "Where's my money?"

"Right here," said Locke. He pulled a sack of coins from his pocket and flung it to the groomsman, who caught it on the fly. "You can count it if you wish. I won't be offended . . ."

"Sooner I'm out of here, the better." The groomsman wheeled his horse around and seconds later was galloping off down the road. The three remaining horses watched him go with clear concern. Perhaps they thought they were being left behind as some sort of sacrifice.

By this point, Locke was pulling off the wig and false facial hair that had disguised his appearance. As he did, Thomas and James went to the horses and started undoing the leads, holding them tightly. The horses were definitely spooked by what they sensed was going on in the woods, and the last thing they needed to happen was to have the horses bolt and leave them standing by the side of the road. Locke quickly came to their sides and helped them steady the nervous animals. "I can't get over that disguise," said James. "I never would have recognized you."

"You haven't before. Then again, you hadn't met me yet, so it's understandable."

"What are you talking about?"

"In the Library."

"I still don't . . ." Then slow realization dawned on James's face. "The . . . the Librarian! The one who tried to beat the crap out of me!"

"Not the 'crap.' Just information." Locke placed his foot in the stirrup and swung himself up into the saddle. "Your interest in balverines prompted me to make certain that you were not part of the conspiracy."

"You manhandled me!"

"And saved your life shortly before when that snow leopard threatened you. Or did you think that knife buried itself? Now get on the damned horses; we've no time to waste, and sitting around here blathering about the past will only guarantee that we have no future." Without waiting for James to reply, he dug in his heels and sent the horse galloping north toward the mansion.

Seeing no choice but to follow him, Thomas and James clambered upon their own horses and urged them forward. The horses required no great incentive to start galloping. They were clearly glad to be putting as much distance between themselves and the forest as possible.

They pounded across the terrain. The sun was settling upon the horizon, the long shadows of evening creeping across the vast, rolling heath. The air that had seemed so fresh and clean now seemed thick and unpleasant. *The stink of evil,* thought Thomas, which he knew was subjective and perhaps even ridiculous, but he couldn't help thinking it anyway. He still didn't know what the plan was, or what Locke had even been talking about. They were going to try and find the three Heroes of legend? But what did the mansion have to do with it? None of it was making any sense to him, and if Locke hadn't proven so utterly capable thus far, he would have thought that the man was insane. Actually, the possibility was still there; they might be following a madman on a demented quest with no hope of success. Unfortunately, it wasn't as if Thomas had any better ideas, short of turning around, heading home, and trying to forget any of this had ever happened.

Yet he knew that that wasn't an option. This was no longer simply about personal jeopardy. Not only were there three innocent people in the clutches of the Balverine Order, but the safety of Albion itself was at stake. If they did indeed manage to spread their influence throughout the ruling class, then there was no telling how much damage they could do. Perhaps they might even be able to achieve their goal and take control of the land itself. No one would be safe.

With all of that to ruminate on, the time seemed to fly by until they finally reined up at the mansion. Quickly, they tied the horses off at a convenient hitching post set off to the side. The horses seemed a bit more relaxed although Thomas was sure he could still see fear in their expressive eyes.

Thomas and James approached Locke. As they did so, Thomas scanned the horizon, and then said offhandedly to James, "I don't see Poxy. Where do you think she got off to? I thought sure she'd be waiting for—"

"She's dead," James said tersely. "She tried to rescue me, and Kreel killed her."

Thomas's heart sank. It was just a dog, a damned dog. Yet James had gotten terribly attached to her, plus she had proven herself a valiant companion. "James, I'm so sorry . . ."

"I don't want your 'sorry,' Thomas. I just want Kreel dead."

Locke was striding toward the front door. He was briskly reloading his pistol as he did so, and once it was ready, he shoved it in his belt. He had already slid his sword back into its sheath so that it once more looked like a normal, common walking stick. The boys caught up with him just as he arrived at the main entrance. "What are we doing here?" said Thomas. "You haven't told us . . ."

"The Triumvirate."

"What about them?"

"They're here."

"Here? In this mansion?"

"Below the mansion, yes," said Locke. "They're entombed there. This place"—and he gestured toward the mansion—"was once their hall. A hall of Heroes. And in a great battle against evil, the Heroes were brought down. And evil came in and has been here ever since. As would be expected when dealing with such chaotic forces, there were turnovers in control of the mansion until the Balverine Order finally took charge of it. It has been relatively stable since then, but the Heroes have remained there, beyond the touch of evil, waiting for successors to come to them and purge the dark forces from this place."

"And we're those successors?"

"That is my hope. But it will require the three of us, working in tandem, to accomplish this."

"Wait, wait . . . I don't understand," said Thomas,

who felt as if he'd been saying that a lot lately. "How do you know this?"

"The *Omnicron*. That's why I was at the Library. I found one of the few copies extant there."

"*I* was looking for that!" said Thomas.

Locke gave him a dour look. "I shall be happy to lend it to you, should we survive. Now listen carefully: According to the *Omnicron*, the way to the Heroes is guarded by the three spires, one representing each of them. Those who would seek the Triumvirate—'three worthies,' as the book put it—must provide offering to each of the spires at the same time, and the way will then be shown."

"Fantastic," said James. "Provide offering? What's that mean?"

"I'm not sure."

"Even better." James looked up with dread toward the three spires, which stood at their respective points on the mansion. "So we have to climb up there, is that it? I think this is the time to tell you that I have a problem with heights . . ."

"That is what I had thought initially," said Locke, "but having walked around the mansion last night, I've concluded that something more down-to-earth is what the *Omnicron* was speaking of."

"The mural room," Thomas said abruptly.

"The what?" James hadn't seen it.

But Locke was nodding, which meant that he most definitely had. "Yes. The mural room. The three of us need to go together and explore those distended spires against the wall, for I believe that it is through there that the secret lies."

"And you are one worthy, and James and I are the other two?"

"That is my belief. You have come all this way on a quest. There is no more classic definition of 'heroic endeavor' than that."

"Then why didn't you come to us during the night?" James demanded. "If you knew that Kreel was leading us all into a trap—"

"Suspected, not knew," Locke corrected him.

"—then why not head it off and have us try to reach the Heroes during the night?"

"That was my intention, actually," said Locke, casting an annoyed glance at Thomas. "I was coming to your room to gather you, except apparently Mr. Kirkman here had other plans for the evening. Had he been where he was supposed to be, rather than otherwise engaged—"

"You're . . . you're not blaming what happened in the forest upon me!" said Thomas.

"No," said Locke. "I remain focused on who the true villain is. And whatever lapse your dalliances last night may have caused in our ability to protect others, we're going to set matters right with our actions now. Come. Let us—"

"Wait," said Thomas. "Who *are* you?"

"I told you."

"You told us your name. That doesn't explain why you're involved in this. Your personal stake. How you happened into this . . . this madness."

Locke nodded in understanding and sought a way to answer simply. "I am here," he said finally, "because I am someone who has an awareness of the world. Of the way things are and the way they could be. And when you are someone who has that sort of insight, you cannot turn away. You must use whatever gifts and resources are at your disposal to have an impact and influence them. And whether you influence them for good or ill is up to you. I, for reasons that will remain my own, have chosen to influence them for the good. You, Mr. Kirkman, are of a like mind. You, Master Skelton"—and he glanced warily at James—"are on the fence, I believe, and could go either way. Let us hope that you make the right decisions."

"What's that supposed to mean?" said James in irritation.

"I believe you know, and we have wasted enough time. We need to return to the temple before midnight if we are to save the others. That is the hour," he went on, anticipating the question as to why that time was important, "at which the others will be transformed into members of the Balverine Order. Most balverines do not transform into individuals who seem relatively normal. Most of them are ravening beasts with only the vaguest recollection of what they once were. A bite at any other time creates a simple mindless beast. But a bite at precisely the witching hour, during a full moon, administered by one who is already part of the Order, will create more of their kind. That is the moment that we are racing against. So, if you have no further questions—?" He looked from Thomas to James, and both of them shook their heads. "Onward, then."

"How are we going to get into the mansion?" asked James.

"Yes, I have a rather cunning plan in that regard."

At which point Quentin Locke strode toward the front door and banged on it. The thumping echoed within and, moments later, the door was opened by a puzzled-looking servant. Thomas instantly recognized him as one of the butlers who had served them dinner.

He took one look at Locke, Thomas, and James, his face twisted in fury, and he yanked out a knife from a scabbard behind his back.

Locke did not hesitate. He strode forward and, before the servant could bring the knife forward, Locke struck him full in the face. The impact of the blow spun the servant around, and he went down in a heap. Locke stepped over him and gestured for Thomas and James to follow.

"Hurry," said Locke. "Hurry before—"

"What are you doing here! What's going on!"

It was another servant, and his cry brought others. And from the look of them and the way they came straight at the three guests who were now clearly intruders, it was obvious that they knew that Locke, Thomas, and James were not supposed to be there. Which meant that they knew exactly what it was that the master of the house was up to.

Thomas braced himself for them to transform into balverines, but they did not. Instead, they charged forward, bearing knives and looking to carve up the new arrivals.

Unfortunately, Thomas and James were weaponless. Fortunately, Locke was not.

"They're not worth wasting silver bullets on," Locke said coolly, disdaining to take out his pistol. Instead, once again, he withdrew his sword from within the confines of his cane. He moved with a speed and precision that Thomas would not have thought possible, like a lethal dancer, deftly stepping between the clumsy thrusts of his attackers and striking quickly and mercilessly.

He killed no one. That was what fascinated Thomas the most. His precise thrusts inflicted wound after wound while receiving none himself. The clumsy way in which the various attackers came at him ensured that they were far more likely to trip each other up than pose a threat to Locke, and he took advantage of their disorganization. He sliced and stabbed and cut with surgical precision, and men went down clutching at wounds to their chests that would not prove fatal, or staggering about because an incision across their forehead was causing blood to get in their eyes, thus rendering them easy victims to a knockout punch. One particularly troublesome bruiser nearly got the better of Locke, clipping him with a blow that glanced off Locke's jaw and knocked Locke off his feet. But Locke simply took advantage of his momentary position on the floor to dart behind the bruiser and slice through the man's right Achilles tendon. The bruiser screamed and went down, flopping about on the floor like a seal, as Locke quickly bounded back to his feet and dispatched the remaining attackers.

Thomas and James would have joined in the melee, but they were mostly concerned about getting in Locke's way. Plus, it was all happening so quickly that there wasn't much time for them to leap into the engagement. By the time that they had picked up knives from fallen attackers and were ready to join in, there was nothing in which to join. Locke was briskly striding away from a circle of half a dozen men who were lying on the floor in various stages of consciousness and blood loss, moaning and holding different parts of their body. Other servants were appearing from other directions, but when they saw the chaos that reigned in the main hall and the fact that the man who had perpetrated it looked more than ready for more, resistance melted away. The trio headed in the direction of the mural room without further opposition.

Within minutes, they were standing in front of the vast three-wall mural that depicted the entirety of the mansion. James, who had not yet seen it, let out a low whistle. "This is it, then?"

"This is it." Locke nodded. "Quickly . . . the two of you each go to one of the spires."

They did as he instructed, Thomas to the right, James to the middle, and Locke at the left. "Now what?" said James.

"Now we all three push against it and see if that does something. On three and one . . . two . . . three."

Together, at their respective places around the room, they pushed as hard as they could against the raised spires. None of them were exactly sure of what was supposed to happen next.

As it turned out, nothing did.

"That was exciting," said James dourly after long moments of no response at all. "Was there anything in the *Omnicron* about what to do if you're completely buggered?"

"There must be some trick, some mechanism to it," said Locke, stepping back and studying the mural. "We just need to find . . ."

"No. You don't."

Slowly, the three of them turned and saw that Sabrina had entered the room. She was wearing a simple green frock. There was a look of infinite sadness in her eyes. "You don't need to find anything."

"Sabrina," Thomas said urgently, "it's all right. We know what he is. We understand everything."

"No," Locke said, "I don't think you *do* understand everything, Mr. Kirkman."

Thomas ignored him. He went to Sabrina and took her hands, speaking as quickly and passionately as he could. "We know what your father is. We saw it. And you must know, too. You do, don't you?"

"Yes," she said, her voice small. "My mother . . . she was his . . . his offering to the darkness . . . his pledge of loyalty to the evil that made him what he is. He didn't run from the curse; he embraced it."

"And you've lived with that knowledge, with that evil, all this time." He wanted to weep in sympathy for her.

"Mr. Kirkman," said Locke.

"Not now."

"Mr. Kirkman," and he was more insistent.

"Shut up!" He turned heatedly toward Locke, and then he was astounded to see that Locke had his sword out and was pointing it toward him. "What are you—?"

"Think, Thomas. Tear the blinders of infatuation from your eyes. Do you truly think that she could exist within this house of evil all this time and remain unscathed by it? Do you not see her for what she is?"

"She is an innocent, caught up in—!"

And suddenly James, who was standing just to Locke's right, took a step back and brought up his knife defensively. His lips mouthed, "Thomas," but he was unable to speak.

Thomas turned back to face Sabrina, and was horrified to see her eyes, baleful and yellow, locked upon him.

"It wasn't supposed to be this way," she whispered, even as she started to grow, fur sprouting all over her face. "We were going to be together, you and I. Father promised. He promised that I would feel so less lonely if I had someone. I hated it . . . hated what he was . . . hated what he made me . . . I told you that." And each word became progressively deeper, more guttural. "Told you that I wanted to be something other than I was! *I told you that! Why didn't you listen?*"

The frock she'd been wearing split down the back,

and she tore it off herself with her clawed hands. That same hideous sound of bones crunching and reknitting themselves filled the air, except within the confined area of the mural room, it sounded even more horrifying.

"Thomas, get out of the way!" shouted Locke.

But Thomas remained where he was, paralyzed, frozen, trying to tell himself that he had simply gone mad, and he wasn't witnessing what was actually transpiring. "Sabrina . . ." he whispered.

"We could have been happy together!" roared the balverine, and she lunged at him.

Thomas barely darted back in time as her claws raked across him. He screamed as his shirt shredded, and five thin lines of blood welled up on the chest that, the night before, she had been covering with kisses. He fell back even as he shouted, *"No! You don't have to do this!"*

"Yes, she does!" Locke called out. "She's in thrall to them, Thomas! She has no choice!"

Locke came straight toward her, his silver sword extended, and the balverine grabbed Thomas and without hesitation flung him straight at Locke. Locke quickly flung his sword arm wide, lest he impale Thomas, but as a result Thomas slammed into him, the both of them hitting the floor. Locke lost his grip on his sword, and it clattered away.

James darted toward the sword, trying to grab it up so that he could return it to Locke or perhaps even use it himself. But he had no opportunity to do so, for the balverine—seeing the weapon lying on the floor—leaped toward it and landed between it and James. She roared at him and thrust forward with her open paw, knocking him flat. Then she kicked the sword away, sending it clattering to the far end of the mural room.

Locke shoved Thomas off him and yanked out his pistol. He took aim and would have had the balverine cold except she noticed him out of the corner of her eye and quickly yanked James to his feet. James let out a cry of stark terror as the balverine held him up as a human shield, keeping him between her and Locke's deadly pistol.

"Dammit!" snarled Locke, trying to get a clear shot and unable to do so.

And James cried out, *"Shoot through me! It's the only way!"*

"I can't!"

"This is no time to worry about me!"

"I'm not worried about you per se," Locke said tartly. "Frankly, I don't like you all that much. But if you're dead, you're of no further use to us in our overall quest."

Despite the tenuous situation he was in, James was somewhat taken aback at that. *"Oh, well, thanks a lot! I'm trying to be noble, and you're just being a prig about it!"*

And then Locke fired.

It was not a shot at the chest, because she was continuing to keep James firmly in front of her. Instead, for half a moment, James's leg had shifted and it gave Locke a shot at the balverine's thigh. He hoped that burying a bullet there would startle her enough that she would drop James and give Locke a clear shot at her heart.

In a rare happenstance, matters did not work out as

Quentin Locke desired. The balverine, still holding on to James, leaped straight upward. The shot went under her, and as Locke swung his pistol around to aim again, the balverine rebounded off the ceiling and plunged straight toward Locke at high speed, still keeping the screaming James between them.

She crashed into Locke with James as a battering ram. Locke held on to his pistol, but the hammer snapped home, and the shot went wide. He tried to bring it around, and the balverine roared, grabbed him by the arm, and flung him to one side, tearing the pistol from his grasp as she did so. Locke struck the far wall with a violent thud and slid to the ground, looking dizzy and confused.

The balverine tilted her head back and let out a ululating roar of defiance, and then she came straight at Locke. Locke's blurred vision focused upon the oncoming behemoth but, bereft of weapons and still reeling from the impact, there was nothing he could do to defend himself.

And then Thomas was directly in her path, between her and Locke, and he was holding Locke's sword, which he had retrieved from the corner of the room, gripping it with two hands. The balverine saw it at the last instant, but she was moving too quickly to slow her forward motion. She slammed straight into it, the impact driving Thomas to the ground and her on top of him, in some twisted perversion of a lover's embrace. The blade drove into her heart, and she cried out, an animalistic howl that escalated into a higher and higher register until it sounded not like that of a creature but instead of a human girl.

Thomas screamed her name, and she tumbled off him. He yanked the sword clear of her chest even as James shouted to him not to for fear that somehow she would mystically be healed by its removal. He need not have been concerned. Instead, the balverine lay unmoving upon the ground, blood seeping from her chest onto the polished wooden floor.

And as the blood pooled beneath her, as if she were a balloon gradually deflating, the balverine started to shrink. The fur fell out, slowly at first but then in large clumps. Her teeth shrank, her muzzle withdrew, her arms and legs and back transformed into human proportions. The yellow faded from her pupils, and she gazed up at Thomas with limpid eyes.

Thomas began to sob as he dropped the sword and yanked off his cloak, covering her nakedness. "Help her," he said in a choked voice to Locke. "Help her . . ."

She reached up to him and placed a bloodstained hand against his cheek. "You *have* . . . helped me," she said, her voice barely above a whisper. "I go . . . to be with my mother . . . thank you . . . thank—"

And then her hand fell away from his face, a bright red stain against it down which his tears were now rolling, leaving little trails in the blood smear on his cheek.

There was a deathly silence then, broken only by Thomas's sobs, and Locke stepped forward, knelt next to Thomas . . .

. . . and slapped him across the face.

Thomas reeled, almost falling over, and he looked in stunned astonishment at Locke.

"We've no time for womanish tears," said Locke harshly. "Whatever else she was to you, she was an enemy to us, and you dealt with her accordingly."

"You bastard," James said, feeling pained on Thomas's behalf. "How can you—?"

"Be quiet and think. The means to reaching our goal has been handed to us, and you two are too busy simpering or displaying indignation to see what's in front of you." He shoved back the cloak that Thomas had draped over Sabrina and placed his palm squarely onto the pooling blood.

"What the hell—!" James was so outraged that he looked ready to take a swing at Locke, or perhaps try to stab him with the knife he was now holding.

"An offering," said Thomas hoarsely.

"Ah. He understands," Locke said approvingly.

Thomas couldn't have given a damn about Locke's approval at that moment. All he cared about was what needed to be done in order to put an end to this horror. His voice was an emotionless monotone as he said, "The spires need an offering to show the way. If great Heroes are within, then proof that evil has been vanquished must be what's required. The blood of a freshly killed balverine will likely do." The blood was still warm as he put his hand in it, and then he said coldly, "James. You too."

James looked as if he had never wanted to do something less in his life, but he did as Thomas bade him although he didn't look down at it, and his face was twisted in disgust.

"Quickly," said Locke. "We need to—"

"Quiet," Thomas said wearily. "We know what we need to do." He wanted to mourn. He wanted to scream. He wanted to curse the day he had ever set foot out of Bowerstone, but none of those were options now. Instead, he simply walked across to the spire on the right, turned, and waited for the others to do likewise.

Without a word, Locke and James went to their respective spires as well. This time there was no need to count. Thomas simply nodded, and, as one, they placed their blood-soaked hands flat against each of the spires.

For a moment nothing happened, and Thomas wanted to scream in frustration. Before he could, however, there was a low rumbling that seemed to be coming from everywhere around them, but mostly from beneath the floor.

Each of the spires simultaneously retracted into the wall.

There was a deafening grinding of gears, and Locke now had his sword at the ready, looking around coolly to see if another danger was about to leap out at them.

Then the source of the rumbling localized itself. It was the front section of the mansion as depicted on the mural. The paneled section of the mural upon which the front door of the mansion had been meticulously rendered detached from the ceiling and began to slide down. They watched in astonishment as it continued its steady progress down, down, and eventually it reached the floor and clacked into place.

Where a section of the wall had been, there was now only emptiness, and what appeared to be a stairway that led down to darkness.

The three of them had now moved away from the spires and stood in front of the opening, staring down at it.

"After you," said James to Locke.

Locke promptly began to stride forward, and then, to his surprise, Thomas put a hand out and stopped him in his tracks. He did not say anything. He did not have to. Locke inclined his head toward the opening and gestured for Thomas to precede him.

He did so. Moments later, the only thing left in the room was the rapidly cooling body of a young woman who had gone to her grave with a heart that had been pierced by silver and lightened because of it.

THE STAIRWAY WAS NARROW, AND THEY HAD to make their way down it carefully. Locke, using some of the incendiary oils in his pack, had fashioned a torch for them, which was fortunate since there was no other light source available. He followed directly behind Thomas and in front of James, thus providing an equal amount of light for all, albeit limited.

There was high-pitched squealing and skittering of feet as rats scattered to get out of their way. The smell in the place was almost overwhelming; it was all James could do not to pass out from the stench. *This is where Heroes lie?* James thought. *It hardly seems a suitable resting place. One would have thought something more grand. Even penniless paupers get something better than this.*

They continued to move single file through the corridor, and then there ceased being rats in their path. James was thankful for that. Hadn't they already faced enough without having to deal with vermin?

His heart went out to Thomas. The poor bastard had given himself over to this girl, had allowed himself to take an emotional plunge, and it had ended with a literal plunge of a sword into her. The first girl he had ever been with—of that James was reasonably certain—and he'd had to kill her. How in the world was he going to achieve any sort of closure as far as his brother's death was concerned when he had a brand-new tragedy to dwell on? James knew that an adventure like this changed people. His worry was that it was going to wind up changing Thomas into someone who was unrecognizable as the friend he'd known for so many years.

"Up there," Locke said, raising the torch slightly. "Do you see it?"

James did, and, presumably, so did Thomas.

There were three sarcophagi lying at the far end of the corridor.

They were upright rather than horizontal, and each of them had a body propped within. They couldn't quite make them out from where they were standing; the flickering torch was sufficient only to provide the general outlines of their forms.

"No lids?" said James.

"Sarcophagi lids are rather heavy. Who would have lifted them on?" said Thomas.

James nodded. "Good point. Still, it's a wonder they weren't—I don't know—devoured by the rats or something."

"I don't see any here," Thomas pointed out.

"Let us proceed carefully," said Locke.

They did as he suggested, treading carefully, wary of perhaps some manner of booby trap that might have been left in place.

Nothing seemed to spring out at them, though, and the closer they drew, the more they were able to make out. The flesh had long since rotted away, and only the bones of the great Heroes remained, the remains of their clothes hanging loosely upon them: a humbling reminder that time and death had no respect even for the mightiest of mortals.

"I see them. The dean was right," he whispered, and the others immediately knew that the "them" to which he was referring were not the bodies of the long-dead Heroes. Instead, they were the icons, exactly as Dean Carter had described them. The arms of the Hero on the farthest left were crisscrossed over a great sword that, miraculously, did not have so much as a speck of dust upon it. The body in the middle had a pistol tucked into a timeworn belt. The body on the far right had a gauntlet adorning its bony left hand. It appeared to be crafted from elegantly spun copper, spanning most of his forearm, and it glittered in the torchlight.

James couldn't take his eyes off it. He had been concerned over the prospect of trying to remove a bauble from a desiccated arm. Now, faced with the reality of it, it didn't bother him in the least. It was as if the gauntlet were calling to him, urging him to free it from its lengthy languishing in the darkness. He could only imagine that the other icons were similarly calling to Thomas and Locke.

"The Black Dragon," whispered Locke. For once even the unflappable Locke seemed overawed. "That pistol may well be the Black Dragon."

"The what?"

"A sister weapon to another legendary pistol, the Red Dragon. Never misfires, perfectly weighted. It's said it's as if you're wielding an extension of your own arm. And that sword," he said, "has to be Quicksilver. It is a silver-augmented melee sword of substantial power; nothing can withstand it. As for the gauntlet"—he turned to James—"I do not know. Magic users tend to guard their secrets, and they believe that names have power. But I'll wager that, should you be able to harness its abilities, you would be extraordinarily formidable."

"Then what are we waiting for?" said James.

As one they walked forward.

Abruptly, the air in front of them seemed to congeal, and there was a sense of raw power all around them. Then, as if they were standing at the beach and slammed by a gigantic wave, a blast of heat that seemed to come from everywhere and nowhere washed over them. They staggered, James squinting and shielding his face,

Thomas doing likewise, and for a moment it felt as if their very skin was going to be flayed from their bodies by the unknowable force that was enveloping them.

Then, as quickly as it had arisen, the overwhelming force dissipated, leaving no sign that it had come through there.

"What the hell was that?" said James.

"If I were to hazard a guess," said Locke, who was the only one who didn't seem the least nonplussed by what they had just experienced, "I would say that we just passed through a ward of some sort."

"What's a ward?"

"It's a mystic barrier," Thomas spoke up. "Something that can be erected to keep people out."

"In this instance," said Locke, "it was doubtless designed to prevent anyone deemed unworthy from approaching the presence of the weapons. We certainly need no further proof than that that the Heroes placed their very essence within these weapons."

"Okay," said James cautiously. "And just out of curiosity, what if this ward thing had decided we *weren't* worthy?"

Locke appeared to be considering that possibility for the first time. "In all likelihood, we would have been incinerated."

"*Incinerated*? And you didn't think to *mention* that?"

"No," said Locke calmly. "It never occurred to me that that would be a problem."

James suddenly felt as if he couldn't get enough air in his lungs, but then Thomas put a steadying hand on his shoulder and looked at him grimly. "James," he said tersely, "it's time to grow up."

There was a tortured look in Thomas's eyes such as James had never seen, and also a cold, burning fury. It was clear that Thomas's mind was back on what had transpired in the mural room, and on the corpse of Sabrina, the girl whom he had slain. He had neither patience nor interest in anything save payback for her, and also for what had been done to his brother.

Without a word, he reached forward and gripped the hilt of Quicksilver. He pulled it from the hands of the Hero of Strength. Even as he did so, Locke extracted the pistol from the Hero of Skill. James, seeing that they had done so, stepped over to the Hero of Will and reached down into the sarcophagus. "Sorry about this," he murmured to a being long dead, and he slid the gauntlet off the arm. He hoped that the action would not cause it to snap off at the elbow and was relieved that it did not do so.

"Now what?" James said.

Locke appeared a bit flummoxed. Even though it was ill timed since they needed him to know what was going on, James took some small pleasure in that. "I . . . am not sure," Locke admitted. "Perhaps there is some incantation that is required to activate them. But there was nothing in the *Omnicron* about it."

"That's just perfect," said Thomas, clearly annoyed.

"After all that?" said James. "After everything we had to do, and with lives at stake, you don't even know how to turn the things on? How are we going to use them if—?"

"Wait," Thomas said abruptly. "We're not all using them yet. We're holding our weapons, but James, you need to be wearing yours. Put it on."

"All right." He slid it onto his wrist. "But I don't see how—"

Then he let out an alarmed scream. The gauntlet had been hanging loosely on his arm when he first put it on, but suddenly it burned white-hot with energy, then shrank and clamped down with such ferocity on his arm that it might well have been alive. Instinctively, he tried to remove it, but he had no chance. Instead, energy lanced out from the gauntlet, striking the pistol and the sword, forming a triangle of pure power that threatened to burn their eyes out of their sockets. All three of them, even Locke, cried out . . .

. . . and then knowledge flooded through them, and memories that were not their own. Their muscles acquired reflexes that they had never had before, which elevated them to levels they had not yet achieved and might never be able to in this lifetime.

And Locke, who had fancied himself a crack shot, was humbled in the face of how much he did not know, and how his beloved accuracy was actually off by millimeters, even inches, and he was shamed and shown how he could do better, would do better.

And Thomas, who believed himself a fair swordsman, saw that he had not even begun to master the blade, and that the true berserker power that a melee swordsman required was not even close to being his, but it would be, at least for now.

And James, who believed himself to be strong-willed and determined, saw how he had not even begun to understand how he could truly manipulate his will, transforming it into a weapon that was as formidable as any sword or axe forged by the hand of man. He saw that if he truly believed that he could be unstoppable, he would be, and nothing and no one would be able to withstand him.

The three came together as one, and just as suddenly as the chamber was filled with the roar of energies being unleashed for the first time in ages, all became deathly silent.

The three who were now operating as one nodded in agreement without having to speak a word.

They strode with utter confidence down the corridor that they had just walked so tentatively mere moments before. Beyond the area where lay the three sarcophagi, the rats were still swarming. When the three of them approached, however, the rats seemed to look at them in unison, and then, without so much as a squeak, the mass of them parted to either side. The way was now clear. The Heroes simply nodded as if that were the natural order of things, and they kept moving.

Before them was the stairway they had taken down into the underground crypt. They strode up the steps, radiating certainty and confidence.

There were servants in the mural room.

They had gathered around the fallen body of Sabrina and were trying to determine what to do. When they saw the Heroes, their knee-jerk reaction was to attack, correctly intuiting that the three were responsible for the death of the mistress of the house. But all they managed was several steps toward the Heroes before the unbridled power that the three of them were radiating froze them in their tracks. They backed down without even fully comprehending why.

The Hero of Will approached Sabrina's rapidly cooling corpse and stood over her. Then he stretched out his hand and a dark force began to issue from it.

"James," said the Hero of Strength sharply. "What are you doing?"

"A useful spell called Raise Dead, Thomas," replied the Hero of Will. "It will animate her and enable her to fight our enemies alongside us."

"Animate her? You mean bring her back to life?"

"In a manner of speaking."

"Meaning her body will obey commands, but she will have no soul."

"Small matter. She was a balverine. She had no soul anyway."

The dark force was building around his hand as he prepared to unleash the spell, and then, to his surprise, a sword gently tapped his hand. He turned and saw Thomas, the Hero of Strength, wielding it. There was no overt threat to the gesture; merely a firm warning. "No, James."

"But she can be of use."

"She had a soul, James. Blackened and burned by the curse of the balverine it may be, but it was there. I touched it—"

"Along with everything else," James said with a coarse laugh.

"—and I will not have you do this," Thomas, the Hero of Strength continued. "It is unjust for her, and unworthy of us . . . and of you. Do you understand me?"

"I understand that you do not seem willing to do whatever is necessary to crush the Order."

"Yes, I am. I just do not believe this to be necessary."

James thought it might well be his imagination, but at that moment he felt as if he could see an aura of light shimmering around his fellow Hero. He closed his eyes and opened them again, but there it still was. It was the damnedest thing.

"Do we understand each other, James?" said the Hero of Strength.

James, the Hero of Will, was clearly considering pressing the matter, and then the Hero of Skill stepped in between the two of them. "We need to be united, gentlemen. We must be precise in our efforts, or they will come to naught. And the united front of the Heroes does not support the issuance of this spell. Will you defer to us, James?"

James's hand had been closed tightly in a fist. Now, though, he opened his hand, and the spell dissipated before becoming fully formed. "If you wish to restrict our resources in combat, then I will abide by that," he said sourly.

"Good man," said the Hero of Strength.

"Come, gentlemen," said the Hero of Skill. "Our enemy awaits, and time is not on our side."

They headed out, James bringing up the rear. He was sure that he was seeing that same strange glow around

Locke as he was Thomas, and could not fathom what it was. He thought perhaps his eyes were playing tricks on him, and as he passed an oversized mirror, he glanced in it to see if his eyes appeared tired or bloodshot.

They were not bloodshot, or if they were, he could not distinguish the tiny vessels within.

Instead, they were solid red, glowing at him ominously. It was as if he were looking into someone else's eyes.

James withdrew, startled, uncomprehending of what he was witnessing. He blinked rapidly and even changed the angle, looking this way and that, to see if it was some sort of trick of light. They remained exactly as they were, scarlet and fearsome to behold.

After he got over the initial sensation of being startled and a bit afraid, he regarded them a little longer and decided he rather liked them. They made a statement that he was someone not to be trifled with and would doubtless strike fear into those who beheld them.

"James!" came Thomas's sharp voice. "You will have plenty of time to admire yourself later on! There is work to be done!"

"Coming!" He smiled at his menacing reflection one final time and then headed out after the others.

They reached the front door without any further problems from servants, who parted in their advancement in much the same way the rats did. When they reached the horses, the animals reared up at first, startled by what they instantly perceived as changes to their riders that—due to their uncanny nature—were enough to cause them consternation. The moment the Heroes drew near, however, the horses calmed, although James noted with annoyance that his horse still appeared a bit nervous around him. He opted not to dwell upon it; what did the reaction of a dumb animal mean to him, anyway.

Moments later, they were galloping at full speed toward the Elderwoods.

The midnight hour was approaching for the Balverine Order. And so were the Heroes.

Chapter 16

LAIRD ETHAN KREEL STALKED THE temple, an uneasy feeling having settled upon him.

It was a vast structure, a seemingly perfect synthesis of architecture and natural cave. It was impossible to determine where nature ended and human—or inhuman, as it were—efforts began. The names of the builders of the balverine temple were long lost, presuming they had ever been known. All that remained were their efforts, which served as a gathering place to balverines to this day. It was their most revered of shrines, and a testament to the fact that they were far, far more than the mindless beasts that many thought them to be.

Towering columns reached from floor to ceiling. It was impossible to determine whether they were supporting the structure within or if they were simply decorative. In a way they were both, for the columns had images of balverines twisting around them, depicting them in full pursuit of cowering so-called Heroes who lacked the nerve to face them.

At the far end of the main cavern was an altar that had been erected long ago. Images of the phases of the moon decorated the front, running from left to right, with the full moon naturally in the middle. It was a wide enough altar that it could accommodate up to six new converts; this evening only three would be taking up space upon it.

"What ails you, brother?" said Lugaru, slowly approaching Kreel. When in human form—as he and Kreel were now, since human bodies were better suited for simple conversation than those of balverines—he very much looked his age. When he was a balverine, on the other hand, he was as agile and powerful as any of his kind, and more so than most. Although he was not a literal brother of Kreel, it was he who had transformed Kreel into one of them and mentored the laird during his transition and embrace of the balverine way of life and death. "You seem distracted. The fire has been extinguished, and the midnight hour approaches. All is well."

"All is not well," said Kreel angrily. "There should be five converts up there, not a mere three."

"Two escaped. Of what consequence is that? We have balverines in pursuit of them. They will overtake them, as surely as I am standing here. Night belongs to us, brother."

"But if they are not brought here before midnight—"

"Then it matters not."

"It *does* matter. The transition must be accomplished during the first of the full moon. Tomorrow night will not suffice."

"Then we will hold them for a month or, if that proves inconvenient, they will simply be fed to our brethren." He looked at Kreel sadly. "You worry too much about things of no consequence."

"But there is something else," said Kreel. "I just . . . I am uncertain what it is. Something has happened, something that fills me with unease."

"You let your imagination get the better of you. Look at this place." And he gestured toward the balverines stalking around, prowling, on guard for any possible intrusion. "Behold our past"—and he gestured toward the altar—"and our future." On the altar, Carter, Laird Shaw, and Lady Molly Newsome were strapped down hand and foot. Carter was lying there, studying the surroundings; Shaw looked to be in shock; and Molly Newsome was still pulling at her bonds with a ferocity that had not lessened. Lugaru watched her approvingly. "That one, in particular, will be a greatly valued addition. Perhaps I shall take her for myself. What think you, milady?" he called out to Molly Newsome, causing her to cease her struggles for a moment. "Once you have been brought over, I may honor you with my personal attentions. You will, at that point, be in a far better position to fully appreciate me."

"The best position for me to be appreciating you," shot back Molly Newsome, "will be when you're a carpet in my den, and I'm standing on top of you."

"Ha!" said Lugaru. "You see, Kreel? This one is extraordinarily feisty. I will enjoy bringing her around to our view of the world."

"Perhaps . . ."

"Perhaps what?"

"Perhaps you are correct," Kreel said. "Perhaps I am worrying about nothing."

"No 'perhaps' about it. Your heart will lighten once you see our brethren returning with young Skelton and Kirkman. You will see: All will be well."

Kreel very much wanted to believe it. And yet he could not shake the feeling that something profound had changed in the last few hours.

FOUR BALVERINES WERE SPRINTING ACROSS the heath, tracking the scent of the escaped offerings, when they saw three horsemen pounding toward them. The balverines were downwind of them, else their own scents would have been detected by the horses. Consequently, they crouched low in the high grass, waiting for the horses to draw within range. The moment they did, the balverines would leap upon them, two from each side, take down the riders, and devour the horses. A worthy meal, for the balverines had had a busy evening thus far, and sating their constant hunger was a priority for them.

As the riders drew nearer, the balverines caught their scents and were overjoyed to discover that it was the ones they had been tracking. Their lives had just become that much easier: Their quarry was coming to them and bringing dinner with them besides. How utterly considerate.

Still, something seemed wrong. It was definitely the scent of their prey, but something had changed, something indefinable. It was enough to give the balverines pause, but only momentarily.

The horses charged directly into the trap, between the two groups of balverines. With a collective roar designed to freeze their enemies in their tracks, the balverines leaped at them from both sides.

The lead rider never so much as hesitated. A pistol that had been in his belt was now in his hand, so quickly that it never seemed that he drew it; it was simply there. He fired twice to the right, transferred the gun to his left and fired again, all while the balverines were still in midair, before the horses had even had time to register that they were under assault.

Each bullet thudded squarely into the heart of its target. The last balverine to be struck had barely enough time to see the first of his group fall to the ground stone dead before he himself was hit. The impact of the bullet blasted him backwards in a manner that would have seemed impossible; no gun should have been able to drive a bullet with that degree of force. But this one did, and the balverine flipped over backwards and was dead before he hit the ground. His brethren likewise lay sprawled upon the heath, and the horses never even slowed their stride.

* * *

THE HERO OF SKILL HAD RELEASED HIS hold on the reins, guiding his mount with the strength of his legs only, and was calmly reloading his gun.

"Locke!" the Hero of Strength called over to him. "How many bullets does that thing fire, anyway?"

"Six, James," the Hero of Skill replied. "A definite improvement over the two that my previous weapon could hold. And with far greater stopping power, as you have seen."

"No kidding! I think you could have knocked over a tree with that thing!"

"Not quite, but I would say that the tree would come away the worse for it."

As they continued to gallop, the Hero of Strength shouted, "James! Did you see that—?"

"It was nothing I couldn't have handled. A simple Time Control spell would have slowed them enough for a child to dispatch them," said the Hero of Will.

Thomas was somewhat taken aback by James's casual dismissal, but the Hero of Skill merely said, "He brings up a valid point. We will be at our most formidable if we are working in concert. The forest approaches."

The three Heroes reined up at the edge of the wood. "It's too dangerous to ride in," said the Hero of Skill. "The terrain is far too uneven. The horses would break their legs, like as not."

"But if we tie them off here, then they would be

prey to any passing balverines," pointed out the Hero of Strength.

"Then we let them go. They will retreat to a safe distance and wait for us," said the Hero of Will.

"Are you sure, James?"

"Yes," James said flatly. "They will wait. I will see to it."

The Hero of Will was as good as his word. He looked into the eyes of each of the horses and, as if they understood his intent, they moved off a short ways away and herded together. Each of them was watching in a different direction so that, no matter which way a balverine approached, they would be able to react.

Quentin Locke, the Hero of Skill, turned to James. "That Time Control spell of yours," he said. "How pervasive can you make it?"

"Pervasive?"

"I see what he's saying, James," said the Hero of Strength. "Midnight is approaching faster than we can reach the temple. But if—"

Immediately, James comprehended. "Say no more. I understand." He closed his eyes, stretched out his hands, and felt the flow of time all around them. He knew that he was endeavoring something that was unprecedented: a combination of single-target localization and employing time control in radial mode. He was going to speed the three of them up while simultaneously slowing down the world. A hundred Heroes of Will could have studied a hundred lifetimes and still never acquired the technique or ability to accomplish such a feat.

But James was not a Hero of Will. He was *the* Hero of Will, unique in the whole of Albion. There was little within the realm of existing spells that he could not perform once he was able to conceive of it.

Energy rippled from his hands, and throughout the forest, as far as the Temple of the Balverine Order. The inhabitants therein were unaware of the fact that they were moving and talking incredibly slowly. To them, there was no change in the world around them.

As it so happened, however, the ripple effect generated by the Hero of Will stopped just short of the altar upon which Carter, Shaw, and Newsome were strapped down. They watched in bewilderment as the balverines, who had been stalking the temple, were now moving at a pace that would have allowed a snail to hurtle past them. Kreel and Lugaru, who had been in the midst of a conversation, had come to a virtual halt, their mouths frozen.

Even Shaw, who had been near catatonic with fear since they had fallen into the clutches of the balverines, was roused from his stupor at the bizarre sight. "What in the world—?"

Dean Carter regarded the strange scene with the same academic detachment he viewed everything else. "It's some manner of time-disruption spell."

"A *spell*?" said Shaw, beginning to sound like his typical doubting self. "What are you saying? That there is a magic user in the area . . . ?"

"Let's hope so," said the Lady Molly Newsome. "Because I think it's going to require something akin to the miraculous to free us from this situation."

* * *

THE WORLD WAS BEGINNING TO SPIN AROUND James.

He had been utterly confident of his ability to hold matters static as they moved through the forest at what was, comparatively, incredible speed. They even passed several immobilized balverines that Thomas was able to dispatch with a flash of Quicksilver.

But he was starting to feel a pounding in the back of his head, and he felt as if he were losing focus. He staggered and nearly fell, and only a quick movement on Thomas's part kept him upright. "I . . . I don't know what's wrong," whispered the Hero of Will.

"I do," said Quentin Locke. "There is only so long you can sustain this type of spell. You can attempt to maintain it, but it may well deplete you of power so thoroughly that you will have nothing left for the battle."

"Don't tell me what I can and cannot do," James said heatedly.

"I know more about these matters than you," Locke said. "But if you desire to put us in a position where we have to function without you, then I assure you that we can triumph without you. Otherwise, you need to cease producing the spell and replenish your energies."

"I'm the Hero of Will, not you! I—"

His legs gave way completely. Thomas, who was supporting him, sank to the ground with him. With a loud, shouted profanity, James released his grip on reality around him. Within seconds the world surged back into its normal time stream, and James pounded his fist on the ground in fury. "Just a little longer," he said. "I needed to . . ."

"It's all right, James," said Thomas. "You've accomplished what we needed. Come. Let's finish this."

James nodded and started to get to his feet. But he got no further than the intention to do so.

"James—?"

"I can't," James said, trying to keep the panic from his voice. "I have no strength . . . not enough even to stand."

"You will," Thomas said confidently. "You just need time to rest."

"Time," Locke reminded him, "that we do not have. We have to leave him."

"*Leave* him?" The voice of the Hero of Strength rose. "To hell with that. I'll carry him—"

"He'll slow us down at a time when we cannot afford it."

"Thomas . . . he's right," James managed to say. "And even if I were present . . . I would be useless in a fight. I would just lie there helpless, and you'd be busy watching out for me. Go. Go, and I'll catch up."

"I'm not sure that . . ." Thomas began, but Quentin Locke had already started moving.

"Go," James said once more, even more firmly.

Thomas squeezed his arm again as a sign of solidarity, and then headed off into the forest.

The moment they were both out of sight, James took a deep breath, released it, and then got to his feet. The darkness that had been surging within him had been brought even more to the fore, and it was that darkness that had prompted him to play up his weakness because Quentin Locke's attitude had greatly annoyed him. He dusted himself off, and then muttered, "Arrogant prig. Trying to order me about. You could have had me at your side, but no. You give me, 'I assure you we can triumph without you.' Fine. Let's see you do it, then."

"THEY'RE MOVING AGAIN!"

Kreel turned in confusion toward Shaw, who had been the one to blurt out the exclamation. "What are you talking about?"

Molly Newsome fired an angry look at Shaw, and instantly his mouth tightened. The comment had attracted Kreel's attention, however, and he approached the altar. "My laird . . . what did you mean by that?"

Shaw said nothing but simply stared blankly at Kreel.

"My laird," and there was an edge to Kreel's voice. "I suggest you speak to me, or—"

"Or what?" Shaw was suddenly defiant. "Or you'll kill me? You have no desire to do that; you want to transform me into one of your own vile kind."

"Want to, but do not need to." Kreel extended a finger, and a single claw extended from it. His control over his form was absolute. "Two offerings will be sufficient." With the extended claw, he carefully sliced open the front of Shaw's tunic, leaving him bare-chested. His torso was covered with thick, graying hair. "Pity this has to happen," said Kreel calmly. "You're already rather hirsute. Growing fur would not have been that much of a change for you. Ah well. Now . . . where to start? When you intend to gut someone from crotch to sternum, it's always hard to know quite where to begin. Let's see, let's see." And he moved the claw up and down repeatedly. "Crotch . . . sternum . . . crotch . . . sternum . . . yes, definitely, it will be the—"

"You weren't moving!" Shaw blurted out. Molly Newsome rolled her eyes in annoyance, but Shaw didn't see it, and even if he had, it would have made no difference. "I mean, you were, but incredibly slowly. If we'd been able to break free of here, we could have walked right past you, and you would never have noticed us."

Kreel retracted the claw, his thoughts racing. "For how long?"

Shaw was staring down at his exposed chest, still clearly terrified at the prospect of being vivisected. As a result, Kreel's question didn't register on him at first. Then Kreel got his attention through the simple expedient of wrapping his long fingers around Shaw's throat. *"For how long?"*

"I don't know!" Shaw cried out. "I lost track . . ."

"How could you have lost track? *How?*"

Shaw was trembling, so terrified that he could not get out a word.

The dean could stand it no longer. In his best academic manner, he said, "It is impossible to be certain of the passing of time under such circumstances."

Molly Newsome looked poisonously at him. *"Men!"*

"Shaw should not have a painful death inflicted upon him simply because he is an ignorant coward."

"As opposed to you, a knowledgeable coward?"

"While there is life, there is hope."

Kreel clamped a hand over the lady's mouth. "Your words are serving no use. You"—and he turned to Carter—"scholar. Speak to me. What transpired here?"

Carter did not hesitate. One would have thought, from the way he was talking, that he was back at the dinner table discussing matters of myth and legend. "The concept is called Time Control. It is something that only a Hero schooled in the use of Will would be able to implement. Except there are no longer any such—"

"Damnation!" The people on the altar forgotten, he turned, and shouted, "Lugaru! Quickly!"

Lugaru immediately came upon being called although it was clear from his expression that he did not appreciate being summoned in that manner. "What is the problem, Kreel? With the midnight hour nigh—"

"They've obtained the icons."

Lugaru's shock was palpable. *"What?"*

"Someone used an act of will to stop time. It is the only answer. And if one of the icons has been attained, we have to assume that all of them have."

Lugaru did not hesitate. Instead, he pivoted on his heel and strode quickly across the vast chamber. With each step he left more of his human body behind until he had reached the full height of his balverine form. At the far side, there was a bust of a balverine mounted on the wall, with its mouth wide open. Lugaru leaned forward, opened his own mouth, and then tilted his head back and let out a howl. The sound was carried up, up a stone shaft, and a second later the eerie sound was carrying to the farthest regions of the Elderwoods.

And then, after a few moments, the returning howls were heard.

Lugaru turned to Kreel and, in his deep growl of a voice, said, "The brethren are coming. All of them. More than enough to handle even three Heroes. And when midnight comes within the hour"—and he turned to the prisoners—"there will be three more to aid us in our endeavors."

THE HEROES OF SKILL AND STRENGTH WERE sprinting through the woods when the uncanny howling drifted to their ears. They stopped dead for a moment, listening to it and the responding howls as well.

"They're summoning additional forces," said Locke. "They know we're coming."

"Let them," said Thomas, gripping his sword firmly. "Let them know. Let them think they have a chance of stopping us. They'll find out how wrong they are."

"We need a plan."

"I have a plan. I'm going to kill anything that stands between me and the bastard that killed my brother. And then I'm going to kill him."

"Thomas, wait—!"

But there was no waiting. The Hero of Strength was

going to depend upon his strength alone, for the blade, Quicksilver, was whispering to him that his sword arm was all that was going to be required to get the job done, and Thomas was in no mood to dispute it. Into the woods he ran, vengeance singing in his head and drowning out everything else, from common sense to the words of his fellow Hero.

The Hero of Skill, realizing that his ally wasn't listening, did the only thing he could: He took off after him as quickly as possible.

JAMES WAS WALKING BACK TOWARD THE horses, but was doing so very slowly. Locke's words still stung him, and he felt that the Hero of Skill had been nothing but an ingrate. Nevertheless, he had a mental image of Thomas going up against potentially overwhelming odds and felt as if he was betraying his old friend by turning his back on him.

Something warned him.

He didn't know what it was: A slight breaking of a branch, or a heavy breath, or a deep snarl that the creature had been unable to restrain. Whatever it was, it was sufficient to warn the Hero of Will, and James brought his hands up in pure reflex as a snarling balverine leaped at him from the darkness.

A ball of fire leaped into existence in James's outstretched palm and straight at the balverine. It struck the creature with full force, and the balverine staggered, its fur going up in flame. Within seconds, James had hurled three more balls of fire, and the creature threw itself to the ground, rolling, trying to extinguish them.

"Fine," said the Hero of Will, "so be it," and with more time to focus, he summoned lightning that blasted from his hands and encompassed the struggling balverine. The creature let out a high shriek and stopped thrashing. Instead, it lay there, unmoving, as the remains of the fire eagerly consumed its body.

Even as the last of its life fled its body, the Hero of Will had already dashed past it. It would have been uplifting to say that he was doing so because he had put aside his own anger and was determined to back up his good and dear friend, Thomas, now the Hero of Strength.

But the fact was that James had simply enjoyed killing the balverine with a wave of his hand, and he was particularly keen to do it again. Even more specifically, he wanted to throw flames and lightning bolts and anything else he could at Kreel, because Kreel was the bastard who had killed his dog, and there had to be justice for that.

Chapter 17

THE HERO OF STRENGTH STOPPED IN his tracks, alerted by a low, warning growl. He had already unsheathed his sword, ready for any attack, so he did not even have to withdraw it from its scabbard. Thomas could feel power flowing from it into his sword arm, although for additional strength he was now holding the sizable blade with both hands. It was as if he were inside his head, looking out—which was usual enough—but also standing outside of himself, looking down at the assemblage of balverines who were converging upon him.

They stopped several feet away from him, forming a ring around him. There were at least a dozen of them, varying colors of fur, their claws extended, their evil eyes fixed upon him. They snarled their defiance.

But none advanced. Instead, Thomas noted with quiet amusement, they were now casting sidelong glances at each other, and he realized what was happening: Each of them was waiting for another to make the first move. Their ferocity was tempered with caution.

"You're right to be cautious," said the Hero of Strength, with a grin on his face that was as wolfish as any of the creatures facing him. "For years—for *years*—your kind haunted my dreams. Not anymore. For now I will haunt yours. Not that you will survive this night, but the slaughter your kind will experience will be so monumental, so traumatic, that it will sear itself into the collective memory of your entire race. Balverines will jump at shadows because they will think I am in them. And in this instance, they will be right. So . . . come on, then. Come on and die." When still they hesitated, he bellowed, *"Come on!"*

Triggered by the shout, they did as he bade them. They converged on him from all sides, thinking that they could take him down through overwhelming force.

The silver blade whipped through the air like a windmill. Several of them froze in their tracks, ducked back, but most of the balverines continued their charge.

They never got near him. Instead, the blade sliced through their necks without slowing. Two of them endeavored to duck beneath the blade and the result was to have the upper part of their heads sent flying.

The power of the Hero of Strength surged through Thomas as he completed his spin and came to a set position, awaiting the next charge. One cycle of the blade and, just like that, eight balverines were lying dead on the forest floor beneath him.

The remaining four spread out, more cautious this time, no longer being able to assume that overwhelming force would carry the day, and cautiously circled him. Thomas countered their moves, and no matter which way they tried to come at him, his blade was always a barrier, as if it were in several places at once.

Suddenly, there was a quick noise from overhead, a rustling of air, nothing more, but that was all the warning Thomas needed to bring his sword swinging up and around. The balverine that had tried to drop down upon him wound up bisected at the hip, falling in two separate pieces.

But the necessary change in Thomas's angle of attack left, for just a moment, his back exposed. That was all that was required for one of the balverines to land on Thomas's back, knocking him to the ground, the full weight of the balverine pressing him down. The balverine let out a triumphant cry and was about to rip Thomas's spine from his back and dangle it in front of his eyes.

Then there was a thunderous explosion, and the balverine was blasted backwards with such force that it flipped over. The remaining balverines tried to scatter, but a second explosion, like a thunderclap on the ground, took down a second one. It fell, clawing at its chest, and then it ceased all movement and simply lay there.

The remaining two balverines melted into the woods and, seconds later, were gone.

The Hero of Strength clambered to his feet and saw,

as he might have expected, the Hero of Skill emerging from the woods. The barrel of his gun was still smoking.

"You may want to rethink your 'run on ahead and nearly get killed if not for me' strategy," Locke said drily.

"Good point," Thomas was forced to admit. "Thank you for the save, by the way."

"You would have managed to fight your way out entirely on your own."

"Maybe not."

"Undoubtedly not," replied Locke. "I was being generous in order to assuage your ego."

"All I need to feel assuaged is to kill the bastards."

"Then let us attend to it," said the Hero of Skill.

They sped through the woods then, and as they did so, they quickly put together what seemed a reasonable plan: the Hero of Strength would handle the bulk of the heavy lifting when it came to dispatching the balverines, while the Hero of Skill would see to rescuing the intended victims of the Balverine Order.

The minimal distance between them and the temple was hardly without difficulties. Balverines leaped out at them with seeming randomness, trying to throw them off step, catch them by surprise, take them down. In every instance, they failed: the Heroes of Skill and Strength were not to be caught off guard, intercepting attacks and ruthlessly gunning or cutting down all opposition. The Hero of Strength carried the lion's share of offense since the Hero of Skill did not have an infinite number of bullets.

They left a trail of bloody mayhem in their wake and,

upon reaching the temple with minutes to go until midnight, saw they had a clear path to the mouth of their goal.

"It's too easy," said Quentin Locke, putting an arm out and preventing Thomas from advancing.

Determined to reach the temple's interior and find the monster who had crippled his family and destroyed so much of his life, it was everything Thomas could do to heed Locke's counsel. "You think they're waiting for us?"

"I surely do."

"But that's the only entrance."

"So far as we know."

"Then we need to draw them out if they're in hiding."

"I suppose, but—"

"Then," said the Hero of Strength, "it is necessary for us to remember the plan. I will draw them out, and you will get to the prisoners."

He half rose to standing, and Locke said sharply, "Getting yourself killed so that you can join your brother is hardly a wise plan."

"That is not my plan."

"I would be hard-pressed to prove otherwise."

"We," said Thomas, "are losing time."

"Then," came a slightly out-of-breath voice from behind, "you are not going to benefit anyone by wasting more of it here."

They turned and saw the Hero of Will walk boldly past them without slowing so much as a step. "James!" Thomas cried out, overjoyed, and suddenly fear for his friend caught up with him. "Wait!"

James did not wait. Instead, he strode out into the open, making no effort to look around or anticipate any manner of assault.

He had taken five paces out into the open and suddenly balverines were descending from on high, like sleet, roaring their triumph.

They had been secreted against the rock face of the temple itself, flattened, waiting, their eyes closed so that their presence would not be betrayed by their gleaming yellow orbs. Now they fell en masse toward their target, far too many to count, anticipating sinking their claws and fangs into the flesh of the lone Hero.

The Hero of Will glanced up at them and spread his hands. The air rippled upward and then blasted like a geyser of pure power.

The name for the spell was Force Push, and it carved a divide between the plummeting balverines, scattering them to either side, halving their forces. Some of the balverines were hit directly with such intensity that they were crushed against the very rock face that had been their shelter only seconds earlier.

The rest of them endeavored to regroup, and James promptly switched tactics. *"Inferno!"* he called out, and a wall of fire erupted from him, blasting in all directions. A number of the balverines retreated in the face of it, but some of them weren't fast enough. They went up in flame, shrieking.

"Going to need some help!" James called. "Flame alone won't do it!"

"My pleasure!" Thomas leaped from the concealing

woods and charged forward, wading into the melee with unrestrained joy. With each swing of his sword, with each balverine head that went flying, with every drop of blood that was spattered because of him, a bit more of the nightmares that had haunted him were shredded and sent screaming off into oblivion. The Hero of Strength was there to rescue not only his friend, not only the prisoners, but first and foremost, himself.

The Hero of Skill, as per the collective plan, sprinted through the battle, avoiding getting caught up in it so that he could reach the prisoners. Even as he disappeared into the mouth of the temple, there were more howls, the sounds of reinforcements.

"Follow Locke!" James said, turning to face the oncoming hordes who had not yet made themselves visible. "He may need help getting to the prisoners!"

"What about you?"

"I can handle it," the Hero of Will said firmly, and his eyes burned red as he spoke. He brushed away some flies that were swarming about him. "Trust me . . . I'm going to enjoy this."

Thomas hesitated, but only briefly. Then he stuck out a hand, and James clasped it firmly. "Remember who and what you are," Thomas said.

"And you," replied James.

Thomas turned and ran into the temple as James wheeled to await the inevitable oncoming mass. He was starting to feel the drain on his will, but he knew this was no time for weakness.

And then, with a collective roar that would have

wakened the dead, a pack of balverines thundered out of the woods toward him.

"Vortex!" shouted the Hero of Will, throwing wide his arms, commanding the winds to do his bidding. It was a temporary spell to allow him time to prepare Blades, a spell that would enable him to conjure multiple magical swords that would, with any luck, cut them to pieces.

The air hardened, and the winds sprang to life, creating a whirlpool of air that picked up the foremost balverines and sent them spinning. Others of them fell back, grabbing at the trees, sinking their claws into the bark, and holding on for all they were worth.

James kept it up for as long as he could, smiling grimly as the balverines spun around him, up and up, tossed into branches or slammed into each other and sustaining terrible damage because of it. And when the balverines regrouped and Vortex had run its course, then came Blades, and after that, Shock, with living lightning flowing through him and into his enemies.

They kept coming at the Hero of Will, and he kept beating them back, keeping them at bay, determined not to let so much as one slip through.

But one finally did.

LOCKE, MOVING QUICKLY THROUGH THE temple, heard a swift footfall behind him, turned, and fired without even looking to see what it was.

It was a rare misstep for the Hero of Skill, and one that nearly had tragic consequences, because he saw to his horror that his target was the Hero of Strength. But the bullet was already flying, and the Hero of Skill never missed.

Thomas reacted without thinking. Instead of trying to dodge, he brought up his sword and slapped the bullet aside. It lodged in the wall to his right, right in the eye of a sculpture of a balverine. They both stared at where the bullet had lodged, and then at each other. "Well, that was a waste of a silver bullet," said Thomas.

"Sorry."

"I think that's the first time I've ever heard you apologize, and it only took you almost shooting me to do it."

"I said it once; don't expect seconds. Come," said Locke, "it's almost midnight."

TWENTY BALVERINES RINGED THE MAIN chamber where the sacrament of the Balverine Order was about to be administered. No timepieces of any sort were required; the balverines, by their very nature, were attuned to the world around them and knew precisely when the midnight hour was to strike.

Lugaru, retaining his full, menacing balverine form, had stepped up onto the altar with the three new converts. His jaw was slightly open in anticipation of administering the bite, and saliva dripped down from it on Molly Newsome's face. She twisted her head away and spat out some that had dribbled into her mouth. Shaw was whimpering; Dean Carter was observing the activities in that same detached manner of his, as if he were endeavoring to make mental notes of everything so that he could tell others all about it.

In his deep growl, Lugaru said, "You are about to begin a new life. I know that all of this may be confusing to you now. But all will become clear to you."

"The only thing clear to me is that I'm going to see you dead," said the Lady Newsome.

A balverine's face was not built for smiling, but his yellow eyes crinkled slightly as he leaned in toward her, and said, "You, my lady . . . you will be first. Do you have a preference as to where to be bitten?"

She spit at his eye.

His head snapped back, and he snarled in anger, wiping it away. Then he leaped up upon the altar, crouching over her, reached down, and tore away a section of her skirt, exposing her bare thigh.

The balverines, as one, raised their voices in a triumphant howl as the midnight hour arrived.

And suddenly, astoundingly, a single voice raised above the collective howls of the pack.

It was that of Thomas Kirkman, Hero of Strength. It was a battle cry of unrestrained fury, and Thomas charged into the assemblage with no plan, no strategy, nothing save to strike down anyone and anything that got within range of his blade.

As plans went, it was rather formidable.

He swung the sword so quickly, so furiously, that it sounded like a swarm of bees cutting angrily through the air. There was no grace or artistry to his attack; instead, scant yards away from the beast that had slain his brother,

Thomas became a butcher with a blade. The balverines tried to attack, tried to come at him with tooth or claw, but anything that drew within range of the sword was quickly sliced off and dropped to the ground.

In such a paroxysm of fury was Thomas that he wasn't even capable of speech. There were no shouted challenges, no declarations of intent to wreak havoc. Instead, the sounds that emerged from him were nothing but inarticulate rage, bellows of fury that were on a par with the howls that issued from the throats of a balverine. For so long had he lived with the image of a balverine rooting around within his sleeping mind that now, faced with his enemy, he had become little better than one. But the philosophical differences between the other animals and him in the vast chamber were of no interest to him. Even concerns about the prisoners had fallen away. All he wanted to do was hack his way through to Lugaru.

He almost made it entirely on his own, but he was betrayed by his own success. A sudden turn caused his foot to slide on some balverine blood that had spread across the floor, and the Hero of Strength slid and fell onto his back.

Instantly, the remaining balverines advanced, seeing an opportunity, and had Thomas been on his own, then his life would have ended there. Transforming him into a balverine was no longer on the mind of anyone in the chamber; they would have torn him apart given the slightest chance and happily feasted on his heart.

Fortunately for the Hero of Strength, the Hero of Skill had his back.

The Black Dragon erupted within the chamber, the blast echoing in the ears of the balverines.

Locke could not have been more precise with his aim, nor the bullets more powerful. Two balverines were trying to get at Thomas and were getting in each other's way, one elbowing the other so that the other was behind him. Locke fired off a single bullet and it drove through the chest of the lead balverine, out its back, and into the chest of the second, piercing both of their hearts in one stroke. The two balverines went down, and Locke fired off another shot, and another, each perfectly placed shot taking down yet another of the monsters.

Kreel, letting out a furious roar, leaped through the air and landed several feet away from Thomas. Thomas turned to face him.

"Your blade is trembling," snarled Kreel. "Does fear finally seize you?"

"It trembles with rage," said Thomas, "for what you did to your wife . . . to your daughter . . ."

"You foolishly believed what she told you, did you?" said Kreel. He moved around Thomas, looking for an opening. Thomas kept his blade at the ready, never dropping his guard. "Don't. She wanted this. She wanted to be like me. She loved me above all others."

"And now she's dead," said the Hero of Strength, "by my hand."

Upon hearing this, Kreel stopped moving, his huge jaw hanging open.

Thomas braced himself, ready for the charge.

And then Kreel unleashed a thunderous roar, one so

violent, so deafening, that it knocked Thomas off his feet. Thomas scuttled backwards as Kreel advanced on him and then got to his feet just in time as Kreel lunged at him. Thomas swung his sword, and Kreel barely managed to dodge the thrust. The blade slid across Kreel's rib cage, leaving a bleeding gash that was painful but hardly fatal.

Then a high-pitched, womanish scream distracted Thomas. He looked and saw that Lugaru, who had not allowed himself to be distracted by anything, was about to bite down on Molly Newsome's leg. The womanish scream had come from Shaw.

Quentin Locke was pinned down, the remains of the balverine pack trying to get at him. He had taken refuge behind one of the columns, and the balverines were proving to make themselves less-than-easy targets. And Locke was at a bad angle, unable to get a clear shot at Lugaru.

The Hero of Strength did the only thing he could think of. He drew back his arm and flung the sword as hard and as straight as he could. It pinwheeled through the air and, just as Lugaru was about to sink his teeth into the Lady Molly Newsome, the hurtling blade sailed past and hacked his right knee through. The lower half of his leg fell away, and Lugaru, with an agonized howl, tumbled backwards off the altar.

His hands empty, Thomas had no time to react as Kreel grabbed him and slammed him against the wall. Thomas lashed out, boxing Kreel's ears, but all it did was irritate him. Kreel's face came right up to his, and Kreel snarled, "You . . . are going to be alive . . . while I eat you . . ."

"Put him down!"

It was Locke. The bodies of the remaining balverines were scattered around the floor, and the Hero of Skill was advancing, his gun leveled.

Kreel immediately twisted Thomas around so that he was a shield between himself and Locke. "Try it, and he dies," snarled Kreel.

"That trick didn't work when your daughter tried it," the Hero of Skill said evenly. "It won't work now. Your only chance out of here is to put him down unharmed. Kill him, you die. Release him unharmed, and you may go."

"Oh, really," rumbled Kreel.

"You have my word as a Hero. His life in exchange for yours."

Kreel was silent for a long moment. "Those weapons you hold . . . they will not protect you forever. They are powered by the essence of long-dead Heroes. But they are tied to their place of burial. You will have to return them, or they will become useless, and the greatness of the Heroes they were once a part of will be forever lost. You will be responsible for killing the spirit of the Triumvirate. Is that your desire?"

Locke said nothing. Neither did Thomas.

"So know this," snarled Kreel. "I release him and leave here . . . but it will never be over between us. Never. I will hunt you down when you no longer have the spirits of Heroes long dead to look over you, and you will die. You will both die, terribly and painfully and slowly. Do you understand that?"

"Perfectly," said Locke.

"And you?"

“Yes,” whispered Thomas defiantly. “I welcome the opportunity to kill you at some future date.”

“Done!”

With that declaration, Kreel shoved Thomas aside and bolted from the chamber.

“Shoot him!” shouted Thomas.

“I gave my word,” the Hero of Skill said calmly, although he kept his gun leveled as Kreel fled into the darkness. “*We* gave our word. And besides,” he continued once Kreel was out of earshot, “I’m out of bullets.”

“Oh.”

JAMES LAY ON THE GROUND, SURROUNDED by the corpses of balverines.

But he was not feeling any sense of triumph. Instead, he was keeping his hand buried deep in his stomach, trying not to think about what he was touching to keep the organs in there.

There had been so many of them . . . so many . . . and yet, even with all that, he had been certain that he would be able to keep all of them at bay.

He had been throwing spells around so quickly, with so little discipline. With death coming toward him apace, he knew that now. He realized his own shortcomings and wished that he could go back in time in order to refight the battle and do it properly. But that was not an option, even for one of his abilities.

Nor would a Heal Life spell serve him. The wound was too catastrophic.

How? How had that one damned balverine gotten close enough to gut him? James kept running the fight through his mind and couldn't conceive of it. He must have left a blind spot during the fray, something that a quick-moving monster could get through and reach him. It had been so fast, incredibly fast. One moment he was beating back the pack, the next he had felt a ripping across his stomach, and the balverine had been right there. A quick twist of his will, and an ethereal sword had flashed downward and cut out the balverine's heart. The Hero of Will had then used that considerable willpower to keep himself going, to put down the last of the balverines, leaving himself triumphant.

"A hell of a triumph," he grunted to himself. His hands were thick with red, and the world was seeming more and more distant to him.

"Well, well, well . . ."

He looked up. There was a towering balverine standing in front of him, and it had spoken, which automatically differentiated it from the other balverines—little more than snarling brutes—that he had been battling. He recognized the balverine, recognized the voice.

Kreel slunk toward him, nose twitching. "The Hero of Will, I take it. Or is it instead poor James Skelton, a mere shadow of himself?"

"Somewhere . . . between the two."

The towering balverine looked around at the carnage. "At least one of my brethren managed to get to you. I could just let you die on your own"—and he drew back his claws—"but in this way I can send a message to your friends . . . of what they have to expect. Any last words, Hero of Will?"

James managed a nod. "Just two . . ." And he stretched out his hand, reached into the deepest, darkest recesses of his soul, and whispered, *"Drain life."*

Kreel looked at him uncomprehendingly for a moment and then suddenly let out a confused screech. A black force had issued from James's fingers, like a malevolent cloud, and it penetrated Kreel's open mouth, driving itself down into him. Kreel tried to get to James, knowing him as the source of the blackness, but was held in place by the fury of the black cloud. He trembled, shook violently, and then his voice vanished, leaving him issuing a silent scream.

James reached out and drew the spell back into himself, and it ripped violently out of Kreel, taking his life essence with him, infusing James with it. Kreel stood there, wavering from side to side, still in balverine form. *He's not changing back to human. No surprise. He's more balverine than man by now,* thought James grimly.

Then Kreel toppled over, thudding to the ground, as heavily as a chopped-down tree and equally lifeless.

Slowly, James got to his feet and, very carefully, he removed his hand from his stomach. There was still blood everywhere, and a deep scar across his belly, but the wound was now healed. Life was flooding through him once. Tainted life, but life nevertheless.

He looked down at Kreel's lifeless body, then kicked it in the side and spat on it for good measure.

"That," he said, "is for killing my dog."

* * *

LUGARU, THE HEAD OF THE BALVERINE Order, was trying to drag himself across the floor, leaving a trail of blood behind him. There was a corridor at the far end of the room that led who-knew-where, and that was clearly his destination.

Quickly, Thomas ran toward him, stopping only to pick up his sword, and seconds later Lugaru saw the Hero of Strength blocking his path to escape.

"You—!" Lugaru said with a snarl, and even minus a leg, he shoved himself forward on three of his four functioning limbs.

He had no chance. The Hero of Strength sidestepped him easily and, with a quick spin, brought his sword around and cut off Lugaru's left arm at the elbow.

With an agonized shriek, Lugaru fell over onto his side, thrashing about in pain. With supernatural calm, Thomas walked around him, studying him as if he were examining a horse that he was considering purchasing.

"Who are the other members of the Balverine Order?" said Thomas.

Lugaru actually laughed at that, despite the agony that he was in. It sounded like no human laugh, but instead the strangled grunt of an animal. "You actually think," he said with a growl, his words barely comprehensible since they were more beast than man, "that I will tell you that . . . so that you can hunt them down? Why would I do that . . . ?"

"I'm hoping that you don't tell me immediately," said

Thomas. "I'm hoping that I have to take my time getting the information out of you. Cutting you to pieces by inches . . . that would give me great satisfaction. It would be the merest taste of the agony that you put me through when you destroyed my life."

"I destroyed your brother's life. I made yours. You would be nothing without me. Nothing."

"I would gladly be nothing with him than something with you." He pointed the sword at Lugaru's left knee. "Tell me, or that goes next."

"You think . . . you are so much better than I," Lugaru gasped out. "In swearing to take joy . . . in torturing me . . . you fail that . . . to which you aspire. You betray the greatness that is in the Hero . . . whose sword you wield. Let me show you . . . how one stays true . . . to others . . ."

And before Thomas could make a move, Lugaru brought his right claw up to his own throat and slashed across his own jugular vein.

"No!" shouted Thomas.

Gurgling, choking in his own blood, Lugaru managed to say, "In the end . . . I was stronger . . . than the Hero of Strength . . ."

And then his head lolled to the side and his tongue hung out of his mouth.

He was gone.

Thomas stood over him, trembling in frustration and also, he was surprised to discover, shame. Because at the last, he knew that Lugaru had been right.

Quentin Locke had released the prisoners from the

altar. Shaw was staring off into space, looking as if he had not truly reconnected with the world around him. Dean Carter was limping; apparently he had injured his leg at some point during the "festivities." The Lady Molly Newsome was helping to support him. He walked up next to Thomas and looked down at the unmoving body of the balverine.

"I wanted to kill him myself," said Thomas.

"Does it matter how he died?"

"It does to me. He filled so much of my life . . . the shadow of him, the memory of him, the curse of him . . . all the times I envisioned my catching up with him, killing him . . . this was never how I imagined it."

"So it's not satisfying, is what you're saying."

"No, it's not." And then he gave a smile that was untouched by amusement. "But it will have to do."

Chapter 18

THE SUN WAS JUST BEGINNING TO RISE when the haggard party of six returned to the mansion.

In quick, broad strokes, Quentin Locke had filled in the others on the specifics of what had happened. Carter seemed the only one of the three who was truly interested and would doubtless have kept on asking questions if a tired James hadn't advised him to shut the hell up, which Carter promptly did. After that, very few words had been spoken during the entirety of the return trip. There were a few muted words of thanks, and some muttering from Shaw, who was attempting to recover some of his bluster now that danger was past and not doing a particularly good job of it.

Matters could have taken far longer if the horses had

not done them the courtesy of remaining in the area, and consequently they were able to ride two to a mount, thus expediting their return.

Upon reaching the mansion, they discovered the front door hanging open. It seemed at first as if it might be some sort of trap, but once they entered, they encountered no one. The servants had all fled, perhaps fearing vengeance to be visited upon them should the Heroes return. The only thing remaining was Sabrina's body. It had been left lying on the floor of the mural room.

"Well, this is simply scandalous," said the Lady Molly Newsome. "Whatever she was . . . whatever her father made her into . . . she deserves a burial, at the very least. Lord Shaw, Dean Carter . . . there must be shovels around here. Find some so we can dig her a grave."

"And are we supposed to return to the woods and give last rites to the bodies of the monsters lying back there?" Shaw said.

"This is different, and you know it's different," said Molly Newsome.

"I will have you know, Lady Newsome, that asking me to engage in such manual labor to—"

She spun and slapped him across the face so hard that it sounded as if Locke's gun had accidentally gone off. Shaw staggered, his hand going to his cheek, and he stared goggle-eyed at Molly Newsome.

"Get to work," she said between gritted teeth.

He did as he was told.

* * *

THOMAS, JAMES, AND LOCKE STOOD IN front of the three sarcophagi, staring at the remains of the Heroes from whom they had taken their heightened abilities. There was a long moment of silence, and then Thomas stepped forward and returned the sword to the Hero of Strength. Locke followed suit with the pistol.

They both turned expectantly to James.

James put a hand on the gauntlet and clenched his fist. His eyes seemed to glow in the darkness.

"James," Thomas said with a sense of urgency. "What are you doing?"

"I'm thinking."

"About what?"

He turned his gleaming red eyes upon Thomas. "You know what."

"James . . . you cannot be contemplating trying to hold on to the power."

"Why not?" James said, his voice rising in defiance. "Why allow it to molder here, far from the eyes of man, when I can put it to so much greater use?"

"It is not our power to keep," said Quentin Locke, "because we have not earned it."

"I nearly got killed using it. How does that not qualify as earning it?"

"James . . . we stood upon the shoulders of giants to acquire it," Thomas said. "But that does not make us giants ourselves. This was never anything but borrowed power. Besides, sooner or later, separated from the beings who wielded these weapons, the power would be lost anyway."

"How do we know that?"

"Kreel said as much . . ." said Locke.

"Oh, and *he's* a reliable source . . ."

". . . and the *Omnicron* said so as well. The power can only be borrowed, not kept."

"But for how long?" James said, desperation beginning to fill his voice. "Does it say *that*? An hour? A year? An age? How long?"

"No," Locke admitted. "It does not."

"Then I say we keep it," said James firmly. "It's not as if our job is done. You both know that. The Balverine Order is still out there. We don't know who they are or what parts of society they've infiltrated. We're going to have to hunt them down, one by one. Figure out who they are, kill them. How are we supposed to accomplish that without the power of the Heroes?"

"The power of Heroes," Quentin Locke said, "lies not in the weapons but in ourselves."

James stared at him. "You're kidding me. I'm talking about wielding icons of tremendous power in an effort to make certain that evil is crushed, and you're giving me trite homilies?"

"That did sound somewhat pathetic, Locke," Thomas had to admit.

Locke looked annoyed. "Fine," he said at last. "Depart with the gauntlet of the Hero of Will."

"Thank you for your permission," James said mockingly with a bow. He turned to leave.

"Presuming," Locke said, "it will let you."

Slowly, Thomas turned back to him. "Let me?"

"We passed through a mystic ward unscathed because our hearts and goals were pure," said Locke. "Has it occurred to you that the purity is no longer within you, and that the same ward might take catastrophic means to prevent you from departing?"

"He's right, James," said Thomas, trying to look sympathetic and not entirely succeeding. "I mean, you were pretty angry when Locke didn't bother to warn us that we might be incinerated upon entry. So really, he's doing what you wanted by letting you know what could happen to you if you try leave while still wearing the gauntlet."

"I felt it to be the least I could do," Locke said diplomatically.

James looked at the gauntlet upon his wrist and then back behind himself, trying to see where the ward was and determine whether it did pose a threat to him. "I don't see why my motives are suspect," he said, sounding defensive. "I told you I want to use the power to destroy the rest of the Balverine Order."

"Except . . . is it? Is that your true motive?" said Thomas. "Or is it more about wanting to hold on to power for its own sake? You better be right about the answer, James, because your life may well depend upon it."

James stood there for a time, staring at the path down

the corridor that led back to the world . . . a world upon which he could have tremendous impact with the gauntlet upon his arm.

Then, finally, with a frustrated sigh, he removed the gauntlet from his arm and placed it back upon the arm of the Hero of Will.

"I would have been magnificent as a spellcaster," he said, his voice choked with emotion.

Thomas draped an arm around him. "You still can be. There is a vast world out there and many possibilities within it."

"That is true," said Quentin Locke. "The icons did not produce attributes from whole cloth. They simply built upon what was already there. That which you have within you, Master Skelton, can be brought to the surface through hard work and study."

"Study? With whom?"

"When the student is ready, the teacher will appear."

"More homilies. Wonderful," James said sourly.

They retraced their steps, James reflexively pausing at the point where the mystic ward had enveloped them during their first entry into the place. When nothing happened he let out a brief sigh of relief and kept going. They trudged up the steps and out into the mural room, and suddenly there was a grinding noise behind them that startled them. The wall, which had remained open all this time, slowly moved upward, until it slid back into place with a resounding thud.

"What a waste." James sighed, and then he saw that Thomas was looking at him oddly. "Now what?"

"It's the oddest thing, that's all," said Thomas. "Your eyes."

"What about them?"

"It could be a trick of the light, but . . . they look red."

James shrugged. "I'm not surprised. I haven't been sleeping particularly well lately." And with that, he walked away, leaving Thomas feeling concerned without knowing why.

SABRINA KREEL WAS LAID TO REST IN AN unmarked grave. Dean Carter said last rites over her body.

The six of them stood around her grave and, when the last words had been spoken, looked at each other.

And then, without a word being spoken among them, they went their separate ways.

I WAIT FOR THE STORYTELLER TO CON*tinue, but he lapses into silence. The sun has almost set upon the horizon, the cold is more profound than ever, and I display more patience than a king ordinarily possesses. Yet still the storyteller says nothing.*

"And—?" I prompt.

"And that is it."

"What is it? That cannot be the end."

"Of course it is not the end, Majesty, because nothing ever truly ends. One action always leads to a reaction; one answer begets another question."

"But what of the Balverine Order? Did they eradicate all of it? Did Thomas and James eventually return home? And what of Quentin Locke? What happened to him? And how did *he know so much about Thomas and James when he first met them? You never explained that."*

"It was all some time ago, Majesty. The details escape me. Besides, life is not about easy answers."

"Do not," I tell him, bristling, "seek to dismiss it as easily as all that, or presume to tell me what life is all about. This is about a story, after all. A fable. The excuses of real life do not excuse lapses in a fable. How do you—"

I hear a calming voice behind me. "Majesty, you sound out of sorts," it says. "Is something amiss?"

I do not bother to get up. I do not have to. These are the benefits of both kingship and old age. Instead, I remain seated as I see a familiar individual coming toward me. "Ah. Terrance, Duke of Overland. It has been an age, old friend."

Tall, slender, with rakish good looks, the Duke of Overland approaches, and says, "Far too long, Majesty. And who, may I ask, is—?"

The storyteller stands and, without hesitation, pulls a pistol from within his cloak, aims, and fires.

The bullet embeds in the duke's shoulder, and he lets out a scream as he clutches at it. "You bastard!" he howls.

I lurch to my feet, the old reflexes returning to me, slowed with age but not entirely gone. "Guards!" I shout, reaching for my short sword. "Assassin! Assassin in the—"

Then I hear a thunderous roar and turn and gape in shock.

The Duke of Overland is transforming before my eyes. His clothes tear away, there is that horrible sound of bones cracking, and white fur sprouts from his body. He is now towering over me, and he looks like nothing that could ever have been human.

The balverine roars, its foul breath washing over me. I am too stunned to move. Death looks down upon me, and I do not attempt to escape it, for I have seen enough to know that I desire to see no more.

The air explodes from the gun's second discharge, and this time, the bullet—silver, I realize belatedly—thuds squarely into the chest of the balverine. The monster clutches at its chest, lets out an agonized howl, and then falls. It crashes onto the stone bench upon which I had been sitting and shatters it.

I stare down at it, dumbfounded.

"Of course, I could have shot him in the heart with my first bullet," says the storyteller. "But then you never would have known him for what he was. The pain of the silver in his shoulder made the transformation inevitable." The storyteller calmly replaces the pistol within his clothes. "I truly did not mean to consume so much of your day with this business, Majesty. Unfortunately, the duke was running late. Still, we found a pleasant enough way to pass the time, did we not, Majesty? Hopefully," he says with astounding calm, "that is the last of the Balverine Order. It certainly took long enough. Still . . . one never knows. Vigilance is the watchword of safety, and even those who walk side by side with danger can never be too careful."

"Are you . . . Quentin Locke?" I say to him.

He smiles cryptically. "I am whoever you need me to be, Majesty. Sometimes I think the best Heroes are those who remain nameless, don't you?"

There is a pounding of feet from the castle. I turn and see that my guards are now running to my defense, albeit belatedly. They see the balverine lying dead upon the ground and gasp at the sight. They approach slowly, their weapons out, as if the corpse were capable of assailing them. Naturally, they recognize it for what it is.

"The king has slain a balverine!" says the captain of the guards.

"Someone certainly has," I correct, "but 'twas not I. 'Twas he."

The captain looks at me in confusion. "He who, Majesty?" he says carefully, clearly not wishing to offend me.

"Why, him," I say impatiently, and turn to point at the storyteller who just saved the life of an old fool.

The storyteller is gone.

The story is ended.

Except, as he said . . . nothing ever ends.

FABLE III
NOVEMBER 2010
LIONHEAD STUDIOS
RATING PENDING
RP
CONTENT RATED BY ESRB
May contain content inappropriate for children. Visit www.esrb.org for rating information.
XBOX 360
Microsoft game studios